Hooked on Trouble

T0352228

ALSO BY KELLY SISKIND

Chasing Crazy
My Perfect Mistake
A Fine Mess

Hooked on Trouble

KELLY SISKIND

New York Boston

Forever Yours
Hachette Book Group
1290 Avenue of the Americas, New York, NY 10104
forever-romance.com
twitter.com/foreverromance

First published as an ebook and as a print on demand: January 2017

Forever Yours is an imprint of Grand Central Publishing. The Forever Yours name and logo are trademarks of Hachette Book Group, Inc.

The publisher is not responsible for websites (or their content) that are not owned by the publisher.

The Hachette Speakers Bureau provides a wide range of authors for speaking events. To find out more, go to www.hachettespeakersbureau.com or call (866) 376-6591.

ISBNs: 978-1-4555-6546-7 (ebook), 978-1-4555-6800-0 (print on demand)

Hooked on Trouble

One

Raven

I don't make a habit of laughing at naked men. Not that every guy I've hooked up with has been Adonis. They've ranged from unimpressive to average to exceptional—with one sexy-as-hell beast I've tried to block out. Still, I never laugh. Not even at the guy who strutted through my room in a leopard-print thong. But none have ever walked around nude wearing nothing but a fanny pack. A lime green fanny pack.

I elbow Shay. "I'm gonna lose it. Like cackle in this dude's face."

She squishes her lips so tight she's barely breathing. "I know," she says from the side of her mouth. "It's so ridiculous it's funny."

Lily fidgets on my other side, her pale skin pink with embarrassment. She digs her flip-flop-clad toe into the sand. "I can't *believe* you guys dragged me here."

I bump my hip into hers. "I can't *believe* you haven't been here yet. A nude beach in a major Canadian city? This place should be a World Heritage Site." I inhale the briny smell of the Pacific Ocean, hints of sulfur and fish mingling with the summer air. Even faced with Nude Fanny Pack Dude, I'd take Vancouver's sea and sand over the constant bustle of Toronto.

Fanny Pack Dude smiles as he passes, his paunch jiggling with each step. The visual reminds me of the Jell-O molds I'd make as a kid. Better to eat wiggly sugar than a plate full of nothing. "It wouldn't be so bad if he lost the accessory," I say. "It's just wrong."

"This place is a time warp." Shay scans the long-haired hippies baring it all to the sun, the majority of whom likely attended Woodstock. Gray hair and sagging skin extend for miles. "I bet they still think it's 1960."

Without warning I get shoved from behind, and I stumble forward, bile rising up in my throat. If someone's dick rubbed against my ass, hellfire will rain. Spinning around, I tuck my limbs tight, clutching my purse to avoid touching anything *naked*.

A clothed man holds up his Frisbee. "Sorry, wasn't looking." He does, however, *look* at my legs in my jean shorts and my chest in my tank top, my black ensemble leaving little to the imagination. "Nice ink." He nods at my exposed skin.

I smile but don't flirt back; younger guys aren't my flavor of choice.

He jogs away to join a rowdy group drinking by the evergreens lining the beach, likely students from UBC. Having a nude beach in Vancouver is odd enough. Having it attached to the city's main university is a whole other level of weird. At least the steep descent from campus is a natural barrier to prying eyes.

"So, what do we do now?" Lily crosses her arms as though people can see through her white summer dress.

"Walk, I guess." Shay plaits her brown curls into a loose braid. "It *is* a nice beach, naked hippies notwithstanding."

"Walk it is," I agree.

Shay and Lily, both in flip-flops, go ahead while I unlace my black goddess sandals from my calves. I carry them as the sand sifts through my toes, the grains hot and coarse. We pass clothed beachgoers, the majority seemingly unconcerned by the naked bodies around them. Two ladies stroll by, their boobs swaying. Behind them a younger woman walks alone, her nudity on display. I slow my pace. Her hair is long and black, like mine. Her eyes are dark, like mine. She's about the right age, too—ten or so years older than me. I study her face, her features. I scan her lips and cheekbones and nose, looking for familiarity. Looking for my sister. Then she smiles, revealing a mess of crowded teeth.

Not my sister.

I run my tongue across the back of my two front teeth, letting it slide between the center gap. As kids, when our mother was busy pickling her liver and my father was betting our rent money at the track, my sister, Rose, would take me for ice cream. Ten years older, she'd use the money she'd earn babysitting, then waitressing, to distract me. We'd count the number of licks it would take to finish our mint chocolate cones, her teeth perfect and straight, mine gapped in the center. My envy knew no bounds.

I haven't seen her perfect smile since I was nine.

I glance ahead. The girls are waiting for me, and Shay shades her eyes with her hand. "You're looking for her, aren't you?"

Lily frowns, then raises her brows in understanding. "Is that why we're here? To find Rose?"

My friends don't miss much. "Yes and no. Yes, I thought it would be a good place to check out, considering she only wore tie-dyed shirts and used enough incense to send smoke signals.

But I also thought, since Lily's only ever seen two penises, that she should have a look at the variety out there. For scientific reasons."

Shay cackles, and the sound eases my tension. A reminder that moving closer to her and Lily was a smart decision. Shay has lived in Vancouver seven months, Lily and me only one. The girls moved to be with the men they love. For me this is a fresh start: new job, new city. And a chance to find Rose, *if* my intel is correct.

Lily attempts to scowl at me, but she can't hide her giggle. "I'm not sure Sawyer would be happy about me being here without him."

Shay links elbows with her and turns to keep walking. My purse bounces against my backside as I join them.

"It's better he's not here," Shay says. "Sawyer would be the first to strip and lounge naked."

Lily cringes. "You're probably right."

The sun beats down, sweat gathering on my forehead. I run the back of my hand under my bangs. "In the name of scientific research, we should work on Lily's penile education."

"I'm in." Shay releases Lily's arm and tips her head toward a naked middle-aged man reading on his towel. "Exhibit A: the Number Two."

The poor guy has nothing more than a string of licorice between his legs. Although unattractive, his nudity sends my mind to a place it often goes, the place I try to ignore. To the beast of a man I woke up naked with in Aspen. It may have been over a year ago, but that's not the kind of thing one forgets. *Goddamn Nico.*

I ignore the unwelcome thought and focus on Mr. Dick Smalls. "If that's a two, I assume your ranking system ranges from one to a hundred."

Shay shakes her head while a silent Lily blushes. "Nope. That bad boy is a two. As in the pencil. Hopefully he's more of an H pencil. If that thing is a B, he's screwed."

"More like *not* screwed," I say, wishing we'd invented this classification in high school. If we'd lined up our hard H pencils and soft B pencils, naming each after a boy in our class, Mrs. Water's gray hair would have caught fire. Thank God for that art class, though. With the amount of pot I smoked and rules I broke, I'd never have befriended Lily and Shay without it.

Lily's so embarrassed she looks sunburned, her white-blond hair blowing across her heated cheeks. "You guys are horrible."

"What's wrong with a little peen humor?" Shay asks.

Lily ducks as though she can hide on the open beach. "Don't use that word."

"Peen?" I holler, drawing annoyed glances our way.

Cringing, Lily covers her face with both hands.

Shay kisses her cheek. "You're adorable. And I'm still in shock we're all living in Vancouver. I've been thinking about us starting that event business. I have a tight deadline at work, but when that's done, we should have our first board meeting."

I nod but don't answer. I love the idea of working with the girls, and we could rock an event business. Lily's attention to detail makes her a natural planner, Shay's interior design skills could transform any space, and I could finally put my photography to use, documenting the events for clients. But a start-up business needs cash, and there's no way I'm returning to teaching art.

Although it had its moments, dealing with a roomful of thirteen-year-olds is up there with getting my ribs tattooed.

My remaining choices are: Live on Wreck Beach with Dick Smalls, or find a new job.

To distract myself, I gesture toward a naked man walking out of the ocean. "Exhibit B: the Hoodie."

Shay coughs out a laugh. "Nice one."

Lily tilts her head and studies the specimen, playing along with our immature game. "I don't get it."

"The Hoodie," I repeat. "The man's foreskin is still intact, covering the coveted *head*."

"Oh my God." Lily studies the sand.

As I'm about to make fun of Lily's perpetual shyness, Shay stops in her tracks. "Goldilocks at twelve o'clock."

It's my turn to frown in confusion. "You lost me on that one."

She tries to gesture toward the Asian man with her eyes, but her attempt at subtlety makes her look like she's having a stroke. "Goldilocks—not too big, not too small...you know, *just right*. I'd bet that man knows how to please a woman." She pinches my side. "You should talk to him."

"To the naked man? On the beach? That sounds about as fun as the time you forced our hot waiter to set me up with his friend. I'm still paying off the restaurant bill that jerk stiffed me with."

Continuing on our mission, we traipse through the sand, the wind in our hair, the sun on our faces. I don't glance back at the cute guy Shay spotted; our definition of Goldilocks differs. My "just right" isn't average. It's thick and long and hard. It's *Thor's hammer* big. It's attached to a tower of tattooed muscle, one I vowed never to acknowledge again. Tequila may have blurred my night with Nico, but I know we didn't have sex. With what he's packing between his thighs, there's no question I would have been sore afterward. What was crystal clear, though, were the secrets I shared with him before the shots flowed, and the fact that he ditched me afterward.

Goddamn Nico.

I've avoided crossing his path since moving here, but he's best friends with Sawyer and Kolton. So unless I stop hanging out with Lily and Shay, I'm bound to suffer his presence eventually. Good thing I have a doctorate in grudges.

Lily grips my upper arm, concern beaming from her gray eyes. "There are a couple of women ahead, and one has black hair like yours. Do you have a picture of Rose? We could help you search if we know what she looks like."

My fingers twitch as I scan the beach. I'd kill to have my camera here, to study the area through my lens—a barrier between me and my past, providing the semblance of safety. If I find Rose, I'll have to apologize for what I did as a kid. Find the words to explain my actions, even though there's no reversing the consequences. If it weren't for me, she may never have left.

Pulse surging, I follow Lily's gaze, but the woman in question has a wide nose and thin lips. Although I haven't seen Rose in seventeen years, those features don't match the girl I remember. Still, Lily has a point: I could use help. The only clue I have that Rose moved to Vancouver is a tip from an old friend of hers who spends her days cashing welfare checks to play the lottery. Not exactly promising.

I reach for my purse and pull it around to my front, but the second I dip my hand inside, I freeze. "Shit. No. *No, no, no.*" I shove my hand deeper, then pull it out and stick my nose in the small opening, hoping to hell this is one of those bottomless Mary Poppins jobs.

"Why are you making out with your purse?" Shay asks.

I drop it and slump back. "Because my wallet isn't inside. I had it when I gave you change for the meter, so how the hell did I lose it between then and—" My jaw drops as realization sinks in. "Fucking asshole." I whip my head around and squint down the beach, but the rowdy group and the guy playing Frisbee are long gone. "That guy who bumped into me. That asshole stole my wallet."

Lily bites her lip. "Are you sure?"

"It's the only thing that makes sense, and my one picture of Rose was inside, along with my driver's license and credit cards and health card and fucking bank card." My purse caves under the pressure of my fisted hand.

Shay's nostrils flare. "That little shit. We better go, then." She attempts to stomp away, but her flip-flops sink in the sand.

"Go where?" I call.

She stops and swivels back. "The police station. You'll have to file a report."

"Yeah," Lily agrees. "And maybe we should cancel tonight? Sawyer was looking forward to seeing you, but we can reschedule."

I wave her off. "No. I haven't seen Kolton and him since moving here. It'll be a good distraction. But I might need one of you to spot me some cash."

"No problem," they say at once.

I offer a half smile and rub my eyes. I planned to visit a couple of photographers this afternoon to hand out résumés and hopefully find a paid apprentice job. Now I have less money than I did an hour ago, no ID, and I have to put off my job hunt. The warmth of the summer air is suddenly suffocating, a bout of heatstroke imminent. Things can only go up from here.

* * *

But things go down. At breakneck speed. A plummet off a steep cliff. Unwilling to ruin both my friends' afternoons, we drop Lily at home, then Shay drives us to the police station. Not my favorite place. A portion of my teen years were spent getting booked for having a rare disease: bad decision-itis. Walking into a station still makes me itch.

We push through the glass doors and are directed toward a counter at the back. Men and women in uniform weave around us, a number of regular citizens among them, including a belligerent man in stained pants who belches as a cop drags him through a set of doors.

Any old day at the lockup.

Except on this particular day, as we near the back counter, a deep male voice says, "Shay?"

My day ricochets from bad to worse.

Cursing my luck, I glance over. Of course Nico is wearing his uniform blues, like he isn't hot enough in his usual jeans and T-shirts. Now I have to endure all that male power packed into drool-worthy clothes. He swivels to talk to someone, and my throat dries. His thighs and ass look delicious, his massive shoulder blades *massive*. The man could be a professional wrestler. I should have known I'd see him here, should have thought this through. Unaware what station he worked from, I'd ignored the possibility. Vancouver's a big city, and getting into it with Shay meant inviting questions. After today's fiasco my stress level has reached capacity.

Now I'm faced with the Sexy Beast.

Shay grabs my arm. "I didn't know he'd be here. I can ask for someone else."

I will *not* be that girl. I will not play hide and seek, worried I'll run into my ex-hookup. "No. Whatever. It's fine."

Nico flips back and lowers his gaze. He scrubs a hand over his buzzed head. "Why are you guys here?" He directs the question at Shay, but his attention darts toward me.

The sensation is immediate, the way his proximity raises my pulse. He shouldn't still affect me. One glance shouldn't have my belly tightening and my arms wanting to slip around his waist. I shouldn't thirst to nuzzle into his broad chest and feel his heartbeat against my ear.

It shouldn't hurt this much.

I shoot him my best glare, and he looks away quickly.

Shay has on a loose tank top with a pair of skis printed on the front, the hem hanging over her shredded jean shorts. She widens her stance and plants her hands on her hips. "Some asshole bumped into Raven on Wreck Beach, and now her wallet's gone. Pretty sure the guy stole it, so we have to file a report, and if I see him again, I will personally reassign his gender."

"What she said," I add, making sure to avoid Nico's blue eyes.

Everything about him is dark and imposing: dark skin, dark stubble if he doesn't shave, eyebrows set in a dark line. All but his eyes. There's something about those light blue stunners that are so *disarming.* They're probably why I opened up to him in Aspen, why I told him things I'd never shared, ever, with anyone. For the first time in my life, I opened my heart to a man, then he blew me off.

A fresh wave of humiliation rocks me, shocking in its intensity.

He narrows that penetrating stare on me. "Some guy on Wreck Beach bumped into you? Naked?"

Swallowing down the sting seeing him revives, I shiver at the thought. "No. I was not accosted by any geriatric genitalia. Some young guy, a student maybe, *clothed*, was playing Frisbee. He probably saw my purse was open and figured I was an easy mark. Which, clearly, I was."

Nico shifts on his feet, his gaze raking over every inch of my body in a very non-public-servant way. Awareness lights through me, a memory of his hands dragging up my thighs fanning the flames. Big hands, heavy hands—the weight of them plaguing me with months of flashbacks. And here he is again, raising the temperature in the room. I doubt all the civilians he deals with get this sort of probing attention. *Unwanted attention*, I remind myself. As hot as he is, as intense as our time was, I do not need to walk that road again. My family has gifted me with a lifetime of disappointment. No point suffering in my personal life, too.

"Come," he says finally. "I'll help you at my desk."

He has us sign a logbook and hands us visitor badges, then he leads the way, and I'm faced with *that* ass in *those* pants, his broad back filling out his shirt, the muscles below flexing as he swings his arms. I'm also faced with the uncomfortable vulnerability that plagued me after Aspen.

Goddamn Nico.

Two

Nico

Raven's been in Vancouver a month, and I'd lost hope we'd have a chance meeting. I've been relying on intel from Sawyer and Kolton, asking them regularly what they're up to and who they're going out with, never getting the answer I want. If I'd kept it up, they'd have stopped answering and started grilling. I can handle a persistent Kolton, but Sawyer's immaturity is grating as fuck. But I don't have to suffer their obnoxiousness.

Not when Raven's right behind me.

I keep my eyes facing forward. One more look at that tattooed skin and those sandals laced up her calves, and the guys at the station will know exactly who I've been fantasizing about for sixteen months. Just wish she wasn't here because of a stolen wallet.

I push through the doors into the office area and hold my breath as I pass Mary Santos and her usual plate of curry stinking up the room.

Alessi hollers, "Message on our desk," as he heads for lunch. Then my partner's gaze lands on the girls. He smirks his porn-star smirk, and I grind my molars.

I've seen that look enough times to know the deviant thoughts running through his mind. Normally I dig the entertainment. Picking up random chicks may not be my thing, but Alessi makes a sport of it: the wide stance, the folded arms, the sly grin that has women biting their lips and getting their ditz on. It's better than hockey highlights.

Except Shay is like a sister to me, and Raven is…*way* off limits.

By the time we get to the desk I share with Alessi, he has redirected his trajectory and strikes his player pose in front of the girls. "I'm Tony Alessi, Nico's partner. Anything I can help you ladies with?"

There's that smirk again.

Shay smiles politely. "Thanks, but Nico's got us covered."

"Speak for yourself." Raven rolls her shoulders back, lifting her cleavage. She flicks her long black hair over her shoulder. "I could use some help."

Alessi tilts his head, eyes traveling places they shouldn't go. "Happy to oblige."

I flex my hands.

Last time I saw Raven, she was in town visiting Shay. She ignored me the entire night, picked a guy up at the bar, and left with him. I pounded back two beers too many and spent the next morning at the gym, doing squats and bench presses until my thighs screamed and chest ached. It didn't kill the unwanted images flipping through my mind, and I have no intention of going through that again. She has every right to be pissed at me, every right to harbor a grudge. But I caught how her lips opened when she saw me, practically felt the heat radiating from her. I'd bet a month's pay she hasn't forgotten our night together, either.

Alessi slaps his hand on my shoulder. "Why don't you break for lunch? I can take care of this."

I crack my knuckles. It's either that or torch his gelled hair. "Not necessary. This is Shay, Kolton's girlfriend, and her friend, *Raven*."

The second I say her name, Alessi's hand stiffens. He peels his eyes off Raven's breasts. "Sure. Right. Sorry, bro. I'll see you girls around."

He pounds my back and slinks away, but not before he winks at me. I've mentioned Raven to him once, recently. He'd been on my ass about spending all my time stressing over my brother and not having a life. With the hours we clock in the patrol car, there's no escaping Alessi; the dude likes the sound of his own voice. If I didn't give him an inch, tell him the only woman I cared to date was moving to Vancouver, he'd have had one of his twenty cousins at my doorstep, condoms in hand.

"He seems nice." Raven licks her lips as she watches him walk away.

I should really torch his hair.

I nod for the girls to take a seat as I search drawers for the Property Report Form. Documenting every detail of every daily interaction wasn't exactly what I'd imagined when joining the force, but I wouldn't have it any other way. Bury me under a waterfall of paperwork, and I'd still sign up. First in line. First day eligible. It was never a choice, really.

When I find the document, I squeeze into my too-small chair and lean on my desk. "You'll have to fill this out. Be as detailed as you can about what he looked like. The more we know, the better our chances of catching him and recovering your wallet. You'll still need to cancel your credit cards, to be safe."

Raven closes her eyes and mumbles, "Shit."

Shay puts a hand on her arm. "I'll lend you money until you get it sorted out."

Raven swallows, vulnerability softening her often hard features. She has sharp cheekbones, full lips, and exotic eyes framed with thick bangs. She's tall and strong, not muscular but fit, always wearing tight black clothes, always displaying her ink, always scowling if she looks at me. Except when we were in Aspen. Her face right now—sad and unsure—is the same as it was that night. Then I screwed everything up.

Instead of saying the wrong thing, I watch her as she fills out the form. Her body is angled, her crossed legs jutting out beside my desk, and *damn*, those sandals. They snake up her inked legs, crisscrossing the waves and fish splashed over her skin. Birds and feathers fly up her arms. Flowers decorate her chest. All black and gray. All sexy as hell. I spent a lot of hours exploring that ink sixteen months ago. Each line is seared on my brain, except for her new sleeve.

More Raven to explore.

She puts the pen down and traces the rose tattoo inside her left wrist. "Anything else you need from me?" She avoids my eyes.

That's okay. I'm happy to work for what I want. My life has been nothing but the job and family drama for too long. I haven't had a woman since Aspen. Since Raven. Maybe that's why I haven't been able to forget her. Or maybe it's my usual thing: Fall hard, fall fast, then lose interest. Whatever the reason, I need to find out.

"No," I say. "We'll contact you if we hear anything. And if any other details come back, give me a call." I push aside some papers and lift my keyboard. No business cards anywhere. I go to lift my message pad and see Alessi's scrawl on the page. My pulse speeds at the name on top: *Luke Woodfield*.

"How's your brother? Any news on Josh's case?"

I snap my head up at Shay's question. At least there's no judgment in her tone. No look of distaste that Josh got arrested for jacking a car. A car he didn't know was carrying a fuck-ton of meth.

"Nothing," I say. Unless this call leads me to the real man responsible for the drugs.

Raven regards me and holds my gaze for a beat. If I didn't know better, I'd say there's a hint of tenderness in her eyes. Could be she remembers the personal stuff I shared with her in Aspen. Could be she's thought about me as much as I've thought about her.

Then her features harden. "Can we go now?"

Man, does she give good glare. I glance at the message pad again, wishing I could walk her out, finally get her alone for a minute to apologize. To explain. But a call from Luke is time sensitive. In an hour he could go underground. No word. No trace. Snitches are unreliable like that.

At least I've got Raven's number now. Another week and I would have gone to Shay, tail between my legs, asking for it. "Let me grab one of my cards from my locker, in case you need to get in touch."

Raven scoffs. "That won't be necessary."

Ignoring her, I stand and cross the room behind them. At my locker, I sift through my clothes and the briefcase I keep shoved inside. Ordered chaos. Alessi's locker is pristine, like his hair and clothes—his shirts and jeans always folded, any papers filed alphabetically in folders. When I shoved my business cards into my locker, he grabbed a handful and said, "Come to me when yours get sucked into the Bermuda Triangle that is your life."

Fucking hate when he's right.

A minute later, I find a couple scattered at the bottom, under my shoes, and I hurry back to the girls. As I approach from behind, Raven leans toward Shay, their heads bent in quiet conversation. "He's not coming out tonight, is he? Because I'm not going if he is."

I hang back as Shay replies. "No. I made plans with the guys on a night he'd be busy. But I don't get why you have such a hate-on for him. Nico is a good guy."

Raven spots me lurking and raises her voice. "I have a thing against people who tell lies to get what they want. There's nothing good about a guy like that." She shoves back her chair, snatches her purse, and shoulders past me, elbows locked, sandals slapping the floor.

If I didn't have the message from Luke nipping at my mind, I'd run after her. Force her to face me. Try to explain how messed up the past year and a half have been. But I'm not smooth like Kolton or funny like Sawyer. My words don't always come out how I plan. If I blow this chance, odds are I won't get another.

Shay plucks the business card from my hand. "Whatever you did to her in Aspen, you need to apologize. Raven doesn't act like this with guys. She hooks up and moves on. So whatever went down must have been bad, and she won't talk to me about it. You need to fix things."

I glance at the door she stormed through. "She doesn't act like this with other guys?"

"That's what you took away from what I just said?" She shakes her head. "Fix it, *Constable Makai*. I love you, and Jackson thinks you're his own personal action hero. I don't want things to be weird when we all hang out."

Shay stands taller, her big hazel eyes uncompromising. She's taken to her role as surrogate mother to Jackson like a pro, which I'm beyond grateful for. When Kolton came home from the hospital, son in one arm, his wife's lifeless body left behind, I did the only thing I could: moved in. Helping him raise Jackson was hard and amazing and heartbreaking, but I'd do it all over again. Now, eight years later, Kolton and Jackson have Shay, and nothing's worth messing things up with them.

I nod. "Consider it done."

She takes a step but pauses. "And no…Raven's never been like this around another guy. Not sure if that will hurt or help your cause."

With a shrug, she leaves, and I rub my neck. Hearing that Raven's reaction to me is different tightens my ribs. Sixteen months is a long time to build resentment. It's also a long time to keep a memory alive. Our night together was hot, but it was the hour before the shots flowed and clothes came off that keeps me up at night, and I'm guessing that's the part that has her perfecting her glare. At least we didn't have sex. Telling her no was excruciating, but she was too drunk by then. Not in the right mind to make that choice. There's that, at least. I still need to make things right.

First step is to change tonight's plans.

For now I have my brother and his sorry ass to save. I trudge to my desk and squeeze back into my chair. Breathing deep, I count to three, then exhale and dial Luke.

He answers after the fourth ring. "Woodfield."

"It's Nico. What have you got for me?" The longer he stays silent, the harder I bounce my heel. If he hasn't found Jericho and I can't get that punk to confess, my little brother is in for a world of hurt.

"He was here, but the dude split."

"What do you mean split?"

"Gone underground. Maybe Mexico or somethin'. He copped to ditching the meth in the car they jacked." A muffled voice carries through the line, then, "Give me a sec."

I rock in my too-small chair as I wait, fisting my free hand. I don't need Luke to tell me the meth didn't belong to Josh. I might not have believed my brother at first, but there's been a lot of hollering the past months, insults hurled and received. Enough tears, too, until I was sure. Josh didn't know the car he was asked to drive was stolen. He didn't know there was enough methamphetamine stashed in the trunk to kill a herd of elephants. But believing him and proving it are two different beasts.

Josh's only chance of an acquittal is getting a confession from the "homies" he once called friends. Anything short of that is jail time.

"Sorry, bro." Luke talks low as if he has an audience nearby. "You know I'd do anything for you, but this one's outta my hands."

I scrub my head and squeeze my eyes. "Testify for me. Tell a judge what you know."

He laughs. "No fucking way. A known felon? They'd kill me up there. And I got my rep to protect."

"Yeah" is all I can say. It was a stupid question. I could remind Luke what I did for *his* brother, standing up for him in court and getting his sentence knocked down. But the facts are the facts—a jury would never listen to a kid like Luke.

We hang up, and my gut churns worse than when I smell that blasted curry.

Another dead end.

I pull Raven's form toward me and run my thumb over her name. *Raven Hunt.* She loops her *R* big and wide, the *A* and *V* and *E* and *N* tight and even, steady strokes like a teacher. No art teacher I had ever looked like her: dangerous, sultry, a body made for sin and a face for film. The rest of my life may be circling the drain, but she's here, in Vancouver, and I could use a distraction.

If it were just Raven's looks, I'd move on. Not complicate things and chance messing up my relationship with my friends. But she's pissed at me for the same reason I can't let this go: We shared more than a bed that night in Aspen. Something passed between us, something deeper than I've felt with anyone in a long while. Maybe ever. It's time to find out if it was the mountain air, or if it was more.

My bet's on more.

Three

Raven

Walking around without a wallet makes me feel as naked as those hippies on Wreck Beach. I hop off the bus, tug down my mini skirt, and check for the millionth time my purse is still zipped, all belongings safely inside. (Helloooo, paranoia.) I scan the restaurants for street numbers until I get my bearings, then I move into step with the other locals out for their Thursday night.

Shay and Lily both offered to pick me up, but I like finding my own way. I ride different buses when possible, mapping out the streets as we bump along. I've already found a bagel shop that bakes fresh, doughy bread all hours of the night and a biker store filled with all things black and leather. Even after today's fiasco, Vancouver is feeling like home.

I spot the restaurant Shay booked and push through the door. An attractive Asian man approaches as I adjust my strapless top. Like me, he's dressed in black, his smooth cheekbones striking in the soft light. If I had my camera, I'd snap a close-up of that chiseled line; the slope of his cheek is as sleek as a sand dune.

He checks a book on his counter. "Do you have a reservation?"

The bar is hopping, all surrounding tables full. When I see Shay's unruly hair, I nod toward the group. "I'm meeting friends."

He motions me on, and the girls wave when I catch their attention. Kolton has his arm over Shay's chair, and Sawyer's hand is on Lily's knee. Both guys are in their usual jeans and T-shirts, like they should be lounging on deck chairs, sipping beers.

Kolton stands. "Nice to finally see you."

"Nice to be seen." I walk into his outstretched arms and sink into his hug.

He rubs my back. "Sorry about the wallet."

"Yeah."

"Looking hot, Hunt." Sawyer winks as he stands to kiss my cheek.

"Save the sweet talking for your girlfriend." I round the table and sit next to Lily. "This place is cool."

She fixes her hair band in place. "Don't you love the walls? Such a fun design."

Bicycle wheels line the top half of the space, all painted lime green. The same color as the naked dude's fanny pack. "Yeah, it's different. Is this for me?" I point to the glass of red wine by my plate.

Shay turns the bottle toward me, and I salivate. Last time I had the Penfolds Shiraz was at her going-away party, along with several blue shots and an obscene number of cupcakes.

"It is," she says. "Tonight's a celebration."

I sip the deep purple wine, thankful my friends can afford the steep price, and I savor the spice and pepper that coats my palate.

"If I get to drink this, I'm happy to pass on dinner. And what are we celebrating? My stolen wallet and potential identity theft?"

"That kid better hope he never sees me again," Shay says, practically snarling. "But tonight is a fresh start, which includes celebrating our new business. And don't even joke about skipping dinner. The charcuterie here is ridiculous."

"The business is all she talks about." Pride sparkles in Kolton's brown eyes. "She's even claimed the office in the basement as your headquarters. And—"

"I've thought of a name," Shay interrupts, talking over him.

Lily squeals. "Let's hear it."

"Three Hot Chicks Do Vancouver." Sawyer's usual humor earns him a glare from each of us. "What? If you slap your pictures on a brochure, every dude in the city will be calling for your services."

I reach in front of Lily and punch his shoulder. "It's an event business, asshole. Not an escort service. I'm pretty sure you don't want a bunch of sleazy men propositioning Lily."

He slides his hand up her thigh. "Only this sleazy guy gets to solicit my girl."

Blushing, Lily plays with the ring on her necklace, her newest tic. If she's not picking her cuticles or chewing her nails, she's twisting Sawyer's promise ring in circles. Better that than falling into her old patterns—shopping to calm her nerves. If I had to guess, that ring is what has her tangled in knots. To say yes to Sawyer's proposal, or not. To trust he won't be a coward and hurt her again, or not. The way he's looking at her now—stars in his eyes, one hand on her thigh, the other at the back of her neck, playing with her white-blond hair—he seems intent on proving his love. If he's not, I'll go for the jugular.

"Ignore him," Lily says, still fiddling with the ring. "Let's hear the name."

Shay holds up her hands as if silencing a crowd. "Painted Heart Events."

I almost snort out my wine. "Are you serious?"

Lily drops her head forward. "The humiliation."

"What am I missing?" Sawyer squints at us.

Shay leans back, pleased with herself. "When we were in high school, we spent a night at a friend's ski chalet and got drunk."

"Annihilated," I cut in. "Someone spiked our vodka with vodka."

Lily sinks lower on her seat. "Please don't say any more."

"No, please do." Sawyer leans closer, as though he's about to be told the Caramilk Secret.

Unable to contain herself, Shay beams. "Our sweet Lily danced around the room in her bra and underwear, and although none of us can hold a tune, we formed a girl band. We called ourselves the Painted Hearts."

God, that night. Growing up in a small town north of Toronto, everyone knew everyone, which meant getting served underage was a no-go. On the evening in question Shay's brother smuggled us booze, and umpteen shots later, we had smudged black eyeliner under our eyes. Shay set up pots and pans and smashed away on them with a wooden spoon. Lily found a recorder and screeched out notes that could shatter glass. I, of course, played air guitar, hopping around the room like the lead singer of the Slits, head banging to my imagined punk tunes.

We were *horrible*.

I grin at the memory. "As much as I loved our band, the heart part makes it sound too wedding specific. But whatever we choose, we could use that picture of us in our underwear and ski boots for the logo."

Lily drops her forehead to the table, and Sawyer rubs her back. "If all it takes is some vodka to get you ladies skiing in your lingerie, then we need to book another ski trip."

Ignoring him, Shay says, "My second choice is Over the Top Events. Less personal, but it gets the point across."

Now *that* name works. "Catchy. I love it."

Lily lifts her head from the table. "It's actually pretty perfect."

Kolton drums his fingers on the table, each tap timed to the hipster music strumming from the speakers. "Can we get back to that ski trip talk? How about Whistler next winter?" He nudges Shay's side. "I'll give you lessons first. Make sure you know how to merge onto a run so you don't cut off any skiers."

I settle into my chair, waiting for Shay to unleash her inner Mike Tyson. Kolton knows she can ski circles around him. He also knows she'll never admit it was her fault when the two collided on Aspen Mountain. But he loves pushing her buttons, and she loves rising to the bait.

Her passive-aggressive reply: "It's okay. I've forgiven *you* for skiing into *me*. We might not have met otherwise."

Sawyer jumps in then, all four of my friends joking about how crappy their lives would be if they hadn't met. The odd woman out, I keep my mouth shut. I'd erase that night if I could. I wish we hadn't spotted the boys in their condo, or Nico, to be precise. The second I saw his massive frame, tight T-shirt emphasizing each inked muscle, I pushed the girls to be wild and crazy, to invite ourselves inside. The casual hookup I'd imagined was anything but.

"Shay said you saw Nico at the station today." When I don't answer Lily, she nudges my elbow. "How'd it go?"

"Fine."

"Fine good or fine bad?"

"Fine, meaning: I'd rather stick my face in a termite mound than spend time with him." I also wanted to crawl over his desk and stick my face somewhere else, but I keep that nugget to myself.

I pick up my menu, determined to let this day go. The wallet incident and being around Nico—all that's in the past. Tonight is about hanging with my friends and celebrating our new business, in name, at least. Tomorrow I'll hunt for a paying job, and there's a chance I'll find my sister soon. My future is bright.

Until a shadow falls across me. "This seat taken?"

At the sound of Nico's voice, my heart flips, *involuntarily*. It shouldn't flip. It should stay exactly where he left it, incinerated on his condo floor in Aspen. Instead of replying, I aim a missile glare at Shay. She shrugs as if she didn't know he was coming. All eyes are on me—expectant, waiting—leaving me little choice.

"The seat is not taken." I lift my menu higher and study the main courses. Chicken *something*. Shrimp *something*. The words blur, like I've left my camera's shutter speed open too long.

The chair across from me scrapes along the wood floor.

Flip goes my traitorous heart.

My table wobbles as he sits, and I clench my jaw. He's probably leaning on his inked elbows, probably staring at me, forcing himself into my space. My world. My body temperature spikes, along with my anger. Not wanting him to ruin this night, I put down my menu and focus on Shay and Kolton. "How's Jackson?"

They share a look and burst out laughing. When Kolton recovers, he says, "Good, but thanks to Sawyer, his latest quirk has us questioning our sanity."

Sawyer pulls back from whispering to Lily. "Every kid should have a drum set."

Shay makes a show of rubbing her ear. "Tell that to my hearing."

"He's actually not half bad," Kolton says. "But he won't put down the drumsticks and insists on smacking everything in whacking distance. Including Shay's ass."

Sawyer beams. "The kid learns fast. We should put on a talent show. Jackson could write a song, my nieces could choreograph a routine, and Nico could roll his hips. We'd rake in the cash." Sawyer picks up his phone and shakes it, taunting Nico with the video he took a while back.

Eager to embarrass his friend, Sawyer showed it to me one night in Toronto. So accustomed to associating Nico with anger, I surprised myself by laughing. Cackling, really. Nico dancing with five-year-olds is a sight to behold. Seeing how cute he was with Sawyer's nieces, how willing he was to humiliate himself for a smile, melted a layer of my animosity.

Then I remembered Aspen.

That night I'd glimpsed what it would be like to feel open and vulnerable and cared for, how I'd imagined having family would feel—unconditional acceptance, an unbreakable bond you can't explain. I had that with Rose, before she left. I had that with Nico, for a minute. And for some messed-up reason I can't let it go. Can't move on like usual.

"That video goes live, and I impound your car."

They all laugh at Nico's joke, but he slides his gaze toward me, and my breath hitches. His eyes, blue as the ocean, lock on mine. My neck tingles. My fingertips twitch. My ability to sit across from him and hide my hurt and anger evaporates. I also can't hide my attraction. Still, sixteen months later, one look from him and my stomach drops and my blood boils and I itch to lick every inch of his body.

His large hand presses against my knee under the table. "Can we talk?"

Jesus, his touch. It's the first time I've felt the weight of his palm on me since Aspen. It's heavy. Huge. Callused. Instinctually I shift forward, my body no longer mine to command. He doesn't move his hand. Just his thumb. It presses harder, dragging downward. I grip my armrests to keep from sliding to the floor. He stares at me, waiting for my answer.

Yes. No. Maybe. I choose silence.

The way our lives are entrenched with our friends, I'll have to spend time with him, and I can't keep pretending I can block him out. Moving here was about starting fresh, which means letting go of this grudge. But talking about Aspen could stir up more feelings, the same way the experience spurred my need to find Rose. If we talk about our time in the hot tub, it could unhinge me further.

Our waiter arrives to take our order, and Nico's thumb moves again, a tiny brush, his skin against mine, sending a pulse between my thighs. My sanity plummets. I shout, "Chicken," like a lunatic as I push away from the table.

Nico's hand slides from my knee, but his eyes don't waver. I feel his gaze on my back as I hurry to the bathroom. The second I get inside, I close the door and lean against it, thankful it's not a public room with several stalls. I take a few deep breaths.

How can that bit of contact turn me inside out? The smallest touch?

Memories of his other touches flip through my mind, snippets of skin and ink, flashes of ecstasy.

My back arching.

His fingers exploring.

The curve of his inked shoulder.

His huge hands.

The sheer size of *him*.

We might not have had sex, and the details may be fuzzy, but there's no doubt it was the hottest night I've ever had. What isn't fuzzy is the time I spent with him in the hot tub prior, and how he took advantage of my vulnerability.

Goddamn Nico. And Goddamn Aspen.

We'd left the group that night, the two of us intent on privacy. Since I'd laid eyes on him, I was salivating to see Nico's hulking frame in the flesh, taste his inked skin, so I suggested a hot tub. We met at his place and stripped down to our bathing suits, a bottle of tequila at the ready, and holy god of gods, that body. I'd seen fit men before—eight-pack, deep V, and carved muscles—but I didn't know where to look first. Tribal tattoos followed the deep cuts of his biceps and triceps, the tail of a stylized phoenix landing in the groove between his pecs. The muscles of his thighs and calves twitched with each step, and his swim shorts were snug enough to show what I'd hoped.

Everything about Nico was huge.

He took an eyeful of me in my black string bikini, letting his hand drag over my ass as he passed me to slip into the outdoor tub. The water sloshed as he sank in. "We should get to know each other better."

I licked my lips. "I'd like to get to know what's under your shorts."

I'm pretty sure he blushed, but the outdoor lighting was nothing but a soft glow, and Nico's uninked skin was smooth and dark, thanks to his Polynesian father, making it hard to tell. He flicked his head toward the seat opposite him. "Sit. Let's talk first."

I wasn't one for delayed gratification, especially being that desperate for oblivion. Talking led to thinking, when all I wanted was distraction. Wanted to pretend the news I'd learned before leaving home never happened.

Unprepared to walk away from him, I huffed out a breath then did as he asked. I sank into the warm churning water, my sore muscles relaxing on contact. Steam curled into the cold air.

I waited and waited until he said, "Tell me something about yourself."

"Or we could do shots." I grinned.

"Shots sound like fun, in a bit."

Was this guy for real? There I was, my bikini practically nonexistent, a sure thing, and he wanted to *talk*. "I like long walks on the beach, collecting garden gnomes, and saving whales."

He didn't crack a smile, not even a smirk, so I nudged his knee with my foot. He caught my ankle and tugged me forward. *That* game I could play. That game led to release and nirvana and the amnesia I craved. I straddled his lap but couldn't get close enough to feel him against me, to medicate my emptiness with his big, strong body.

The more I wiggled, the firmer he gripped my hips. "If you want me, tell me something real."

It was a trip to be so tightly wound and forced to hold back. I dug my fingers into his shoulders, kneading the ropy muscle. "I don't do real."

"I don't do casual." He leaned forward and kissed my neck, his tongue darting out for a taste. My head dropped back, and I tried to shift forward, but he held firm.

Frustrated, I planted my feet on the bench to push away, but his vise grip didn't budge. "You live in Vancouver, Nico. I live in Toronto. This is the definition of casual. If you're not interested, that's fine. I'll find someone else to have fun with on this trip."

He eased his grasp. "If you want to go, then go. I won't keep you here. But if you want what I want, tell me something real."

The heat from the pool and his body clouded my mind, my heart buzzing faster than a tattoo gun. I never did real. I did fun and easy and quick escapes. Real was a broken heart. Real was tearstained cheeks the day you turned nine and walked into your sister's room to find everything *gone*. No note, no good-bye. Real was learning your grandmother had tragically died.

I should have taken Door Number One and left him sitting here, not played his game, but I looked into his ocean eyes, and I was drowning. The urge to share a piece of myself with him over-whelmed me, to release some of the turmoil simmering below my skin, but I didn't know how.

"I don't do real," I repeated, quieter, hoping he'd convince me otherwise.

He tilted his head and brushed my bangs aside. "Why?"

The men in my life liked sex and good times, not searching con-versations. They didn't look at me like I was special or precious.

They didn't look at me like Nico did. "Real gets you hurt." I gripped his shoulders.

He traced a line down my cheek to my chest, fanning his huge hand over my heart and breast. My nipples pebbled. I rocked forward again, needing friction, but this was his game, his rules, and he held me steady. "I won't hurt you," was all he said. He might have used his words sparingly, but they hit on target. He leaned in as if to kiss me—his wide lips too full, his narrow hips too close, the churning water too hot. "I promise," he whispered.

I wasn't one to share, to cry or whine or complain about my lot. Life was like poker: You got what you were dealt. Believing and sharing only led to disappointment.

But those eyes. That promise. I was a goner.

Confused and lost in the moment, I lifted my left wrist and looked at the rose tattoo over my pulse point. That was for my sister, but it was the feathers inked up my arm I found myself pointing to. "I got these for my grandmother. I only met her once. I was sixteen, and she showed up out of the blue at my house. She sat beside a fire and told me a person can only know who they are and where they're going if they know where they're from. She'd said if I stared at the moon too long, its energy would pull me into the sky. That the earth we take for granted grew from the back of a turtle."

I sucked in a shuddering breath, entranced, reliving every word she spoke, once again greedy for knowledge—a history of my First Nations' ancestry that was bigger than my small town and absentee parents and disappeared sister.

Eyes burning, I looked up at Nico. "She lived on the street and died a week ago, exposure to the cold. I can't imagine what that

would feel like, your blood turning to ice." I shivered, still horri-
fied over what she'd endured. "I never got a chance to thank her.
To tell her what that visit meant to me."

I didn't dare mention what a mess I was at sixteen. That meeting her had changed my life in ways she'd never know. But that was
more than I'd ever shared with a man. More than I'd even shared
with my best friends. Then I told him about Rose. Not the tough-
est part, but enough.

He didn't say he was sorry, didn't look at me with pity. He
pulled my arm to his lips and kissed the inked feathers, then the
black and gray rose. The intimacy of the moment caught in my
throat, my chest, reeling me in.

He pointed to part of the tribal piece on his left pec—two
semicircles with repeated patterns like a candelabra. "This is *enata*,
a Polynesian symbol of the sky guarding its people. I've had to help
my mother raise my sister and brother, my father's in jail, and my
siblings attract trouble like bees to honey."

I traced the lines, water dripping from my fingers down his
broad chest. "You tell that story to all the girls?" I forced levity into
my words, but even I could hear my uncertainty. My insecurity.

He shook his head, those blue eyes piercing. "No."

The relief was instant. "Why me?"

"Don't know. There's something about you, Raven."

He said my name low and deep, a quiet murmur that rumbled
in my dark places, lighting them from within. Everything about
him was big and safe and reassuring. He felt like…*home*.

Fresh tears pricked my eyes. "I don't understand what I'm feeling."

"Me neither." He pressed his forehead to mine. "Is it okay?"

I nodded. "As long as you keep your promise."

He kissed my shoulder, the dip at my throat, tender and sweet. "I'm a man of my word."

The man is a fucking liar.

The memory scrapes at the scar tissue left in his wake, and heavy knocks thump on the bathroom door, bringing me back to the moment. Back to the awareness of Nico's too-large presence once again thrust into my life.

The sound is followed by the fucking liar's voice. "Raven, let me in. We need to talk."

My heart accelerates, racing for cover. The air suddenly feels too warm, my throat too tight. Instead of pacing between the cream walls in this cramped room, I plant my feet firmly. "You are *persona non grata* in here. Not wanted. Go away."

"I'm not leaving."

Damn him and his stubborn self. Last time he forced me to talk to him, to *share*, I got steamrolled. But he's best friends with Kolton and Sawyer. Not talking to him will be more challenging than having this discussion.

I yank the door open and face the Sexy Beast. "Talk."

"Can I come in?"

I step back and he steps in, the small space smaller with his huge frame inside.

"I'm sorry," he says as the door clicks shut behind him.

Tapping my toe, I cross my arms and study the pink tile around the oval mirror. I count the number of sticks poking out of the air freshener, the scent of eucalyptus permeating the room. Better to focus on that than the smells of man and musk and bad decisions that followed him in here.

When he realizes those two words won't cut it, he inches closer. "I'm sorry. Really sorry. Our time in Aspen meant a lot to me. I think it was intense for both of us, and I should have called. Should have gotten in touch with you. But the stuff with my brother took over and other things went down. I couldn't think straight. And part of me was ashamed."

He studies a crumpled paper towel on the floor, then looks up. "I told you stuff about my family in Aspen, but admitting how bad things really were was hard for me back then. I was embarrassed, so I shut down. Once I realized I was being stupid, too much time had passed. I didn't know if you'd want to hear from me. Figured I'd fucked everything up and that was that. Then I heard you were moving here, and I thought about you more. Knew I needed to explain."

I body-check him with my eyes. "You got the fucked-everything-up part right. You broke a promise to me and didn't even apologize. Only a dick would do that."

He winces and rubs his shaved head, his hurt and disappointment clear as day, and *God*, I feel bad. I know what his family means to him, how much of a burden he carries. In a few simple words, he shared that with me in Aspen. And embarrassment over family is something I'm intimately acquainted with.

I just wish my heart hadn't gotten caught in the crossfire.

"I'm sorry," I say, and his face brightens. "About the dick part," I clarify, "not about the rest. Yes, you fucked everything up. I won't trust you again on a personal level. But…" *But* your chest should be bronzed and your forearms rival the Rock's. "*But* I need to move past this. We're going to see each other a fair bit, and I'm tired of being angry."

He stands taller, moves closer. "Friends, then?"

I shrug as if his proximity isn't sending goose bumps up my arms, as if I don't want him to pin me against the wall with his powerful thighs. But what I want isn't what's good for me. "Looks that way."

He leans down to my ear, his hot breath ghosting over my skin. "Go out with me."

Maybe he's imagining my legs around his waist, too. My nails digging into his neck. Too bad he burned that bridge. And torched the surrounding villages.

I try to shove him back, but I'd have more luck moving a tank. "What part of 'I won't trust you again on a personal level' did you not understand?"

That big and dumb thing really *does* go hand in hand.

He takes my not-so-subtle hint and steps away. "Can't blame a guy for trying." He lingers a moment, then pulls a piece of paper from his back pocket. "I really am sorry. I've thought about you a lot since that night. Haven't been with another woman since." He unfolds the paper in his hand, blinks at it, then passes it to me. "I've read this more times than I should admit. See you at the table."

He leaves, taking the air in the room with him, and my mind whirls. Nico hasn't been with another woman since Aspen—*since me*—for sixteen months? I look at his note. Scratch that, *my* note. My handwriting loops across the page, the familiar words taking me back to the morning after.

I woke up early and wanted to get changed at my condo. Thanks for the tequila. And the bed. But especially the hot tub. I'm still freaked out, but I trust you. I don't want this to end when we leave.

Can't even believe I'm writing this down, but I've never felt this way. Text me when you get up and we'll meet later. Can't wait to see you again.

x Raven

Reading my words revives the sting of his betrayal as I checked my phone for days and weeks afterward. Normally I'd have no issue calling a guy. But he forced me to open up, promised he wouldn't hurt me, then he vanished without a word. My pride was on the wrathful side of unimpressed.

I glance at the painful note again, and warmth worms its way under the hurt. He kept it. Reread it. The wrinkled page tells as much, and he hasn't been with another woman since Aspen. I should rip the paper up and finally put the incident behind me, move on as I told Nico I would. And I will. The aftermath I endured wasn't worth that fleeting moment of wholeness. Still, I fold the note into four so I can slip it inside my purse at the table.

Four

Nico

I roll my shoulder, the joint stiff after yesterday's workout. And Wednesday's. And Tuesday's. Every day's since Raven walked into the station. I've lifted enough weights the past week to win one of those World's Strongest Man competitions. All that's left is pulling a transport truck.

Alessi slams his fist into my arm. "You're not listening, bro."

"You still talking?" After three years together, the guy's voice has become white noise.

"I need some advice."

"Definitely get that rash checked out."

He snorts. "Fucker."

He turns the patrol car down Hastings Street for a final pass, easing his foot off the gas. We scan the homeless people crammed against walls, legs sticking out from under blankets and cardboard. Fidgety men and women huddle together by barred-up stores while an old man pushes his life in a grocery cart. East Hastings is as seedy as Vancouver gets.

It also used to be the place my brother called home.

Alessi drums his thumbs on the wheel. "My cousin, Lucia, is getting hitched next month, and since their having, like, ten thousand people stand up for them, she's asked me to be in the wedding party. Normally I'd be all over that. The suit, the bridesmaids—sign me up. Turns out her maid of honor is a chick I banged last month. Had no idea I'd have to see her again, and now she's texting me. Lucia gave her my number and expects me to take her to the wedding. The whole thing's one big clusterfuck."

I crack my neck and massage my temples to stall the headache building at the edges of my vision. "So take her. What's the big deal?"

He brakes at a stoplight and flings his hands in the air—his Italian sign language. "I've told you a million times how crazy Lucia and her sisters are. If I take this Mara chick, they'll have us before the priest by the end of the night saying 'I do.' If I *don't* take her, they'll rip into me in front of my folks about banging random chicks. I'll get lectured for the next millennium."

"My advice is to stop using the word *bang*."

Eyes forward, he accelerates. "I need a new partner."

"You need new life skills."

"Says the dude who has the hottest chick I've ever seen in front of him and doesn't seal the deal."

Man has a point. But being with Raven isn't about getting laid. I might have a lot of pent-up sexual frustration from the past sixteen months, and the thought of being inside her gets me hard like nothing else, but I have to do this right. I'm at fault here. I hurt her. I need to prove she can trust me. Leaning back, I resume rubbing my temples. "I'm giving her time."

"Bad idea, bro. With a body and face like that, she won't stay single long."

I narrow my eyes at him. "Don't even think about it."

A young boy in the car beside us waves, and Alessi gives him a thumbs-up. To me, he says, "I may like to *bang* chicks, but I wouldn't go there. I prefer both my heads to remain intact. What about when you're done with her? Still a no-go?"

I bristle at the jab, but my history speaks for itself. At sixteen I fell at Tammy Eisen's feet and professed my love. Three months later I avoided her calls until I had the courage to end things. I chased Jasmine Lee for weeks, fell hard and fast, serenaded her at our high school graduation, then I couldn't muster up enough interest for a basic conversation. Even Lisa, my last girlfriend, lost her appeal. Never anything specific. No cheating escapades or massive arguments. They each meant something to me, I thought I was in love, then I wasn't.

What I experienced with Raven in Aspen was different. Bigger somehow. More intense. Josh was living on the street then, my sister sliding downhill fast, and I sensed sadness under Raven's tough exterior. Unable to fix things at home, I wanted to ease Raven's pain, feel useful for a change, but her vulnerability hit me hard. Before I knew it, I was telling her about my family, too. Confessed how terrified I was to be anything like my father.

Even for a night, she had the power to ease my troubled mind.

It doesn't mean I won't lose interest, the same cycle spiraling. But the idea of Alessi taking her out, even if that happens, has me wanting to snap his neck.

"Definitely a no-go," I say. He nods, and I stare out the window. The busy city flips by. "I'm giving her space, okay? She's pissed at me. But I'm not walking away."

"Just sayin', I'd be careful how much space you give."

"Noted."

But wary. Last week, after I apologized to her in that bathroom, she sat opposite me for the night. I'd said my piece, but I hated admitting I'd been too embarrassed about my family to call her, hated how juvenile it sounded. When Josh pulled himself out of the gutter and started working toward his GED, I pushed that bullshit aside, knowing he needed someone to be proud of him. He needed a stronger hand guiding him, too. Consequences for recklessness promised and dealt.

Now Raven knows the truth.

She didn't glare or snap at me afterward. We hung out with our friends, laughing and joking. Still, tension hung between us. My knee would brush hers, and she'd freeze. Her calf would touch mine, and I'd fist my hands. Like at the gym, when I'd exhaust myself, every breath pushed awareness into my muscles, my joints. Near Raven, I was hypersensitive, and I'm pretty sure she was, too, always catching her breath the way she was. Unfortunately, when I tried to give her a ride home, she barely looked at me, said no, and walked to the bus alone.

I'll give her another few days. Time to let my apology absorb and to read the note I kept…the note *she* wrote—a reminder of what she felt, too. Then it's full steam ahead. I've spent too many hours stroking myself, reliving our night in Aspen: her inked skin rubbing against mine, her sliding on top of me, working her way down. Her head between my thighs. Her hands and lips and tongue working me over.

Falling asleep with her tucked into my side.

"You going to the rec center tonight?" Alessi asks as we pull into the station.

I shift on my seat, thoughts of Raven always making me half hard. "No. Seeing my family. I need to get in as much time as possible the next couple months. Things are looking bleak for Josh." Just like that, the heat in my veins cools.

He parks, turns off the ignition, but doesn't move. "There's a bust going down soon. I don't know the details, but I'm pretty sure some of Josh's old gang are about to get it up the ass. I'll keep my ears open. All we need is one weak link."

I shove my door open. "Appreciate it."

I trudge to my locker, looking forward to seeing Josh, but sick to my stomach. I haven't told him my lead fell through, haven't busted his bubble of hope. He's been toeing the line since he got out on bail. Partly born of determination to avoid the punks who led him to drugs, the street, and enough bad decisions to seal his fate, but I've lain down the law since this shitstorm began. His arrest was the last straw. If he screws up again, he's on his own. Cutting him off from the family would gut me, but lax rules are what led us here. He needs to be accountable. Culpable. Our nephews are getting older. Watching. Learning.

If he stays strong and honors himself, I'll stand by him. Be there for him, whatever he needs. If he falls, I won't be his safety net again.

* * *

I pull into my mother's driveway and note the broken gutter on the sloping roof as I shut my door. Must have been last night's storm. The air smells like earth and wet leaves. A few torn branches are scattered over the lawn. Mentally, I add the gutter to my to-do list, after patching the back deck and repainting the white siding.

When I get a foot inside the door, Jack rushes my legs, chanting, "Cake, cake, cake."

Colin hangs back, hands stuffed into the pockets of his oversized shorts. "Hey, Uncle Nico."

I ruffle Colin's dark hair, the little guy too big to be picked up. Too big to get excited to see me. Jack is a different story. Tiny for seven, the kid is pale with fair hair to match and weighs less than my gym bag. I lift him up by his armpits and tuck him under my arm like a football. "What's this I hear about cake?"

Jack wiggles in my grasp. "There's cake but we're not allowed to have it, but it smells *so* good, and it's chocolate and I'll die if I don't eat some."

I carry him into the kitchen while Colin walks beside us, slouching, eyes as puffy as a hungover frat boy. I duck under the narrow door frame and twist to avoid smacking Jack's head into the side. The entranceway is small, the kitchen not much bigger. The brown plaid wallpaper and green counters are the same as when I was a kid. My mom's famous chocolate cake sits on top of the oven, the sweet smell filling the room.

She baked that piece of heaven for every birthday in this house, two layers of chocolate cake and icing an inch thick. It was also the cake she baked each time my father got out of jail. The last parole, when I was thirteen, it sat there for two days and got tossed when he never turned up.

Since it isn't anyone's birthday, and my father is behind bars, the cake is a mystery.

"My son isn't a football. Put the kid down before he pukes up his dinner." My sister crowds into the cramped kitchen, arms folded, the skin around her eyes puffier and darker than Colin's. She smiles, though, a sight I wasn't sure I'd see again.

Not wanting to upset her fragile balance, I kiss Jack's head and put him down. I nod to the cake. "What are we celebrating?"

"I want cake!" Jack cries again.

Too tough to care about cake, Colin leans on the fridge and kicks his heel into the base. The appliance looks more yellow than white, the dent still there from when I punched it the day Josh stormed out, the day it all went to shit. I should buy them a new one.

Nikki smacks Jack on the bottom. "Into the living room with you. No one gets cake 'til Uncle Josh gets home."

He runs out and Colin rolls off the fridge, trudging after his brother.

I shake my head. "Who pissed in his Cheerios?"

Nikki twists her long brown hair around her finger, chewing her lip the way she's done since rehab. She's still skinny in her ripped jeans and AC/DC tank top, but not as gaunt as she was. "He's ten going on fifty. Life's hard, he tells me. Too much home-work. Shitty sleep habits. He doesn't know hard."

"How's the crowd he's hanging with at school? Anything I need to worry about?" That's all it takes, one bad seed and the crop is spoiled. Or maybe I have it backward.

Maybe it's the earth.

My father, uncle, and a few cousins have all done time. Drugs, burglary, car theft, assault—you name it, my family has bragging rights. All us kids could have walked that path, but the punks

Nikki and Josh fell in with tipped the balance.

When it came time for me to go to junior high, my mother's cousin lived in a different district. Without consulting me, they lied about my address and shipped me off to a posh school in a posh neighborhood, my sneakers never in style, my clothes never quite right. Sawyer and Kolton didn't seem to care. We hung out and fucked around, but never crossed certain lines. Unlike my siblings. A family argument meant Josh and Nikki went to the local schools. Their friends offered them heroin instead of beer, nights stealing cars instead of watching movies.

If that had been my life, I could have spiraled downhill, too.

Nikki leans on the small table at the center of the kitchen. "His friends seem all right. For now, at least. Better than the crowd Josh ran with." Her blue eyes are glassy, rimmed red around the edges. Not dilated like when she gets high. Just tired, hopefully.

"If you even get a whiff of something, I want to know. I won't see those boys messing up their lives."

Blinking rapidly, she places her hand on my forearm. "You're too good to us."

More like not good enough. I should have been firmer with Josh when he was younger, gotten in his face when he'd ditch class and spray paint walls, locked Nikki in her room when she blew curfew. I know better now. But then? With our father either looking to score or in jail, and our mother working two jobs to keep us fed, I was scrambling. She never asked me to step in, never made it my burden. But Nikki and Josh weren't given the same chance as me. I at least owed them that.

I jut my chin toward the cake. "Still don't know what the fuss is about."

She grins wider than usual. "It's a surprise."

"Last time there was a surprise, I ended up in a Superman costume for Jack's birthday."

"And I still plan on framing those pictures."

I'm about to threaten her with jail time (not the best joke in this house) when the front door swings open. My mother kicks it shut, struggling with an armful of full of groceries. I duck through the door frame and take long strides to reach her, grabbing her bags in one arm and hugging her shoulders with the other. She may be tall, but her head fits under my chin.

She squeezes back. "Is Josh home yet?"

"Nope. What's with the mysterious cake?"

She shoves me with her hip and glances at the boys in the living room. Jack's pushing my old Tonka Truck around, skirting the cigarette burns in the brown carpet. Colin's sullen face is hidden behind his iPod. Nikki flops on the couch beside him and smooths his dark hair. He raises a shoulder to ward her off, and she winces.

Sighing, I carry the groceries into the kitchen and help Mom unpack. She kisses my shoulder. "How was work?"

"Not bad."

She side-eyes me, my two word answer not cutting it. I don't fill silence needlessly like Alessi, but I usually offer up more than two syllables. But talking opens the door to questions, often about Josh and his case. Questions I prefer to avoid.

I choose deflection. "Colin seems quiet. Everything okay with him? Nikki doing all right?"

She tosses a bag of dill pickle chips and M&M's on the counter. "He's just being a kid. Nothing serious. And Nikki is…better. Definitely better. Good days and bad." She reaches up and pinches my cheek. "But *you*, I don't have to worry about. Josh is lucky you're in his corner."

The smell of the chocolate cake sours, my gut turning over. *Lucky* isn't the word I'd choose.

"Could you empty those bags in bowls? Josh will be home any minute."

Happy to busy my hands, I grab the yellow plastic bowls from the cupboard and dump in the chips and candy—Josh's favorite. Whatever the celebration, he's at the center of it. Maybe if I don't mention Jericho and the confession I won't get, Josh can enjoy his last weeks as a free man. Not worry about the rationed food and prison bars and empty days. The inmates.

No point destroying what's left of his time on the outside.

The front door slams open again, and Josh ducks inside. He scratches at his dark scruff. "Where are the rugrats?"

Jack, of course, throws himself at his uncle, head butting his thigh. Colin comes to life and loiters in the hallway, his clenched hand held up for a fist bump. Josh obliges and crouches down, a stack of comic books on his knee. "I was with a buddy, and he was getting rid of these. You two want 'em?"

Jack crows, "Yes!" and tries to swipe the stack.

Pushing to his feet, Josh looms over the boys. He pulls a few comics from the stack. "These, little man, are for you." Jack grabs them and disappears into the living room. He holds the rest out for Colin. "And these are not for your brother's eyes. They're too gory. Got it?"

Colin bobs his head and takes the stack of comics. "Thanks, man. These are awesome."

Josh squeezes his shoulder and pushes past him toward the

kitchen. Instead of slinking off, Colin follows, his focus locked on his uncle, like Josh might do or say something brilliant at any second. A couple weeks back Colin was all over Josh, playing new songs from his iPod, eager to impress his uncle. He even wears his jeans low on his ass like Josh, a fucking travesty. I should be happy Josh brings Colin out of his shell, but it eats at the hollow in my gut.

Josh's conviction will reverberate through this family.

"Nico," Josh says in greeting. He tosses his sketchbook on the table, the thing glued to his hands these days, then he rounds the table and pulls me into a hug.

I pound his back, holding on longer than usual. There was a time, before his arrest, that he wouldn't talk to me, let alone give me a hug. The silver lining, I guess.

I release him and nod to the cake. "Someone want to tell me what's up?"

Josh folds his arms and sucks on his lips, pressing them tight. His eyes shine brighter than I've ever seen them, like he's swallowed a lightbulb.

"Seriously," I say. "Someone tell me something or I'm taking Jack and that cake, and we'll eat it ourselves."

"I got my GED." Josh grins so wide *my* face hurts. "My fucking GED," he repeats, then winces. "Sorry, Ma."

Mom doesn't yell at him to watch his language. Her chin trembles, and she fans her face to keep the tears at bay. I scrub my jaw then cover my mouth to hide the extent of my emotion. *His GED.* Every grade since his arrest has been hard earned. Late nights. Determination. Desperation to be better. As tough as it's been, it validates the harsh line I've set for him.

Choked up, I grab his T-shirt and pull him back into my arms. "So proud of you." I cup the back of his neck and kiss his head. "So proud," I say against his hair.

By the time I let him go, Mom is crying, Nikki's leaning on the door frame wiping her eyes, and Colin shifts on his feet, unsure what to make of all the hugging.

"Can we eat cake now?" Jack pokes his head around Josh's legs and bats his lashes at my mother. "Please, Anna, can we?"

Anna. No one chooses to become a grandparent at forty, but having your grandkids call you by your first name won't change the facts.

She nods, still too emotional to speak.

Josh smacks his hands together. "You bet. Cake and chips and chocolate. It's a party 'cause your uncle is the bomb."

I stand back as they crowd around the cake, failure coating my throat.

This small house has witnessed enough yelling to crack the walls. It has withstood enough tears to be washed away, enough anger to light it on fire. But it's still standing. *We're* still standing. How many disasters can we weather, though? If Josh gets convicted, Colin could pull so far away he sets Nikki off. If she starts using again, Jack suffers and Mom loses another kid, possibly her grandkids, too. It's all so damn fragile.

Josh shoves a plate of cake into my hand, and they all pile into the living room, but I can't sit. Can't get comfortable. Can barely swallow a mouthful of chocolate. Jack's face is stained with icing in seconds. Colin badgers Josh about his recent sketches. Nikki puts chips on her plate, alternating bites between them and her cake, more content than I've seen her in ages. My mother is radiant. We're the reason she fought for her receptionist job at the dental office and worked nights bagging groceries. We're the reason she didn't fall apart when my father went to prison, *each time*. And she thinks this is the beginning of something, a new start for our family.

How do I confess the truth?

She leans into the couch, her body rounder than when she was young, her dirty-blond hair streaked with gray. Those light blue eyes never age, though. My eyes. Josh and Nikki's eyes. Eyes that pleaded with me when Josh was arrested to do *something*. To save him. The warmth in the room strangles me, the facts I haven't shared tightening the noose. I can't let this happen. Can't stand by while he's sent to jail. Not when he's trying so hard to be better. I have to work the streets again, hit up the vagrants on Hastings. For months I questioned and investigated, even uttering threats. Maybe I missed something. I had to have missed something.

There's too much at stake.

Five

Raven

I'd rather put on a pink dress and twirl a baton for a beauty pageant than share my photographs with another artist. Unfortunately, that won't get me the job I want. I saw Sasha's advertisement in the paper this morning. As soon as I read *Paid Photography Apprenticeship*, I hurried out the door, portfolio in hand, and hunted down her address. Now I'm sitting across from her, chewing my cheek, dreading the moment when she asks to see my work.

She holds out her hand, probably unsure why I have my leather album in a death grip. "Can I see your work?"

Yep. Dreading this moment.

"Sure," I say, wowing her with my intellect.

Her platinum hair is cut in a severe bob, framing her straight black brows and purple eyes. Not blue irises with a tinge of violet. Those suckers are Barney the Dinosaur purple. It takes dedication to wear colored contacts, serious style commitment. A friend in Toronto does special-effects makeup, and every time we'd go out, she'd change her eye color and apply a faint scar for kicks. Hopefully my ordinary black hair and wardrobe aren't marks against me.

Unable to delay my blistering insecurity, I hand over my album.

The photos are from last year's trip to the Sandy Lake First Nation Reserve. My first trip there. Only accessible by plane most of the year, I drove in with a supply truck on their winter ice road. I snapped action shots of teams playing broom ball, close-ups of kids chasing stray dogs, stills of elders digging in at a community feast. My favorite is of a young girl ice fishing, brazen, holding her catch by the gills. I see myself in her: the shape of my face, the color of my skin, the shine of my hair. My grandmother was born in Sandy Lake. My trip there was a way for me to say thank you and good-bye.

Sasha analyzes each image.

Unable to handle the suspense, my gaze drifts to the spiky wall clock above her diamond-backed dining chairs, then down to the triangular coffee table between us. One wrong move in this place, and I could slice an artery. I pull her album toward me, flipping pages as each excruciating second drags. Two images in, my insecurity doubles, because holy shit is her work *sick*. Each photographic portrait is unique, the setting and lighting telling a story.

"Your work is solid," she says. "You have a good eye for composition."

I sit up taller, hand frozen mid-flip. "Thanks, that means a lot. Your photos are unreal." I study one of an older black man, deep lines etched in his face. Gray stubble dots his chin and cheeks, longer whiskers above his lip. Light reflects off his smiling eyes.

Behind him, blurred tombstones fill the space; it's a portrait of love and loss.

She crosses her legs, and her boxy skirt crinkles. "Thanks, but this job isn't about taking those shots. I need an assistant, someone to help with the grunt work. It's not glamorous. You'll be hauling gear and setting up lighting. And Vancouver's weather can be a bitch. We can't always reschedule, so rain and cold come with the territory."

I nod as I flip the page. A young girl beams at me, ankle deep in a puddle, her pigtails flying, water splashing as rain pounds in blurry sheets. It's glorious.

Sasha points at the photo. "That one took close to a hundred frames. I had to convince her folks to let her splash around."

Overwhelmed and impressed, I shut the book. "If you'll have me, I'm in. I've taken enough classes and worked on my own to know the basics, but this stuff"—I point at her book—"this is what I need to learn. Getting to the heart of people, seeing beyond the frame. If you give me this job, I'll work my butt off for you."

She bounces her platform shoe, her purple eyes intense and trippy. "Okay. I'll give you a shot. Can you start next week?"

Once we iron out the details, I hurry from her loft, camera and portfolio in hand, barely fighting the urge to dance in the street. My credit cards have been replaced, and I secured a job before cashing my last teaching paycheck. Things are looking up.

Most things, at least.

There is still the Sexy Beast Issue that's plagued me the past week. That man is trouble. I tried to toss the note I wrote him, tried to put it out of my mind, but it's hard to ignore the truth in my own words. *I don't want this to end. Can't wait to see you again.* I've seen him, all right, in nearly every dream this week, even when zoning out while awake. Sitting across from him at dinner the other night, his knee brushing mine, was worse than getting tattooed without ink—all the pain and no pleasure.

I curl my fingers around my camera, itching to snap some frames. Sasha's work was beyond inspiring, and it will help me shake thoughts of Nico.

I tuck my portfolio in my purse and start walking. No direction. No plan. My black Doc Martens pound the pavement, my shorts and tank top not quite warm enough as evening sets in. Pumped to shoot, I ignore the chill. The neighborhood gets seedier with each passing block, more bars on windows, more litter on the streets. Bring it on. The rawness of life is what I'm after. The ugliness people try to ignore. Too often pedestrians march past homeless people, gazes averted, as if they don't exist.

My grandmother existed.

I scan the streets, breaking the scenes into pieces with my mind. Angles cropped. Compositions imagined. Even before I raise my camera, I fracture the world into frames.

A man and his dog catch my eye, a bulging garbage bag by his feet. He's asleep on a step, and his filthy shirt has ridden up, exposing sores on his side, red and seeping. The slope of his strong nose and long black hair tell me he's First Nations, but I don't know his story. I lift the camera hanging from my neck, hoping to conjure it.

Snap. His fisted hand by his chin.

Snap. His mangy dog resting its muzzle on his leg.

Snap. His gaunt face beside a newspaper article: *Meatloaf Mondays.*

A man knocks my shoulder as he hurries by, and I tug my purse closer. I'd rather not have a repeat of Wreck Beach. All personal property present and accounted for, I skirt around a lamppost. The smell of pizza wafts from a restaurant, and my belly rumbles, until the sickly-sweet scent of raw sewage overpowers it. Holding my breath, I hurry along, then stop short.

A couple of women have their backs to me, similar hair to mine. Squinting, I stare harder. Having black hair doesn't mean one of them is Rose, but—*there's always a but*—one of them could be. Every time I spot a woman with a familiar trait, my pulse taps a nervous beat. Would she be happy to see me? Pissed I tracked her down? Does she know I'm the reason our father beat her senseless the night before she left? She may hate me. She may not forgive me. But she's my last chance to have an Unconditional Someone.

Every Christmas and Thanksgiving, Lily and Shay go home to their families. I'm always invited and often tagged along, but they aren't my people. They don't joke with me about childhood stories or boast about my accomplishments.

With my grandmother gone, Rose is all I have left.

Tonight, at least, I have my camera. My security blanket. I raise it and snap frames. Hands. Knees. Slim legs. When the girls angle their shoulders toward me, I lower my lens. Way too young for Rose.

Another cool breeze sends goose bumps down my neck, gradual darkness turning the concrete from gray to iron. People lurk in the growing shadows. The vibe on the street creeps into *creepier*. I'm about to hurry to a bus stop when a huge, hulking man comes into view.

My heart does its flipping thing.

Illuminated by a streetlight, Nico's hands are planted on his knees as he leans forward to talk to a boy seated on the sidewalk. His face is intense, as though he's in cop mode, but he's not in his uniform blues. The kid looks to be in his twenties, a baseball cap pulled low over his eyes. I should look away, *walk* away. Instead I lift my camera.

Click. The head of the phoenix curling up Nico's neck.

Click. The bulging bicep that stretches his short sleeve.

Click. The set of his square jaw.

Then I shoot an ass montage.

Every angle and viewpoint I can manage, wide shots and close-ups, details and panoramas, because God in heaven, that ass. Twenty shots later, his head whips around, and his sights lock on me. I freeze, sure he knows I was scoping his chiseled form, practically drooling. He says something to the boy then straightens. His long strides eat up the distance between us, and I enjoy every purposeful step. Dark jeans hug his hips, his white T-shirt tight enough to outline every edge and groove of his arms and pecs.

Forget the ass montage; the man needs a portfolio for each muscle.

When he reaches me, I realize my camera is still in front of my face. He puts a finger on the lens and presses it down, forcing me to acknowledge him. I'm not a short girl. I've dated guys taller than me and some shorter, but Nico's massive frame towers. "You taking pictures?"

I rock on my feet, unsteady in his presence. The hair on his buzzed head is the same length as the scruff on his jaw, his lips slightly parted. If he didn't ruin things after Aspen, I'd press to my tiptoes and rub my cheek against his five o'clock shadow.

Since he *did* ruin things, I say, "Can vegetarians eat animal crackers?"

He frowns. "Excuse me?"

A bus screeches by, and I drop my camera around my neck, looking anywhere but at his eyes. "I have this thing where if someone asks me a stupid question, like something really obvious, I reply with the dumbest question I can think of." *Don't look into his eyes. Don't look into his eyes.* I drag my gaze up, and my heart stutters. Those ocean eyes.

He rolls his tongue over his teeth. "Are you calling me stupid?"

So hypnotized, I almost fall into him. "No, I'm calling your *question* stupid. Yes, I was taking pictures." I jiggle my camera. "That's usually why people carry these contraptions."

"I don't remember you having such a smart mouth in Aspen." He licks his lips.

I so want to lick those lips. "Selective amnesia. Sarcasm is my signature move."

His gaze drifts down to my boots. "I remember other moves."

Although not verbose, the Sexy Beast likes to banter. "Do you, now?"

He steps closer, his chest brushing my camera lens. I tense my abs, heat spreading south. "Some," he says. "I remember you smiling."

My lips twitch, but I keep them flat. His charm is a weapon I'm ill equipped to handle. Standing here, so close, I can easily forget the nights I spent staring at my cell phone, plotting his demise. Dismemberment by captive killer whale was high on my list, a close second to pitching machine shots to the balls. Still, some twisted part of me wants him to ask me out again. If he did, I could wrap my arms around his waist and kiss his stubbled cheek and say, *yes, yes, yes.* Or I could turn him down and flip him the finger. Also a feel-good option.

He doesn't ask, though. "You shouldn't be in this neighborhood at night. It's dangerous."

A moment ago these shadowed streets were the last place I wanted to be. But with Nico's size and presence, I feel safe. Physically, at least. Emotionally, not so much. "I was heading home. Didn't realize how late it was."

He looks at his black boots, then at the streetlights, then at me. "Can I give you a lift? There's something I need to do, but if you come, I can drop you home after. I'll be worried if you take the bus on your own."

Worried. About me. A shiver courses through my body, and I don't think it's from the cold.

When I first flirted with photography, I couldn't get the shutter speed and aperture right. Too slow or too fast, too much light or too little—whatever I did, my shots weren't crisp. I'd download them to my computer and trash everything. Fastest index finger in the West. Then I photographed Shay at the bottom of one of her ski races, and the images rocked. Each one was clearer than the last: blue sky, bright snow, excitement in the air. Everything just *clicked*.

Like my night with Nico.

For years I'd kept men at arm's length, didn't even realize I was lonely. Then the Sexy Beast slammed everything into focus. Maybe it was my vulnerability that trip, or simply our connection, but once back home, when I returned to my easy nights with men, no strings, no emotion, I knew what I was missing. One night with

Nico, and I craved that closeness—someone to confide in, total honesty. My thoughts shifted to Rose. If I could have a sister in my life, real family, I wouldn't miss the feelings Nico inspired. I would have an Unconditional Someone.

But Nico's the one in front of me, asking to give me a lift home. I could stay aloof like I did after dinner last week, not let him any closer than need be. He hasn't pushed me since then. Hasn't called or sought me out. Maybe he's just being a good guy.

"Sure," I say. "Lead me to your chariot."

He presses his hand to the small of my back, firm but gentle. His hand is so big the tips of his fingers span to my ass, probably on purpose. I should shake him off, not let him cop a feel, but I'm greedy for his touch. We walk in silence, him guiding me through the streets, *hand on my back*.

When we get to a parking lot and his truck beeps, I plant my feet. "So there's this thing, called global warming, and it's liable to melt the world. Maybe you've heard of it?"

He faces me, a smile spreading. Not a full grin, just the corners of his lips tugging upward. Boyish for such a masculine man. "Sounds familiar."

"I'm pretty sure your truck is responsible for vaporizing half the ozone."

"Doubtful." He moves around me and opens the door of his Ford F250, massive like him. Imposing, like him. He holds out his hand. "Your chariot."

What he lacks in words, he sure makes up in charm.

Once on the road, he turns his ear-bleeding country music down. "Why were you on Hastings this late?"

"I, if you must know, just got a job."

He glances at me, then back at the road. "That's great. Teaching art?"

"No." I point to the camera still around my neck. "Gopher girl for an awesome photographer. I'm not cut out for teaching. The whole being around kids thing was a challenge."

"I imagine a roomful can be tough. But photography, that's your passion?"

"It is." I run my hand over the grooves and edges of my Nikon D750. Ever since Lily came by my house on my seventeenth birthday, she's made a point of buying me gifts. When she asked my dad what we were doing to celebrate that day, he sneered at her and said, "Celebrate what? That she drains our bank account?" He was pissed I'd used his track money to buy *vegetables*.

I pull the camera over my head and secure it in my purse. There's a *Sports Illustrated* magazine on the floor. Swimsuit edition. Considering Nico hasn't dated in sixteen months, I bet the pages are sticky.

Chuckling to myself, I say, "Lily got this for me. I love shooting street life. That and colors. I've been going to Kitsilano Beach in the morning, early to catch the sunrise."

He turns the wheel, edging onto a side street. I'm not sure what errand he has to run or where we're going, but I watch each shift of his wrist, each twist and tilt. Thick veins pulse under his dark skin. I don't normally ogle men as they drive, don't study their movements and hand work, but Nico's forearms flex in the most delicious way. Forearm porn.

He fists the wheel at ten and two. "I'd love to see your shots sometime."

I eye the portfolio tucked in my purse. "Maybe." Art is personal, those pictures a window into my world, my heritage. Keeping my distance from Nico doesn't include sharing that. "What about you?" I ask. "What were you doing in that fine part of town? Detective stuff?"

Frown lines pucker his brow. "Things aren't looking good for Josh—my brother. Have the girls told you about it?"

"A bit, not much. I know he stole a car or something."

One hand clutching the wheel, he rubs his neck with the other. "Or something. They found meth when they impounded it. He had a minor drug charge the year prior, so they got a search warrant. He's been out on bail for seven months, but the trial's not far, and we're running out of options."

"Did he do it?" I wince, unsure he wants me butting in, but he doesn't shut me down.

He seems to contemplate the question, then he shakes his head. "No. No way. He made a lot of bad choices, but he's not a dealer."

"So you spend your free time looking for leads?"

He nods. "That, and I volunteer at a rec center in my old neighborhood twice a week. It was a haven for me growing up, and I like to give back. Try to keep the kids there involved and off the streets. One of them did something stupid recently, and we're about to teach him a lesson."

At those ominous words, I glance in the backseat but don't see any ropes or duct tape or weapons. That rules out kidnapping. "Am I about to participate in an illegal activity?"

He keeps his focus on the windshield. "I'm a cop, Raven."

"Are you implying cops never break the law?"

"You watch too many movies."

"You don't watch enough."

Smirking, he keeps driving. We pull up to an apartment building, the porches crammed with plants and tiny barbecues. I wait as Nico disappears inside and reappears with a boy. The kid's skinny as a sapling, probably thirteen or fourteen, a dark mop of hair covering his eyes as he drags his sneakers in an attempt to delay whatever torture the big guy has planned. The boy slides into the backseat and crosses his arms.

Nico shuts his door. "Tim, this is Raven. She'll be coming along with us."

Smiling, I offer a small wave.

A mumbled "Whatever" drifts forward.

Instead of starting the car, Nico pauses. "Pretty sure that's not how you greet a lady. Mind trying again?"

Tim's eyes are hidden under his hood of hair, but I bet he's rolling them. "Nice to meet you."

At that display of teenage sincerity, Nico grunts and reverses onto the street. A silent ten-minute car ride later we pull up to a white building. Several cars are parked outside. The lawn is tended, small flower beds lining the entryway. A large Canadian flag hangs over a sign that reads, *Royal Canadian Legion*. Nico nods for me to get out, and we wait for Tim to join us. If molasses were thickened and forced through a pinhole, it would move faster than this kid.

Nico places a hand on his shoulder. "When we go inside, you straighten up and give these folks your attention." His voice is stern, his wide stance intimidating, even for me. "You show respect. You return what you stole, then you apologize and listen. Got it?"

Tim's Adam's apple bobs down his neck. "Got it."

I follow the boys into the open space. Round tables, plastic chairs, and what looks like a small kitchen fill the room. The average age of the twenty-odd people seated, mostly men, hovers around a hundred and five. If I hadn't seen the sign outside, I'd guess these seniors were here for a game of bingo. But this is a gathering of war veterans.

A man stands when he sees us and motions Tim forward. When the kid doesn't budge, Nico nudges him. Tim's sneakers squeak on the floor as he trudges toward his punishment.

Nico comes to my side and lowers his voice. "Tim stole from their collection cup last week. I heard talk of it at the rec center and told Mr. Miller about it." He gestures to the old man lecturing Tim. The veteran's white eyebrows are as thick as a forest. "We decided making him return it in person would be punishment enough. Have him apologize and learn what the money's used for. If there's a next time, it'll be a different story."

Tim shoves a hand in the front pocket of his baggy jeans, pulls it out, and passes over a wad of bills to Mr. Miller. More words are shared and Tim stands taller, nodding and shifting his feet. Even from this distance, I sense a change in the boy, who then proceeds to meet with every person in the room, shaking hands and speaking softly.

A glance at Nico tells me how important this moment is for him. "Do all the volunteers at the center do this sort of thing?"

He shrugs. "Doubt it. Most of them do it as résumé work, not to make a difference."

"But you think you can? Make a difference, I mean. You think delinquents like Tim can really change?"

"If my brother and sister can turn things around, anyone can."

He doesn't elaborate, and I take the cue, touched how much he cares for not just his family, but for punks from his neighborhood. Only a good man would go the extra mile, give up his free time and devote his energy to others.

If someone had taken a second to talk to my grandmother when she lived on the streets, to connect with her, maybe she'd still be alive. If someone had spent time with me, maybe I wouldn't have nearly burned Gord Dwyer's barn to the ground, *on a dare*. That was the last night I hung with Mitch Harris and his band of losers, smoking pot and vandalizing the town. The possibility of hurting Gord's horses had me sick to my stomach, but it was my grandmother's brief appearance in my life that night that woke me up.

Rose had taken off years prior. My parents alternated between ignoring me and yelling obscenities. I was angry. All the time. Didn't know how to channel the guilt and loneliness broiling inside me. Then my grandmother turned up. She shared her stories until the sun rose and told me I was a good girl, as though I were still a child. Like I hadn't done despicable things. Overwhelmed, I broke down. Confessed to the hell I'd caused that night.

She didn't shout at me or write me off. She touched my face and said, "There is darkness in all of us, but there is light, too. Yours still shines, Raven. How brightly is up to you. Find a way to make amends and always remember the sickness you feel now."

The next day, I marched into the police station and faced the music.

Nico must see potential in the kids he helps, see them for what they are: full of crap. The pricklier the pear, the sweeter the fruit. Like my grandmother saw me. My awareness of his size and strength and beauty, inside and out, amplifies as we wait. If he asked me on a date right now, my answer would probably be yes.

Back in the car, Tim sniffles a few times. Nico asks him what he learned, and the two discuss how vital the money he stole is to the programs offered by the legion, how members of the serving and former Canadian Armed Forces are often in financial distress, loved ones sometimes unable to support themselves after losing a spouse.

Then Nico's tone hardens. "You did good tonight, Tim. Real good. But this was a one-time pass. You steal again, you face the full punishment, and you won't be welcome back at the rec center. Do I make myself clear?"

I can almost hear Tim swallow. "Clear."

Tim's heartfelt apology when we drop him off is more rewarding than landing my job, but Nico's intensity lingers as he drives me home.

I try to bite my tongue, not stick my nose where it doesn't belong, but the longer he broods, the tougher it gets. "Seems kind of harsh, warning to cut him off. I mean, I get the one-time-pass thing—if he does the crime, he does the time—but won't pushing him away ruin the good work you've done?"

"No." There's no hesitation as he flexes his hands around the wheel. "One thing I've learned from my brother and sister is give them too much slack and they fall. I was too easy on them. Offered too many chances. My brother screws up again, he's on his own. Tim makes a bad decision, he won't have me to bail him out. They know right from wrong. Real consequences push them to be better."

Uncompromising much? "You could be right, or you could be

setting yourself up for a lonely, disappointing life."

If my grandmother had laid into me and told me one more screw up would ruin my chances at a bright future, I'd have gotten defensive. Instead she showed me compassion, and I soaked it up like the needy sponge I was. Nico's hard-nosed ways make me wonder what he'd think if he saw my record. Arson. Vandalism. Heroin possession. Would he still want to ask me out? Would he think I'd worn out my chances?

Do I still want to say yes?

Silence extends as we drive, my mind spinning to the stupid stuff I did as a teen, circling around Nico's honor and his stringency. Shaking my head to clear it, I focus on his forearm porn. An excellent distraction. The clench and release of his muscles have me clenching, too. I'm a little sad when we get to my place.

As I reach for my things, he puts his hand on my wrist. Tingles flutter up my arm, making my belly dip. Definitely lots of clenching. "I'm sorry, Raven—about Aspen. I wish I could go back and do things differently."

Keeping my distance from Nico would be a hell of lot easier if he wasn't so freaking nice. If he didn't give his time to others, asking for nothing but goodness in return. Sighing, I lean back. "You don't have to keep apologizing. I already forgave you."

"Doesn't feel like you forgave me."

I fight my instinct to lean into him. "Why? Because I wouldn't go out with you?"

He smiles at his lap. "Yeah."

Seriously. This guy rumbles out one syllable, and I want to crawl over the center console and straddle the real power in this mammoth truck. There's no mistaking the thick line pressing against the zipper of his jeans, the zipper I'd love to tug down with my teeth.

"See something you like?" he asks.

My eyes snap up to his. Forward Nico takes this attraction I'm avoiding to a whole other level. "Wouldn't you like to know?"

His boyish grin makes an appearance. "I would." Then, "Will you go out with me?"

There's that question I'd hoped for earlier, but none of my options feel right. Saying yes means facing potential hurt again when I'm gearing up to find Rose. If my search for her falls apart and he kicks my heart to the curb, I'm not sure I'll snap back so quickly. But flipping him the finger after he trusted me with Tim and gave me a ride home doesn't sit well, either.

I settle on a straightforward "No."

"So you haven't forgiven me, then."

"Persistent, aren't you?"

Instead of answering, he hops out of his side of the truck and has my door open before I've collected my bag. He grabs my thighs and angles my body toward him, wedging his waist between my legs. "Go out with me." This time there's no question in his voice. "We can take it slow. All I'm asking for is one date." His hands travel up my thighs, just an inch. Enough that my eyes nearly roll back in my head.

He isn't making this easy.

Unable to resist a touch, I place my fingertips on his forearm and trace the grooves that flexed each time he turned the wheel. His grip on my legs tightens. I lean toward him, my lips brushing his ear. "Thanks for the ride."

Grabbing my bag, I try to hop down from my seat, but he

barely moves, so I end up sliding down his (rock-hard) chest and thighs, then I duck under his arm.

Looking for Rose is about as much drama as I can handle right now, and everything about Nico is too much. Too much charm. Too much heat between us. Too much *him*. And he doesn't know the details of my past, the stains on my character. I've never hidden my infractions from people. I was a stupid kid who did stupid things. It's not who I am now. But I'm not so sure Nico would see it that way. Better to focus on my job and finding my sister, not giving the guy who hurt me a second chance.

Without a backward glance, I slip into my apartment.

Six

Nico

I should be hitting the streets and using any free time to search for possible leads. Instead I'm up at the crack of dawn, hoping for a chance meeting with Raven.

When I was a kid, my mother would yank off my covers, toss clothes at my face, and shove me out the door so I wouldn't miss the bus. Now, the second my alarm blares, I shoot out of bed. The possibility of seeing Raven is the only motivation I need to slap on my running gear and head to the beach before the city rises. It's been a week since I drove her home, since I touched her thighs and felt her breathy voice by my ear. Since she told me she likes to photograph the sunrise. I've jogged this route each morning, desperate for a glimpse of her. So far my efforts have been for nothing.

The air is damp as my sneakers hit the pavement, the humidity dripping down my back. My lungs ache in that good way, my thighs burn. Working my body is the best natural high there is, the best form of therapy. The day I arrested my father for dealing drugs, I hit the gym for five hours. When I found out Nikki got knocked up at sixteen, I ran across the city and back. The night I rushed her to the hospital, a needle hanging from her arm, I worked the punching bag so hard, my knuckles bled. Learning Josh got arrested while I was in Aspen had me tied in knots. I had no outlet, no release for my anxiety and anger. I sat in a cramped airplane seat for two and a half hours, mind racing, jaw clenching, as I imagined the little boy I'd carried on my shoulders living behind bars.

Each heavy fall of my foot strikes the unpleasant thoughts from my mind, blood pumping through my limbs. The clouds above shift, the sun just rising. As soon as I stepped outside this morning, I knew the sky would be spectacular—the clouds hung low in rippled layers with breaks at the horizon. It set the stage for the type of sunrise Raven would photograph.

I pick up speed down Alma Street and hit the beach as the sky burns pink. I stop at the sight, hands on my knees, heart pounding in my ears. The colors intensify, coral deepening into red. The calm ocean looks like a river of blood. I grab my T-shirt by the back of my neck and yank it off, using the drenched fabric to mop the sweat dripping into my eyes. The few people out at this hour have stopped, too, mesmerized by the glowing sky, and disappointment fists my gut.

No sign of Raven. No girl with a camera stuck in front of her face, snapping frames.

Lungs still on fire, I walk closer to the water's edge. If I'd called her after Aspen, even sent a stupid text, she wouldn't have turned me down. She'd let me take her to dinner, a movie, a picnic on the beach. Defeated, I grab a rock and skip it into the water. It bounces twice then sinks.

As I reach for another one, my pulse picks back up. *Raven.* She's sitting on the sand, resting against a large log, one of many lining the beach. Her camera hangs loose around her neck, a far-away look on her face. She's in her usual black shorts, tank top, and tall boots. Boots I'd like to undo one lace at a time. Her arms rest on her knees, her face so open I want to take that camera from her neck and snap shots. Like this, quiet, the red sky reflecting off her inked skin, no sarcasm barrier, she's the prettiest thing I've ever seen.

I approach and gesture to the empty place beside her. "This seat taken?"

She startles at my voice, her charcoal eyes going wide then falling heavy with longing as she soaks in my sweat-slicked body. My heart kicks against my ribs.

Just as quickly she purses her lips. "Does looking at a picture of the sun hurt your eyes?"

I almost ask her what she's talking about, then I remember her stupid-question rule. The sarcasm is back. I lift my shirt to put it on as I think of a witty reply, but her eyes keep darting to my chest. I drop my shirt on the sand and sit beside her. "If olive oil is made from olives, what is baby oil made from?"

We sit side by side, arms stretched over our bent knees, the bloodred sky above us. She glances at me, smirks, then focuses ahead. "How do you spell ESPN?"

"Do they hurl compliments in a civil war?"

She tips her head back, chuckling. "You're pretty quick for a big guy."

For a big guy. Most people assume I'm a dumb jock, a gym rat who builds muscle to compensate for something. Can't say they're all wrong. When my father would tell me I'm no good, that I'm a waste of space and a stupid loser, I'd lift weights. I found barbells at the dump, and I'd pump them daily, tearing my muscles until I felt bigger, stronger, *invincible*. One day I wanted to be so tough his words would bounce off me.

I also like knowing I can keep a girl like Raven safe. If she were in trouble, I could protect her with my body or my badge.

If she'd let me.

She rests her head on the log at our backs, the length of her neck close enough to taste. I swallow. "Thought I'd try to get you smiling, maybe see those teeth of yours."

She slaps a hand over her mouth, as if embarrassed, and faces me. "What do you mean, my teeth?" she asks through her fingers.

"The gap in the middle. It's sexy."

Still covering her mouth, she says, "Maybe you have cataracts. There's nothing sexy about my teeth."

Everything about her is sexy. The vines and feathers inked up the side of her left leg, the way her dark eyes narrow when she scowls at me. Her independence and defiance and spirit. Those teeth of hers add innocence to her wildness. "Whatever you do, don't smile." I grab her wrist and lower her hand.

She rolls her eyes. "I'm not five. Reverse psychology doesn't work on me."

"Then *do* smile."

Her cheeks crease as she shakes her head and rolls her eyes *again*, the inevitable smile spreading across her face. Tentatively, she widens her mouth. I brush my thumb over her bottom lip, and she sucks in a breath. "Yep," I say. "Definitely sexy."

Sexy as hell. That mouth of hers fit perfectly against mine in

Aspen, nothing about her shy or bristly back then. If I lean forward now, I could kiss her senseless and pull her onto my lap and remind her how good we feel together, show her how much she turns me on. My dick nudges me to make the move, my bent legs thankfully hiding my growing hard-on.

Ignoring the heat in my groin, I face the water. "Why aren't you taking pictures? The sky's spectacular." A kaleidoscope of color.

She presses her hand into the sand, digging and filling a trench. "No reason."

So that's what I get. Two words. It's like talking to Colin, forcing my nephew to string a sentence together. Maybe this is a lost cause. The determination I like about her might keep us apart. Still, the way her gaze raked over me just now and last week in my truck, there's no doubt she feels something, too.

She crosses her legs and leans forward, picking up handfuls of sand and letting the grains sift through her fingers. Finally, she says, "Sometimes I have to remind myself to enjoy a moment. To just be. Not get caught up in capturing it. And I have a lot on my mind these days."

"Anything I can help with?"

Seagulls swoop overhead, several landing nearby, fighting over a banana peel. The sky fades, the bold colors muting as the sun comes up, like my football jersey after years of washing.

"Why are you here, Nico?"

Her question catches me off guard. I'd debated showing up at her apartment, asking her out again, but that wouldn't fly with Raven. She's doing her best to keep me at a distance, and forcing the issue would only push her farther away. I could lie and tell her our meeting is a coincidence, not let her know I can't get her off my mind. But lies don't breed trust.

Jamal, the man who ran the rec center when I was a teen, was even bigger than me. Not as thick, but a full head taller. *Honesty*, he'd tell me. *Honesty and trust are what makes a man.* I dispense the same advice to the kids who come to play sports and escape the streets. Punks like Tim. Can't be sure they always listen.

I inhale the ocean air, the salt and fish pungent. Raven deserves a man. "You said you come here to take pictures, so I've run this way every day since I dropped you off, hoping to see you. And I'm not a morning person."

She doesn't shoot me a dirty look, but she closes her eyes for a few beats. "Is that why you smell like shit?"

I lean down and sniff my armpit. *Not* roses. "Sorry. I smell like I've been rolling in a bowl of curry."

"Curry? Curry is divine. *You* smell like a locker room."

"Curry is nasty, but yeah. I could use a shower."

Her gaze slips over my arms and chest languidly. I wonder if she's imagining what I am—us in the shower, water pounding our bodies, me on my knees, her hands gripping my scalp, my face between her thighs.

My erection thickens.

She blinks, wipes the sand from her hands, and fiddles with the camera around her neck. "That's a lot of effort just to see me."

"You're worth the effort."

"You could have called."

"Would you have answered?"

She huffs out a laugh. "Probably not."

She touches her wrist, looping her index finger over her rose tattoo, then traces the feathers on her arm. The ones she told me about in Aspen while straddling my lap, while telling me secrets, while looking into my eyes. Maybe it's selfish of me to want this time with Raven, to focus on myself instead of my family. Good or bad, right or wrong, I'm not willing to walk away from her again. Not twice.

"Remember I told you about my sister?" Her quiet words are nearly drowned by the water lapping ashore.

I lean heavier into the log. "Yeah."

"I think she's here, in Vancouver. It's one of the reasons I wanted to make this move. After Aspen, I thought about her more. Wondered what happened to her, and…I don't know. I thought maybe there was a chance she missed me, too." She rests her elbows on her crossed legs, hunching forward as if there's a weight between her shoulder blades.

I place my hand on her back, and her body stiffens. "I bet she does."

"That's not a bet I'd take. And why am I even telling you all this?"

"Because I asked, Raven. I care."

Her nose twitches, like she's sniffing out my honesty, then she relaxes into my hand. "Things are complicated with Rose. She took off the day I turned nine, and I'm kind of the reason why. So I'm not sure she'll want to see me. But I can't let it go. This need to have family kind of dug its roots into me. I can't fully explain it. I mean, I have my friends, but Rose lived in the same hellhole as me growing up. She knows me in a way others never will. Or knew me, I guess. And I have so much to apologize for. Bad stuff I can't seem to move past."

I rub soothing circles on her back. "It sounds real. Important.

Can I ask you something personal?"

A muffled snort drifts toward me. "Since I'm in a tell-all mood, why not? It's pretty much your MO anyway."

She's right about that. This need I have to know her has been there from day one. "What happened when she took off? Why do you think it's your fault?"

"That's two questions, hot shot." We're back to her signature snark, but her voice waivers. We watch the rolling waves. She seems ready to ignore me, then she places her hand on my thigh. "I appreciate the asking, but I can't talk about it yet."

Although it's a warm summer morning, a quiver runs through her shoulders, as though her memories are sending ice through her veins. Whatever happened was bad. Painful enough to reduce the strong woman I know to quaking limbs. Unable to keep my distance, I grip her hips and hoist her onto my lap, facing me. She wraps her legs around my waist. Just like in Aspen.

I cup her cheeks. "It's okay. Tell me when you're ready. I shouldn't have asked. I'm sorry."

For dredging up painful memories.

For ditching you after Aspen.

For making it all worse.

She drags her teeth over her bottom lip. "What are we doing exactly?"

Isn't that the question? One I have no problem answering. "We're starting over, getting to know each other."

Tentatively, she places her hands on my chest, and my muscles jump. One touch from her is like an electric spark. "Then I guess it's your turn to open the vault."

Barely able to focus, I say the first thing that comes to mind.

"I hate curry."

Smirking, she flicks my shoulder. "Yeah, big guy. I figured that out. Not exactly breaking news."

Or the type of sharing that breeds trust. I touch her nose, the arch of her eyebrow, the dark strands of her hair, some tinged red by the eerie lighting. If we're going to find our feet, there has to be honesty, which means divulging the hard stuff. She's not ready. I get it. Best way to pave that path is to offer my truth. Find a way to voice the nasty thoughts that have plagued me recently.

I clear my throat. "When my father got arrested, my sergeant hauled my ass into his office for a 'heart-to-heart' about my family. My character was put into question, and things were sketchy for a bit." I lower my head and sift through the tough realities I haven't wanted to poke. Steeling my resolve, I look Raven in the eye. "Insisting I'm not involved with their drama may not go well a second time. I sometimes wonder if I'm working so hard to clear Josh's name more for me than for him."

Embarrassment creeps up my neck. Here I am, worried about my job when Josh could go to jail. Older Brother of the Year Award.

She traces the *enata* symbol on my pec. "It's natural to look out for yourself, but from what I've seen, you care a lot for those around you. You're also hard on them. And probably too hard on yourself. You're a good man, Nico."

I press my thumb below her jaw, to feel her pulse point, judge her sincerity. It's all there. In the tenderness lighting her ebony eyes. She has no idea how those words lift me up. It's exactly what I've worked toward. To be good. To prove my worth. To not be my father. From her, it means everything. "Thank you."

We sit like this awhile—her hands on my chest, mine in her hair. Seeds of trust planting. I shift her weight on my lap. "What leads do you have on your sister?"

She narrows her dark gaze on me. "You really want to help?"

"I really want to help." My family's fate keeps slipping out of my hands, but Raven has the chance to patch hers up. A small patch, at least.

She stares at me so long I almost flinch, then she says, "I did some digging at home. Found out she might be living here, but I don't know where to look. Every time I'm out—like at Wreck Beach or on Hastings—I study women, but it's like searching for a needle in a haystack."

I rub her arms, slow and gentle. "Let me look into it, see what I can find."

"It's a lot to ask." Her head dips forward, a curtain of black hair covering her face. We're close. Intertwined. Not pressed together the way I want to crush her to me. My body is heating, though, my cock thickening. She must know it, feel it.

I push the strands aside, and my knuckles brush her jaw. "I *want* to help. Let me do this."

She leans into my touch, so I uncurl my fingers and grip her neck, slip my thumb below her ear. She tilts her head and parts her lips. My heart jogs faster than it did on my run. My attraction to her is always intense, but this, right now, has my skin on fire. "Babe, I need to kiss you."

A soft sigh escapes her lips. "Do you make out with all potential private eye clients?"

Always cheeky. "Just the ones I want to date."

"In that case, let's see what you got."

Her eyelids flutter closed, and I surge forward, needing to ease her worries and erase the emotional distance between us, get to a place where we talk without thinking and touch because we have to. I close my lips over hers, groaning at the contact. Noses brushing, I thread my fingers into her hair. Savor the way she bends toward me. Pretend she's mine. I swipe my tongue over the seam of her lips, easing them wider. She invites me in, and my dick pulses. She tastes like honey. So good. So sweet. Our tongues twirl, a sensual dance that has me pressing my hips upward, but I don't grind against her. I'm wet and sweaty. We're in a public place. But I don't let up.

I've been starved for her too long.

When she gasps and says, "Fuck," against my mouth, I growl.

Eventually we come up for air. A pudgy kid runs after a group of seagulls, the noisy birds taking flight. The sun rises higher, the ocean waking up, waves rolling with the increasing wind. Feels like the start to a perfect day.

"You actually smell pretty good. Manly," she says in a deep voice. "And that was quite a reunion kiss."

"The first of many." *My* voice sounds scratchy.

Her heated gaze dips down my pecs and abs, and sweat collects along my waistband. Digging her heels into the sand, she uses my shoulders to push herself up and off my lap. "I need to get home. I'm having brunch with the girls."

I grab her ankle. "When can I see you again?"

"So persistent."

"I know what I want."

She stands facing me, her feet planted wide, the toes of her boots brushing my sneakers. I want to reach up and feel how wet she is, how turned on from kissing me.

She chews her lip. "Here's the deal, *Captain Persistent*. What happened in Aspen, with us, changed me. Not just the fact that you took off and didn't call." I wince, but she doesn't stop. "More how I felt with you. Vulnerable, I guess. I hadn't felt like that since Rose left me, and I didn't like it. I *don't* like it. It makes me feel weak and out of control—emotional. Things I'm not used to dealing with. And finding Rose has become this obsession for me, but it also terrifies me. Because"—she pauses and blinks—"all this stuff I'm feeling could go south if it doesn't work out. If she hates me or brushes me off…I'm not as tough as I was. Then there's you."

Her eyes haven't wavered from mine. I grip both her ankles now, trying to show her I'll hold her steady.

"There's something between us, Nico. I can deny it all I want, but it's there. I just need to take this slow."

That's a hell of a lot better than her usual glare. "I'm in no rush, babe. I'm in this for the long haul. I want the whole package."

The way she's eyeing my tented gym shorts, I'd say she wants *my* package now. I almost groan, imagining her lips wrapped around me, pumping me until I spill into her mouth.

But we'll do this at her pace.

I release her ankles. "I'll start looking for Rose tomorrow. Might take a while, but I'm heading to East Hastings on my next day off, to poke around about Josh. There's an abandoned building filled with squatters. It's not somewhere you should ever go alone, but since you like to photograph that stuff, you might want to come." More like I want any excuse to spend time with her.

"Sounds like a date." She turns to leave but glances over her shoulder. "And slow doesn't mean stopping. I expect a dinner invitation. Maybe some sexting."

I chuckle and adjust myself in my shorts. "Noted."

More people appear, running or walking on the beach. Once Raven's gone, I pull my phone from my pocket and send her a message:

You taste sweet. Like honey. Hated that you had to go.

Her reply comes shortly: You taste like trouble.

Trouble? Not on her life. If one of us is dangerous, it's Raven with the soft vulnerability she hides under her hard edges. Edges that can cut.

I did like watching your ass as you left, though. That part was nice.

Is this your version of sexting?

I'm better in the flesh. When you're ready, I'm gonna make you feel real good. My thighs flex in anticipation.

Like I said, trouble.

Maybe she's right.

My phone buzzes again, and I smile down at my screen, expecting her name to appear. It's Alessi. Call me if you're around.

I toss on my shirt and dial right away. "If this is another hair gel emergency, I'm not running around town looking for beauty products."

"You can fuck off. This is about Raven."

I sit straighter. "What about her?"

"I was at the station because I *maybe* ran out of hair gel and had some in my locker. Turns out her wallet came in with a bust. Some student at UBC has been busy picking pockets. Her cash and cards are gone, but her ID is intact."

"That's great." I get to my feet and dust the sand from my sweaty ass. I just got myself another excuse to see my dark-haired beauty.

Alessi clears his throat. "Yeah, there's just one thing…"

I pause mid-swipe. I know that tone. "What's wrong?"

"Probably nothing. But the guys had put her name into the system before they realized you knew her, and she has a record. Thought you might want to know."

With the upbringing Raven had, it's not surprising she rebelled. Josh and Nikki aren't exactly saints. "Give me the Cliff notes." When he doesn't answer, I jam my toe into the sand. "Spit it out already."

"Typical teen vandalism, but there's also an arson charge that got settled out of court, and a charge for heroin. Possession."

The briny air lodges in my throat. "You sure?"

"Positive. Sorry, man."

All I can do is grunt my thanks and hang up. Arson? Heroin? That's not your typical teen stupidity. That shit screams danger and tosses up a massive red flag. I'm falling for Raven. Falling fast and likely hard. And having a woman in my life means she'll be around my family, including my sister, who's still recovering from her own heroin addiction. Raven might be right for me, but if her past has lingered into her present, she could be trouble for my family.

I chew on that unwelcome possibility as I jog home.

Seven

Raven

My walk to meet the girls for brunch is a hazy blur of tattooed muscles. *Sweaty*, tattooed muscles. Straddling a half-naked Nico—the sky above us bleeding passion, his hands on my hips, his lips devouring mine—nearly short-circuited my brain. And that wasn't just any kiss. It was an apology and a promise and a *prelude*. Another second and I would have licked every inch of salt from his body.

Instead he shared an intimate fear with me.

There's just something about Nico. His quiet presence maybe. His deep voice and sincere questions. He's trying to ease the gap between us. A gap I'm nervous to close.

I step into the cramped café and squish my elbows to my sides. This place is beyond tiny. Tables are crammed together, barely enough room for servers to get around. The walls are covered with picture frames of newspaper articles and celebrity photos. There's no sign of Shay or Lily, but I spot a free table in a back corner and try to catch someone's attention. Both waitresses glance my way…and ignore me. When a group of four push into the place, I take matters into my own hands.

Two strides toward the table, someone says, "Those tattoos don't scare me. Seat yourself, and I'll have you doing dishes."

I spin around, squinting at the waitress with the snarky tone. "Excuse me?"

Her hair is in two blond braids, her ripped jeans and faded Mickey Mouse shirt not exactly professional. She winks at me. "I don't like it when girls rush me. I'm all about the slow burn."

The patrons laugh, as if it's just another Sunday and I wasn't propositioned by their server. I stand my ground, unsure if I should return to the door or take a seat.

Shay pokes her curly head through the waiting customers and waves. "Rave!"

Mickey Mouse Girl says, "Stop taking up space. Sit your asses down already."

More laughter. More confusion from *moi*.

Lily and Shay join me, neither of them fazed by the nutty service. Once we're seated, I cross my arms. "The food here better be insane, or I'm leaving."

Shay waves a hand in the air. "It's what they do, like their shtick. They harass the customers."

"And people pay for this?"

Lily slings her purse over the back of her chair. "Sawyer brought me here my first week. When I ordered sausage with my eggs, the waitress asked if I could handle all those inches. Sawyer, of course, told her I'd had lots of practice." She blushes so pink telling the story, I can't imagine how she looked that day.

I relax into my chair. "That sounds more my speed."

"Plus," Shay says, "the home fries are amazing."

A few patrons glance our way, probably thinking we make an odd bunch. We've always been a mash-up of music genres and styles. Shay in her trendy platform shoes, skinny jeans, and fitted pink T-shirt is our Pop girl. Lily looks as though she walked off the cover of one of her hipster CDs, flowy lace top, jean skirt, ankle boots, and all. My black outfit and inked skin scream old school punk. The three of us are as different as different gets, but they're my closest friends, and I need their advice.

Attention focused on their menus, they don't notice me twisting my hands on the table. Probably best to blurt it out. "I kissed Nico."

Their heads fly up at once.

"What? When? Why? I thought you hated him," Shay says.

Grinning, Lily leans forward. "Details, please."

I never told the girls the Aspen specifics. I'd never even told them I'd met my grandmother, let alone the fact that she'd passed. Skilled at bulldozing my emotions and masking the wreckage with sarcasm, I cracked jokes and teased them about their love lives, and we had fun in Aspen. Back home, it all hit me so hard. The worse I felt, the snarkier I'd get. I'd hook up with guys. When I couldn't shake thoughts of Nico, I'd lie on my bed and blast the Clash loud enough to wake the dead. I'd use the time to perfect my Ten Ways to Kill Nico List. Talking to the girls back then meant reopening old wounds, and I was squeaking by.

But I kissed the Sexy Beast and his offer to help me find Rose means we could be spending more time together. Avoidance is no longer an option. "Apparently he's been running on the beach each morning because I told him I go there to take photos."

"Tenacious," Shay says. "I like it. So you made out on the sand?"

I nod. "He had his shirt off and everything. That man's body should be illegal."

And his lips should be black market contraband. But it's his sweet nature that has me shredding the napkin in my hands. Nico has apologized more than once. He's devoted to his community, to his family, and he's offered to help me find mine. He's the type of man girls dream about. Why am I still holding back?

Shay and Lily exchange glances, then Lily drags her chair closer and lowers her voice. "You must have your reasons for being quiet about what happened in Aspen, but we can't help if you don't let us in. If it were me, I'd be upset if a guy didn't call after hooking up, but you've never cared about that. Why Nico?"

Because he looked into my soul that night. Because for the first time in my life, I wanted more. "Because he pushed me to share personal things with him and promised he wouldn't hurt me. Then he blew me off."

Lily bites her lip. "I'm sorry, Rave. I wish you'd talked to us about it."

I drop my shredded napkin and trace my rose tattoo, the first ink I ever got. The way Nico kissed it in Aspen made my chest ache. "I should have. But I didn't know what to do with everything I was feeling. And it seemed ridiculous. It was one night, and I fell so hard for him. It fucked me up, to say the least."

"And now?" Shay asks. "You're willing to give him another shot?"

My roaring libido and nervous stomach seem to differ in opinions. "Aside from the fact that he's the sexiest thing on legs, Nico and I have an intense connection. We've both been through a lot as kids, fucked-up family stuff. And I know he didn't mean to hurt me. But part of my move here was about finding Rose. He's offered to help, and I said yes, but I'm having second thoughts. I'm worried if we spend time together, I'll fall harder. The idea of looking for Rose *and* getting in deep with Nico scares the crap out of me."

The snarky waitress interrupts us and blows the bangs from her face. "What do you ladies want? If it's me, I get off in a couple hours, but it takes a lot of work to *get me off*."

Well then. "I'm good with the menu," I say, chuckling.

The girls rattle off their orders, and I choose pancakes on the fly. When I ask for coffee, the waitress says, "You have feet, get it yourself."

I smile as she marches off, getting into the vibe of this place. "If my apprentice gig falls through and our event business doesn't take off, I could probably waitress here."

"You do have a PhD in sarcasm," Shay says.

Lily elbows her. "Back to the Nico problem. I have a suggestion."

I bounce my leg, eager for advice. Advice I could have used when I let a friend tattoo a guitar on my hip. The proportions are off, the lines wonky, and the neck is a blur of muddy colors. It resembles a choking chicken. If I push Nico away again, odds are my regret over the choking chicken tattoo would pale in comparison.

Lily smooths the napkin on her lap. "My vote is that you should let him help you find Rose. He has the resources, and it's important. If you don't look for her, you'll always wonder. As for Nico, I get why you're hesitant. I don't believe for a second he'd hurt you again, but relationships can be messy. I'd take it slow, but I'd give it a shot." She looks at Shay, who nods in agreement.

I tap my fingers restlessly. "Slow might be a challenge. I mean, you have seen him, right? And that kiss was unreal. Plus, things get intense when we talk. *Slow* isn't in our vocabulary."

On the beach, I was a heartbeat from spilling about the hell that sent Rose running. The horrific beating. How I pissed myself that day. It's not a story I want to relive, and if he asks again, I'm not sure I'll be able to swallow it down. But never knowing if my sister and I could reconnect would be harder than sharing my worst day as a person. Nico's a cop. He's got access to databases and driver's license info. All I've been doing is scanning random people on the street.

I sigh. "If we spend time together, fighting this thing between us won't work. But yeah. I want his help finding Rose. I'll just have to hope for the best."

Hope my heart doesn't get trampled.

Lily twists the ring on her necklace. "God, can you imagine what it would be like to see Rose after all this time? Did she look like you?"

The reality of finding my sister whispers through me, leaving a chill in its wake. The same unease that seized me at Nico's questioning. Holding out hope for a relationship with her is dangerous business. She could be a drunk like our mother. Violent like my father, who raised us both. She could blame me for it all. The smell of bacon and waffles veers from heavenly to acerbic. "Yeah, we looked a bit alike, but it's hard to remember. We're both a quarter First Nations. She had dark hair and eyes like me and our mother, but her father was Scottish, so her skin was fair. And she had the most perfect teeth."

Shay makes a choking sound. "Honestly, you and your teeth.

The gap in the center is hot. Totally in these days. Tons of models have it."

And Nico likes it, I don't say. For the first time in my life, I didn't want to hide my smile.

We discuss our website for Over the Top Events, but my thoughts drift to my upcoming outing with Nico. An idea's been brewing in my mind for a while, a concept for a photographic essay on street life. Ever since I learned my grandmother spent time on the streets, I've been drawn to the people there. The stories.

Something else Nico wants to help me with.

His offer to visit that homeless community has emotion rising thick in my throat. This is the whole package he alluded to: a man in my life who cares about my interests, plays my stupid-question game, and kisses me like I'm his last breath. My mind fills with all things Nico—his chest, his lips, his eyes. His sexy grunt when our tongues brushed. Yep, there's no resisting him.

I pull my phone from my purse. Someone needs to teach him how to sext.

Do you prefer lace, silk, or leather?

Seconds later, my phone buzzes.

Can't talk right now. I'll pick you up Thursday night at eight.

I frown at his reply, a niggle of uncertainty curdling my gut. No cute banter. No hint we'll chat over the next four days. The man really needs to work on his dirty talk. Either that or he's brushing me off. I give myself a mental slap. I don't do insecure. I don't do needy. I'm just worked up about searching for Rose and dating Nico. Slow is good. Slow is what I want.

My phone lights up again. Your wallet came in. No cards or cash, but your ID is inside. I'll drop it in your mailbox.

Drop it in my mailbox? How did we go from pawing each other to "drop it in my mailbox"? Where's the sweet guy who told me he wants the whole package? I scowl at my phone and attempt to ignore my unease. Technology has a way of twisting words and meanings. That's probably all this is, and I'm just being a nutjob. He was nothing but affectionate on the beach.

Eight

Raven

Rundown neighborhoods have a smell about them. Sometimes pungent, sometimes subtle, but there's always an undercurrent of stale cigarettes, body odor, and exhaust. The alley Nico leads me through is no exception. Eau-de-vomit hangs in the air as we pass an entranceway blocked by two men passed out on the stairs. Graffiti decorates the crumbling bricks and barred windows, bold slashes of yellow, white, and green crisscrossing in random patterns.

If done well, graffiti elevates a neighborhood and empowers teens. These walls look like they've been painted by a blind seeing-eye dog.

And I love it.

I've been in fast forward all day, the prospect of getting photos for my project like mainlining Red Bull. At work, I had Sasha's gear loaded in her car in record time. I helped set up a couple of shots, even suggested we take a client's reflection in a puddle. Afterward she scrolled through the images with me, explaining why each one sucked or rocked. Every day my brain expands with knowledge, my creativity hurrying to catch up. The more I can practice on my own, the better.

Nico slows as we near what looks like a construction zone and stops at a chain-link fence. He tips his head toward the gaping hole. "Once we're in there, I don't want you wandering off. Most of these folks are just down on their luck, but some will take advantage if they think they can."

I was a tad disappointed when he picked me up today. A small (large) part of me hoped he'd be in his uniform, providing a tasty image to add to my ass montage. Although he's in civilian clothes, the view is still mighty fine. His jeans stretch over the expanse of his thighs, his worn black belt tilted forward along the slide of his hips, his snug gray T-shirt practically painted on. I force my eyes to his face. "You could leash me if you want. I'm not opposed to bondage."

His Adam's apple bobs down his throat. "I'm serious, Raven. No playing around in here."

I'm serious, too, about our outing, and possibly the bondage. But he doesn't crack a smile. I gesture for him to go ahead. "I promise to stay on your heels."

There are other parts of him I'd like to be *on*, but Nico's body language has been as cool as his minimal texts. I'd given up sexting him after the first fail, and he never initiated. All I got was a peck on the cheek when I opened my door today. My taking-it-slow speech must have made him extra cautious. Nico is proving to be sweet like that.

He ducks and tilts his wide frame to fit through the gap in the fence, and I follow close behind. Once inside, he juts his chin toward the pile of rubble at our left. "The city was set to flatten this whole place, but there was a dispute over the land. The demolition stalled partway through. More squatters show up every month."

Half of an apartment building fills a section of the fenced area, as though it's been sliced through with a knife. A few toilets are visible in the open rooms that climb toward the sky; pipes and wires hang, attached to nothing. On the ground, people huddle in groups, piles of clothes and garbage bags and mattresses dotting the area.

We hang back, taking it all in. "Not exactly homey," I say.

"No." His tone is clipped, the lightness in his eyes clouded. "My brother lived here for a while. Six months or so."

"Josh? Before he got arrested?" A whiff of smoke joins the sickly-sweet smells rising from the earth, and I wrinkle my nose.

"Yeah." He kicks at the loose gravel. "We had a nasty fight the night he left. I'd dropped by to find out he'd stolen money from our mother. I lost my shit. Called him fucked up and heartless and weak. He railed at me about how I'm not his father. Took off after screaming himself raw. He thought his punk friends were his real family." He scans the decrepit building, the trash littering the ground. "Turns out his friends were more than happy to use him as target practice."

I nod, too aware of how welcoming a band of thugs can be. Like Josh, before I met Shay and Lily in art class, I bonded with my fellow high school delinquents. Throwing bricks through windows and pulling fire alarms were all in a day's work. With each stupid prank, my guilt over Rose would ease momentarily. The badass brigade would pound my back. They'd praise my aim. They'd tell me I was awesome. My parents told me I'd amount to nothing.

Now I have a man like Nico wanting to care for me.

His cheekbones are sharp, intensity in his eyes as he studies these ruins, relives his worst days. No longer able to maintain this slow pace I requested, I move to slip my hand into his, but he clasps his fingers behind his neck.

The avoidance stings, hits me straight in the chest, but this is painful, what he's sharing. "Sounds like it was the wake-up call your brother needed. And he probably wouldn't have made it out if it weren't for you. I bet he knows how lucky he is, no matter how the trial goes."

He tips his head back and studies the sky. "Maybe. Josh doesn't know my leads have dried up. He still thinks I've got him covered. Can't bring myself to tell him."

I almost hear his heart cracking, and mine squeezes in response. That's quite a burden for one man to carry. A burden I'd like to help shoulder. The more I've thought about him the past four days, the more I've realized I'm ready to let him in. Give this thing with us a shot. Seeing him with Tim showed me who he was at his core. I told him about Rose because he truly cared, and it just felt right. I've also relived our kiss numerous times, how he smelled like sweat and man and beach and tasted like a fresh start.

The grudge I've harbored has blurred like a photograph exposed to too much light. Too much Nico. He may hurt me, intentional or not. It's a chance I'll have to take.

For now I need to get his mind off things beyond his control. "I visited the Indian reservation where my grandmother grew up this past winter, took a ton of shots. I used to look for her, before she died. Would check homeless shelters, hoping to show her I'd made something of myself. Since I can't do that, I started thinking of ways to make a difference. It's why I went there and photograph places like this. If I get enough images, I'm hoping to put a show together, bring attention to the homeless community."

He brightens. "Sounds cool. Bet it was a great trip."

"It was. I'll show you pictures sometime." The offer is out before I realize the thought even existed. More secrets shared with Nico. More vulnerability unleashed.

He considers my proposition and lowers his voice. "I'd like that."

I'm surprised how much I'd like that, too. "They're nothing special. No swimsuit photos," I say, remembering the *Sports Illustrated* magazine in his car. "Might not be your thing."

He cracks a smile. "Were you wearing a bikini when taking the shots?"

"Nope. It was northern Ontario. Middle of winter. I would have lost a nipple."

His gaze drops to my chest, and the nipple in question salutes him. Abruptly, he looks away. Still distant. Still barely flirting. The evening sun dips behind the rotting concrete, and a wolf-like dog darts in front of us. I focus on its matted fur—a welcome distraction from Nico's confusing behavior.

He places his hand on my back, like that day on Hastings—his palm low, his fingers brushing lower. "We should head in. There are a few regulars who talk to me, one in particular who hangs with Josh's old crew. I hit him up from time to time. The ring leader, Jericho, split, but I'm hoping someone knows something."

I played poker in high school, for kicks and for cash. I usually read a bluff like nobody's business. Except the time I lost my favorite Clash CD to Simon Wright. He played the entire hand like he was having a stroke, touching his nose and blinking and swallowing and generally acting like a douche to throw me off. His plan worked. But Nico isn't trying to hide his turmoil. The rigid set of his lips and deep crease of his brows are telling. He's grasping at straws.

We walk ahead. A couple of women wearing skirts the size of headbands sneer at us, smacking their gum as they slip into the shadows. Twenty or thirty men and women lounge around their makeshift homes and stare or look away. Rose could be here. She could have ended up like our grandmother, homeless and alone. Nico has been looking for her, but hasn't offered an update. I haven't asked; my nerves have turned me into an overworked painting, one muddied step from falling apart.

"Fucking hell. Which one of them punks stole my blanket?" A woman gestures wildly, her gray hair a ratty mess. Her loose shirt and trousers are covered in stains.

"That's Betty Leroux," Nico says. "She's been here awhile. Doesn't drink or use. When she lost her husband, things went downhill. You okay if I talk to her?" I nod, and he strides her way, familiarity in his easy smile. "What seems to be the problem, Betty?"

He towers over her, the contrast between the two almost comical, but I don't laugh. Before, with him next to me, I didn't worry about my safety, didn't feel the need to keep alert. Now my senses heighten. Gravel shifts beside me, and I whip my head around. Just an oversized rat. I tighten my grip on my camera and focus on the reason I'm here: photographic journalism.

This place is my Mecca.

The hardships of life are emphasized by the half-demolished building. Deterioration. Destitution. Luck turned on its ass. Nico and Betty are a perfect example of the haves and have-nots, the juxtaposition of their size and positions in life impossible to ignore. I lift my lens.

Click. Nico's huge hand on Betty's shoulder.

Click. Betty's arms flung in the air.

Click. Nico's black boots facing her ripped sneakers.

There's a chance I snap one of his ass.

Once Betty calms down, his attention drifts behind her, to two guys on milk crates. He looks over at me and holds up a finger to tell me he'll be a minute. Absorbed in my craft, I return to my living canvas. I snap an image of the mangy wolf dog licking a McDonald's wrapper, and several frames of two women spooning in their sleeping bag, the moment almost too intimate to shoot. I glance behind me once, my neck tingling with intuition, as though someone is watching me. Probably just the wind.

Through the remnants of a concrete wall, I spot the source of the air's smoky haze. Flames lick from the inside of a garbage bin. A teenage boy and an older woman huddle close to the fire, and the poster behind it makes the scene a photographer's wet dream: A mouthwatering burger is pictured, the caption reading, *Grilled to Perfection.*

Nico's crouched in front of those guys, deep in conversation. Instead of interrupting, I walk a wide circle, making sure no one's behind me, looking for the perfect angle. I lose sight of Nico as I round a half wall of concrete, the garbage fire coming into view. I stand in what must have been a kitchen corner, lift my lens, and play with the focus.

It's not a cold evening. I'm in jeans and a T-shirt, not shivering in the slightest, but I've eaten today. The boy and woman stand close to the fire as if it might warm their skeletal frames.

If I put enough work together and stage a proper show, I could effect change. Maybe people would donate to their local food shelter instead of buying a fifth pair of Jimmy Choos. Maybe they'd remember to care. I snap a number of frames, adjusting the shutter speed and aperture as I go, getting lost in the camera's clicks and pops, the sounds like insects in my ear.

"Hey, pretty lady."

My spine snaps straight at the unfamiliar voice. The *sleazy*, unfamiliar voice. Slowly, as though not to disturb a wild animal, I lower my camera. A disheveled man with boots too big and pants too low sways from side to side, his feral gaze locked on me.

I glance around for Nico, but he's hidden behind the slabs of concrete. Hoping the man's harmless, I force a smile. "Hi."

I step to my right, trying to make a quick exit, but he's faster. He blocks my way.

Maybe not so harmless. There's no crowbar or pipe around. No shards of glass to use as a weapon, and screaming could set him off.

"You sure are pretty," he says in a singsong. "You taking pictures?"

It's the same stupid question Nico asked me on Hastings Street, but my snarky reply dries up. Ready to crack the man over his head with my camera, I shift left. His body sways with mine. I dodge right, but he mirrors my move. My pulse thunders in my ears, my voice lodged in my throat. When he reaches down and pulls his dick out of his pants, I'm left with one option.

Nine

Nico

Another useless conversation later, I push to my feet. At the mention of Jericho, Matt and Derek exchanged glances. They confirmed the little shit split, disappeared underground or farther. Maybe Mexico, South America. Nowhere I can find him and force a confession. Jericho was the first to take Josh under his wing, invite him to ride along on their drug runs. Asking him to drive this car here, drop that package there, giving him enough information but not too much.

Smart for a street kid—when things go sour, always good to have a patsy.

I drag my hand over my head, discouraged. Another disappointment in an already challenging day. Being around Raven has me twisted in knots. Talking to her on the beach was a window to how good we could be together, my attraction to the woman has me ready to crawl out of my skin, but that call from Alessi has muddled my mind. I've thought of little else since. Tried to figure out if Raven's history could push its way back into her life.

Heroin is no joke. I see the grip it has on my sister, how every day is a battle. Nothing about Raven hints at a drug problem, but she's heading into stressful times, and those demons sneak up on you when least expected.

Rubbing the invisible ache in my chest, I glance around. Betty's still grumbling about her blanket, most other people ignoring me. The first time I came down here, they scattered like crabs on a beach. They're used to me now; know I'm not here to arrest them. And sometimes I bring food. I twist farther, but don't see Raven. Apprehension grips my gut. She was just there, snapping pictures. I swallow hard, hoping to push down my rising unease. I told her not to wander off, told her these folks can't be trusted. Sure, most of them are decent enough, but lots carry blades and hold grudges and would love to take advantage of a pretty girl. My mind flashes to stab wounds and bruised faces, too many cases I've worked ending poorly.

Then someone shrieks.

I played football in high school, my size and power an asset as a defensive end. I was quick, too, considering. When that ball snapped, I'd be on the quarterback or running back in seconds. That cry has me moving faster than at our championship game.

Loose gravel flies underfoot, dust churning the air as I peel around a block of concrete. Some guy is on the ground curled in a ball, moaning, Raven above him, camera shaking in her grasp. She looks scared as hell, but she's in one piece. Wish I could say the same about me.

I wrap her in my arms and squeeze.

"Easy, big guy." Her light tone doesn't hide her trembling shoulders, or how tight she's fisting my shirt. "I can barely breathe."

I ease my hold. Slightly. "You okay? Please tell me you're okay."

Still breathing hard, she looks down between us at her legs. "Technically I'm fine. But I need to burn these jeans. My knee made contact with bare testicle."

Fury nearly blinds me. "That man exposed himself to you?"

She nods, and my pulse rages. How could I have let this happen? I shouldn't have brought her here, should never have let her out of my sight. I barrel over to the man, ready to slam his head into concrete. He's already lifted himself up and is sitting hunched over, cradling his nuts. *Enjoy them while they exist, buddy.* When his shifty gaze slides my way, my adrenaline crashes. "Fucking Christ, Joe. What the hell are you doing?"

"You *know* him?"

I curse under my breath, avoiding Raven's shocked glare. "Joe here has some mental health issues. I met his sister once and said I'd watch out for him. But"—I crowd Joe until he cowers—"I ever catch you whipping out your junk in front of a lady, it's a one-way ticket to lockup. You understand?"

"Yeah. Sorry. Sorry. Joe understands. Sorry." He prattles on, hand between his legs, as he hurries to the demolished building's inner sanctum.

"You certainly know how to pick your friends."

I whip my head around. "Did he touch you?"

"No. Just looked…and touched himself. Now I feel bad, though. He probably didn't realize I was scared."

I cringe and scratch my jaw. "He's never done that before. Not that I've seen, at least. For the most part he's harmless, but exposure isn't cool. You sure you're okay?"

Unable to keep away, I move in front of her and run a hand

down her arm. She nods and shivers at the touch, but I can't tell if it's from me or the shock. I never should have suggested this. I should have taken her to dinner instead of a slum. Somewhere with candles on the table and white napkins. I'd order the red wine she likes and hold her hand and have her to myself for a while. I'd treat her so damn nice.

I still want to do that for her, with her. Build on our new foundation. But I can't get past Alessi's call. Every second together, it's harder to maintain my cool. When she flirts, holding back is agony. Even now my arms itch to circle her again, pull her against me. Instead I release her arm. "We should probably leave."

She rolls her camera from hand to hand. "Can we stay a bit longer? There are a few shots I'd like to catch. But only if you keep close."

I may be messed in the head where she's concerned, but she'd have to pry me away with a crowbar. "Yeah. I'll keep close."

Nodding, she touches my waist, a gesture of reassurance maybe, but the sensation travels to my groin. I've had dry spells before. Unlike Sawyer in his day, I don't get off on meaningless flings. But this is the longest I've ever gone, and shady past or not, this is the most desperate I've been for a woman. I even love how tough Raven is. How she can hold her own with a man like Joe. Not branding her with a kiss is the worst kind of torture.

For the next half hour, I stand where she stands—legs wide, arms crossed—like her personal bouncer. The blue sky fades to navy, evening encroaching. A couple more fires are lit, people returning from begging on the street. It's easy to point fingers and assume these folks made their beds. Some have. But Betty didn't ask for her husband to die, leaving her with a mountain of debt.

Joe, who's got one chance left with me, can't always make sense of the world around him. And Raven gets it. I'd never have brought a woman here before, never have shared this part of my life. It's all easy with her.

"You ready?" I ask as she lowers her camera.

"Sure. I just want to make sure I got these last frames." She glances at me. "You want to see?"

She lifts the camera, and I lean over her shoulder. The digital images flip across her viewfinder, some detailed close-ups, others wide-angles. I'm no photography buff, but she's captured something, all right. The grittiness of the street. The heart, too. All with her charcoal eyes. By the time she lowers the camera, I'm so close my chest touches her back, her ass flush with my thighs. Before I know what I'm doing, I wrap my hands around her hips, so small in my grasp. I lower my mouth to her ear. "This is what you're meant to do."

Her breath catches, but she doesn't speak. Then, "You really like them?"

"They're remarkable." I don't tell her how remarkable she is, but I need to talk to her about her past soon. Ask outright if anything could come back to haunt her, find its way to my doorstep. My family's. This is what I do, though. Internalize. My mother gives me shit about it. *Broody*, she calls me. *Always letting things fester.* I just don't like to speak until my mind's clear. Not say regretful things like I did to Josh the night he took off. And Raven could get pissed, defensive. If my words come out wrong, if I'm making more of this than I should, I could lose her trust again.

Thoughts tangled, I step back.

She lets her camera hang loose from her neck. "Thanks for

bringing me here, even with that whole Joe thing."

I grind my molars, still pissed I wasn't there for her when it counted. "Sorry about that, but I'm glad you got some good shots."

She glides her fingers down my forearm. "Me, too."

And damn, the look she gives me? One glance from her sultry eyes is like sixty thousand cheering football fans, and I don't want to give that up. I want another kiss, deeper, wilder, nothing but need and lust in her breathy sounds.

Frustrated, I nod toward the fence and spread my hand on her lower back, guiding her. It's my favorite place to touch. In Aspen I kissed my way down her spine, explored all that sexy ink, pausing at the top of her ass and tracing the lines of the pirate ship sailing across her tailbone. I never asked what it symbolizes, what most of her ink represents. Only her rose and feather tattoos. She shared those with me. She also offered up another vulnerable piece of herself at the beach, and here I am, tossing in an anchor, halting our progress.

She breathes deeper, as if trying to press into me. "Have you made any headway, looking for Rose?" Her voice is as soft as the breeze, but there's a nervous undercurrent.

I pause, unsure how much to share. I don't want to get her hopes up, only to have them dashed. "Nothing concrete, but there's a chance she's living in Fraser Valley."

Her shoulders shoot toward her ears. "That was fast."

I stop at the gap in the fence. "She hasn't lived at the address on her license for five years, but one of the women there said she'd moved to an apartment downtown. That led to two more places and a guy who thinks she lives on a farm in the valley. Some sort of communal agriculture thing. Might be a long shot, but worth checking out."

"That must have taken hours."

I nod. "My partner owed me a favor."

I pull back the metal chain link and help Raven through to the other side. Once I join her, she grabs my wrist. "I know it's a lot to ask, but will you come with me? When I look for her? If not, it's no big deal. I can ask Shay or Lily or go on my own. It's just—"

"We're doing this together." My tone is more vehement than intended. I've barely recovered from what could have happened with Joe. She doesn't know what she's walking into. It could be dangerous. Physically. Emotionally. I plan to be there for her, regardless of this other crap screwing with my head. "I have night shifts starting tomorrow, which means it'll be a bit before we can go. Probably five days. We should plan to stay overnight, in case we need to follow leads."

She exhales a slow breath. "Thank you."

We walk on, and she interlaces our fingers. I let her. Crave the feel of her smooth skin. Her hand is so tiny in mine. So soft. It feels so good. A few steps later, she swings our hands like we're in grade school. "Although I'll be so nervous I might puke, this trip could be fun. I mean, now that I know you'll be *coming*, there's lots to look forward to."

I'm not sure what happened to the Raven who wanted to take things slow, but her teasing voice drips with innuendo, and I can't resist playing along. "What if I decide I don't want to *come*?"

She drags a nail down the meaty part of my thumb, rough and deliberate. "It would be a shame. You said yourself you haven't been to the Valley in a long while. I bet you really miss it."

I groan—a pained sound from the back of my throat. Can't even find my voice to reply.

That doesn't stop Raven. "I hear it's quite warm down there. It would be a shame to miss out, unless you don't remember how to find your way." Her suggestive wink almost kills me.

I shouldn't keep flirting, not when I haven't been honest with her about my concerns, but it's too tempting. "I know my way just fine. Enjoy the scenic route, actually. Taking my time. Finding secret places to explore."

It's her turn to whimper, and my skin tightens at the image of a naked Raven writhing on a bed. My cock gets heavy. I'm breathing hard by the time we reach my truck.

She leans her back into the door and grabs my belt loops, pulling me in front of her. "Thanks again for everything. For today, for looking for Rose. It means a lot."

She tips her chin up, drags me closer, and everything else fades. My uncertainty. My questions. I can't deny myself this. I plant my hands on either side of her and dip my head down, taking a taste, a soft brush of our lips. Heat suffuses my chest, hunger fires my gut. The kiss deepens, and I suck on her bottom lip. She nips mine. My dick throbs, reminding me just how long it's been. Tongues tangling, her fingers dig into the base of my skull, and I push my thigh between hers as we move closer. And closer.

Before things pass the point of no return, I create some distance. "Damn."

She hums. "Yeah."

I run my thumb over her swollen lips. "That was quite a thank-you, but it's not necessary. I'm helping because I want to."

"Okay, but if I buy slushies for our drive as a not-a-thank-you, what flavor would you want?"

Even after the Joe disaster, she has me chuckling. "Those things are bad for you."

Her attention drifts down to my waist. And lower. "Sometimes the stuff that's bad for you tastes the best."

Isn't that the truth? Whisking her home and having my way with her is becoming harder to resist. If I don't get my head straight, spending a night alone with her in Fraser Valley will kill me.

We hop in the car and chat lightly on the drive, but I'm wound up. By the time I drop her off, I'm restless, the Joe incident and Raven's proximity feeding my agitation. I could hit the gym or pound out some miles on the pavement, run until I can't feel my legs, but a beer with the guys is what I need. A sounding board. Time to unload and decide how best to approach Raven about her past.

I pull out my phone to text Sawyer. You in for beers?

Definitely. I'll check with Kolton.

Meet at Diamonds in ten.

* * *

I have a pitcher, three glasses, and a booth claimed by the time the boys arrive. They slide in opposite me and pour themselves a round, not bothering with a word until they toss back a generous swallow.

Sawyer plants his glass down with a thud. "Beer is shit as always."

"Tunes are shit, too." Kolton winces as some classic Hank

Williams strums from the speakers.

Classic, meaning old, like everything in this place: the juke box that doesn't work, the pool tables with the cigarette burns on the felt, the bartender, Doug, who likely survived World War One. The beer is never cold enough, the dartboard falls every time you hit the target, but we've been coming here since they'd serve us without IDs.

"You guys don't know from good tunes." I could listen to Hank all day.

Sawyer sticks a finger in his ear. "Tell that to my eardrums." He turns to Kolton. "Has Shay been working on this new business as much as Lily?"

Kolton shrugs. "She clocks a lot of hours. Locks herself in the basement office."

I nod to Sawyer. "You feeling left out?"

He scowls into his beer. "All I know is, between designing for us part-time and selling purses and starting up this new event gig, Lily hasn't had much free time."

Kolton pats his back. "Never thought I'd see the day."

"It's like he's learning to walk," I say. "Except his feet are tied together. The man doesn't know how to function on his own anymore."

"The man, for your information, is sitting at this table. And I could eat a bowl of alphabet soup and shit out a better joke than that."

Kolton drums a thumb on the table. "Probably not spelled correctly."

Ignoring him, Sawyer drains his beer.

I kick his foot. "That ring's still on Lily's necklace, not her finger. You making headway in the marriage department?"

"Wish I knew. She twists the thing all the time, like she can't stop thinking about it. Drives me crazy. Every time I look at her, I glance down, hoping to see it on her finger. Maybe I haven't done enough. Time will tell, I guess."

Kolton grins. "If you asked me a year ago what was more likely: Sawyer proposing to a girl or Sawyer winning gold in rhythmic gymnastics, I'd have bet my savings on the leotard and ribbon. Goes to show you."

"That you're so dumb your Patronus is a snail?" Sawyer chuckles at his own joke.

Kolton's reply: "Someone should have told you sniffing paint kills brain cells."

We sip our beers.

"Is it hard on you, too?" I ask Kolton. "Shay working so much?"

"Nope. She does better when she's busy. Loves working and having a project on the go. Best for all parties involved. We still find time to hang out, with Jackson and on our own."

He leans forward, his long hair barely covering his smile. Shay may push his buttons, the two of them often arguing, but they fit, like joists aligned in a house. Like Lily and Sawyer work, although I have no idea how she tolerates him. I frown, unsure our meet and greet in Aspen will have as happy an ending for Raven and me.

Kolton knocks his glass against mine. "Were you working tonight?"

"No. I was out with Raven."

"Things okay with Josh?"

I bristle at the question. "My last lead disappeared, and the punk just got his GED. I don't have the balls to tell him it's not worth planning for the future."

"Sorry, man." Kolton empties the pitcher into his glass and stands. "But you should be proud. And maybe something will come together last minute. I'll get this round." He walks over to the bar and sits on a stool, jug in hand, waiting for Doug to stop chatting with the regulars. Might take a while.

Sawyer stretches out on his side of the booth. "Let's rewind to the part where you said you were out with a certain tattooed vixen. What's the deal?"

I spin my glass on the table, wanting to rewind farther. To the way she felt against me at my truck, how her soft lips yielded to mine. "I'm into her."

"Right, but that's like me saying I love a particular comic book. You always fall hard for the ladies."

He's seen too much for me to tell him to fuck off. "She's different. I can talk to her about Josh and the stuff I do at the rec center. It's easy." And there's that deep connection I can't try to explain.

"So what's the holdup?"

Sawyer knows me. Gets that he has to ask questions, force me to reveal the hard truths. The man is as good as family. "You know how some punk stole her wallet?" He nods, and I go on, "Someone at the station found it, and they put her name into the system. Turns out she has a record. Intense shit that kind of shook me." I lock eyes with him. "There's a charge for heroin possession."

"Jesus."

"Yeah. I'm wary to get involved, have her around my sister. The kids. I don't know who her friends are outside of Shay and Lily, if they'll visit her here. What that might bring. But I'm already hooked. I'm helping her find her sister, and it's brought up a lot of heavy stuff for her, too. She doesn't want to spread herself thin, and I'm using it as an excuse to keep her at arm's length, but I'm struggling. Not sure how to process it all."

Sensing my agitation, he plants his elbows on the table. "So you're saying you think she's using? That she's used recently?"

"No. I'd be able to tell, and I haven't even asked her about it." I rub my hand over my mouth. "Things are really fragile with Nikki. With Josh. I just heard the word *heroin*, and it freaked me out."

"Bro, honestly? You're getting way ahead of yourself, and you're judging her without giving her a chance. From what I know of Raven, she's a cool chick. Solid. You can't expect to meet someone without a past. Can't expect perfection. Except from me, obviously."

I'd chide him for his last comment, but his words hit below the belt. He hasn't had to take a sibling to the ER with vomit caked to her skin. Hasn't wondered if his brother would wind up on the five o'clock news because he'd killed someone or been killed. The people closest to me need rules. Tough love. Strict boundaries. I need the rigor, to get me through. But he's right. I haven't given Raven a chance to explain. I've done nothing but let my imagination run wild.

"Assuming you're right, and I'm being an overreacting prick, how do I broach this without pissing her off?"

Sawyer squints at me like I'm nuts. "You sure you want to be asking me that question? I'm the guy who broke my girlfriend's heart because I thought I was doing her a favor. Your instincts have *got* to be better than mine."

"Solid point."

"Actually, scratch that. You sending that dodge ball into Eve

Hamilton's face to get her attention was classic. Worst plan in the history of the world."

I cough on my beer and pound my chest. "Seemed like a good idea at the time. And how was I supposed to know she wasn't wearing her contacts?"

"I'm surprised she didn't relocate your nuts. Should we make a wager, though? Bet that your tact still hovers around the sixteen-year-old mark?"

Sawyer can be a total asshole, but at least he gets me laughing. Loosens me up. "Last time you lost a bet, things didn't work out so good for you."

He shrugs a shoulder. "Lily liked my smooth legs. And I only cried for the first half of the waxing."

I'd rather have my leg hairs ripped out one by one than piss Raven off, but we're overdue for a serious conversation. My ability to read people is usually fine-tuned. Comes with the job. With Raven, my emotions are too invested. Everything's too clouded with the heat she stirs in my blood.

"One word of advice," he adds. "If you do hook up with Raven, maybe hold back the 'I love you' crap until you're sure, especially with these unknowns. You set speed records with the mushy stuff."

I grunt, and we sip our beers and listen to George Jones sing about his broken heart while Kolton gets sucked into conversation with Doug. The ancient dude could talk the oxygen from the air. A commercial flashes on the silent TV behind the bar—an ad for a high-tech superglue. I immediately want Sawyer to challenge me on another bet. The possibilities with that glue are endless.

Kolton plunks a fresh pitcher on the table. "Apparently Doug's alarm clock went off late this morning, and the paperboy's been tossing his paper too deep on his lawn."

"Good to know." Sawyer juts his chin toward the crappy pool tables. "Should we rack 'em up?"

We both nod, and I stretch my legs. Smacking a bunch of balls around should help get my mind off Raven awhile. Stop me picturing us in a motel room, my rough hands charting a map over her inked skin. Her ankles digging into my shoulders. Our sweat-slicked bodies sliding. My deep thrusts.

The pool should help, but it doesn't. I barely sink a goddamn shot.

Ten

Raven

I've been staring at the front door so long I'm surprised I haven't burned two holes through the wood. All I've done the past hour is stand and stare, sit and stare, pace and…*stare*. My eyes sting from lack of blinking, the inside of my cheek raw from chewing on it. Nico should be here in thirty—I glance at my stove clock—scratch that, twenty-nine minutes, each nanosecond I wait making me twitchier. I haven't eaten in twenty-four hours.

My phone buzzes from the countertop, and I nearly jump a mile. I stub my toe on nothing as I lunge for it, smacking my cell to the floor with the back of my hand. The thing tumbles in slow motion, my anxiety spiraling with it, before it lands on the mat by the sink. Diving to my knees, I grab it, but I don't look at the text. For sure Nico is canceling. We had to delay his pickup time to one o'clock already. Something probably came up at work or with his family.

Not seeing him since that scorching car kiss has been challenging, but if we don't look for Rose today, *if* I have to endure another minute or night or week waiting, I'm liable to tie my intestines in a knot.

I exhale at the sight of Shay's name on the screen: Open your door.

I scramble to my feet and do as requested. She and Lily are climbing the stairs and push past me, arms full of thick catalogs. They drop them on my kitchen counter with a thud.

I scan the six gargantuan books. "To what do I owe this honor?"

Lily shakes out her wrists. "We stopped by a few stationery places and collected catalogs. Since we were passing by your place, Shay wanted to show you and wish you luck today and…" She trails off as Shay tosses a plastic bag at my head that I barely manage to catch. "I had nothing to do with this," Lily adds.

Inside are three boxes of condoms. "They're extra-large," Shay says.

I cough out a laugh. "What? No banana for me to practice on?"

She grins. "They weren't big enough."

She doesn't know the half of it. Although most parts of my sexy-Nico-Aspen night are blurry, the one thing that's clear as day was waking up next to him and lifting the covers to take a peek. I immediately touched my jaw, wondering how I didn't dislocate it, and realized there was no chance we'd had sex; I'd for sure have been tender and sore. Now I'm dying to know how it would feel to be joined to him, filled up with him, *ridden* by him.

That's a lot of man to handle.

Lily can't look me in the eyes. "Nico would die if he heard you talking like that."

"More like he'd be smug as hell," Shay says. "Besides, I'm just trying to focus on the fun part of this field trip. How are you holding up?"

Instead of replying that I'm a jumbled mess, I open one of the catalogs and flip through it. Looping calligraphy, printed stationery, and colored envelopes fill each page. "These are great. Lots of options for our future customers."

"Right?" Shay flips through another one. "We'll figure out pricing, but there are tons in here."

Lily stills my busy hand. "Seriously, Rave. How are you?"

Noxious. Terrified. I might have to face my sister and my betrayal. There's also a chance I might find forgiveness. Find someone to order Chinese takeout with for Thanksgiving, because neither of us knows how to cook a turkey. Someone to remind me I was a shy kid who chased snakes and actually wore dresses.

I run my fingers over a cream invitation. The dainty ribbon enclosing the page is so sheer it looks ready to snap. "How many hours without sleep are considered dangerous?"

"It's that bad?" Shay asks.

"I've been waiting to find Rose for seventeen years. There's major buildup with that, and it could be a disaster."

"Or it could be great," Lily says. "Whatever happens, you still have us."

She's right. I know she is. But she's always had family. Her birthday doesn't pass unnoticed by her kin. Hallmark displays of Mother's Day cards or "Sisterly Love" don't make her want to spend the day at a gun range. I yawn into my elbow, my sleeplessness catching up to me. "I know I have you, I just might not have my sanity."

"Because Nico might literally fuck your brains out?" Shay wiggles her eyebrows.

We all burst out laughing, even Lily tossing her head back with a hearty giggle. Man, do I love these girls. "The guy is dead sexy," I say.

"No argument there." Shay fixes her bra strap, the red lace a match to the ruby lips printed on her tank top. "Seriously, though, you're still good with your decision? To take things further with him?"

"I'm still nervous, but there's no use fighting it. He's been nothing but good to me since the Aspen fiasco, and the attraction is too intense. Time will tell if it's the right move."

At the slums, our bodies touched so many times I may as well have smoked a joint. The way his thighs bracketed my ass while he looked at my photos, how his hands curled around my hips— every point of contact snapped through my bloodstream, leaving me a hazy mess. When he lowered his lips to my ear and said photography was my calling, my body melted into his.

Then, *that kiss.*

A girl could get used to that sense of connection, that swoopy feeling in her stomach. Very, *very* used to that. And sleeping in his arms might calm the anxiety keeping me awake at night. *After* he fucks my brains out.

We flip through the books, pointing out our favorite invitations. Mine has a large black raven swooping across the page (obviously). Lily's choice has branches of coral layered over handmade paper. Remembering *my* to-do list for our business, I grab a stack of menus from my room and fan them over the books.

"I checked out five catering companies and chatted with the owners about what we're doing. I think we should narrow it down to three. They all said we could crash a party to see them in action—taste their food and check out the presentation. I can get on that when I'm back. Just let me know if you want to come."

Shay scrunches her face. "Is that a real question? Free fancy food? Sign me up."

Lily stops chewing her cuticles long enough to say, "I'm in."

Pounding sounds from my door then, one glance at my clock telling me my Sexy Beast is on time. Thanks to the girls, my nerves are less overwrought, but when I open the door, I nearly dissolve, my insides turning to goo at the sight of Nico.

Must be the sleep deprivation.

He smolders at me. "Hey."

Definitely some form of deprivation. "Hey, yourself."

He's in his non-police uniform: tight black T-shirt—the stitching across his biceps holding on for dear life—dark jeans, black boots, and sunglasses covering those eyes. Come to think of it, this could be his *on*-duty wardrobe. Everything about him screams COP.

I stare at my reflection in his glasses. "Is that what you're wearing?"

He looks down at his (I'd love to lick whipped cream off of it) chest and back at me. "Yeah."

Nico excels at single syllables.

I huff out a breath, realizing neither of us is dressed right. He looks like a narc, and I could pass for a punk rocker with my black ensemble. The Rose I remember wore bell bottoms and flowered tops and tied ribbons in her hair. If we show up at a hippie commune looking like this, no one will talk to us.

"Hi, Nico," Lily calls from behind me, both girls weighted down with their books.

He steps aside to let them pass. "That stuff for the event business?"

"Yep." One foot out the door, Shay pauses. "You're welcome in advance for my gift." With that, they traipse down the stairs, leaving me with a confused Nico.

He doesn't close the distance between us. He removes his sunglasses and walks into my apartment, positioning himself on one side of my laminate countertop. I stand opposite him, my back to my living space, a two-foot barrier between us. There's an emotional gap, too. The same coolness I felt at the slums. It does nothing good for my anxiety.

He studies the room. "Not what I expected."

I shrug. "It came furnished, and I haven't had the cash to redecorate."

My apartment in Toronto was cool. The walls were deep purple, black-and-white photographs decorated the space, and I had a cool beanbag chair and black leather couches. Not to mention the gothic mirror by my bed. This place is beige. Walls, beige. Couch, beige. Carpet, beige. Beige kitchen cupboards and curtains. It hurts my eyes.

What doesn't hurt my eyes is the colossal giant taking up my kitchen.

He drops his head a moment, like he's upset or nervous or I don't know what. My agitation doubles. When he looks up, determination sets his jaw. "There's something I need to ask you, and I didn't know how to bring it up. Not sure this is the right time, and I'm not accusing you of anything, but we're about to spend a couple days together, and I need to get this out."

Excuse me? *Accuse?* I don't know where he's going with that train of thought, but my knees lock, and I cross my arms. "What exactly is it that I've done?"

He mumbles something under his breath and rubs the back of his neck. "Nothing," he says louder. "Absolutely nothing. But when your wallet was found, your record came up."

"My record? You looked into me?"

"No. It wasn't like that. Alessi called, filled me in. Thing is, I haven't told you, but my sister is a recovering addict. Heroin. She overdosed shortly after Josh got arrested, and it's been a long haul to get her back on her feet. So when I saw the possession charge, it kind of stopped me cold. I want you, Raven. You have to know I'm falling for you, but drugs are a hard no for me. Can't risk Nikki being near anything. So I need to know I'm being overly cautious here. That drugs aren't a part of your life now."

His words slam into my chest. "What you're being is an *asshole*. You think I'm using? Or dealing? You think that little of me?" My knees go from locked to weak, and I grip the counter.

"No. Babe. Fuck. No." He squeezes his eyes shut, then exhales. "I'm just scared. Scared how much I like you. Scared all the time something will set Nikki back. Scared I can't keep my family together. Just scared."

How do I stay mad when those blue eyes plead with me? I don't like it. The accusation stings. But my stress over searching for Rose doesn't hold a candle to the weights Nico bears. I press my hipbones into the counter. Closer to him, but still apart. "I'm sorry about Nikki. I didn't know, and I don't do drugs now. Haven't for years. Weed was my thing in high school, nothing harder, but I was out with a friend one night. We got pulled over for a busted taillight. Turns out the idiot had enough heroin in the glove box to slap him with a possession charge, but I told the cops it was mine."

The big guy frowns. "You took the fall?"

"He was a loser, but not all bad. The reason we were out was because he wanted to talk about getting clean. Asked my advice. He took care of his younger sister. Was really good to her. She needed him around or she'd end up in foster care. So I paid a fine and spent a week in jail. I'd just turned eighteen, had an open record, so all the crap I did when I was younger was tattooed on my file."

Nico's cheekbones sharpen. His light eyes take on a darker tone. It's the same intense look he gave Tim when doling out his final warning. Like he doesn't approve of the choice I made.

"Look," I say, tightening my grip on the counter. "I've done some messed-up shit in my life, but that's not who I am now. You and I haven't spent that much time together, but we both obviously want more. I'm nervous to get involved with you, too, for my own reasons. We either trust each other and give it a shot, or we call it a day. If it's the latter, I'll go to Fraser Valley on my own."

He doesn't hesitate. He lays his hand palm up on the counter between us. An offering. An invitation. Inexplicably drawn to this man, I place my palm on top of his. His fingers are twice the size of mine. Calluses toughen his skin. He should be intimidating, scary, but he's a gentle giant. "I'm all in. I just needed to know for sure. I'm sorry for asking. For being distant recently. Can we start over?"

My rush of relief is instant, and surprising. Searching for Rose on my own isn't what I want. *Nico* is what I want. Him joining me on this adventure. His strong arms to wrap around me if things don't go my way. Even right now, with all the sexual tension knotting me up, I also want to press my face into his wide neck and feel his pulse against my cheek. Let it lull me.

When I nod, he rounds the counter, closing the space between us in long strides. His lips capture mine, his huge hands wrapping around my hips. He kisses me so slowly I fall into him.

"Now what's this about a gift?" he asks against my lips.

Breathless, I nod to the plastic bag on my floor. "Shay thought we might need condoms. You know, *just in case*."

The man blushes. It's so sweet, I nearly drag him to my room, but we have more pressing issues, as well as a night in a motel to look forward to. Our overdue fresh start.

First up, new wardrobes.

I extricate myself from his grasp. "We need to make a stop on our way."

I grab my bag, but he takes it from me and follows me to his car. Our conversation and Nico's judging gaze sit heavily at the back of my mind, but I'm tired of holding grudges. I'm all about new beginnings these days. With him. With Rose. As of right now, Nico and I are undercover detectives on a mission. Hiding him in plain sight won't be easy. Good thing a Value Village isn't far.

***

Speed shopping isn't Nico's thing. I drag him around the thrift shop, holding up clothes that might fit his large frame, a deep frown on his face the whole time. Shoving him in a change room proves a challenge. The only reason he agrees is that I promise to listen to his country music for the drive. (He doesn't know I cross my fingers.) By the time we're in our new outfits, our bag of old clothes clutched in his hand, Nico is highly unimpressed.

He stops at the exit and plants his hand on his hip. "I'm not going outside in this. I look ridiculous."

Ridiculous is an understatement. "But you don't look like

a cop."

"I look like a freak." He grimaces at his baggy jeans, the waist cinched with an awful fabric belt, the pink ends hanging down his hip. His loose Hawaiian shirt hides the build he often emphasizes, but it's the wig and hat that puts his outfit over the top. Brown "hair" hangs to his jaw, a red beret pulled over his forehead.

"If you saw the losers my sister hung out with in high school, you'd understand. Plus, if I'm wearing this, there's no way you're changing." I flutter my light blue dress, the stitched yellow flowers undulating with the movement. Add the white ballet flats and wide-rimmed sun hat, and I practically look virginal.

Gently, he stills my hand with his. "You look nice."

The reverence in his tone sends warmth curling through me. His fingers linger on my skin, little brushes that speak volumes: *He's sorry*, I think each one says. *Forgive me. Let me make it right.* Like he's worried his concerns and questions have set us back. Or maybe he's thinking about the motel in our future. Whatever the reason for his increased PDA, I need these moments of connection today.

I kiss his shoulder. "Thanks, but I look like I should skip through this place humming 'The Sound of Music.'"

"You really think this is necessary?" He scratches at his wig.

I play with one of the buttons running down the front of my dress, and his eyes follow my movement. "I think it's our best chance of getting people to talk to us, and it makes me feel a bit protected. Like if she's there, I can hide under this stupid hat and decide if I want to approach her."

He tugs up his jeans, resignation on his face. "Fine. I'll do it. Because it makes you feel better, but the hat and wig can wait 'til later." He yanks them off and adds, "You better not take pictures."

"If I do, might you arrest me? With handcuffs?"

That earns me a smile—dark and mischievous with a dash of me-ow. "Tempting. And the answer to your text from after the beach is silk."

My cheeks heat, like the revirginized girl I am. I can definitely do silk.

A chaste kiss later, we're on our way. Once outside the city limits, I try to ignore my mounting unease. The high-pitched twang vibrating from the radio doesn't help. Cars blur by; trees and light posts break up the landscape. I yawn. I shake my head. No matter what I do, my eardrums feel as though someone's drilling into them with ice picks. "I can't take it anymore."

I reach to fiddle with the radio, but Nico puts his hand on mine. "We had a deal."

"That was before I was faced with losing my hearing at twenty-six. And I'd prefer to avoid awakening every dead dog within a thirty-mile radius."

Smirking, he returns his hand to the wheel. "I like this music."

"I like curry, but knowing you hate it, I wouldn't lock you in here for two hours just to watch your face turn blue."

His smirk widens. "Okay. I'll give you two songs. Then we'll alternate."

I flip the dial, passing static, something French, a classical guitar, and coffeehouse yodeling that goes with our outfits. When a scream blares from the speakers, followed by a heavy bass, I stop fiddling. Nico winces but doesn't say anything. He endures two metal tunes and then changes the station back.

This is how the drive goes: his songs, my songs, his stupid shirt showing off his forearms as he drives. My dress shifting across my sensitive skin. *His* gaze raking over my body.

And we talk.

He tells me about the school trip with Kolton and Sawyer that ended with Nico locked out of their room, only to wake up on the hotel floor, a mustache drawn on his face. I regale him with my tales of delinquency, complete with the time I shoved a banana up my principal's tailpipe. He listens without interrupting. Nico always listens.

Once we leave the highway, farmland blankets the valley floor, mountains bordering the lush land. I relax more, the scenery as calming as Nico's rich voice.

Until he pulls up to a sign that says, *Neverland Farms*. "You nervous?" he asks.

"Do they speak Portuguese in Portland?"

He chuckles. "Right. Stupid question." He takes my hand, uncurls my fist, and laces our fingers together. The kiss he places on my pulse point hurts my racing heart. "I'm here because I care about you. That won't change. No matter what happens with Rose, I'll see you through this."

That boyish grin of his appears, sneaking into places I usually keep locked. I'm not sure how he got the key. "Bet you weren't counting on this much baggage, dating me."

He looks at me then, really looks at me, and his eyes have never been so blue, burning bright with so much emotion I'm forced to glance away. "Raven," he says, drawing my attention back to him. He cups my jaw and brushes his thumb over my cheek. A cut or callus scratches my skin. "I'm all in. Wouldn't want to be anywhere else."

His gaze is unwavering, his jaw as strong as the mountains around us. His shoulders are big enough to carry this burden of mine, and his family's, and the kids he helps at the rec center.

He is such a *good* man. And he needs to know it. "What I wrote to you in Aspen is true. I've never felt like this before. With anyone, even after all this time." The radio is off, but I'd swear a heavy bass beats in my chest. Nico presses his forehead to mine as though he wants to read my mind. Learn what drives my heart. I'm not sure how long we sit like this, his large hand on my cheek, my heart pounding in my ears.

It's a good thing we brought lots of condoms.

He kisses my wrist again, then we drive under the arched sign. Flowers line the road, as wild and untamed as I feel, but my hand is secure in Nico's grasp. When he parks, he releases me to stick that hideous wig on. I pull on my sun hat. As soon as my feet hit the gravel drive, he's at my door and laces our fingers together again. It feels different this time—possessive, seductive. A promise of what's to come.

Unfortunately, I laugh. "I really need a picture of you in that beret."

"You obviously don't value your life."

"Come on. I could use it to bribe Sawyer. He'd clean my apartment for a month to get his hands on that."

"Make that a double homicide."

"Even if I promise to listen to country on the drive home?"

He tugs me forward. "Not a chance."

Deep purple rows of lavender extend under darkening clouds, as does a multicolored fence. Other crops grow in sections, some tall, some short. The main house is painted pink and orange and every color under the sun, sculptures of dragonflies and butterflies stuck to the siding. My maybe-boyfriend is in a hideous outfit, holding my hand, while we search for my estranged sister at some whacked-out hippie farm.

The idiocy of the situation takes the edge off. *Slightly.*

Nico knocks on the door and pulls me closer. Someone calls, "Coming!" and that edge I've been balancing on sharpens. I tap my ballet flat and nearly hyperventilate. When the door swings wide, I tense and lower the rim of my hat, but immediately exhale. Not Rose. Still, I give myself a mental thumbs-up for dressing undercover.

The woman's foot jingles from her stacked anklets. A baby is perched on her hip, her flowing patchwork dress as busy as the outside decor. "Can I help you?"

Although Nico is dressed like an overgrown hippie, his wide stance and stiff posture probably give him away. "We're looking for a woman," he says. "An old friend. Heard she moved out here a while back. Maybe a few years. Is there anyone who could help us?" He slides his hand over my lower back and grips my hip as though holding me steady. I press into his side.

The woman bounces her baby. "Sure. I'm Wispy, but Lake has lived here longer. He might know something." She nods for us to come in.

Nico leans down to my ear. "You should probably call me Spirit."

The big guy made a joke. "How about Starbright?"

Or Dusk. Or Ocean. Or simply *Mine.*

"Whatever you want," he says.

We follow Wispy into the open floorplan. Like outside, it looks like a paint set exploded. Large pillows fill the area instead of couches, knit blankets draped everywhere in yellows, peaches, oranges, and greens. On the floor, a man has sunk into an oversized beanbag chair, his dark dreadlocks tied in a knot on his head. He strums a guitar with lazy strokes.

Wispy motions to us. "These folks are looking for someone who might have lived here."

With that introduction, she floats off, lowering the top of her dress as she goes, exposing her breast. She begins feeding her baby. The simplicity of the act intrigues me, the innocence of it—our bodies doing what they were built for. Makes me wonder if I was breast fed. If I was ever held and loved and doted upon. The hard places under my bones assure me I wasn't, but the beauty is so alluring I wish I hadn't left my camera in the car.

Nico, however, blushes fire-engine red. He angles his body toward Lake. "We're looking for a girl who might have lived here, or near here, a few years ago."

Lake doesn't interrupt his lazy tune. "Name?"

"Her name is Rose. Rose Hunt." I'm thankful Nico's the one speaking. Between our impending night together, this nutty place, and the possibility of finding my sister, I'm not sure I'd be able to string two words together.

A few more unhurried strums later, Lake says, "No. *Your* names."

God, like I'm not nervous enough without him drawing out the agony. Nico scratches the back of his wig and huffs out a sigh. "I'm Spirit, and this is…Petal." He presses his lips tight.

There will be retribution.

Strum. Strum. Strum.

Strum.

"Welcome to Neverland." Lake sings the words with his guitar, and I kind of want to smash the instrument over his head.

"So," Nico says when we've listened to eight bars too many of Lake's impromptu song. "I was told Rose lived here a few years ago. She has long dark hair, dark eyes. She's from outside Toronto, originally." He nudges me. "Anything specific you can add?"

I want to add a black eye to Lake's stoned face, but he means to Rose's description. The first thing I always look for when scanning faces are the teeth—straight and white and perfect. Considering the nipple unveiling, there's a chance Lake has seen the birthmark on Rose's hip.

I point to the spot. "She has a large birthmark here, shaped like a heart."

Strum. Strum. Strum.

Strum.

"Yeah...Rose...sure. I remember her."

Strum.

My internal organs migrate toward my throat, nausea and excitement shaking my foundation. Nico's strong hand grips my waist.

When Lake doesn't go on, a growl rumbles from Nico's chest, almost too low to hear. He keeps his voice even. "Does that mean she doesn't live here anymore? Do you know where she is?"

Strum. Fucking. *Strum.* "I think she left a year ago. A friend of hers, Clara, might know where she's at. She's gone for the day but will be back for our potluck tonight. You're welcome to come."

My churning gut calms a bit, but the room spins. It looks different, the space filled with shadows of my sister. I imagine her working the fields or sitting on a giant pillow or cooking at the stove. I imagine her smiling her bright, white smile. She could also have dreadlocks and four kids named Rainbow, Butterfly, Rock, and Leaf.

Nico doesn't reply, but he watches me, waiting.

"We'll come," I say.

"Groovy." Lake's incessant melody continues. "Bring something vegan to share with the farm." He leans back and closes his eyes.

Our cue.

At the car, the first drops of rain fall. Nico spins me to face him and hovers over me. My personal umbrella. "You okay?"

Although my hands are shaking, all limbs are intact. Major organs haven't shifted. I reek of patchouli oil from the incense burning in the house, but other than that, I survived our undercover operation. "Yeah, but I need a shower." I slide my hands around his hips and pull him and his ugly jeans closer.

He tips my hat back to see my face. "You need help undoing those buttons down the front?" His gaze drops to the pearl snaps over my breasts.

Man, oh man. My dress is so thin his hard-on is unmistakable as he presses closer. But he steps away. "We might not have time. We need to find a motel and figure out what to bring tonight."

Right. Vegan potluck. Not Nico's large fingers struggling with my dainty buttons. "We can pick a bunch of flowers and grass and roll them in seaweed."

He moves to open my door, and the light rain dances on my arms and legs. It's pleasant. Refreshing. And knowing I won't see Rose tonight melts some of my remaining tension. A breeze blows up my skirt as I slide into the car, and Nico groans from behind me. The sound travels up my skirt, too. This will be the longest (and only) vegan potluck I'll ever attend.

Eleven

Nico

The smell of sweaty feet wafts through the farmhouse, bowl upon bowl of curried vegetables filling up the kitchen. I gag once and inhale through my mouth. Raven puts our containers of store-bought salad beside something that looks regurgitated. Her long hair meets the top of her blue dress, the girly look not my first choice on her. I like Raven dark and edgy, exactly how she is. But those buttons on the front catch the light—winking at me, teasing me—and her black bra is visible below the fabric.

Tonight can't come soon enough.

Back at the motel, we dropped our bags, both of us eyeing the queen bed in the middle of our room. I ached to fling her on the mattress and show her just how much I've missed her since Aspen. But making love to Raven won't be quick business. It will be slow and intense and deep. And as tough as she's being, this still has to be hard for her. Her sarcasm doesn't hide the way she's picked her cuticles raw since leaving earlier, the way she studies every woman she sees.

She bends forward now to move bowls around, her dress shifting over her round ass, and I grab her waist. It's more than this piercing attraction, though. I want her close. Want her to know she can lean on me.

She straightens and falls against my chest.

"As soon as we talk to this Clara woman," I whisper, "we're getting out of here."

She presses the curve of her ass into my groin. "I couldn't agree more."

I grunt and push her forward, unable to handle the contact. These free-loving hippies might not bat an eye at two people going at it in the kitchen, but I want Raven all to myself. No prying eyes. No interruptions. Just her and me and a lot less clothing.

I grab her hand to keep her close as we weave through the twenty-odd people in the house. This place looks like a rainbow puked on it. So do the guests. Unfortunately, *so do I*. I can't stop scratching at the wig, the hat is ugly as sin, and I'll be burning this Hawaiian shirt the second it leaves my body. Raven doesn't seem to mind. She keeps glancing at me, her eyes as dark as I've ever seen them, like I'm in nothing but my boxer briefs.

The briefs barely containing me.

She was smart, though. If I were in my black T-shirt and aviator glasses, I doubt Lake would have given us the time of day. I spot him in the same beanbag chair as earlier, same guitar in his hands, probably still plucking out the same damn tune. I stop beside him, and he doesn't glance up. Raising my voice over the crowd and music won't win me any favors, so I fall into the beanbag chair beside him, all arms and legs. Sawyer and Kolton would have a field day with me in these clothes, in this chair, my knees bent up to my ears. When I stop shifting around, Raven sits between my legs and tucks her knees to her chest. Suddenly, this stupid excuse for a piece of furniture doesn't seem so bad.

I wrap my arms around her. "Lake," I call, but the dude doesn't budge.

Raven leans forward and taps his thigh. When he doesn't twitch, she smacks him harder.

His lids flutter open. "Oh, hey." His pupils dilate like a cartoon character. A stoned, dreadlocked cartoon character. He sways toward us then pulls back. "Spirit, right?"

Yep, the guys would kill themselves laughing. "Yeah. You mentioned Clara would be here tonight. Has she arrived?"

He glances around the room, but I'd bet all he sees is a blurred rainbow. "Yeah. Probably." Then he closes his eyes, his fingers strum, and he returns to his corner of the world.

Fucking hippies.

Raven sighs. She leans heavier into my chest, tilts her head, and brushes her nose against my neck. A bolt of heat strikes my groin. She kisses me, a slow taste with her tongue that has me crushing her to my chest. If she had any doubt what effect she has on me, my hard-on against her back should reassure her. Needing a taste, too, I nuzzle my face into her hair until I have her ear between my teeth. Her replying whimper is all the reward I need.

"Like I said, *Petal*, let's find Clara and get out of here."

"You sure, *Spirit*? Because I'm pretty comfortable."

"I'm sure. My plan for your petal doesn't involve a room full of people."

She laughs. "I like it when your inner hippie talks dirty." She grinds backward, but I still her hips.

Slow, intense, deep, I remind myself.

When Raven admitted she's never felt this close to anyone before, my heart nearly busted through my ribs. All my nerve endings shot to life—being near her hurt, swallowing hurt, looking at her hurt. This morning it was a relief hearing she'd never done hard drugs. I didn't like learning she'd lied to cops to cover for some punk, but that was years ago. I won't second-guess her. If she says that part of her life is done, it's done. All I want now is to make up for the months I've wasted since Aspen. The time I've wasted the past couple weeks.

Starting with making love to her tonight.

"My inner hippie plans to get you nice and high, naturally. But not here." I grab her hips to lift her up and give myself a minute to avoid embarrassment. Then I push to my feet and search for the only other person we know. Hopefully Wispy's breast is tucked away tonight. Nikki used to do that in the house, breastfeed on a whim. I get it. I approve of it. But damn, if it doesn't make me uncomfortable.

Sixties music comes from a nearby stereo, guests swaying, some with their hands in the air. The smell of pot is unmistakable. I smoked once in high school, but it wasn't my thing. I prefer my mind sharp, in control. Occasionally I drink too much, but I've never been face-first in a toilet like Sawyer and Kolton. I never let things go that far.

When I spot Wispy, her flowing dress is intact. She's with a couple of women, their eyes closed and heads swaying to the music. I move in behind them and tap her shoulder.

Without pausing, she opens her eyes. A lazy grin sweeps across her face. "Spirit, hi."

Raven snorts, and I ignore her. The sooner we get the information we need, the sooner we get back to the motel. "Lake mentioned a girl named Clara would be here tonight. You know her?"

She nods and sways, and nods and sways. She nudges the red-head beside her. "Clara, these folks wanna talk to you."

That was surprisingly easy. Unlike Wispy, Clara stops dancing and studies us warily, eyes lingering on my wig and beret. "Do I know you?"

Her red hair is in two braids, like a doll my sister had. She tugs one, bites her lip, and swallows, everything about her shifty. I'm about to speak when Raven pushes in front of me. "I'm looking for my sister. Rose Hunt? Lake said you might know where she's living."

Clara stops fiddling with her braid and settles her weight on one hip. "I didn't know Rose had a sister."

Raven sags forward. Hurt maybe? Upset Rose doesn't talk about her? I move closer, pressing my chest to her back. "They haven't seen each other in a long time," I say. "Any chance you know where we can find her?"

More swallowing and braid spinning, and worry snakes up my spine. I've been around enough skittish criminals and degenerates to sense when someone has something to hide. After she's twirled her hair umpteen times, she says, "Last I heard she was crashing at a friend's in Vancouver. A guy by the name of Russ Adams. Around East Hastings, I think."

Raven's shoulders stiffen at the mention of Hastings. She's been there. She knows the types that live in the area. As do I. I've been so focused on helping her and getting my mind right, I didn't stop to consider the implications. Sure, emotionally, this was bound to be tough, but connecting with her sister could mean learning truths better left ignored. The bad elements I worried about might still shove their way into Raven's life.

Lead settles in my gut, but this isn't about me. I owe Raven my trust, and she has so much riding on this. She's built Rose up in her mind for seventeen years. That comes with expectations, hopes that could go up in smoke.

I school my features. "You have an address?"

Clara shakes her head as a waft of curry hits my nose. I fight the urge to gag. Once we say our thanks, I pull Raven after me, inhaling the damp air outside like I've been drowning. My gym bag smells better than that.

"Indian food is amazing. I bet if you tried it, the smell wouldn't bother you so much."

"How about I take your word for it." Give me meat and potatoes any day. I scratch my wig and suck in a few more breaths. "Looks like our search continues."

She's back to picking her cuticles, her shoulders nearing her ears. "We're getting closer, though. Can you find the address? Or I can look it up back home."

"I got this, babe. Don't worry about a thing." I press my lips to hers, and she hums against me. Two gentle kisses later, her posture relaxes, but I'm still leery. I pull my phone from my back pocket. "I'll send Alessi the name. Get him to put it in the system and see if we get any hits."

She grabs her skirt and swings from side to side. "That's awful kind of you, Spirit."

Raven keeps hamming it up, swaying her shoulders and giving me bedroom eyes. Likely masking the turmoil still brewing in her mind. Hopefully we're both overacting. Clara's shifty behavior was probably because of my ridiculous outfit, this wig enough to put anyone on edge.

Either way, Raven needs a distraction. I could use one, too. One that doesn't involve the virginal role she's playing. I spent a night with her in Aspen—her nails left marks on my neck, and memories of her sexy moans kept me up nights afterward. She may have been too drunk to remember much of what we did, but I wasn't. I remember it all.

"I need us back at that hotel," I say, my voice gruff.

She licks her lips. "Yes, please."

I rip off my hat and wig and drive faster than an off-duty cop should.

* * *

She's out her side of the car before I come to a complete stop, her door slamming as I pull my keys from the ignition. If she thinks she's as desperate as I am to get naked, she doesn't have a clue. She races up the steps to the motel's second story, teasing me by turning twice. Each time a new button on her dress has been undone, and I quicken my strides. Her key is in the lock when I reach her.

She swings the door wide, but I grab her hips from behind and pull her against me. "I want you so fucking bad." Her dress is soft, the fabric sliding over her curves as she rubs against me, her ass pressed to my thighs. I can't get close enough. I cup her breast and bite her neck and walk us forward into the room. Kicking the door shut, I spin her around, latch an arm around her waist, and haul her to me. My lips are on hers in seconds. She grips my neck, the flat of our tongues connecting as our kiss deepens. Moans trade, teeth bump. I'm hungry for her. Starving. Like nothing I've ever felt.

She comes up for air and sucks a trail down my neck. "I'm so wet," she says against my pulse.

The throbbing point nearly tears through my neck.

I grab her ass and lift her up. Sensing what I'm after, she latches her legs around my waist. Her heels dig into my hips, her thin dress riding up, her underwear nothing but air between us. Grunting, I push her back into the wall and grind into her. A picture frame rattles.

"Jesus, you're hard." She rolls her hips into my growing cock, my zipper ready to bust. Another hip rotation, and I see double.

"That's all you." I rub against her. "That's what you do to me." I bite her neck.

She wiggles around, dropping her pelvis to get me exactly where she wants me, my confined erection hitting her sweet spot. All I want is for her to feel good, better than good. For her to get off on me, like this, her legs and arms around my body, my mouth on hers. Watch her fall apart before I strip every item of clothing off her and start again.

We move in time, her riding me, me grinding against her. Kissing gets messy—just lips and tongue and a lot of groaning. Needing to touch her, I slip my hand between us. Her underwear is drenched, the tender flesh below soft. Wet. *Glorious.* I sink one then two fingers inside her, using my thumb to coil her tighter and push her further and give her what she needs.

What I crave.

"God, I'm…" Her words are muffled against my neck. "I'm so…" Again they slip down my skin, but I think she says she's *close*.

I roll my hips once, twice, as if we're having sex, and my hand mirrors the movement, rocking into her. She rocks back. Raven isn't a woman who gives herself freely. Growing up with her parents' negligence must have been like marinating in bitterness. Her sister's abandonment toughened her skin. With me, she's thawing, letting me glimpse the girl beneath the attitude. It lights a fire low in my gut.

She squeezes her knees into my ribs, her nails raking my neck. "God, Nico. I'm so…" She cries out then, high-pitched and animal, her teeth clamping my shoulder as her legs tremble around me. I hold her up. I always will. When she's spent, her body still, she sinks her full weight on my hips.

I keep her pressed to the wall, my balls aching and my dick rock hard. I kiss her collarbone, the hollow at the base of her neck, the tender spot below her ear as I ease my fingers out. "You're sexy as hell when you come."

She reaches between us and runs her hand over my cock. "If that's what you can do with our clothes on, I'm dying to know what happens when the beast is unleashed."

I kiss her mouth hard. "Soon. First we play a game."

Pouting, she releases her legs from my waist and slides down my body. I'm aching to be inside her, but this is about more than sex for me. Nikki tells me I care too much, that I'm always trying to be the hero. Maybe I am. But learning more about Raven means I can be here for her when it counts. Pick her up when she falls. And I need to know, without a doubt, she's willing to do this with me. Not close down when I pry.

I brush her bangs aside and tilt her chin up. Her well-kissed lips are red and swollen. "I planned on us getting naked slowly."

Her quiet "Okay" is the perfect amount breathless.

I leave her at the wall and glance around the room. The curtains and comforter are red and gold, the brownish carpet a little worse for wear. A couple of sailboat paintings hang on the cream walls, my mind instantly on the pirate ship sailing across Raven's tailbone. An interrogation is what we need. Two chairs flank a small table, so I drag them to the foot of the bed and face them toward each other.

I nod to the far one. "Have a seat."

She adjusts her twisted dress and pats down her flyaway hairs, eyes narrowed as she follows my instructions. "Are we playing spin the bottle?"

I turn off the main light and switch on a lamp, then I sit opposite her, my legs wide and arms crossed, my dick throbbing. "I'm curious about your ink. For every answer I get, I'll remove a piece of clothing. Same goes for you. Think you can play this game with me?"

"Sure, big guy. I'll play your silly reindeer games." Her tone is playful, but she's tracing her rose tattoo, something she does when she's uneasy.

Eyes locked, I ask, "The skull at the top of your left arm, how it dissolves into a flock of birds. What's the significance?" It's a sick tattoo, the mass of wings flapping down to her wrist.

She glances at it and smiles. Must be an easy one. "I had Lily and Shay each design something for the piece. Shay did the skull, said it was badass like me, and Lily did the ravens—an homage to my name." Pleased with herself and how little she had to share, she sits taller. "Pass over your shirt."

My fucking pleasure. I yank the offensive blue-and-orange-flowered top over the back of my head and toss it at her. She eyes my chest and bites her lip. I get harder. "Your turn."

She tilts her head, her dark gaze practically drawing lines over my body. Over both tribal sleeves and the large area inked on my left pec, down to my baggy pants, zeroing in on the bulge I can't hide, and up to my neck. "The phoenix," she says, motioning to the tail that hangs in the middle of my chest. The bird's body curls over my trap and up the back of my neck, flames licking at its wings. "Tell me about it."

"Typical symbolism. The phoenix burns and rises from the ashes, reborn. I decided on it when I was thirteen but didn't get it 'til I was older." The day comes back, the emotions less potent but there. Always there. "They'd arrested my father the year before. He was high on something that day and grabbed me by my shirt and told me I was a worthless piece of shit. A year later he was paroled. My mom had baked a cake, like she did the previous two times. She was excited to see him, but I was dreading it. Wished he hadn't been released. He never came home, and I imagined that as the start of my life—reborn like the phoenix. Next time I saw him was fifteen years later. The day I arrested him for dealing."

It's been a while since I've spoken about this, but a familiar anger flashes behind my eyes. A father is supposed to support you, not break you down. Not leave your mother a crying mess. Not force his son into a position where he has to choose between family and what's right, even if that family deserves jail time.

Her gaze doesn't leave mine. "How old were you when you finally got the tattoo?"

"Eighteen."

She nods, emotion brimming in her eyes. "What do you want of mine?"

Your heart, I want to say. "Your dress," I ask for instead.

She stands and steps closer. "Mind helping me with the buttons?"

This, I like. The slow seduction. Getting pieces of her before I take what I want. "Sure."

I stand, too, towering over her. Before I touch her dress, she traces the lines of the phoenix, and the edge of her nail drags across my skin. "You're remarkable."

It's the same word I almost used to compliment her at the slums, but I don't reply. I've never shared that much detail with a woman. Sawyer and Kolton know the shit I've dealt with, how hard it was to put my own father away. *Remarkable* isn't the word I'd have used to describe myself, but from her, I'll take it.

She stands, shoulders square, chest up, waiting for my big fingers to fumble with the tiny buttons keeping her body and stories hidden. She took care of the top two on our way in, so I start with the third. It pops out easier than I thought. I open the neckline farther, her breasts rising faster, then I undo the next.

And the next.

It goes like this. I spread the fabric apart, release a button. My fingers graze her chest, her breasts, her ribs, then I reach her waist. I slip the straps off her shoulder, and the blue dress pools at her feet, revealing a skimpy black bra and thong. Goose bumps flare across her skin.

"You're skilled with your fingers." Her voice is nothing but a hum.

I almost stop this game right here, almost drag my hands all over her. Seventeen months is a long time to go without a woman. But this is Raven, and I want more. Slowly, I back up and sit. Different flowers float across her chest, waves and petals flowing down her right arm. All black-and-gray ink, like mine. All shaded beautifully. Two wild horses decorate her left side and rib cage, a tattoo that probably hurt like hell, but it's the shitty image on her right hip that has me curious. "Is that a chicken?"

She startles as if woken up and snorts. "Actually, it's a guitar." When I frown, she moves between my legs and angles the piece toward me. "I had a friend who wanted to practice. He'd just started tattooing, and I was high at the time, so I let him do a guitar on my hip. It is now affectionately referred to as the choking chicken tattoo." She doesn't smile at the comment. Her usual sarcasm barely covers her irritation.

"You regret it?"

She blinks several times, then reaches forward and grips my shoulders. "I don't like how stupid I was. I slept with boys when I didn't want to. I nearly burned down a barn. There were horses inside, and I could have killed them." Her voice drops lower. "You wouldn't have liked me back then. I hardly liked myself."

I run my hands up her thighs, grip the edges of her hipbones, and pull her closer. "Why did you do those things?"

"To fit in. To feel like people liked me. Why does anyone do stupid stuff?"

She answers too quickly, like there's more to it than that, but I get it. The draw to feel wanted. Still, my whole life I've worked to avoid the things she regrets. If kids at school were up to no good, I'd walk the other way. When punks at the rec center stand too close to the edge, I sit them down and list every person from the neighborhood who's dead or in jail, painting as clear a picture for them as I can.

The thought of Raven breaking laws is tough to swallow, but she didn't have anyone to set her straight. No parents who cared enough or siblings to keep her in line. But she turned her life around, and if she hadn't done those things, she probably wouldn't be here right now, gripping my shoulders, telling me secrets, her body about to become mine.

I lean forward and press a kiss to the ugly tattoo. "Our past choices shape us, but our future ones define us. I wouldn't change a thing about you. Now give me your right shoe."

She glances down. "Do shoes count as clothing?"

"In my game, they do. I still have lots of questions."

An eye roll later, she has one shoe off and is seated again. For the next while we swap stories and shed clothing. Shed our boundaries. My feelings for her morph into something bigger than this moment. She tells me about the pirate ship on her back, how she dreamed of sailing the seas as a kid, away from home. She also wanted an eye patch and a peg leg. I tell her about the stars across my lower abdomen, the largest for my mother, then two for my siblings, the smallest two for Jack and Colin. The vines up her left leg are woven with feathers, symbols of her First Nations heritage. Telling her about the large Libra scale on my back is the hardest. Weights and measures. Choices. How easy it is to tip the balance. I got it after I sent my father to jail. It reminds me there's no gray area. Only right and wrong.

She clams up once. When I ask about the dragonfly on her right ribs, she says, "Not yet." Two words that I respect. The small insect has bright red eyes, and its wings are burning. I'm guessing it's linked to her sister taking off.

After a spell, all that's left are her thong and my boxers. Her pink nipples are tight, begging to be touched. Licked. The head of my cock pokes out of the top of my briefs, so fucking hard. The air buzzes between us, along with silence. We stare, take our fill, neither of us asking more questions. We're both ready for what comes next.

Twelve

Raven

As mesmerizing as Nico's ink is, I can't look away from the beast between his legs. My underwear has been wet since our potluck, this game of his heightening my arousal. And feeding my soul. Like in Aspen, sharing my broken pieces with him opens a floodgate of emotion. The more I say, the more I want to divulge. Unload every story that's been locked up for so many years and confess that, although I admitted a fraction of my feelings in his truck, I'm truly terrified to fall for him.

But I don't confess. I couldn't even share my worst story. It lodged in my throat, that dragonfly forever a reminder of what I did. The damage I caused. Thoughts I'd rather not face tonight. Right now all I need is to have his skin touching mine.

And to get those boxers off.

My gaze shoots to my bag on the floor, then back to his barely contained erection. "So…I brought Shay's condoms. But since you're so"—mammoth, huge, *terrifyingly* large—"big, I'm not sure they're the right size."

Grinning, he reaches down and pulls a foil packet from his jeans on the floor.

"Come here." He widens his legs, and I don't waste a second.

Breasts loose, I straddle him on his chair, nothing but two thin pieces of fabric between us. And God, the *feel* of him. It took all of two minutes for him to make me come against that wall, the world tipping sideways. I'm not sure how I'll handle being filled with his girth. He trails kisses down my neck, his hands spanning the width of my back, and he takes my nipple into his mouth. Moaning, I drop my head back and arch into him, his wet mouth busy on my body. *So freaking good.*

Rotating my hips, I lower my hand. The tip of his cock sticks out of his boxers, a few drops of pre-come glistening on the crown, and I spread it around. He hisses out a breath. Next thing I know, he's on his feet with me around his waist, carrying me like I weigh nothing. The comforter gets ripped off, and we're in the middle of the bed, Nico above me, lust etched in his weighty gaze.

He pauses. "You're the prettiest thing I've ever seen."

My throat burns too hot to speak.

"You sure you're ready for me." This time his voice rumbles.

Forget being afraid to fall for him. I'm already gone. "I hope so."

That's all the answer he needs. He peels off my thong and stands to remove his boxers. The second his cock springs free, heat spikes between my thighs. His eyelids fall heavy, the ridges of his abs contracting with his breath. Shadows flex from the grooves of his hipbones as he tears the foil packet and rolls on the condom.

My memories from Aspen were spot on—he's Thor's hammer huge.

"Is this the part where you tell me not to worry? That objects appear larger from this angle?" My attempt at levity falters under my shaky voice. I'm no virgin, but my body has never accommodated something that size.

Gripping the base of his shaft, he kneels on the bed and nudges my knees apart. His eyes flick up to mine, that usual liquid ocean now blue flame. "This is the part where I show you how good a man can make a woman feel."

Then he pushes in.

I gasp, and he pauses. He kisses me so soft and deep the room spins. I catch the wave of his breath and dive with him, moving my lips to his addictive rhythm. He shifts forward, filling me, inch by inch, until we're flush. He stays there, running his lips and tongue over my neck and breasts, giving me time to adjust. The fullness is toe curling. His thickness stretches me, every nerve ending alight. I shift my hips, and he settles deeper into my body. My life. My heart.

Like this, with him, it almost doesn't matter what happens with Rose.

I clasp his shoulders. "Don't hurt me again."

He pushes up and fans his large hand over my chest. "Never."

When he pulls out and glides back in, I cry out. He does it again. And again. More cries follow. His hand stays on my chest. Each drag transports me places I've never been. Physically. Emotionally. I'm not sure how many erogenous zones a woman has, but he hits every spot. Like with his game, I open wider, let him in farther. He takes his time with me, his strokes smooth and firm.

"I'm so deep inside you," he says on a groan and lowers to his elbows.

"So deep," I repeat.

The next roll of his hips lifts me out of my body. I rise up to meet him. Our chests connect. He's powerful enough to crush me, but he's so tender, worshiping me with his mouth. I grab his ass, the muscle solid, and try to force him faster. The man doesn't comply. Even thrusts. In and out. Slick and hard. He works me over with a steady rhythm, my whispered name rumbling from his throat. When he looks at me dead on, his name catches in mine. His eyes always overwhelm me, but there's more there tonight, our shared pasts lighting them from behind. It *unhinges* me.

His next thrust hits me hard and deep. "*Fuck.*" I'm not sure which one of us cries the word, but I arch my back and widen my legs, needing more, all of him. God, he's big. I drag my hands up his spine, exploring the muscles on his back. They shift with each exertion.

"I'm close," I say.

"Eyes on me. I love watching you come."

I could watch him all day: the deep cuts along his arms, his bunched shoulders, the length of him moving in and out of me. A wave of pleasure gathers in my core, building, coiling. When my lids flutter, he says, "Eyes," and I snap them open.

Then he lifts and tilts his hips just so.

I fly apart, unintelligible words tripping off my tongue as I claw his shoulders and clench around him. I'm an electric current, aftershocks seizing my body. His sheer size draws out the longest orgasm I've ever had.

He keeps moving. The veins along his neck tighten, his jaw flexing with each pulse. He doesn't speed up, so I thrust, urging him on. I want him to let go. Steal his pleasure from me. This man is a giver, and I prompt him to *take, take, take.* Like before, he doesn't follow, but the cracks in his armor show—his grunts get ragged, his breathing hot and heavy. He drops to his elbows and kisses me, our tongues tangling. His calloused fingers are rough on my cheeks. Steadily, he pumps into me, my name passing from his lips to mine. Then he lets go. His body shudders, all that brawn putty in my grasp as he thrusts and his heat rushes between my legs.

When he comes down, his lips get back to work, kissing my neck and throat and chest. He spends extra time on the flowers above my breasts. "I could do this all night."

He takes my nipple into his mouth, and I hum. "You wouldn't catch me complaining."

Instead of holding true to his word, he lifts up and pulls out of me, hopping off the bed to deal with the condom. The loss is instant. To be so full then empty has me curling into a ball, the effect hollowing. I'm raw and sore between my legs, as I'd imagined I'd be, but the deep need to have him here, next to me, is unexpected. Or maybe it's not. This has been the way with us, even the first time we fooled around. But we've opened up more, given each other more, and this longing is *more*.

The bed dips when he returns. The minute he curls around me, peace descends. We're on top of the sheets, in the middle of the bed, his naked body cocooned around mine. And I can breathe.

His thick bicep settles on my arm. "You okay? Did I hurt you?"

I squish closer to him, not that it's possible. "I'm perfect."

Against him. With him. Being his.

He flattens his palm on my belly. "So am I."

This is how we fall asleep. But not how we wake up.

Somehow I end up under the sheets, but Nico's big, warm body isn't behind mine. The room is too dark for it to be morning. The

clock reads 5 a.m., and a sliver of light shines from the ajar bathroom door.

Nico's voice carries out. "When? How many? Was Jericho
busted, too?"

I sit up at Jericho's name. Nico mentioned him when discussing
Josh's trial, something about him being important. I squint as if it
will allow me to hear better.

After a pause, he says, "What exactly are you suggesting? That I
force this Tyler kid to lie? To take the fall for Josh?" Then, "I know
I'm running out of options. I don't need you to tell me that."

The door shuts the rest of the way, blocking me out, but unease
coils under my breastbone. From the sound of things, Nico has
the chance to clear Josh…but at what cost? Nico's entire family is
counting on him, not to mention the pressure he puts on himself.
Would he cross the line to help? Break the law? I probably would.
Forget probably. My moral compass is as wonky as Justin Bieber's.
But Nico's whole life has been a test of integrity. The Libra scales
on his back are a permanent reminder of the choices he's made to
walk the line.

He emerges a few minutes later. My eyes have adjusted enough
to see his face, but I wish they hadn't. A thick groove has sunk
between his brows, his full lips flattened. He's in his boxers, his
hands fisted at his side. When he looks at me, his shoulders drop.
"Did I wake you?"

I roll the sheets back. "No. I just missed you. Come to bed."

He smiles at that. Slightly. He places his phone on the night table, lies down, and pulls me into him. I wish I could spoon him
from behind, hold him close, take care of him the way he cares for
everyone else, but the man is just too large.

I tug his arm more tightly around me. "Who called?"

He kisses my head and sighs. "Alessi. He got the address for that Russ guy. I might not be able to go with you for a few days, though. Something's come up at work."

"Anything you want to talk about?"

He tucks a large, sculpted leg over mine. "Nothing important."

The lie stings. He's pushed me to open up and be honest. Let him in. I haven't told him all my secrets, and I doubt I've learned all of his, but this feels like a step back. Not that I should be surprised. If he goes so far as to do something illegal to clear his brother, he wouldn't tell a soul. He'd live with the guilt. Alone. Nico the Martyr.

I lie awake the next couple of hours. I'm pretty sure he does, too. He pushes his nose through my hair and kisses my temple from time to time. Each brush of his lips tingles down to my toes. Soon we'll have to get up and leave, but the prospect seeps through me like acid. I've never felt closer to a person than I do Nico. Last night solidified him in my life in a way that can't be undone. It cemented him in my heart. But that call and what it implies is powerful, too. The address he got holds enough weight to crush me. For now, though, for these last minutes, it's just him and me in this room, tangled on this bed.

I twist in his arms and force him on his back. I kiss the *enata* symbol on his pec—the sky guarding its people. Nico guarding those he loves.

Time for someone to put him first.

I trail my lips over the ridges of his abs, and his soft groans float down with me. I kiss each star that represents his family, pulling his boxers off as I go. Nudging his knees apart, I lick a line up his cock, following the vein on the underside. His dick twitches, and his quads flex. His thighs are huge, bracketing my head with power. I plant a hand on one, then I fist his shaft and circle the head of his cock with my tongue.

"*Jesus*, Raven." The words are guttural, his hand pushing back my hair. "Move to the side so I can watch you."

Pleased he's asking for what he wants, I move my body perpendicular to his and take him into my mouth, as deep as possible. I swallow a few times, knowing he'll feel it where it counts, then I slide up, leaving a trail of wetness for my hand to follow. His hips buck. He cups my breast, my angle giving him easy access. He's too big for me to take all of him in, so I use my hand and mouth and tongue and throat to work him over, traveling his full length. He massages my breast and rolls his hips, eyes on me the whole time. I suck his head and pump his shaft until his muscles tense, his cock hardening in my mouth.

"Babe, I'm there. I'm gonna come."

At the last second, he drops his head back, a gravelly "Christ" ripped from his chest as he pours into my mouth. I stroke him until he stills.

Most guys would be comatose by now, totally passed out. Not Nico. Growling, he pulls me up and rolls me over. He kisses me hard. "Whatever I did to deserve that, remind me to do it more often." His brow isn't creased like it was after that call, the stress no longer visible on his face.

He travels downward, tracing my body with his lips the way I did his, but I lock his waist with my knees. If I'm going to date this man, he'll have to let me care for him, too. "Save this for next time. That was just for you."

Shifting his body forward, he cups me between my thighs. The
Sexy Beast fights dirty. "Right now I want to eat your pussy. Consider me a starving man."

Seriously dirty and I'm unarmed, drenched from going down
on him. At least the sentiment was there. "As long as you know
that's not why I gave you head."

He grins and replaces his hand with his face.

Holy Jesus.

Thirteen

Nico

I push into Diamonds, my body wound as tight as my mind. The place is half empty as usual, Alessi's gelled head nowhere to be seen. I walk over to the bar and fall onto a stool. Doug's at the end, rambling on with a regular. Hunching forward, I plant my elbows on the wood, the ancient surface peeling and dented in spots. It looks as worn as I feel.

Being with Raven was better than I'd imagined. She didn't hold back, didn't keep me at a distance. I rocked into her, and she came undone in my arms. The way her pulse pounded when I gathered her to my chest, I'm pretty sure it was intense for her, too. And her mouth on me this morning melted my mind. Unfortunately, the phone call between those slices of heaven has me ready to split nails. But I can't stop living. Not the way I've been all about Josh and work the past seventeen months. This won't be a repeat of Aspen.

I pull out my cell to text her.

Last night was amazing. So was this morning. When can I see you again? Her reply doesn't come, and Doug saunters my way. He's thinner than he was when we started drinking here, his wrinkled skin revealed below his cuffed sleeves. His mustache and eyebrows are bushier, the same cowboy hat he's had since forever pulled low on his forehead. "You drinkin' alone today, son?"

The endearment always makes me smile. "Meeting a friend, but I'll take a beer."

He mimics my pose, leaning on his elbows. It's always like this with Doug—talk first, drinks after. "Got myself a new cash register this week." He nods to the purchase. "Last one died. Outta the clear blue, just up and croaked. Couldn't even get out the cash."

The story goes on, details about the make and model and how hard he had to bargain for the price, years of smoking cigarettes roughing up his voice. The boys joke about how painful Doug's stories are, but he always calls me *son* and speaks politely. There are days I come here just to listen. Eventually, he spins around and pours me my glass. A flyer rests by my fist, an ad for some sort of Fright Night. Josh draws stuff like this, creepy yet realistic. Fantastical creatures. Has a real talent for it. Another thing that will go to waste if he gets convicted.

Unless I act on that call.

The burden has me sinking heavier onto my stool. I don't normally unload on Doug. I never bend his ear about my life. But I couldn't talk to Raven about Alessi's offer, and I sure as shit can't talk it out with my family. The pressure builds, the words expanding in my chest. Before I think better of it, I say, "Would you do something you shouldn't to help someone you love?"

Doug pushes a coaster in front of me and places my glass on top. He rubs the gray scruff on his chin. "Depends on the something and the someone."

Fair point. But I can't go into detail, can't risk anyone connecting the dots if I choose to break the law. "Just some personal stuff. Bending the rules to keep someone's life on track."

He squints at me, his gray eyes clouded with age. "Look, son, I've known you a lot of years. Seen you grow into the man you are. You and your friends, you're good people. You talk nice to my customers and never mouth off to me. Far as I can tell, you're a respectable man, and a respectable man should always trust his gut. Like my granddaddy used to say, 'The only person you're forced to live with is yourself.'"

He goes on about the time his granddad caught him spray painting a neighbor's barn, how he and his friends were just playing a prank, but I tune out. I know what my gut is telling me. It's been twisting so damn hard, it's impossible to ignore. Breaking the law and risking my job are things I swore I'd never do. I've seen shit go down at work. I've been aware of cops coloring outside the lines. But that's not me. If I force a false confession, the time I put in at the rec center, teaching kids to do the smart thing, would all be a lie. The man I am, the things I've done, would all be worthless.

But not doing it means my innocent brother goes to jail.

Alessi walks in and scouts the place for me. Doug barely takes a breath as my partner comes over and leans on the bar. The old man goes on about his grandfather's rules and wisdom for a few more minutes, then he gets Alessi his drink. After one last story, the two of us retire to a booth for privacy.

Usually Alessi would bust right into a story about some chick he picked up, but his face is drawn. "They arrested five guys with enough meth to close the case quickly, but none claim to know where Jericho is. No matter what you decide, the Tyler punk will end up with jail time. A confession from him to clear Josh will only add more years to an existing sentence."

Only add more years. As if forcing a false confession is child's play. "This can only end badly."

He locks eyes with me. "This Tyler kid's a major screw-up. Even has a history of assault. I promise you, if we do this, Josh will walk."

"How the hell can you promise that? You have a crystal ball or something?"

"Keep your fucking voice down." He scans the room and sinks lower in his seat. "I'm doing what I can here. You need a goddamn miracle, and I'm offering you one."

A country singer croons in the background about his life stalling worse than his truck. The soundtrack to my turmoil. My gut churns, my fists clenched so roughly my nails almost break skin. "This isn't a miracle. This is coercion."

Before, thinking about Josh going away was bad. Worse than bad. I'd pace at home or hit the gym for hours. As much as it gnawed at me, it never felt as sickening as this…this nausea. My head pounds. Sweat breaks out on my temples.

It reminds me of being eight years old and dumb. In a rare moment of affection, my father took me out for a cigarette run. It was a stupid car ride, a nothing twenty minutes together, but he didn't call me worthless and didn't snarl at me in anger. I watched him grab sunglasses from a rack and shove them in his pocket. Back in the car, he gave them to me. A gift, he'd said. The only one I'd ever received. I was pumped and wore them inside all day. Felt special. It was also the first night I heard him hit my mother. I'd seen the odd bruise, but they always came with excuses. Hearing the thuds and cries filled me with rage and shame.

Here I was, an idiot, coveting a fucking gift from the man, when I should have been protecting my mother. Instead of crushing the glasses, I hid them, sure the cops would bust down our door any minute. I was a sweaty, panicked mess until I snuck them back into the store.

Now I'm considering coercion.

Alessi leans closer. "You don't have to be involved. I'll do it, keep you out to avoid suspicion. Give me the go-ahead, and I make the charges against Josh disappear."

"It's not that simple."

"It can be."

"Shit always finds a way of getting out. Nothing is as easy as it seems." I should be saying no. Should have said no the second he walked through that door. What the hell is wrong with me?

"I'm telling you, this is open and shut. I could turn Tyler on a dime. He has a brother up on charges, too. Some pornography thing, but the evidence is nonexistent. If I promise to get his brother off, he'll sing whatever tune I play."

My heart knocks in my ears. My throat dries. I wipe the sweat from my forehead.

"Okay," I croak. *Fuck. Fuckfuckfuck.*

"Okay?" He looks as shocked as I feel.

I can't say it again, can't even believe it came out of my mouth. The room sways, and I dig the heels of my hands into my eyes, verging on a panic attack. *What have I done?* Everything I do bleeds through the ranks, to Josh, down to Colin and Jack, too. Those boys need to understand the difference between right and wrong, and here I am, just another dirty cop. I hear Alessi punching numbers into his phone. Hear his hushed voice say things like *yeah* and *he's in* and *keep it quiet.*

Sudden fury has me wanting to ram my head into a wall, rip the phone from Alessi's hand and smash it with my fist. Send a punch into *his* ribs. *He* taunted me with a poisoned apple. Coaxed me to take a bite. I did it, willingly, but he set these wheels in motion, and it feels like a betrayal.

I reach across the table and grab his wrist. "Call it off."

He stares at the phone then at me. "Come on, bro. Think this through."

My night with Raven flashes in my mind, how she confessed her regrets, and the words I spoke. *Our past choices shape us, but our future ones define us.* My own truth taunts me, reinforcing what I already know: I can't do this. Can't break the law, even to save my brother.

I shake my head, nearly giving myself whiplash. "No. Discussion done. I won't do it. Won't be able to live with it. Josh will know it's bullshit. He'll know I broke the law to help him. That's not okay. *Call. It. Off.*"

I'm a second from a goddamn heart attack.

Slumping, Alessi backtracks on the phone then jams it into his pocket and passes his beer from hand to hand. The glass bottom drags along the table. "If you change your mind, let me know. Josh may have fucked up, but he's a good kid. Doesn't deserve to go to jail."

He's got that right, but it's no excuse. "I won't be changing my mind. And if you ever suggest something like this again, for any reason, I'll be asking for a new partner."

When shit went down with my father and Josh, Alessi never questioned me, never looked at me funny like the guys at the station, wondering if I was dirty, too. I've been to his huge family barbecues, and he sat with me in the hospital when Nikki overdosed. He's even helped make sure she attends her meetings, but backing me into a corner with a decision like this is bullshit.

We have a stare-off, then he nods. "Got it."

I swish a sip of beer around my mouth, the stale brew as warm as always. Part of me wants to leave him sitting here, get out and get some air. Let my anger at his request cool. Quell the fury aimed at myself for giving in. I said *yes*. I gave him the okay. Freaking out afterward doesn't change my primal instinct. But standing up and moving feels like effort.

He kicks my foot. "That name you asked me for, what was that about?"

"I'm helping Raven find her sister."

He scratches his neck and frowns.

"What?" The word comes out as a bark.

"Might be nothing, but the guy I looked up for you has a history. I checked into it a bit, in case you needed more info. Minor drug charges."

The unease Clara left me with at Neverland Farms returns. "Rose might not even be staying there. It's just a lead."

He doesn't push, and a strained silence resumes. When he's drained the last of his beer, he leaves me with a solemn nod. Working together with tension between us is bad business; in our uniform blues he's as important as my vest. My frustration with him will dissipate. In time. For now I need to stop thinking about the things I can't control and focus on the things I can.

Seeing Raven again tops that list.

I flip over my phone, hoping for a reply from her. I'm not disappointed.

Is it normal that I miss you already?

Fuck, did I need to hear that. Don't know. But I feel the same. I'm walking around in a fog.

Dropping you off killed me.

Sleepover tomorrow?

Last night, in the motel, with our bodies pressed together, her steady breaths calmed my anxiety. Hopefully she can perform her magic again, make me forget what just went down, because all I feel right now is guilt blooming in my chest, thick and heavy. I'm hungry to be inside her, moving with her, making her moan. But it's more than wanting to blow her mind and quiet mine. I still hate how I reacted to her police record. She seems to have forgiven me, but an urge to prove myself swells. Prove I trust her one hundred percent.

I have a dinner tomorrow, I write. But I'd love you to come. Sleepover after.

Count me in. Not sure what time my photo shoot will end. Text me the address, and I'll meet you there.

My thumbs hover over my phone. Instead of telling Raven she's coming to my mother's house, I type out the address and hit Send. This could be a huge mistake. Raven will be pissed when she realizes where she's going. She might even knee me in the balls, send me sprawling like Joe in the slums. But something tells me I'm on a timeline with her. If things don't work out with her sister, she could shut down. My life could become a shit storm at any moment.

Meeting my family doesn't fit with her take-it-slow plan, but she needs to know, before we find her sister, that I'm serious about us. Better to risk the nut shot tomorrow than leave things to chance.

Fourteen

Raven

I hop off the bus and walk until I'm at a small white house on a residential street. The number matches the one Nico texted, but there's no music thumping through the walls, no cars lined down the street. He didn't give any details about this mysterious dinner, and I didn't ask. All I cared about was seeing him again. In the twenty-four hours since he dropped me off, my stress levels have spiked again. Getting closer to finding Rose means I'm closer to everything I want, and everything that terrifies me.

Nico is the cure I crave.

Now I'm outside a random house, no idea whose party I'm crashing. His gas guzzler is parked on the driveway next to a rusted Honda Civic. A sullen, dark-haired kid pushes by on a skateboard, his skills not half-bad. I used to be okay on a board, ear buds in, the Sex Pistols blaring as I rolled down the street. I'd felt pretty badass.

The kid in question flips his board around, skates toward me, and stops at my feet. "You Raven?"

I glance around, unsure how he knows my name. "Last I checked. And you are?"

He kicks up his board and scratches his hip, nearly sending his shorts to his knees. At least his basketball jersey hits mid-thigh. "I'm Colin. Nico's my uncle."

With that he walks to the door, and I stare after him.

Nico is his uncle.

Unsure what to expect tonight, I wore a black mini skirt, tank top, and my favorite heeled boots laced to my calves—the type of outfit that would draw a certain Sexy Beast's attention to my legs. In that particular fantasy, Nico growled and dragged me into a dark corner to have his dirty way with me, but his nephew didn't make an appearance in my imagined scene. Not even a cameo. Now I'm about to meet his family while wearing a pair of hooker heels. Not that I have anything pleated or khaki in my wardrobe. Still, if I knew where I was going, I might not have chosen such a short skirt. I might not have gone so heavy on the eye shadow.

What if they don't like me?

Shocked at how fast my heart races, I swivel on my heels to leave. I'm two stomps away when the man himself calls, "Raven!"

Heavy footfalls pound behind me, but I don't glance back. No point acknowledging a traitor.

"Raven, babe, I'm sorry."

I flip around and poke a finger at his (I'd kill to lick chocolate sauce off of it) chest. "Don't *babe* me. At what point did you plan on sharing the fact that I'd be meeting your family? What did you even tell them about me?"

He has the decency to look guilty, and his hand, for some reason, hangs over his (I'd kill to lick chocolate sauce off of it) groin.

"Tonight was a bit of a celebration. Josh got his GED recently. We had cake that day, but my mom wanted to do a proper dinner, too. Make a big deal of it. She's been planning it for a while, and I told them I was bringing a friend who just moved to the area."

"A friend, huh? Meeting the family?" Feels more like a lamb being led to the slaughter. I've never walked the meet-the-family road. Never worried if I'd pass or fail some arbitrary test. With Nico, I suddenly care. A lot.

"I'd rather tell them you're my girlfriend, but that's up to you." He sighs and stabs his toe into the curb. "I don't want to rush you, but this is important to me. Important for me to *show* you how wrong I was the other day. I want you to know my family. To really know me."

That sweet vulnerability softens my shoulder blades down my back. "You want to tell them I'm your girlfriend?"

It's touching how hard he's trying to make up for his actions, but I can't focus on much besides that word. That label. I've never been anyone's girlfriend.

He slips a hand around my back and hauls me to him, heat in his eyes. "You're mine, Raven. We're together. You and me. I'd like to announce it to the whole goddamn world, but I'll let you set the pace."

The pace I'd like to set involves the sound of skin slapping as he pounds into me.

Unfortunately, someone calls, "Dinner's ready!"

I jump back and tug down my too-short skirt as the reality of this evening slams home. The door shuts, and I glare at Nico. It's either that or hurl myself at him. "I still think springing your family on me was an asshole move, but I will be the better person in this situation and join you…as your girlfriend." I struggle to fight my grin. He licks his lips, not bothering to hide his perusal of my legs. The exact reaction I'd hoped for when choosing this outfit. "Don't get all cocky, big guy. You still have atoning to do."

"You name it, it's yours."

Now those are the kind of parameters I can work with.

* * *

By the end of dinner, I've completely forgotten about my outfit. Josh has the table in stitches, telling a childhood story about the time Nikki dared him to shove peas up his nose. Across from me, Nico laughs around a bite of mashed potatoes, shaking his head at the memory, while his nephews each grab carrot sticks and imitate Josh's stunt.

Every member of Nico's family greeted me warmly when I came in. No measured glances. No searching questions. His mom, Anna, asked about my move and job, never lacing judgment into her tone. Instead of raising an eyebrow at my wardrobe, his sister, Nikki, admired my tattoos, and Josh talked about one he was sketching for himself. Both young boys hung off Josh, bugging their uncle to listen to *this* song or show them *that* karate move. At dinner all conversation flowed around Josh, too. His GED. His sketching. Stupid things he did as a kid.

The entire family orbits around him.

It was one thing for Nico to share how broken up he was about Josh's future, how scared he was to tell his brother the case was falling apart. But now, seeing how Josh lights up his family, dread settles in my bones. Nico may be big and strong, but even great walls tumble.

"You boys were raised by wolves." Nikki reaches over the table to tug the carrots from the kids' nostrils. The action knocks over the gravy, spilling it across the plastic tablecloth and onto Josh's jeans. Nikki freezes. "Shoot."

Josh squints like he's going to backhand her across the face, and I hold my breath. Once, at home, I spilled juice on my father, and he threw a knife at me.

Josh leans toward his sister, who winces and tilts away.

"Here we go," their mother says.

"Don't do it," Nico warns, his tone more playful than I'd expect.

I study each of them, unsure what's about to go down. Then Josh smears spilled gravy across Nikki's cheek.

"Bastard." She digs two fingers into the mashed potatoes and plops a mound on Josh's nose.

The youngest boy, Jack, erupts into giggles. Colin tries to play it cool, snorting to himself. Nico drops his fork on his plate and leans back. "Bunch of idiots."

"Idiots?" Josh grabs a slice of roast beef and places it on his head. "Who you calling an idiot?"

A high-pitched laugh bursts from quiet Colin, the exact reaction Josh was after. Nico's mother slaps a hand over her mouth, her cackle pushing through, and Nikki gets up to walk around, wiping giddy tears from her eyes and gravy from her cheek.

I sit, mesmerized.

"They haven't done this in years." Nico's mother fans her face as she catches her breath. She glances at me, sheepish. "You must think we're heathens."

"Not even close." This is rolling in mud and singing in the shower and dancing in the rain. This is *family*.

My grin nearly splits my face.

Nico watches me from across the table. My brooding giant has been quiet tonight. Talking here and there, but zoning out with a scowl etched on his face, too. When not frowning, he turns his watchful gaze my way. While his family is relaxed around me, it's as though he's working something out. It could be that call at the motel. Nerves. Anxiety. A heavy reckoning weighing on him. But I have a feeling I'm at the center of this particular silence. Like he's assessing how I fit into this family photograph. Judging me again maybe.

I'd never do anything to disrupt the fragile balance in this home. Nico says he trusts that. Trusts *me*. This evening was his way of showing me just how much. But what if Rose is involved in something shady? Living on Hastings isn't a good sign. I stiffened when Ruby mentioned the address. Nico did, too. If she's wrapped up in something bad and I try to help her, he could cut me off. Force me to choose between him and my sister.

Unaware of the storm gathering in my chest, he leans forward and says, "Thank you." His eyes are bright against his dark skin, layers of sky, indigo, and electric blue swirling together. And there, *just there*, under his happiness is gratitude. Peace maybe.

"For what?" I ask.

"For being you."

Boom goes my heart. And the storm dissipates.

Josh dumps the meat from his head onto his plate and wipes at his dark hair. "I should go shower."

If Nico grew out his hair, I bet it would look like that—thick and shaggy with a slight wave.

As Josh pushes his chair back, Nikki makes a throaty sound. "Perfect timing, as usual." She fans a hand over the dirty dishes.

"It's my party. The guest of honor doesn't clean." He squeezes past Nico's chair, clocks his brother on the back of the head, then ducks under the doorway to the hall.

"Actually," Nikki says, "you guys mind if I take off, too?" Her attention darts toward her older brother. They share the same light eyes, but hers look brighter. Or maybe that's because they're off-set by dark, puffy circles. "A friend is playing guitar at a pub, and I thought I'd catch a few songs."

Nico's good humor dampens. "You sure that's smart?"

Nikki twists a strand of brown hair around her finger and chews her lip. "It's fine. I'll be back in an hour."

He holds her stare. "An hour."

"That's what I said, *warden*." Although sarcastic, there's no malice behind her words.

She kisses her boys good-bye, and my boy broods.

With dinner done, Colin and Jack head outside to goof around with the skateboard, and I'm relegated to the living room while Nico helps his mother clean up. I relax into their couch and take in the small space. The burns on the carpet remind me of my child-hood home, the water stains on the ceiling familiar, too. The more time I spend with Nico, the more I realize we have in common. But my family would never bust a gut laughing together.

They also wouldn't hang one of my sketches.

On the wall opposite me an insane portrait fills the space. Josh's name is signed on the bottom, and my jaw nearly hits floor. It's an emotional piece. A boy with venom in his eyes and fisted hands has his mouth wide, the barrel of a gun pointing out from his lips as if he'd swallowed it. The muzzle is aimed at the man he's con-fronting, the message loud and clear:

Words are as powerful as bullets.

A large sketchbook is on the coffee table, and I snatch it up, greedy for more. The first is a detailed hand, the center of the palm transformed into a gory mouth with jagged teeth.

A-freaking-mazing.

Next is an octopus with two heads and eyeballs hanging from its tentacles.

Perfectly grotesque.

I gawk at a woman with a mask sewn over her mouth, horns sprouting from her head.

Hells yeah.

"They aren't that good." Josh steps into the room, his wide shoulders hunched forward.

"You're right. They aren't good. They're unbelievable."

He straightens and beams at me. "Yeah?"

"Your shading is sick, the detail you capture is spot on, and you have the creep factor nailed. How long have you been drawing?"

Moments like this one, right here, were the times I loved teach-ing art. Seeing raw talent in kids, fostering it, and watching them improve. Then I'd have to holler at the class to focus and clean up and deal with the sarcastic dipshits who didn't want to be there, my last nerve stretched so far it would snap. Teaching in a class-room wasn't my calling.

According to Nico, photography is.

My chest warms at the thought, and Josh falls onto the couch beside me. He runs a hand through his damp hair. "Don't know. As long as I can remember, I guess."

I flip a few more pages and land on one of a sea creature. Barnacles surround its mouth, spikes curve along its spine. I almost snap a picture and send it to my friend, Talia, in Toronto. She and her special effects friends would eat it up. "Have you ever thought about art school?"

"Naw. Not sure I could handle drawing a fruit basket. I toyed with the idea of tattooing, but sitting still for hours would drive me nuts. I'm thinking of getting a job at a gaming store in town, maybe work my way to manager."

I visited Talia at her studio once. She wore yellow contacts that day and had applied a small scar to her chin, messing with her appearance as she often did. Everyone moved around the space, sculpting, molding, painting props and prosthetics, rock tunes pumping from the speakers as their creations came to life.

"What about makeup?" I ask.

He snorts. "As much as I'd like to put lipstick on a hot chick, probably not my style."

"No, like special effects makeup. You can't just do what you want. It's about working with a team and taking direction, but you'd get to use your skills. Create gnarly creatures like this."

He scratches the back of his neck. "Never thought much about it. Didn't have my high school diploma. Didn't have many options." He leans toward me and studies his own sketch. "You think I'm good enough?"

"Honestly? These are amazing. I could put you in touch with a friend back home. You could find out more, see if it's something you'd be interested in. I'd be happy to research programs in Vancouver."

"What program?" Nico's hulking frame steps into the room.

Fifteen

Nico

Josh and Raven are head to head, the two of them poring over his sketchbook. Raven has that look about her—hands restless, electricity in her eyes—like when she sets up a photograph. All night my focus has been glued on her. How she never seemed to judge the peeling paint in the dining room. How she laughed at Josh's stupid jokes and complimented my mother's food. She didn't get grossed out or turn her nose up when my siblings smeared gravy and mashed potatoes on each other.

My last girlfriend, Lisa, refused to spend time in my apartment. She said it was too cramped, but I saw how she'd scrunch her nose at the used coffee table and sparse furniture. Alex, before her, would always have plans when I'd invite her to my mom's. With me, my girlfriends were sweet and fun, but it was like they wanted me to be something I wasn't. Tonight they would have curled their lips in distaste, and I would have apologized later and would have somehow felt *less*. Having Raven here makes me feel like I'm *more*.

Josh bounces his knee as she mentions something about an art class. "What program?" I ask.

He shrugs, but there's nothing casual about the way he's vibrating. "Raven thinks I could be a creature designer or something. Maybe go to school for it."

"She does, does she?"

She glances at me, questioning. "These sketches are unreal, and he has a flair for the morbid. I offered to hook him up with a friend who does special effects makeup."

"Sounds cool." Perfect, actually. Exactly what Josh would love. His talent has always been undeniable, but I don't know much about art and how to make a living doing it. One night with Raven, and he sees clearer, dreams bigger. A knot forms in my gut, a tug-of-war pulling me apart—pride and excitement for Josh warring with false hope. Dreams purchased with fool's gold.

Gold I could have offered up.

Even after that fucked-up meeting with Alessi, I've found myself contemplating his offer again. Being a dirty cop. Crooked. Corrupt. Makes me sick all over again. Can't believe I keep giving the idea life. Gut hollowing, I shake my head. What matters is the now of things. Raven showering my brother with compliments and telling him how *good* he is. That matters. Keeping that light and laughter in her eyes is important, too. I sit beside Raven as they talk their art talk. My knee brushes hers, that tiny skirt riding up nice and high. If Josh weren't here, if we were at my place, I'd slide my fingers up the soft flesh of her inner thigh. I'd graze my thumb over her underwear to see if my closeness turns her on as much as hers does me. I'd slip my fingers inside and touch her and stroke her and make her feel so damn good.

When I can't wait any longer, I lean toward her ear. "I need to get you home." My voice sounds huskier than I'd like.

She shifts her weight, and her hip presses into mine. "I'm ready."

I bet she is.

We say our good-byes. My mom hugs Raven, and Raven hugs her back. Josh and her exchange numbers. When we get outside, she does a little jump and runs over to Colin. "Mind if I have a go?"

He looks at his skateboard and frowns.

I smile, loving how excited she is. "You know how to ride?"

Her sassy smirk appears. "I'm pretty good at *riding*. I'm used to more girth, but I can make do."

Colin is oblivious to her double meaning, but I raise an eyebrow. "This board is the perfect size for you."

"Remains to be seen."

"I beg to differ. It's been seen and *heard*."

It sounded something like *fuck, yesyesyes, don't stop.*

She laughs, no witty reply in her arsenal.

"So…" Colin glances back and forth between us, confusion knitting his brow. "Did you wanna have a go?"

"Definitely." She rubs her hands together. "I used to skate circles around the boys."

Jack is on the other side of the street, sitting on the curb waiting his turn. Colin shoots the board to her with his foot and stands back—legs wide, like me, arms crossed, like me. The little guy is growing up fast. Raven doesn't hesitate. She hops on the board and pushes off the pavement, knees bent and weight even. She picks up speed, carves to the right, then spins in a circle and skates toward us, finishing by hoping off and kicking the back so it flies into her hand.

Fucking awesome.

Colin's jaw drops. "Fucking awesome."

I smack his arm. "Language."

He rubs his elbow, staring at Raven like she granted him three wishes. She pats his shoulder. "Thanks for the ride. I actually have my old board at home. The thing's just collecting dust. If you want it, you could give one to your brother. Show him some tricks."

Colin puffs out his skinny chest. "Sure."

A band tightens around my ribs. Raven's been full of surprises tonight: going with the flow at dinner, giving Josh direction with his art, and now Colin. Coaxing the broody kid to hang with his younger brother is no easy feat. Making him think he's bigger and better for it is downright impressive. I could wrap my world around this girl.

Instead of rushing to get her home and get us naked, the urge to have her in my arms, the sand under our feet strikes me. "You up for a stop at the beach before heading home?"

She grins up at me. "I'd like that."

* * *

We park and walk to the beach in silence, the night sky bending over us, stars shining down, Raven tucked under my arm. Our boots beat out a peaceful tune. When we hit the sand, I lead her to the log we rested against the morning I sought her out and kissed her and asked for her to give us a chance.

Now she's mine.

I shake out the blanket I brought from my car, throw it around my shoulders, and sit on the sand. I pull her down between my legs.

Sighing, she nestles her back into my chest. "I've never done this."

I wrap the wool blanket around us. "Sat on a beach?"

She jabs her elbow into my side. "No, jackass. The girlfriend-boyfriend thing. Sitting together. Just being. Not flirting as a prelude to the main event." Her deep inhale forces us closer. "This is just...*more*. I've never had more."

Exactly how she makes me feel. I squeeze my knees around hers and dip my head to kiss her cheek. "It's why I suggested this. I can't control myself around you. Knew we'd be sweaty fast at your place, which is pretty fucking amazing. But I like this, too. A lot."

She twists her head until our lips meet. A slow kiss later, she says, "Not that I'm complaining about the naked parts. Just so we're clear."

I brush her nose with mine. "That mean I get to see your ink again tonight?"

"How do you get off a nonstop flight?" She matches my stupid question with her own.

"Carefully," I say. "Or with a parachute or a really long zip-line."

Her body relaxes into mine. "You into that stuff? Extreme sports?"

"Nope. That's Sawyer's thing. I have enough excitement with my job. Enough adrenaline with Nikki and Josh to last a lifetime. You?"

"I've always wanted to jump from an airplane. Love the idea of how liberating it would feel. Like flying. Same reason I wanted to be a pirate as a kid. Freedom to escape life for a while. But it's always been too expensive, and the move sapped my savings. Maybe if our event business takes off."

If it doesn't, she could seek the nomadic life she once craved. We might not find her sister, and she could get frustrated and move on. The thought has me tightening my arms around her. "But you plan on staying in Vancouver? You like it here?"

"I love Vancouver. The mountains. The ocean." She reaches behind her back and cups my dick over my jeans. Little devil. "Everything's bigger and better than back home."

A man strolls past us, his beagle tugging him along, not another soul visible on this stretch of sand. Under the cover of the blanket, I could unzip her jeans and touch her and let her stroke me until I spill onto her hand, but that's not why we're here. I pull her hand away and brush my lips over her black nails. "Good. I like having you here."

"Enough that you'll pose for me?"

"Pose?"

"Yeah, pose. As in model for some photographs. You owe me one after tonight's ambush." Her fingers drift over my forearms, along the muscle, then circling the bone at my wrists. "I snuck some ass shots of you a few times, but I'd like to add a few in the buff."

I'm no exhibitionist, but there isn't much I wouldn't do for Raven. "Don't those always end up on the Internet?"

"Only if you're a movie or reality TV star. So unless you plan to pilot a show called *Hot Cops of Vancouver*, I think you're safe."

I came down here to cool the fire between us, but her hand on my cock just now and picturing her studying me, naked, through her lens, aren't helping. "I'll pose. On one condition."

"Does it involve listening to more country music?"

"I get to take some of you." Study every line and dip of her body.

She purrs and nestles farther into me. "You have yourself a deal."

I also have myself a hard-on.

Waves lap into shore, the sound rolling over us, her ass flush against my erection. Instead of dragging her back to her place, I enjoy the slow burn, the sweet anticipation. The briny air on my tongue. We trade stories like in the motel. Our clothes are on this time, her hair tickling my jaw when she moves. She tells me how hard teaching was for her. How the kids were draining, and that she got in shit for playing inappropriate music to inspire them. I tell her about my first day in Police Foundations; I was so damn nervous I sweat through my shirt. The longer we talk, the more I learn, the more I want to know.

"Josh is crazy talented," she says after we listen to the waves awhile.

"He's always been good. Guess I didn't know what to do with that, how to foster him. That's a big deal, what you suggested tonight. I could tell he was excited." His skills might not translate to sculpting like Raven explained, but it eats at me he won't get the chance. Won't reach his potential.

I must sigh loudly, because Raven takes my hand and plants a kiss in the center of my upturned palm. She traces the dips between my fingers, stopping on the fleshy part between my thumb and forefinger. She seems intense, all at once. Focused on that one spot on my hand, like she's a fortune teller about to read my future.

"I took my mother's brooch," she says quietly. "It was the day before I turned nine, and I snuck into her room and took it."

The day before she turned nine. The day before Rose left. It's the story she wasn't ready to share. Until now. I kiss the top of her head. It's warm under the blanket, the two of us wrapped up together, but she shivers.

She keeps tracing my hand. "It was really beautiful. A dragonfly brooch with red eyes and delicate wings, and I'd always wanted to wear it. We didn't have parties or celebrations growing up, but I'd found a neat top at the Salvation Army. This black leather thing, that in hindsight was hideous, but I'd been mowing lawns and had some cash, so I bought it. Wanted to wear it to school for my birthday. Thought my mother's brooch would look sick. I didn't know my father planned to pawn it that day."

"Shit." I picture the dragonfly tattoo on her ribs, its wings burning. Her world burning.

Her answering laugh holds no humor. "Yeah. He assumed Rose took it. Demanded she return it. Started that conversation with a backhand across her face. I was there for the whole thing. Watched him hit her harder and harder. Smash her head into the wall. Her mouth was full of blood. Her shoulder was hanging all wrong. She kept telling him she didn't have the fucking brooch. Screaming. Crying. He kept calling her a liar, beating her. I kept my mouth shut and pissed myself. Just lost my bladder. Rose left the next day." She doesn't break down. Doesn't get mad. Her shoulders shudder slightly, the only indication she's upset. Always trying hard to be strong.

But *Goddamn*. I can't listen to stories about a young Raven so terrified she wet herself and not want to destroy the man who shattered her world. Fucking fathers. People need a license to fish. A permit to drive a car or breed dogs or sell houses. But any asshole can be a father.

I twist her around until her legs are straddling my waist and I have her locked tight. "You were nine. It's not your fault. She can't blame you."

Biting her lip, she places her palms on my chest. They rise and fall with my breaths. "It's completely my fault. If I'd confessed, he wouldn't have beaten her so badly. She wouldn't have left. I let her take the fall, and I'll never forget the look on her face. Like she was dead. Defeated. I'd never seen my sister anything but defiant, and he broke her. Broke us."

A tear finally slips out, and I brush it away with my thumb. "He would have hurt you instead. How would that have been better?" When she doesn't answer, I lower my voice. "Did he abuse you, growing up? Hit you?"

Or worse? My pulse revs, the edges of my vision turning as black as the night sky.

She digs her knees into my ribs. "He'd lash out occasionally. There were some bad days. A bloody lip or two. Nothing I couldn't handle. Nothing like that day with Rose. I think what he did actually freaked him out. He never touched me after that. Barely looked at me."

Lack of affection is abuse, too. "I'm sorry, Raven."

"Me, too." But her whispered words aren't meant for me. They're meant for Rose.

This search for her sister holds more water than I'd realized. If Raven doesn't find her, if forgiveness doesn't come or Rose is in a bad way, Raven will blame herself. I understand the guilt that comes with failing those you love. It could end badly for her. For us, if she can't move on.

"Whatever happens with Rose, please take your time with her. It's been years. She might not be the girl you remember."

She doesn't reply. She leans forward and rubs her cheek against mine. Soft against rough. Delicate against hard. Her lips follow next, coasting over my jaw and neck and up again. She wants contact. She wants to forget. I'd like to forget, too. Pretend my brother can go to school, and I don't have to worry about Nikki at a bar. That I never said yes to Alessi, even for a minute. Live in a world where good things happen to good people, and the bad get their just desserts.

Just plain forget.

Twenty minutes later, we're in her apartment, grunting in short, sharp bursts. We don't make it past her hallway, barely manage to close the front door. I pin her to the wall while she fumbles with my belt buckle, and I somehow dragged her thong down over her fuck-me boots. We wind up on the laminate floor—her skirt at her waist, her knee-high boots scratching my hips as I pump into her. My girl, *my future*, meeting my steady thrusts.

She releases a long, low moan. "How can you feel this good?"

Her pussy clamps down on me, sending points of light behind my eyes. "Fucking heaven." I bury myself balls deep and pause. Wait. Feel her contracting around me, writhing under me, getting a little angry with my pace.

Love that gleam in her charcoal eyes.

"You better move, Nico." She tries to roll her hips, but I'm too deep, pressing too close. I mimic her movements, but don't pull out. Just roll into her and grind my pelvis where she needs me, leaning down to suck her nipple between my teeth. Still not sliding in and out. Driving her crazy. Driving myself insane. Wanting it to last forever.

Fuck. It's just too damn good, and I want her to feel nothing but me.

No sadness. No pain.

Just me.

When I finally ease my hips back then sink into her, we both curse. Our lips collide in a frenzied kiss. Messy. Desperate. I'm careful not to unleash all my angst from the past months. She's too raw emotionally. I'm too worked up. I keep my movements contained, just on the edge of savage. We lock eyes, and she lets me into her depths, no secrets between us. I see her fear, though. For what's to come with her sister, her uncertainty in opening her heart. It hurts a bit, the worry shining up at me. Makes me hold her tighter. I cup the back of her head and press wet kisses over her heart, hoping I can shield it from the world.

My orgasm builds from my feet, barreling up my thighs, and we come together as the rush and heat of my release threatens to knock me out.

This woman has flattened me.

She's also stolen my heart. I'm in love with Raven Hunt. As sure of it as the day is long. If the guys could read my mind, they'd be on my ass, telling me this is what I do. That I use those three words too freely. I may have, in the past. Always looking to fit in, to belong, to be loved, I may have jumped too soon, only to land awkwardly. But I've never been so attuned to a woman. Never felt so completely myself.

I'll hold back the words this time. Enjoy the feel of them on my tongue and knocking around in my chest. I won't say them until this uncertainty melts from Raven's dark eyes. Until this gut rot from my conversation with Alessi lessens and things with Josh aren't weighing as heavily on me. This time, I'll wait, and hope the unknowns in our futures don't derail us before we get there.

Sixteen

Raven

I walk down the block, past the Middle Eastern man selling street meat, and he gives me an odd look. Probably because I've passed him twelve times. Effort thirteen goes about the same. I near the address on East Hastings Nico gave me, I slow down, my heart rate speeds up, and I keep moving. If Nico were with me, I'd be braver. With him at my side in Fraser Valley, my nerves didn't best me. But he's been broody(er) since the call I wasn't supposed to hear, more distracted. He stares at nothing with his fists clenched tight, and I didn't want to add to his stress.

Instead we've given each other exactly what we need: distraction. Reliving the day I let Rose down reopened a fetid, old wound. It thrust my shame to the forefront. Each remembered blow she took that night reverberated through my body, snapshots from the horror unsettlingly vivid. The blood that bubbled from her mouth. The deafening screams. The smell of my urine lingering on the carpet for days. Until I find Rose, I can believe she loves me and misses me and wishes she could find me, too. That leaving me was the hardest thing she's ever done. That she forgives me. Until we meet, I still have that.

So, the past two weeks, I've hit pause on my search. Nico's day shifts have given us the freedom to walk on the beach and kiss under the stars and get sweaty between the sheets. My house. His house. We've allowed ourselves to live in the moment.

This morning, however, I woke up pumped. Rejuvenated. It could have been the three orgasms or waking up with Nico's talented tongue between my thighs. Whatever the reason, I knew I had to stop putting off my search. Unwilling to add more drama to Nico's life, I asked the girls to come—to see them and have their support. We've barely talked recently. Shay and Lily are bogged down with their day jobs, our joint business venture not getting much attention. But both were busy. I almost gave up, delayed things for another day or week, but I was too wired and Sasha didn't have any clients booked.

That leaves me wearing a path on the cement.

I tap my toe and eye the door to the apartments as a couple of boys strut by. The taller of the two runs his tongue over his top lip when he sees me, a crude gesture that has me crossing my arms over my chest. I should text Nico and let him know where I am, but he'd be pissed I came here on my own. Better not to poke the beast.

"Let's do this," I mutter to myself, tired of my delay tactics.

Another internal pep talk later, I march straight for the door and step inside. A synthetic strawberry scent hits me, barely covering thick wafts of mildew and cigarettes. Without pausing, I climb the stairs up the narrow space. Apartment 201 is at the top. Just a door. In a building. But Rose could be behind it. Unlike at the farm, I came as myself today. No hat to hide behind. No floral dress. Tight black skirt, boots, and a Death Metal T-shirt. Take me as I am.

I squeeze my fists a few times, then blow out a breath and knock.

Nothing.

A ratty pair of shoes is outside the door, an open garbage can covered in something sticky beside it. My stomach feels sticky, too. Leaving would be easy. But the thought of not seeing Rose today, of living in limbo another minute, is as suffocating as this nasty strawberry smell. I knock harder.

"Yeah, yeah...coming!"

I freeze at the male voice, my knuckles hovering in midair.

"What do you want?" The door doesn't open, but the voice is closer.

My neck tingles, as though someone's eyeing me through the peephole. "I'm looking for a woman. Rose Hunt."

"Why?"

He doesn't ask who she is, doesn't sound confused by the name. She could be in there right now. Excitement and nerves spiral through me. Like with Clara, I sense the need for honesty. Stories and excuses will likely shut this Ross guy down.

I clear my throat. "She's my sister."

A lengthy pause. Then, "Your name?"

"Raven Hunt."

A chain jostles, and the door swings wide. The man looks to be in his forties, tall and lean with a thinning ponytail. His gaze dips down my body. "You have the same eyes, but she wouldn't be caught dead wearing that."

"Are you Russ?"

He nods, letting the silence extend between us.

I chew my cheek. "I heard Rose was living here. Is she around?"

Yawning, he leans on the doorjamb and stubs his bare foot into the frayed carpet. "She left a month ago. If I had to guess, I'd say she's at the local shelter."

Homeless shelter? My heart stutters to a stop. The smells disappear. My worst fear is realized: Rose's life has careened downhill. His green eyes are red-rimmed, but he doesn't look high, not like Wispy and Lake. Sadness darkens his sunken features.

"Were you guys dating?" I ask.

The corners of his lips tilt up. "Something like that."

We study each other, me twisting my hands, him jamming his foot into the floor. Awkward, meet Uncomfortable. But this is different than the hippie den. When Clara said she didn't know Rose had a sister, it cut deep. Here I am obsessing over her, searching for her, and she's barely given me a thought. Or she's blocked me out, chosen to forget the sibling who betrayed her. But Russ opened the door when I said who I was. "Did Rose talk about me?"

"Yeah." I hold my breath until he goes on, "Said you were a cute kid."

Is that how she remembers me—cute? Shy? The kid who'd beg her to watch cartoons? If it were only that simple. The weight of his earlier admission snaps me back to the moment. "Why would she be at a shelter?"

Standing upright, he steps back and grips the door. As if to close it. As if to cut this conversation short. "Rose's priorities aren't what they should be. Keep that in mind if you find her." With that, he shuts me out.

His warning rings in my ears, reminding me I haven't seen my sister in a lifetime. She may be the girl who took me to catch frogs and taught me how to skateboard, but playing games doesn't help you survive on your own. Not when she was thrust into the world with a dislocated shoulder and a collection of gashes and bruises. Who knows what she's done to stay afloat? Hopefully his advice was the caution of a wounded man, his glassy eyes hinting as much, and Rose talked about me. She stood on this spot and dated that man, each bit of information teasing me like a cloud I can't quite grasp.

I could wait and visit the shelter with Nico, but I missed her by a month here. There's no telling what a day or two might impact.

When the cocktail of odors gets too much, I hurry down the stairs and bust out the door, but the fresh air I crave is thwarted by smoke. A woman blows a thick stream as her sneakers shuffle down the sidewalk. I pull out my phone and search for shelters. Not surprising, there's one close by. A number of others appear, but Russ called it the "local" shelter. I don't pause, don't pace in front of the hot dog guy. Cell shoved in my purse, I hoof it to the address without a backward glance.

* * *

The shelter isn't hard to find. A queue leads to a kiosk-style window—people lined up for a bed. If I had a camera, I'd take shots, my street-life essay that much closer to conclusion. Even without it I squint, splitting the scene into frames. Each blink is the snap of my shutter.

Blink. A young boy plays with a cigarette butt.

Blink. A girl in sweats flips through a fashion magazine.

Blink. An emaciated man feeds his dog.

There's more humanity in that gesture than in most people's souls.

This lifestyle isn't so far from my reality. Another time, and I could have been here for a very different reason. But as Nico said, I'm defined by the choices I make now, today, not the mistakes I made in the past. His mysterious phone call comes back, the thought like poking a bruise. He hasn't breathed a word about it, and I haven't asked. What happens to the man who values right over wrong if he breaks the law to save his brother? How much of his soul does he lose? As I stew over the unsettling implications, I join the line, until I'm next.

A Plexiglas divider separates me from a black woman, her braids pulled tight, revealing tired eyes. "We're full up tonight. But if you leave your name, you'll be near the top of the list tomorrow."

My spirit dims. There are at least ten people behind me, including two kids. But they're not why I'm here. Maybe they'll find room at a different shelter. "Actually, I'm looking for someone."

She pulls a binder in front of her and opens the book. "Name?"

I dig my nails into my palms. "Rose Hunt."

The wall to the side is covered in spray paint, vibrant colors and bold lines layered to create a word I can't quite read. I study it like it's one of those 3-D posters with a hidden image. No dinosaur appears, but slowly, letters emerge, and the word *terror* expands across the brick. It's as though the artist, with the use of exploding flames and jagged edges, has captured my self-portrait.

The lady clears her throat. "Rose should be inside. I can have someone call her out."

Forget terror. This is zombie-apocalypse scary. But I won't flake out. I'm the girl who moved across the country without a job. I'm rocking my apprenticeship, my photography is improving, and I have a whole lotta man who looks at me like I'm his last drink of water.

I attempt a smile. "That would be great."

"Who should I say is asking?"

The girl she left behind. The girl who ruined her life. "Her sister."

The woman says something to a man then nods to the next person in line.

I step aside to wait. And...*wait*. My attention doesn't waver from the front door. There's a massive dent in the steel. It must have taken some kind of force to bend it. A bat, maybe, swung really hard. I run through several scenarios that could have resulted in the vandalism, when the metal door pushes open, and my breath rushes out. *Rose.* She emerges like an apparition, and my pulse beats an unsteady rhythm, every apology I've ever imagined saying to her vanishing in an instant. All I can do is stare. And try to breathe. Her eyes are dark, like mine. Her hair is long, like mine. The recognition spills over me as tears well up.

My sister.

She squints and blinks, scanning me from head to toe. "Raven?"

She's not as pretty as I recall. Her gaunt cheeks highlight her cheekbones, her fair skin pasty white, and I don't remember her having freckles over her nose or the thin scar crossing her upper lip. But there's no doubt who she is. We stand like this awhile, assessing each other, a couple feet apart but seventeen years between us.

I wipe at the corner of my eye, unsure when it got wet, and she approaches me. She shoves her hands into the pockets of her cords, her baggy tie-dyed shirt hanging over her wrists. "How'd you find me?"

I'm about to answer, when I notice her mouth. Gone are Rose's perfect teeth, an ochre-stained smile in their place. I run my tongue over my gap, the space Nico finds sexy. The space that always made me feel inferior. For years, I'd imagine her grin brightening up a room like a silly toothpaste ad. Now it's gone. Or did I remember it wrong? How much of our relationship have I fabricated?

I clear my throat. "It's a long story, but Russ said he thought you'd be here."

"Russ? *That* asshole?"

I wince at her biting tone and shrug. "He seemed nice enough."

She waves a hand. "Sorry. There's history there. So...are you living here now? In Vancouver?" Her eyes dart as she speaks, landing on me and flitting about. Restless. Wary. Must come with living in places like this.

I nod. "Almost two months. Heard you moved out West and figured I'd poke around. Do you mind that I'm here?"

She shuffles her feet. "It's fine."

The worst word in the English language. Fine is pissed off. It's passive-aggressive for "mind your own damn business." I used that word for the majority of my teen years. How odd, after all this time, after all my visions of this moment, to be here, facing Rose, talking to her with words like *fine*. I can't even bring up my ninth birthday. Can't fathom what I'd say.

Unlike with my grandmother, there's no hug. She hasn't made a move to wrap her arms around me. No tears collect in her eyes. Mine dry up, awkwardness filling the void. She may not be mad I turned up, but she doesn't seem overjoyed.

"I wasn't sure if I should contact you, you know, since you never called." The bite in my voice surprises me. And *God*, where does my anger even come from? What right do I have to be mad?

"Living in that house was a bad scene for me, Raven. It was either get dragged down or move on."

My resentment cowers under her harsh tone. We both lived in that house. We suffered through the drunken fits and unpaid bills. But I unleashed my father on her, the final blow. I'd have run far and fast if I'd been her. Never looked back. "I'm sorry. This is all just…weird."

"You're telling me." Her attention drifts behind me, her dark eyes narrowing. "You here on your own? Not married or anything?"

Twisting, I follow her gaze. A blond man in army pants and a wife beater stares our way, right at Rose. He doesn't blink. Doesn't bother to hide his perusal. He tongues a tooth, revealing a gap much larger than mine. If Nico were here, I doubt this guy would have the balls to stare so openly. I move to block Rose from view.

"I'm seeing someone, but we're not married. You know that guy?" I gesture to the creep with the crooked nose.

She shakes her head quickly. "No." But she smiles at me, *really* smiles. Her teeth may be stained, her top front tooth chipped, but the gesture melts the strain between us. "Sorry. This was just unexpected. I'm not exactly proud to be living here. But…" She grabs my shoulders, hesitates a beat, then pulls me against her chest.

"I've missed you."

My remaining apprehension thaws, because *this. This. This.*

But there's another reason I'm here. Gripping her back, I gulp down my hesitation. This could be my only chance to speak with Rose. She could disappear again. We could go our separate ways. It's now or never. "I took the brooch," I say, "that day. I took it and said nothing."

My pulse chases out the words, leaving my heart pounding in my ears. I don't remind her of the horrors she endured. Don't tell her how terrified I was. I doubt she's forgotten.

She doesn't answer at first. My throat burns, like each swallow is barbed. Then she runs a hand down my hair. "I know. I always knew. You think I'd have let him touch you?"

Oh God, *she knew.*

I choke on a sob, the messy kind. A garbled, wretched sound. *She knew all along.* She took those blows for me. Protected me. It makes the whole ordeal worse and better. "I'm so sorry," I whisper.

She stiffens but doesn't release me. "*Don't* apologize for that man. Don't take the blame for what he did. I'm sorry I left you there. Wish I'd been strong enough to take you with me. But don't go thinking anything in that house was your fault."

Sounds so easy, to shift the blame. Rational even. But I know what I did. I also know so much in that house wasn't right. There's plenty of blame to go around. I'll own mine. Live with it. Finally have the chance to pay Rose's actions forward. I wipe my runny nose, and we go back to standing near but far, discomfort returning.

The line of people has thinned, but more appear to add their names on tomorrow's list—too many in need, too few beds. If Rose weren't here, maybe the elderly woman in line wouldn't have to sleep on the street tonight. Mid-September means cooler nights, the kind frail bones don't tolerate well. My apartment is a palace compared to this facility. A *beige* palace, but roomy nonetheless. I came here to find my sister, to have her in my life.

Why not start with offering her a bed?

Her attention is back on the guy behind me. Another reason to get her away from here. Away from people like that. Whatever knocked her off her feet, she deserves a second chance.

"Move in with me." I've come this far, no point tiptoeing around the subject.

She chews her lip. "I couldn't."

"Sure you could."

"It wouldn't be fair." She studies the ground between us.

Seriously? Fair? She took a beating for me. "My place is plenty big, and you can use the time to find a job. Assuming you don't have one."

Again, her gaze flits, like she knows the creep eyeing her. When I look, he's gone and her posture relaxes. "It wouldn't be for long," she says. "I'd get out of your hair as soon as possible."

My mood lifts, the weeks and months of imagining this moment worth the worry and unbridled hope. "Yeah. Whatever. However long you need is fine. It'll give us time to reconnect."

"Okay. Let me get my stuff." She scans the street again, then touches my arm. "I really appreciate this."

She disappears inside, and I bounce my knees instead of pumping my fist in the air. Things may have started sketchy, but that's to be expected. Springing a reunion on someone isn't kosher. Doing it at the shelter they call home makes it that much worse. But Rose hugged me and said she missed me. She forgave me my sins.

I suddenly can't wait to tell Nico.

I grab my phone. You'll never guess who I just met.

He replies in seconds. If it's an old fuck buddy, give me his address. There's an empty cell at the station.

I like my man jealous. No. But I dig the idea of being locked in a room. With you.

Now you're talking.

Unable to wait, I write: I found Rose.

His excited reply doesn't come. The pause drags so long I almost dial his number.

You went without me?

I cringe, imagining the frown on his handsome face. Sorry. You have so much going on, and I didn't want to dump more on your lap. Forgiven?

Always. And my lap is yours to do with as you please. Now I'm picturing that lap and my tongue and a couple of ice cubes when he adds, What was she like?

Awkward at first, but nice. If you come over tonight, you'll meet her.

You having her for dinner?

I hesitate before sending my reply. Nico is cautious, always worried about the people in his life. A few times he's mentioned I shouldn't get my hopes up where Rose is concerned, that, if I find her, it's best to go slow and feel her out. Asking her to move in might not be what he had in mind. Still, it's my life, my family.

She and that Russ guy used to date. He told me she was at a shelter. She's moving in for a while. I reread my text and add, Please be happy for me, then I hit Send.

A scuffle breaks out, two men shoving each other, claiming

rights to their spot in line. I glance down as Nico replies, I'll be over tonight.

That's it. No congratulations. No tender words. The softy he is, our texts often end with him saying how much he misses me and thinks about me and wants to fuck me. (His sexting has improved.) I, of course, detail how I'd like to cover him in chocolate sauce and lick him clean.

But no messages follow this last one. Only dead air and disappointment.

When he meets Rose, he'll understand. She'll loosen up when she's away from this place, that hug a reminder of the girl she was. Nico has said himself how people on the street are often here because they fall on hard times. He devotes his life to helping others. I'm just doing my version of the same, helping my family any way possible. He of all people must understand that.

Seventeen

Nico

I pull up to Raven's apartment, my frustration with her ebbing as I park. Apparently my advice wasn't worth following. I've told her as many ways as I know how to take her time with Rose, that if she finds her to ease into things. Now they're living together. But Raven is smart, capable of handling herself, and I haven't seen her since this morning. The thought of kissing her is enough to subdue my irritation.

I knock on the door, and Raven's voice drifts out. "Come in!"

Every time I'm in her place, I chuckle to myself. The apartment is drab and sterile, nothing about it reflecting the girl I've fallen for; Raven's clothes and ink and personality are loud enough to shake walls. Her back is to me as she unloads groceries. A couple pizza boxes are on the counter, and the smell of melted cheese makes my stomach rumble. Or maybe I'm hungry for the curves she's flaunting in her tight skirt and short T-shirt.

Her sister isn't around, so I come up behind her and latch my arms around her waist. "It's been too long since I've seen you."

She sighs and leans into me. "A whole ten hours. You getting needy on me, Constable?"

"Fucking desperate for you." She squirms against me, her teasing tone telling me she's as hard up for contact as I am. I cup her breast and press her into the counter, leaning down to take her ear between my teeth. "You shouldn't have gone to Hastings alone."

"If you need to punish me, I won't complain."

I flip her around and cage her between my arms. "I'm still pissed, but I'm glad you found Rose."

She grins so wide I have to kiss her. She tastes as delicious as she looks, like burned sugar, dark and addictive. Already, I'm half-hard. When I release her, I spot an open chocolate bar on her counter and pop a square in my mouth. "Where's Rose?"

"Showering."

"Then we have a few minutes on our own?" I'd like to taste her as the square melts on my tongue, the rich sweetness mixing with all things Raven. I grip her ass.

She pushes at my chest. "Back off, big guy. And stop with the sexy eyes. She'll be out any minute."

Sulking, I give her space. Then I notice the couch made up with sheets and Raven's book on top of a pile of her clothes on the loveseat. The chocolate turns bitter. "You moved out of your room?"

She lifts one shoulder. "I wanted her to be comfortable. She's been at the shelter for a month. It's the least I could do."

"How long is she staying?"

"However long she needs."

"You know why she was at the shelter?"

"No. I haven't asked yet. I didn't want to pry." She crosses her arms. "What's with the third degree, *Sherlock*?"

Intuition is a gift. And a curse. When my sister brought her new boyfriend, Aaron, home, I had him figured out before he opened his mouth. Nikki ignored my warnings and overdosed in an abandoned warehouse. Sensing doom but not being able to prevent it is a special kind of hell. I haven't met Rose, haven't even laid eyes on her, but her presence here just feels *wrong*.

I shrink under Raven's glare. "Just looking out for you, babe. That's all."

Footsteps thud behind us, the woman who's infiltrated Raven's life making her appearance. "I can't tell you how nice that felt. It's been ages since—" Rose stops short when she sees me.

Her dark hair is wet, her loose jeans and floral top not as bohemian as the outfits at our vegan potluck, but I can picture her swaying to the music. She's paler than Raven with freckles on her nose and thinner lips. She's skinnier, too. I zero in on her arms and thankfully don't see track marks.

Wanting to get a handle on things, I stride over and hold out my hand. "I'm Nico, Raven's boyfriend."

Her smile falters, stained teeth flashing. "Rose. Nice to meet you."

I grip her hand firmer than I should. "I'm a cop, so if you need anything, if you want to talk about how you ended up at the shelter, I might be able to help." If Raven insists on rushing into things with her sister, I need to suss out the situation. Best Rose learns who I am.

She yanks her hand back and folds her arms, eyes darting, lips twitching. "Thanks. But it's not that kind of situation."

She breathes more rapidly, still fidgeting. The exact reaction I don't want.

"He's big but harmless," Raven calls from the kitchen.

She can't see the way Rose lifts her chin in challenge, how she sucks her teeth. "I've dealt with scarier," she replies, but her double meaning is clear. She's on to me.

And I'm on to her.

That's all it often takes with me. One interaction. One exchange with a perp or possible victim to sense if they're lying. Last week, Alessi and I were doing a compliance check, making sure a repeat offender, Marlee, was following her house arrest. Her father answered the door in nothing but his boxers, belly hanging out. He swore Marlee was asleep and Alessi was ready to go, but the man tapped his toe restlessly and blinked a few times too many. When I insisted he wake her up so we could make sure, his resolve crumbled. Marlee's now faced with new charges.

It's more than Rose's demeanor, though. Her shifting life, Clara's reaction, and Russ's history are all marks against her. Living at the shelter could be nothing more than a woman down on her luck. Or it could be a woman grasping at anything to stay afloat, and I'll be damned if she grasps on to Raven and drags her down. Better to be wary.

"It's nice of Raven to have you here," I say. "I'm sure we'll see a lot of each other."

"Looking forward to it." Her rigid posture says otherwise.

We hold eye contact, judging, assessing, then we make our way to the kitchen. Rose keeps her distance from me, remaining on the far side of the counter.

Raven beams at her. "I wasn't sure what you liked, so I bought a bunch of stuff for breakfast. There's two percent milk and almond milk. Tofu bacon and regular. Eggs. Cereal. Unless you prefer fruit and yogurt. I could go out and get that."

Rose's scowl transforms on a dime. Too quickly. She leans on her elbows and reaches over the counter to grab Raven's hand. "Like I said, don't go to any trouble. It's nice enough that you gave me your bed."

"I'm just glad you're here." Raven bites her lip.

And my gut churns. Raven's cheeks are glowing, her skin practically sparking with excitement. If she notices Rose's shiftiness, she probably assumes it's nothing more than a woman turning her life around. A person like that would be worried I'd read into her past, scared I could mess up her second chance. There's a chance that's all this is.

I set the table while the two of them talk. Raven leads the conversation with stories of their youth, and Rose jumps in when a memory strikes her. During dinner, I eat pizza quietly. Watching. Taking everything in. They keep to the past, reliving the good times they shared.

"Remember Bobby Jeffery? That day he came to pick you up?" Raven tears off a piece of crust and pops it in her mouth.

"God, I almost forgot about that."

Raven snorts. "I doubt he has. I bet he still needs therapy."

"You gonna leave me in the dark?" I'm at the head of the table, the girls opposite each other, and I kick Raven's foot.

She nudges mine back. "Our mother was wasted, and Bobby comes by the house dressed in his finest bell bottoms."

Rose tosses her napkin at Raven. "Enough about the clothes."

Raven throws it back at her. "So, Bobby goes to introduce himself, shakes Mom's hand, and the woman passes out. Falls like a rock into him. Bobby was so shocked that he lost his balance and ended up on his back, her face in his crotch." The girls cackle.

I force a smile. If I'm wrong about Rose, this could be the start of something amazing for Raven. A real family member to ground her. Her desperation to tell Rose stories and make her laugh is written all over her face, like Colin's need to impress Josh. To be noticed. It's such a simple thing, the swell of pride that comes from inspiring family. As rough as things are with Josh and Nikki, having them in my life gives me purpose. A place in this world. I want that for Raven, too.

I edge my elbows onto the table. "What do you do for work, Rose?"

"I'm between jobs." She keeps eating, not a glance my way.

She doesn't get off that easy. "What about before?"

Rose places her slice of pizza down and pushes her plate aside. "Different things. Retail. Waitressing. I did a stint on a farm." She flexes her fingers, once, twice, then she shifts on her seat, scratches her nose, and angles away from me.

I keep peppering her with questions.

"So you've been handing out résumés?"

"Yeah."

"No luck, then?"

She swallows. "Job market is rough."

"Have you checked online? The Canadian Job Bank is a decent resource."

"Yeah. But my timing must be off. They've always hired when I get 'round to applying."

Her shoulders relax a fraction, my job questions repetitive enough for her to drop her guard. Time to shift gears. "That Russ guy, the one you were staying with, turns out he has a history of drug charges."

Her body tenses, like a rod has been fused to her spine. Raven prickles with irritation, a steady glare aimed my way.

A beat later, Rose says, "I wouldn't know anything about that."

We might not be in the interview room at the station, but I don't let up. "I thought you dated." At least Raven seemed to think so.

Annoyance flashes across Rose's face, followed by balanced composure. "We had fun, and he gave me a place to crash for a while. Nothing more. I'll find a job soon." She focuses on her sister. "Raven showing up proves things have to turn around eventually." A wide grin spreads across her face…a second later than it should. A delayed reaction. False emotion.

Raven returns the smile, hers sincere, then she shoves her seat back. The chair legs stick on the carpet before smacking into the counter behind her. Everything about this room is small: the tiny table and four chairs crammed between her living area and kitchen counter, the low ceilings. But there's nothing diminutive about the scowl Raven directs at me.

"Rose and I have a lot of catching up to do. Would you mind if we cut our night short?" Her words barely make it past her pinched lips.

I glance again at Rose, who seems pleased, then nod to Raven. "No problem."

But her flared nostrils are definitely a problem.

I try to help with the dishes, but Raven doesn't give an inch. She pulls open the front door and waits for me. I tip my head to Rose, holding eye contact until she looks away, then I follow Raven outside.

At my truck, she swivels around and pokes my chest. "What the fuck was that?"

I rub my neck. "What?"

"*What?*" She gawks at me like I asked the sum of one plus one. "That inquisition you held at my table. All that was missing were a set of floodlights and instruments of torture."

"I'm just curious."

She makes a gravelly sound. "Don't bullshit me. That was Constable Makai in there, not my boyfriend."

I glance at her bare feet. Her black polish is chipped on her big toes, the curve of her right ankle pink from where I nipped it last night. Without her boots on, she's smaller. More vulnerable. I lift her by her waist, so she can rest her feet on my boots. Stand on me. Lean on me. All I want is to protect her.

I turn us so her back is pressed to my truck. "I'm sorry. I'm just worried. Have you brought up the brooch yet?"

She rests her hands on my chest. "She knew," she says quietly. "She covered for me."

Still so much sadness in her voice, but the news has my shoulder blades loosening. Rose endured a beating to save Raven. That took guts. Love. Traits I hope the streets haven't stolen from her. "Sounds like she was a great sister. But I'm still going to worry about you."

"I know. But not everyone you meet is a criminal. Rose has had a rough go of things. You say all the time that people don't ask to live on the streets. Circumstances are often beyond their control. Why do you assume she's different?"

I trace the frown lines between her eyes. "So much is riding on this for you. I don't want to see you disappointed."

Or hurt.

We're just finding our feet together, the nights never long

enough, the days apart an eternity. Everything I've searched for in a relationship, I've found with this woman. I also know what it is to be let down by family. I've seen the scars it leaves behind, healed but always puckered. Toughened yet raw. Nikki will never fully recover from what she went through, and I question everything she does, worried a simple night at a bar will send her spiraling backward. If Rose uses Raven and discards her, it will affect everything. Even us.

She pulls the front of my T-shirt down, exposing the *enata* symbol inked on my chest. She brushes her nose against it, followed by her lips. "You have to let me figure this out on my own. I know she has a history. So do I. I promise to keep my eyes open."

I span my hands over the ship on her back and rock into her, wishing we were at my apartment. In my bed. Nothing between us. "Maybe I'm jealous."

"Jealous?" She works her toe under the cuff of my jeans, dragging it through the hairs on my leg. "Do tell."

Just her toe makes me crazy. I tilt forward, forcing her to look up. "I won't get to see you as much. Won't get to wake you up with my tongue." Won't get to sink into her and forget my worries. I kiss her neck, her cheek, her ear.

She trembles, a whimper escaping. "You, Constable Makai, are dangerous."

Pretty sure she still has that backward.

She wraps her leg around mine, urging me closer. My growing hard-on presses into her belly, and my heart presses against my chest. She reaches between us and cups me, and I nearly lose my mind. We don't kiss. We stare at each other. During sex, it's like this between us. Each time I fill her, our eyes lock. She tries to get me moving faster, harder. And *fuck*, do I want to let go with this woman. It takes every bit of restraint I have to keep from slamming our hips together. But she's so small next to me. When I'm on top, my arms caging hers and my chest hovering, my size and power are emphasized. She looks at me with want and trust, a seductive cocktail that reminds me to stay in control. Always in control. It's a fraying wire.

I open my truck's back door, needing some privacy to touch her. Get her off. I ease her off my boots and inch backward on the seat, curling my finger so she joins me. "Get in here. And close the door."

She glances at her apartment, then at the parking lot, a wicked grin widening. "Have you always been this naughty?"

"Only since I met you." I've enjoyed women, but the urge to please and touch and taste has never consumed me like it does with Raven. I've never dragged a girlfriend into the backseat of my truck. In a public area. This woman spins me like a top.

She wets her lips with her tongue, slow and sensual, then kneels on the seat. I bend my legs, too big and long for the space, and we laugh at the awkwardness, but when she shuts the door, the heat between us singes all humor. She reaches for my belt buckle, but I stop her. My behavior with Rose, the way I challenged her, was for Raven. Raven's my priority. Even now, giving her pleasure is more important than seeking my own. Sliding down on my back, I plant my boots on the door and guide her hips closer, over my waist, past my chest, until she's straddling my face.

Her strained "*God*" becomes a gasp when I push her skirt up. And pull her hips down.

I kiss her wet underwear, and she shudders, gripping the seats to anchor herself. She better hold tight—to the seats, to me, to *us*. The urge to bury my face in her blurs my mind, a heady haze of love and lust. I move the strip of lace to the side, revealing her, and my dick twitches, my body set to unravel. Palming her ass, I bring her closer and lick her once. Her thighs tense. Her breath catches.

"I like you naughty," she purrs.

I groan at her admission and tease her with my tongue, slow movements as I taste my fill. I lick; she moves. The heat in my truck climbs to scalding. When she rocks her hips, searching for more—needing it, needing me—I spread her wide and give her exactly what she wants. Show her I'll always take care of what's mine. Each suck elicits a mewl. She barely contains her cries.

I could live off this. Pleasing her with my tongue and fingers and my cock, memorizing the clench of her thighs and hitch of her breath when she's about to come.

The ecstasy on her face.

She sways her hips, small shifts from side to side with a final jerk and hiss when I'm exactly where she wants me. I sink my tongue into her, moving her wetness around, bringing her to the brink. *Loving* the taste of her. My girl. My woman. Mine to enjoy. Her hand slams onto the roof, her knees gripping my head. I work my tongue faster and suck, pushing her to the edge, until she tips over. My name spills from her lips, her body shaking and boneless. I hold her up until I've wrung every last ounce of pleasure from her, then gently cover her with her underwear and adjust her skirt.

She slinks down my body, straddling me. The depths of her dark eyes shine. "I'm pretty sure we can get arrested for that."

I chuckle, my boldness with Raven surprising even me. "Only if people see us. Maybe you were fogging up the windows so you could clean them."

She leans down for a kiss, deep and wet, sucking my tongue, tasting herself on me. "Maybe," she says.

Again, she reaches for my groin, but I stop her. "You should get inside. Rose might come looking for you."

She wiggles her hips once, killing me, then she pouts. "I hate that I'm not sleeping with you tonight."

"That makes two of us." Three if you count my raging hard-on.

"It might be a while. I want to spend time with Rose and make sure she feels settled."

I drag myself up, frustration edging my movements. Maybe my jealousy comment earlier wasn't so playful. I like having Raven to myself. Making dinner. Talking. Walking on the beach. *Not* talking. I don't want to share her.

We scoot out of my car, her cheeks flushed, her bare feet adorable on the pavement. She tugs her skirt down. "I'm happy to fight daily if every apology feels like that."

"Who says that was an apology?"

"Your tongue did. It begged my forgiveness."

I pull her to me, my jeans tight as hell. I plan to relive my supplication in detail at home. "Did it work?"

"Like a charm." She lifts her face to the sky, the sun dropping toward the horizon. It's warm for September, fall and winter on their way. Soon the days will be shorter. Darker. "But be nice to my sister," she says. "And be happy for me."

As a cop, I choose to work the beat. The community, the people—that's where I belong, where I make the most difference. I see shit every day, good and bad. I've learned to question motives and behavior. Listen to my gut. Exactly what Raven's asking me to avoid. For now I'll step back. Give her space to get reacquainted with her sister. Her happiness is my priority.

"Done." I kiss her softly.

Eighteen

Raven

September falls into October in a tumble of days and nights. The cool air is thinner, the leaves sparse, but my life has never been so full. So full, it's a juggling act keeping afloat amid work, the event business, Nico, and my sister.

I check my watch and pack Sasha's gear faster; this morning's photo shoot ran longer than expected. Rose and I planned an afternoon of movie watching, and it's been a week since I've seen my Sexy Beast. Seven days without his big, strong hands on my body. We text and call, but it isn't the same. And he's been edgier. Josh's trial is in two weeks, each day that passes another shadow added under his eyes. There's been no mention of his brother being cleared. No word of a confession in the works. When I ask about the case, Nico says the bare minimum, more words swallowed than spoken.

Tonight, I plan to give him release.

Sasha leads her client to the door, the pregnant woman glowing from our session. She was shy when she arrived, but Sasha played music and talked softly, and an hour later the woman was naked, lounging on our props like she owned the place.

As I take down the strobe light and umbrella, Sasha returns and helps me pack up. By day, half her apartment serves as her studio; by night, it's her living room. When we're done, she stands back and crosses her arms. "I need a favor."

I run my hand under my bangs, looking forward to the cooler air outside. "Anything."

"Something's come up, and I can't do tomorrow's shoot."

"The tattoo one?"

She nods. "I already moved the date once and don't want to cancel. Can you step in for me?"

That's like asking if black is my color. "Are you serious?"

I've been looking forward to this session since we booked it. A woman who suffered an assault had flowers tattooed over the scars, turning the horrific experience into something beautiful. We were given permission to shoot privately at a botanical garden.

Sasha's leather pants crinkle as she picks up the fur blanket we used as a prop. She tucks it under her arms, then focuses her purple eyes on me. "Your skills have improved, and you know my gear better than I do. I thought it would be a great opportunity, and the tattoo theme is up your alley. You think you can handle it?"

"Definitely. I won't let you down." I better not. Sasha's gone way beyond her job as employer. She encourages me to stage shots, even letting me direct some. And she asks to see my work. When I told her about my goal to shine a light on street life, using my lens to access the heart behind the heartache, her face lit up. We discuss my photos regularly—critiques that have forced me to up my game. She's even mentioned helping me put on a show.

"You'll do fine," she says. "We'll go over the angles and expectations, but you'll be in charge. The more confident you are, the more relaxed the client will be."

By the time we're done discussing the details, I practically run to the bus. My feet barely touch the ground, Vancouver's signature rain chasing me. My move here has proved more rewarding than I could have imagined. My photography is taking off. We've finished the website for Over the Top Events. I'm nervous about documenting client parties on my own, but the skills I'm learning are invaluable. Transferring them to my own business, being in control of everything from the direction to the shots to the final product, sets my head spinning. I have Nico, and a sister, too. I must have done something right in a past life, because the crap I pulled in high school couldn't have led me here.

Still buzzing, I turn down the drive to my apartment as a guy in baggy clothes pushes out my front door, a small white box clutched in his hand. His shaggy blond hair covers his face, but I catch his profile as he slides into his car, and his crooked nose jogs my memory, a fleeting moment of recognition I can't quite place. The troublesome kind, like an unidentifiable stench. He was obviously visiting Rose, but I've never met any of her friends, and she never volunteers much information. She's careful to maintain a certain distance between us.

The visitor drives off, and I try to shake my unease. Rose's acquaintance may be on the seedy side, but who am I to judge? My old crowd makes that guy look like a librarian.

I hurry inside, hang up my raincoat, and run into Rose's room, eager to share my good news. "You'll never guess what happened today."

Her Greenpeace shirt is creased as if she picked it up off the floor, her jeans stained on the cuffs. She looks up from the *Vanity Fair* magazine I bought her. "Judging by the strange dance you're doing, I'd say the news is good."

I shift from foot to foot, my excitement bubbling up. "My boss can't do our photo shoot tomorrow and asked me to fill in. Run it on my own."

She lowers the magazine. "That's awesome, Raven. You haven't even had the job that long. She must be impressed with your work."

I wave her off. "More like she was in a bind and needed a warm body to take her place."

"Sure, but this is her business. She wouldn't take the time if she didn't think you had promise. And she certainly wouldn't leave you with a client if you couldn't pull it off. I'm proud of you. Seriously," she adds when my gaze drops to her sweatshirt tossed on the floor. "This is a big deal."

It is a big deal. Sasha's been the perfect mentor, explaining why she does everything, not just shoving menial jobs my way. But the bigger deal, the thing that has unfamiliar warmth looping through my chest, is the word *proud*. When I buckled down in high school and my grades climbed out of town-idiot territory, my mother squinted at my report card and said, "You're a Hunt. No point tryin' to be somethin' you ain't." My father shrugged and turned back to the TV.

But my sister is *proud* of me.

"Thanks," I say, the only syllable left in my vocabulary. But the appearance of the man at my front door gnaws at me. "Who was the guy who just left?"

She pauses so long, I almost repeat the question. "Did you talk to him?"

"No, but he looked familiar."

"Just a friend. He's been here before. You probably saw him at his car or something."

That lame excuse smells like leftover tuna casserole, but maybe his appearance could be the thing to bring us closer, a way to ease her into opening up. "You should invite him over. I'd love to hang out."

"He's not the hangout type." With those clipped words, she shoves her magazine to the side and claps her hands. "We should celebrate your job. I bought ice cream last night. Mint chip. You inhaled the stuff as a kid. Figured it was a safe bet. Then we can watch a movie."

Her usual avoidance grates on me, but I need to rein in my expectations. Could be he's a boyfriend or ex she'd rather not discuss. I haven't exactly opened up about Nico, either. I suppress a sigh. For now she wants to celebrate my job and watch movies and use words like *proud*.

I grab her arm as she passes. "I'm really happy you're here, Rose."

She blinks at my hand and chews her cheek. Then she smiles. "Thanks for giving me a second chance."

The doorbell chimes, and her smile fades. She shoves past me, nearly body checking me into the wall to reach the door first. Annoyed, I rub my arm, wondering if that guy is back.

I poke my head around the hallway to see Nikki and Colin. A much nicer surprise. "You guys finally made it."

Nikki holds her hand out to Rose. "I'm Nico's sister, and this is my son, Colin. We're here about a skateboard."

Rose offers a polite hello, then slinks off to the couch, always wary with strangers. Nikki frowns at Rose's cold shoulder but brightens when she looks at me. She nudges Colin inside, his sullen demeanor as fierce as ever. I hurry to my room and return with my skateboard. When I pass it to him, he actually smiles.

"Cool stickers." Eyes wide, he runs his fingers over the skull and crossbones on the underside.

"Remember what I said. Use this to teach your brother."

"Yeah. Sure. Thanks." But he's busy spinning the green wheels.

Nikki and I chat for a bit. She looks less tired. Less drawn, maybe. It's nice getting to know her, Colin and Jack, too. Adding them to my circle of friends is special. Nico trusting me with his family means the world.

With a final thank-you, they leave, and I join Rose on the couch. I hand her a spoon and position the mint chip between us. "What are we watching?"

"Tom Hardy's lips."

I laugh, but seriously—I could happily lose a day or five drooling over those lips.

Partway through *Mad Max*, my attention drifts to Rose. She may keep her distance, and we're certainly not the type do each other's nails or sing about summer love, but some nights she tells me stories. According to her, she's spent the last seventeen years "finding herself." Normally that kind of hippie talk would have me miming my demise (death by vampire bite), but I can't learn enough about Rose.

She's curled up on the opposite end of the couch, and I kick her butt. "What's the first job you had in the city? After you moved out."

She squints and tucks her bottom lip between her teeth. "Busking, I think. I'd sing while a friend played bongos. We weren't half bad."

She'd probably laugh her ass off if she saw the girls and me rocking out as the Painted Hearts. We were on the atrocious side of horrible. "I loved when you'd sing to me, so I'm not surprised."

Her eyes shine at the admission. "Some of the few happy times in that house."

She's right about that. "Favorite jobs you've had?" I ask to keep her talking.

More squinting. More lip biting. "Probably my summer tree planting. Although the mosquitoes were insane. And I liked working at Neverland Farms. Growing stuff. Remember that African violet Daniel Putnam gave me? The one in that awful yellow pot?" When I nod, she goes on, "I actually carted it around for ages. Couldn't stomach tossing it."

I twist a lock of hair around my finger, building my courage to pry further. This type of sharing isn't new. We talk about our pasts, but she rarely mentions the present. When I bring things up, she gets quiet and avoids questions, and Nico's warning not to trust Rose so quickly resurfaces, but she flips back to pleasant and always apologizes. A reminder that reunions like ours don't blossom overnight. I should probably drop things after her evasion earlier, but this is the most relaxed she's been. "You know that Russ guy who told me where you were? What was the deal with you guys? He seemed like he cared about you."

She sighs and runs her fingers over the cushion at her side. "You're nosier than you were as a kid." She tickles my foot. "Let's watch the movie."

More avoidance, but at least I got her talking a bit. It still amazes me how different Rose and I are. I'd rather swim in raw sewage than plant trees in the Canadian north. One week at Neverland Farms would have me hanging myself with Lake's guitar strings. But the comfort that comes with our shared history isn't replaceable. She taught me to ride a bike. At Christmas she'd hide homemade jewelry in a stocking under my bed. We'd eat cereal for dinner, our legs intertwined on the couch—a habit we've revived.

Her presence is my own gravitational force, grounding me with familiarity. It makes me wonder how I lasted all these years without her.

Smiling to myself, I return my focus to Tom Hardy—because, *those lips*.

By the time the movie ends, I'm eager to pack a bag and spend the evening with Nico, including a lengthy anatomy session between the sheets. Rose's cell rings and she hurries to her room. She's taken a job at a delivery company that specializes in weekend and evening service. It's on-call, so her phone's constantly going off. I can't tell if she likes it, but she seems to earn good tips, even if the hours are messed up. Nico keeps asking when she'll have enough cash to move out. He hasn't grilled her since that first night, but he's pissed I'm still on my couch, frustrated that I lent her money.

I owe her a lot more than a bed and a few bucks.

* * *

Too impatient to wait for the elevator, I take the stairs in Nico's building two at a time. Being apart this long has me restless, and it won't hurt to build my stamina. We need to make up for our days apart. I also plan to break his defenses. He's always so careful with me in bed, asking for what he wants, but never letting go. Not completely. I bet those blue eyes ignite when he takes charge, his inner beast unleashed. I walk faster.

As I turn down the hallway, I catch Sawyer leaving the big guy's apartment.

"Sneaking out after a quickie?" I ask.

He grins. "Just getting him ready for you."

"Thoughtful."

The hallway is as gray as my apartment is beige. He leans his shoulder into the wall. "The gentleman I am, I won't ask the purpose of your visit."

"No need to pretend around me."

"But you talk to Lily, and Lily's still wearing my ring around her neck instead of on her finger, so…" His words aren't laced with his usual confidence, and he shoves his hands in his front pockets. He focuses on the carpet between our feet.

Is he digging for information? "Are you digging for information?"

"Is there information I should know?"

This is my first conversation with Insecure Sawyer. He's usually the first to crack a joke or put on a costume and parade around for the amusement of others. He dressed as a magician for his nieces' birthday and has sent Nico pictures of the Iron Man outfit he's ordered for Halloween. At his recent office karaoke party, he sang a Beyoncé song complete with choreography. This new, insecure Sawyer is adorable.

"I have no intel," I say. "Even if I did, I wouldn't tell you. Lily will put the ring on when she's ready."

He drags a hand through his hair. "I guess."

Seriously adorable.

"What about you?" He smirks, a gleam in his brown eyes. "Has the giant proposed yet?"

I match his smirk and raise him an eyebrow. "Your erectile dysfunction medication must be confusing you. You should take the pills with food."

"Come on," he says. "No need to play coy. I know my boy. He probably professed his love on date three. A ring can't be far."

My laughter catches in my throat. The guys joke about Nico's tendency to fall quickly for women, the big guy a total softy. I've known that about him since day one. But I've never measured our relationship against those of his past, like he's never judged me and my promiscuity. We exist as a clean slate. New city. New love. But hearing he's looked other women in the eye and said *I love you* scrapes at my heart. He's never shared those words with me.

Avoiding Sawyer's comment, I say, "My money's on you two tying the knot first."

I hike my bag up my shoulder and move past him, but he places a hand on my arm. "Nico finally told Josh about the trial—that things aren't looking good. I stopped by to make sure he was okay. He needs you right now."

My stomach lurches. "I'll do what I can."

As I grab the handle, he adds, "If you guys want to cancel tomorrow night, let us know."

I'd almost forgotten we'd made plans for all six of us to hang out. I miss my friends, but it's up to Nico. Nodding, I push in. His apartment is larger than mine, airy with its minimal furniture, masculine with its dark colors; a dresser, night table, and king bed barely fill his bedroom. Like mine, the space isn't special or particularly nice, except for the fact that it smells like him. Like man and muscle and comfort.

He's sitting on his navy couch, elbows on his knees, head in his hands. When the door clicks shut, he glances up. "Hey." His voice is scratchy, roughened with emotion.

"Sawyer told me. Are you okay?"

He answers with a shrug. "Josh had sent his portfolio to that school you showed him. He was excited. Talking about the future. I couldn't keep lying."

Dropping my bag, I walk over and stand between his legs. I run my hands over his buzzed head, wishing I had the power to absorb his pain. "How did he take it?"

"As you'd expect. He got mad. Took off for a run. I waited until he got back, and he apologized. Said he deserves whatever he gets. That he may not have stolen that car or bought the drugs, but he wasn't a saint…" His voice trails off as his hands slide around my waist, pulling me to him.

Holding his head against my stomach, I feather my fingers over his scalp. "Do you want to talk about it?"

With his nose, he pushes up my shirt, kissing my belly button. "No." Then, "I've missed you."

But he doesn't love me.

The thought startles me, Sawyer's words still swimming through my mind. Maybe things aren't as serious between us as I'd assumed. Maybe he's not falling as hard as I am. Because right now, the only words I want to say are *I love you so fucking much*. It would be the first time I've ever whispered them to anyone, but his rejection after Aspen unraveled my life. If he doesn't feel the same now, his admission would bury me under an avalanche of indifference.

"We don't have to talk," I say, pushing the thoughts away. Tonight is about him. Helping him the way he always cares for others. This I can do. This I can offer. Show him my love without words. Soothe him while guarding my heart.

He drags his hands up my sides, lifting my top with the movement—up my arms and over my head—then he tosses it on the floor. The air is cool, goose bumps spreading from his nearness, his touch. With a twist of his fingers, he unlatches my bra, and the fabric gathers at my feet. His calluses scratch my back, rough yet gentle. At the gym, he works his body hard, stretching his muscles, building his strength, only to treat me with such care. I arch as his lips skim my nipple, groaning with each pass. Then his hands are on me, caressing, squeezing.

His mouth is hot on my skin.

Suddenly, he picks me up and flips me on my back, splaying me on the couch below him. He doesn't speak. Not with words. He traces my tattoos: the flowers on my chest, the stallions on my ribs. The choking chicken. Still silent, he leaves me on his couch and returns with a pillow for my head. Always sweet. Always making sure I'm comfortable. He drops a few condoms on the table and licks his lips. Taking his time, he kneels, lifts one of my legs, and unlaces my boot. Before he drags it off, he places a kiss between my thighs, over the thick denim. Heat gathers in my core, the material wet in seconds. *God*, this man.

Has he worshipped every woman he's been with? Has he treated them like queens?

He starts on my other leg.

When he peels off my jeans, my uncertainty dissipates. He stares at me, takes his fill. The bulge in his pants grows, and he grabs his T-shirt and yanks it over his head, his jeans and boxers hitting the floor next. Like this—naked and glorious, inked muscles flexing with tension—I lose my sanity. I'm not sure when I fell in love with him. Probably Aspen. But knowing it, acknowledging it, spikes my arousal. Want swells deep in my belly, heat pulsing in waves. I need him inside me.

Instead of breaking the spell, I drag my fingers down my body, finding the center of my heat and moving my hips. I spread my wetness around, showing him what he does to me. His eyes spark, unrest brewing behind blue flame. So much turmoil in his heart. He rolls the condom on, then kneels again and lifts my ankles onto his shoulders, placing himself against me.

Help me, his eyes plead. *Erase the pain.*

I thrust upward.

He pushes in, and I gasp like always. So big, so *full*. So much emotion locked in my chest. Hiking me higher, he seats himself deeper, not a breath between us, and a ragged groan pushes from his throat. He rocks in and out, rolling his hips in an endless current, each wave taking me deeper. His lips and tongue and teeth are on my ankle, biting, tasting. I reach behind me and grip the arm of the couch, arching farther. In the past I've needed friction to take me that last mile—my hand or a man's between my thighs. Not with Nico.

His size and the way he looks at me are a one-way ticket to nirvana.

He plants one hand beside my head, his even thrusts stoking

the heat shooting up my legs. I grab his neck and pull him close, our eyes locked. This is love. This is the thing I've missed all my life. This is home. If he doesn't feel the same, it will gut me, the rawness of it already breaking my walls. Pushing up, I kiss him, show him. Then he tilts his hips, and a string of dynamite lights under my skin, igniting in sharp bursts.

My orgasm blinds me.

It's sudden and fierce, my cries strangled against his lips. He holds me tight as I clench around him, pulsing until I collapse, the warmth between my thighs exquisite.

Gradually, I stir and lower my legs. He stills his hips. Nico is a caring lover, always making sure I come first. Usually making me come again. *And again.* Tonight, though, the roles get reversed. The turmoil clouding his gaze is the stormiest I've ever seen it, and it's time for the storm to break.

Nineteen

Nico

There it is: that look in her eyes, vulnerable yet fierce. The one I've been waiting for. To see how much she loves me. It cracks me open, makes it hard to breathe. I can't swallow. Can't speak the words I've wanted to say for weeks. In the past it was easy. I'd tell a woman I loved her, she'd say it back, and it felt right in the moment, but it was never hard. The unspoken words were never cut glass in my throat. But now's not the time to force them out. Not with Josh and the trial and my ten thousand worries. When it's just us, none of this bullshit in the way, she'll get all of me.

But damn, do I love this girl.

Her pupils are glazed, her lids heavy with pleasure. I slide out and then in, moving slowly, easing her back. But she grips my hips. "Not like this. This time, you're going to fuck me."

My dick twitches, that dirty mouth of hers too hot. "Did I not make you feel good?"

She shoves my chest, and I slide out of her, immediately craving her tight heat, her body beneath mine. She moves to her knees, too, and grips my chin. "You make me feel so good, I worry I'll never come down. But you always hold back. I want you to take me. Fuck me. I want you to *let go*."

I curl my fingers around her hips, the tip of my cock pressing against her belly. "No. I'll hurt you." But the thought of moving without restraint the way I work a speedball at the gym, hard and fast, has me digging my thumbs into her inked skin.

She kisses me. Once. Softly. Then she smooths my brow. "You won't hurt me, big guy. But I need this. You need this. Just *take* for a change."

She peels off my condom and curls her hand over my length, pumping me, coaxing me. I move with the motion. Eyes closed, I push my day away. The fear in Josh's eyes. The guilt hibernating in my chest. I forget about the thin line Nikki walks, and the father I put in jail. That I nearly broke the law for my brother. I move faster, guiding her, thrusting roughly. My lungs burn. I open my eyes, and Raven's face is flushed with excitement. She knows exactly what she's doing to me, pushing me to break the shackles I wear.

What happens if I go too far?

But she mouths *fuck me* and something inside me snaps. The need to slam into her catches, sparks lighting down my spine. I flip her over and prop her ass in the air. I rip open another condom, rolling it on with haste. Positioning myself at her entrance, I hesitate, but she grinds into me, so I do as she wants. I let go. I *detonate*. I push into her. Swift. Hard. I tug her ass against my groin in a violent motion. She grabs the couch arm, and I grip her shoulder, keeping my other palm on her hip, anchoring her. I thrust hard—deep and dirty. My need for release surprises me in its ferocity. Our skin slaps. She cries out with each contact, her breasts bouncing and legs shaking. I move faster. I pound into her. Relentlessly. Heat sears my skin like needles, tattoos inked from within.

My grunts turn into growls, pleasure coiling up my thighs. "Oh, fuck. Oh *fuck*." My words sound strangled, savage, my dick so hard and deep inside Raven, I nearly combust. A few more thrusts are all it takes. My orgasm rips a path down my spine as I slam the last of my energy into the woman I love.

Spent and winded, I barely hear her sob. Her fucking tears. My arms shake. My heart hammers in my ears. Oh, God. Oh, *fuck no*. I slip out of her, terrified to turn her over.

What have I done?

Tossing the condom, I rotate and slide under her, gathering her on my chest. I wrap my legs around her, my arms over her. I kiss her everywhere I can. "Please tell me I didn't hurt you. Babe, I couldn't…I didn't want to…"

She looks up, tears like fireflies in her eyes. "I'm fine." She places my hand over her heart. It's beating as wildly as mine. "That was just intense."

Relief quiets my pulse slightly. "You sure?"

"I might avoid spin classes for a while, and that horseback riding lesson will have to wait, but"—she smiles, tentative and shy—"I'm okay."

I kiss her cheeks, salt coating my tongue. Raven rarely cries. She doesn't risk vulnerability, just like I don't lose control. Not like this. But she gave that to me tonight. She gave that to us. Words curl up my throat, but I swallow them down. When I'm no longer living with this twisting in my gut, I'll tell her the truth. Confess the depths of my feelings. The rest of my life may be crumbling, but she'll hold me together.

We lie this way awhile, breathing in time. She nuzzles into me. "I don't need a mattress when I have you."

"You telling me I'm getting soft?"

"Only one part of you."

The way she wiggles, it won't be for long. But she's had enough for tonight. "Way to bruise the ego."

"Trust me, big guy, you have nothing to worry about in the performance department. Sentences might not be your strong suit, but I like you quiet."

If she only knew the words I'm holding hostage. "Thank you," I whisper. "For tonight."

Her breath skims my chest. "It was as much for me as it was for you." Her back expands and pauses, as though she wants to speak. To say something more. Only air comes out. Then, "Are you still up for drinks with the gang tomorrow? If you want to stay in, that's fine."

"No. I'd like to go. It'll help get my mind off things, and I like having you on my arm in public. Showing you off."

"How Neanderthal of you."

If Neanderthal means swinging her over my shoulder and having my way with her in a cave, I could get behind that. "You can parade *me* around all you want."

"Or line dance with you to that crap music you like." She pops onto her elbow. "Forgot to tell you, but Colin and Nikki came by today. Your nephew actually smiled when I gave him the skateboard."

"You should have taken a picture."

"Totally should have. And Rose seems to be getting more shifts at work, which is good."

My jaw locks, all the tension I'd released still simmering below the surface. I've kept my mouth shut where her sister is concerned. Raven sleeps on her own couch, gives the woman money, and falls over herself to please Rose. I don't like the hours Rose keeps, don't understand why she won't introduce Raven to her friends. The intuition that serves me well on the job blares like an alarm when Rose is in spitting distance. I can't explain it, can't see past it. But Raven asked me to let her navigate their relationship on her own, and I'm doing my damndest to let her.

"That mean she'll find her own place soon?" A guy can hope.

Raven narrows her eyes, that sexy glare a little scary. "She'll stay with me as long as she wants. Do you have a problem with that?"

Last time this came up, she stormed out of my apartment and left me tossing in bed all night. She's still not ready to see Rose as anything other than the perfect sister she imagines. She thinks she owes Rose a debt. It's tough to argue with that, and there's no way I'm risking a fight tonight. I slide my hands over her hips. "How does a bath sound?"

"Delicious."

I kiss her nose and untangle our legs, leaving her to watch my ass as I go fill the Jacuzzi tub—the one decent perk of this apartment. The guys love mocking my baths, but my muscles get sore, and my mom always ran them for me as a kid with salts to ease the ache.

I watch the water run, the sound becoming white noise, the white-tiled wall so stark my vision goes hazy. My mind coils tight again. Letting go with Raven felt cathartic, but it was temporary abandon. My family knows the score now, knows I didn't come through. Before I told them, I had a moment of weakness. A spell where I dialed Alessi then hung up. Nearly begged him to just *fucking do it.* Bait those punks. Plant evidence. Force confessions. Whatever it takes. Nearly puked up my dinner. Had to remind myself that as a kid I couldn't sleep, knowing my father had stolen sunglasses. Lying for Josh is coercion, not petty theft.

Yet I almost took the easy way out again.

My breathing gets shallow. The room starts to spin, and I hunch forward, hand braced on the tile wall. I don't realize how close the tub is to overflowing until Raven dips under my arm to shut off the tap. She's all gorgeous inked skin and rounded curves. Makes my mouth water, just looking at her. She kisses my chest and guides me into the warm suds. I let her. Need her. My heart is thudding so damn hard, I'm worried it'll crack my breastbone.

The water sloshes onto the floor as I sink in. Raven moves to clean the mess, but I grab her wrist. "Don't go."

I can't say if my face looks as twisted as my insides feel, but she cups my cheek and bites her lip. "Baby. I'm not going anywhere."

I tug her toward me, and she slips into the water, her spine curling into my chest. I gather her close, wanting to fuse our bodies together and forget how weak I was today. Pretend I never dialed Alessi's number.

She runs her lips over each of my knuckles. "There's something else, Nico. Something you're not telling me."

Of course she senses it; she's the woman who owns my heart. The last person I want knowing about my actions. But she strokes my hands and traces watery circles on my knees and calves. I lean the back of my head into the hard tile, jaw clenched. She doesn't speak, but her feathering fingers loosen my vocal chords. "I almost broke the law to save Josh."

Shame seeps through me as the words croak out.

Her hands freeze. The bubbles stop their lazy spin. "Does this have to do with the call in the motel? Forcing a false confession?"

My pulse revs. "You heard that?"

"Part of it. You didn't want to talk about it, so I didn't push. But I've been worried. I know how much pressure you put on yourself to walk a narrow line."

The bottom half of her dark hair has sunk into the water. I push it aside and press my face into her neck. Her damp-soft skin envelopes my forehead. "Twice," I say. "Twice, I almost gave Alessi the go-ahead. Actually said yes the first time he asked, and I'm sick about it. Makes me want to punch a wall."

She twists her head to kiss my temple, runs her nose over my ear. "You're just a man, Nico. Only human. You almost made that choice because you love your brother, not because it served you or your job, or because you were going to score cash. No one is perfect."

"But I need to be. *I'm* the example. The one who models right from wrong. And I was ready to break the law. I'm a fucking *coward*." That last word sucks the air from my chest.

"No, no, no." She squishes closer to me. "You're as honorable as they come, but life isn't as neat and tidy as you'd like it to be. I took that fall for my friend in high school because I thought it was the right thing to do. Sometimes we let our hearts drive our choices. There's no shame or cowardice in that."

Wish I could agree with her, but I know the thoughts going through my head today were wrong, and I don't like that she lied to the cops, even back then. But Raven knows better now, and her calm acceptance has my limbs loosening. We breathe in time—her upper back rounding into my pecs, my abs cradling her spine. My lungs and heart fill with all things Raven. "Thank you."

"For what?"

I press my toes on top of hers. "For understanding. For not judging me."

"Isn't that what couples do? Support each other? Us against the world."

"Us against the world. I like that." Warm water and suds and Raven are a remedy I could live on. I just wish we'd stop fighting about Rose. Wish my family wasn't so damn fragile. "Not sure what I'd do without you."

Sinking lower in the tub, she sighs. "Good thing you don't have to find out."

Twenty

Raven

"This place is a hole." I wrinkle my nose at the dark stains on the floor, each gathering of blotches shaped like constellations. The walls are filled with plug-in beer signs and sports memorabilia yellowed with age. Even worse is the country twang screeching from the jukebox. "Why on earth do the guys hang here?"

Shay rubs the tabletop with her napkin before setting her elbows on it. "It's a bromance thing. They've been coming here since they were teens."

"I think it's cute." Lily plays with the ring on her necklace. "And the bartender was sweet. He told me all about his rose garden. This place has character."

Only Lily could find charm in a rundown dive bar. The boys are at the back, playing pool, sipping beer, and cracking jokes. Three buddies. Our boys. Nico was right—I like being his, knowing he's mine. Every inch of his towering frame at my disposal. And it has been *disposed*. If last night were a statutory holiday, I'd name it:

National Thoroughly Fucked Day.

The ache between my thighs echoes what we shared, after-shocks still tingling. Nico let loose, unleashing all the power he keeps locked up. He pounded into me, and I took it, trading pieces of ourselves. He also offered me his vulnerability. My strong, pow-erful man whispered his fears into my skin. But he didn't tell me he loved me. Not that I confessed, either.

I couldn't risk hearing silence in return.

Pushing the thought away, I focus on my girls. "The website looks great. Can't believe it's live."

Shay sips her beer. "I'm still not sure about the logo, but for the most part, I'm happy with it. We'll add content later."

Our different strengths have facilitated our start-up business. Shay designed our logo and decided on content, Lily used her computer skills to make it happen, and I worked the layout and found stock photos. Expanding on that is my forte. "Once we do our first event, I'll choose shots to include. Maybe have separate pages—some black-and-white, some color. A mix of artistic and candid stuff."

Today I ran my solo photo session like a champ. The client, Ashley, was shy at first, hesitant to show me her flower tattoos and the scars beneath. But I came prepared with the music she liked and talked to her about my ink. Before the hour was up, she hugged me, happy tears threatening to fall. My favorite image is of her beneath a cherry blossom tree. The blooms are long gone, the fall leaves amber and orange and gold. Ashley's bare back is toward me, bark and leaves crisscrossing her inked scars in a tapestry of hope. She'll have that image because of me, just like the future clients of Over the Top Events.

Shay taps her nails on the table, timing each click to the shrill country tunes. "I guess we have to get ourselves a job."

We stare at one another. We hum. We sip our drinks. When a solution doesn't present itself, I say, "Please tell me this won't be a repeat of the carwash."

Shay's mouth drops open, as though I claimed the earth is square. "The carwash was the best."

"If we were auditioning for a slutty mud-wrestling show, maybe."

"I'm with Shay on this one," Lily says. "It was a blast. We should do it again."

Or not. After I set fire to Gord Dwyer's barn, the girls suggested we raise money. I was upset, and my community service wasn't going to help him rebuild his stalls. Unfortunately, the day before our planned carwash, it rained hard enough to strip paint. Shay's brilliant idea: Pour muddy water on the clean cars parked at the Freshco, then set up our carwash at the exit. I got overeager and tipped a bucket of mud over Lily's head. She hurled hers at me. In minutes, the three of us were doubled over, dying of laughter, muddy bubbles squirting from our noses.

A year later I dropped an anonymous envelope of cash in Gord's mailbox, but our joint business venture tanked.

"We'll have to advertise," I say. "In one of the local papers, or in a mailing or flyers."

Shay nods, too slowly. "Sure...but if we hold one awesome gig, it'll snowball. People will talk. But it'll have to be impressive."

"Like male-waiters-wearing-diamond-encrusted-thongs impressive?"

Shay smirks at me. "More like what's-between-Nico's-thighs impressive."

I snort, nearly choking on my beer. She has no idea. I glance at Lily, sure she's blushing ten shades of red, but her gray eyes are downcast, her fingers still fiddling with her necklace. This is quiet, even for her. "Everything okay?"

That's when the blush comes, her cheeks staining pink. "Amazing, actually. And I think I have a solution to our problem." Without another word she reaches behind her neck, unclasps her necklace, and slips the ring from the chain.

Holy freaking shit.

Shay smacks her hand on the table. "Holy freaking shit."

Lily turns the antique ring over. The center pink stone reflects her rosy complexion, the surrounding gray diamonds a match for her eyes, all bound with detailed gold filigree. Sawyer couldn't have a chosen a more perfect ring. She slips it on her finger, and Shay and I barely contain our squeals. Sawyer will lose his mind.

Drinks forgotten, we all lean close. "Why now?" I ask. "What changed?"

Lily fixes the strap of her blue dress, the color similar to the one I wore to Neverland Farms. The virginal look is much better on her. "Nothing changed, really. But I was talking to my mom last night about visiting home, and as much as I miss them, the idea of being away from Sawyer was unbearable, even for a short while. It clicked, I guess. I love him so much it hurts, and I trust him. I'm ready for forever."

Shay sits taller. "Does this mean we get to plan your wedding?"

Beaming, Lily glances at her ring. "It does."

I refrain from jumping over the table to hug her. "It would be an honor."

"It'll be the most beautiful ceremony Vancouver has ever seen,"

Shay adds.

A gut-busting laugh comes from Kolton. Sawyer does some weird kung fu move then cuffs him on the back of the head. I stare daggers at them. "With Sawyer as the groom, beautiful might pose a challenge. He might push for a samurai theme."

Lily's skin blanches. "He wouldn't...would he?"

"He definitely would," Shay says. "But we'll cut the bastard down at the knees. Kidnap him if—" Flustered, she flaps her hands to quiet us. "*They're coming back.*"

I do a *Flashdance* solo, running my feet on the spot under the table, and I nearly kick Lily. "Are you freaking out? Because I'm freaking out, and I don't do freaking out."

My smile is too wide and too toothy to be natural, my heart tripping over itself, a beat that pounds faster at the sight of Nico walking our way. Kolton punches him in the shoulder as they approach, and Nico whacks him back before shooting me a devilish grin. Then his brows slant, as if chastising himself for having fun. Since last night, his moments of levity have been fleeting, but at least they exist. We might have to add more crazy monkey sex to our weekly regimen.

He slides in next to me, the other guys leaning against the sides of our booth. Kolton nods to Lily. "I apologize in advance for Sawyer's Halloween costume."

Lily's hand is on the table, her ring in plain sight. To me it's a pulsating, glowing thing. The boys are clueless. Wary, she studies Kolton. "I thought he ordered that Iron Man one."

"He did, but he just lost a bet."

These guys live to embarrass one another.

Lily's *Oh God* is barely out when Kolton swigs the rest of his beer and plants his glass on the table. "Your boyfriend will be a Power Ranger this year, complete with spandex unitard."

"In pink," Nico adds.

Shay's focus shifts from them to Lily's hand, back and forth, like she's a bobblehead doll ready to burst. I probably don't look much better.

Still unaware he's about to get his wish granted, Sawyer shrugs. "I'll wear it with pride."

"No socks stuffed down the front." This from Nico, who's packing a heat-seeking missile between his legs.

Sawyer scoffs. "Like I need the boost. Any bigger, and the trick-or-treaters will—" He stops mid-sentence. He blinks. Then he blinks again, his gaze glued on Lily's hand. "You put it on," he whispers.

I grab Nico's knee, and Shay fans her face. Lily and Sawyer get lost in each other's eyes, a silent conversation passing between them. Then he says, "Get over here."

Impatient, he reaches over Shay and pulls Lily up until she's standing on her bench and walking on the table and falling into his arms. And *God*, their kiss. Of the three of us, Shay's usually the one for PDA, but Sawyer and Lily are in their own galaxy, their bodies molded as he kisses her senseless. For the second time in two days my eyes burn with happy tears.

"Any longer, and the regulars will pull up stools to watch." The old bartender tips up his cowboy hat, revealing crinkled eyes.

Lily barely manages to unlock her lips from Sawyer's.

Nico angles his body toward mine, planting his massive forearm on the table, caging me. Eyes soft, he brushes my bangs aside like he often does. "Looks like we have a wedding to attend. Will

you be my date, Raven Hunt?" He says my name slow and deliberate, as if tasting the syllables, savoring them. Each letter spirals
through my belly.

Did he make the women before me melt like this? Did he
turn their names into poetry? I frown, unsure why I'm running in
circles again, questioning his feelings. Probably because this is the
guy who's known for falling hard and fast.

And he's still standing.

He looks about to speak again when his phone rings. He slides
out of the booth to take the call. Shay and Kolton are already
headed for the door, a final congratulations shouted as they disappear. I get up and try to hug Lily, but Sawyer won't release her
hand. I settle on kissing her cheek. "I'm so happy for you and can't
wait to plan the wedding."

Sawyer drapes his arm over Lily's shoulder. "What color cape
should I wear?"

She gawks at the question, so I jump in. "There will be no
cape, no weird sound effects, nothing spandex, and definitely no
lightsabers."

"What kind of boring wedding are you planning?"

"An adult wedding."

"For geriatrics."

"Don't test me, Sawyer. You won't win."

"You're no match for my superpowers. Right, babe?"

Lily's answering silence unnerves me. Pulling this wedding together may be more challenging than expected. We can't make our
mark as event planners if the thing is a gong show. "You can always
back out, Lil. It's not too late."

Sawyer pokes a finger at my chest. "One more comment like

that, and you'll be the entertainment, wearing a tutu and dancing with my nieces."

I shudder and give Lily a reassuring squeeze. The man's immaturity will have to be tamed.

As they leave, Nico appears from the back, practically vibrating. If Shay looked ready to burst with Lily's news earlier, Nico is a piñata about to pop. His grin is infectious. "Are you excited because Sawyer threatened to put me in a tutu?"

"No, but I'd love to see that." He inhales deeply and shakes his head as if dazed. "I just got a call."

"I know, big guy. I watched you leave to answer it."

He scrubs a hand down his face. "The impossible might have happened. We could get a confession to clear Josh."

My heart jumps, this much good news difficult to ingest. "Seriously?"

He nods, his blue eyes shining with a thousand emotions. "We've had leads before, so I don't want to get too excited. But I need to head to the station."

"Go, go, go. I'll bus home. Call me as soon as you know anything." I wrap my arms around his wide shoulders and squeeze him as hard as I can.

A deep kiss later, he hurries out, and my levity slides. I desperately want this for him. To see him at peace, his family intact. Erase that brooding frown from his face. But if this confession isn't solid, my mountain of a man could tumble.

My phone buzzes, and I look down to see Rose's name. The sight exacerbates my nerves. I've been stewing over her avoidance of personal subjects, unsure what it will take to bridge the distance between us. Maybe Nico is the key. If I tell her I'm in love and share my fears for his happiness and his silence on the L-O-V-E topic, she might offer a secret of her own. I bite my lip, thoughts of *love* grounding me. No matter his hesitations, I am pathetically moony over him. Memories of my Sexy Beast and how we defiled his couch last night have me grinning again, my newborn sappy side stretching its legs.

Then I read Rose's message.

I'm in trouble. I need your help. I'll call you as soon as I can.

Trouble? What does trouble mean? My breathing grows shallow, unease twisting my gut. Something bad has Rose freaking out, but for the life of me, I can't figure out what. I scan the room, as though the answer will magically appear. Or Nico. I wish he were here to tuck me into his side and tell me not to worry. That this churning in my stomach will cease. But I'm alone with my galloping pulse. I race out the door.

Twenty-one

Nico

I jog into the station and catch Alessi's eye the second I near the desks. I drag him into an empty interview room and shut the door. "What's the deal?"

Neither of us is in our uniform blues, but Alessi has on his date attire. His eyebrows are as slick as his hair, his dress shirt and pointy shoes probably more expensive than my entire wardrobe. Arms folded, he bounces his knee. "Crenshaw knows we've been looking for Jericho, so he nearly blew his load when he realized who he busted."

"Drug dealing?"

"Not even close. Robbery, fraud, and uttering threats. The fuck-nut pulled a fake gun on some lady outside the Pacific Centre. Full under-the-coat job. Forces her to unload cash at the ATM, then bolts. But she saw his car and called it in, and Crenshaw picked him up. For a guy lying low, Jericho needs to work on his game."

"Are they questioning him?"

"Yeah. The victim already identified him in a lineup, and there was a witness. Pretty cut and dry."

The whitewashed walls are stark, the desk and chairs between us as ordinary as furniture gets, but I'd swear a swarm of bees circles my head. "Have they asked him about Josh? If I know that little shit, there's no way he'll cop to the drugs and car."

"Normally I'd agree, but today is your lucky day."

I grip the edge of the chair. "Elaborate."

"Jericho didn't pull this stunt on his own. His kid brother was in the back of the car, playing video games, while big bro was claiming the World's Dumbest Criminal Throne. When Crenshaw pulled them over, he booked them both, now Jericho is ready to shit out a lung. Apparently he has feelings for his mini-me."

I shift on my feet, spinning through the possibilities. This kid is leverage. If we use him as bait, real or implied, it could be the key to getting Josh cleared. Jericho might be willing to offer information in exchange for the kid's freedom. One brother for another.

I flex my hands and work my jaw, too wired to get excited. With my family history, not every cop would back me up. I'd kill to be the one in there instead, staring Jericho down, but I'm not a detective, and I'm way too close to this thing. "Does Crenshaw know? Is he willing to go to bat for me?"

Alessi slicks back the side of his hair, nodding. "He knows the deal. He asked some blunt questions about you, and I answered. He's cool. I just wanted to clear it with you first. But Jericho has to give us something we don't already know about Josh's case, otherwise his confession might not hold up. Something specific that proves he was the man behind the plan."

"Get it done."

He salutes me and takes off. I clasp my hands behind my neck and hang my head, relieved Crenshaw is in my corner, but panic seizes me. If this fails, nothing changes. Josh knows the score. Life stays status quo. But there's that stirring of hope, rumbling through me like thunder. It clogs my throat and jams my shoulders, my entire body a giant knot. I've never wanted anything so badly.

Unable to stand still, I walk a frazzled line, back and forth, the walls too close, my legs too long. This could take forever. If Jericho shuts down, it could be hours before they get him to talk. Fisting my phone, I text Alessi to message me the second he hears something. Hanging around will only drive me insane. Instead I hop in my car and head to the rec center.

* * *

Sanchez is volunteering tonight, and she has a group of four doing basketball drills on one end of the court. Groans and squeaky shoes bounce off the ceiling as she blows her whistle and hollers at the kids to kick it up a notch. She gives me a curt wave. A few girls are in the adjoining room, practicing a dance routine, and Tim is at the far basket, solo, shooting three-pointers.

He hasn't been in trouble since he stole from the Legion, the lesson he learned sticking for now. If he stays focused on what's important, he could thrive. Just like Josh. I wonder sometimes if I'll have the guts to ban Tim from the center, or cut Josh off from the family—his nephews and home—if either boy screws up again.

Hopefully I'll never have to find out.

Tim's next basket bounces off the rim, his baggy shorts practically dragging the floor as he rescues it. When he sees me, he nods. "Looking for a game?"

"Looking for a miracle, but a game sounds good."

He shrugs at that and passes me the ball. Not ideal running the court in jeans and a long-sleeve shirt, but I'll take a sweaty game with Tim over pacing in a windowless room at the station. I find my rhythm. The ball slaps the court as I maneuver around him. He's a quarter my size, barely able to see from under his mop of hair, but he's quick, blocking me at every turn. Until I spin and sink a jump shot.

If Raven were watching, she'd probably wink and say, "Not bad for a big guy." After watching our friends get engaged, I hated leaving her. Wished I could be inside her, whispering her name as my thighs clench, growling it as I explode. Sweat gathers on my back at the thought, and I play harder.

Tim handles the ball well, trying to get some space to shoot over my size, even driving into me to push me back. He'd have better luck moving a wall, but I give him an inch.

Then the shit talking starts.

"Come on, Goliath, show me what you got!"

"Don't wanna destroy you, kid. I gotta answer to your mom."

"Big guys are always cowards."

"Big guys like me eat little guys like you for breakfast."

"Bring it, Makai."

So I do. Sort of. I play the feisty kid, never dominating. But man, do I love his spirit.

Twenty minutes and a shit-ton of sweat later, my phone rings. The vibration in my pocket rocks me like a five-alarm fire bell. I toss Tim the ball and wipe my forehead with the edge of my shirt, gritting my teeth for the news, reminding myself to expect the worst, repeating it over and over. One hand on the door, I say my good-byes and welcome the blast of cool October air. My suctioned shirt sticks like frost on my skin, and I inhale until my lungs hurt, then I pick up my phone.

Josh is in the clear.

My eyes sting; unshed tears clog my throat. I crouch, forearms on my knees, head in my hands, as the largest weight in the history of the world lifts from my shoulders. My breaths come fast and shallow. Eighteen months. It's been eighteen months since Josh got arrested. Eighteen months of frustration and angst and long nights. Of fear and helplessness. Just like that, it goes away—legally.

I push to my feet and dial Alessi. "Give me the details."

"It took a bit, but once he realized his kid brother could face juvie, he started cracking. There might have been a false threat or two, but he came clean."

"Will the confession stick?"

"Like glue. He told Crenshaw about an extra kilo sewn into the backseat. The charges against Josh are history."

"Jesus fuck."

"My thoughts exactly. Now get off the phone and go tell your brother. I need to bounce. Scott Baker got brought in on drug charges earlier."

Scott fucking Baker: informant by day, worthless piece of crap by night. I'd bet my Jacuzzi tub he sold the meth to Jericho. "You know how I feel about him. Let the asshole rot in jail."

"Whatever, bro. He gives us good eyes on the street."

"Alessi," I say before he hangs up, "I owe you one."

"I'll take payment in hair gel."

I chuckle and disconnect. It's almost dark, a few clouds on the horizon, but the evening sky has never looked so clear. I should call Raven, but Josh needs to hear this first, face to face. As I slam my door and turn the ignition, I falter. There's a chance Josh isn't home. Last night's acceptance of his fate could have been temporary. He could have snapped. He could have snuck out, given up, gone back to the crew, hopelessness trumping resignation. He could be screwing up his life just as he gets his free pass.

My truck's engine roars, my panic screaming louder. The ten-minute drive to my mom's feels like fifty. I fly out of the car and through the door, letting it slam behind me. Colin is on the couch, his face stuffed in the pages of a comic book. Jack is coloring some sort of penis-shaped cloud as he kneels over the coffee table.

"Hi, Uncle Nico." Jack scratches his forehead, leaving behind a smear of orange crayon.

Colin waves unenthusiastic fingers.

"Uncle Josh around?"

Both kids point at the ceiling, and I exhale for an eternity. Clinging to hope is scary business. But Josh hasn't given up. Even facing jail, he plans to stand tall with dignity. Maybe I didn't do such a bad job raising him.

"Nico, that you?" Mom pokes her head through the kitchen doorway, Nikki behind her, the two of them knitting. It was Mom's idea, hoping the hypnotic rhythm of the clicking needles would be therapeutic for my sister, keep her mind and hands busy. I think she likes it just fine.

I point upstairs. "Need to speak with Josh. I'll be down in a sec."

A sad smile quivers over her lips, the same one she wore after I broke the news yesterday. When I broke her heart. I doubt there's a pattern she could have stitched to fix the hole Josh's sentencing would have left behind. Now she won't have to.

I take the stairs two at a time and barge into his room. He's hunched over his desk, earphones on, his pencil flying over paper. Creating creatures. Worlds. His checkered comforter is half off the bed, shoes and a backpack thrown about, socks crumpled beside his laundry basket, but it's the sketches taped to the blue walls that floor me. So much *talent*. Anything I draw looks like Jack's penis-cloud, and here's my brother, breathing life into lizards and the undead, the creepy images practically jumping off the wall. I cover my mouth, overwhelmed. He gets to do this. Be this. Find out how far he can push himself. Whatever it costs, I'll help pay his tuition. He will make something of himself.

Sensing me, he looks over his shoulder and knocks his headphones off. My hand is still over my mouth, my eyes probably glassy as hell. He pushes to his feet and approaches, worry slanting his brows. "What is it? What happened?"

Blowing out a breath, I clap my hands on either side of his head and pull his face close. I swallow to steady my voice. "Jericho confessed. You're cleared. There won't be a trial."

He blinks, the clouds in his eyes clearing. "Are you fucking with me?"

"He was picked up on unrelated charges, and they got him to come clean. It's over, Josh. You're free. You can go to school. Plan your future. You can do whatever you want."

His throat bobs, once and again. Then he grabs my shoulders and drops his head to my chest, a sob following, pushing into me so hard I stumble back. I wrap my arms around him and cup his head, my own tears falling into his dark hair.

"Thank God," he says between pants, gripping me tighter. "Thank fucking God." He trembles, choking on his words.

I hug him like his life depends on it. "It's over," I say a few more times, to comfort him. Or maybe me.

It's finally fucking over.

Not sure how long we stay this way, snotty and crying like kids. When he straightens, he wipes his eyes and smears his nose on his sleeve. "You smell like ass."

I peel my sweat-damp shirt from my chest. "Played some ball with a thirteen-year-old while waiting on the verdict. Kid kicked my ass."

Exhaling heavily, he chuckles. "Sounds about right. You can borrow a shirt." He glances at the door then back at me. "Mom know yet?"

"Nope."

We both grin. I tip my head toward the door, and he bangs his shoulder into the frame in his hurry to get downstairs. I glance again at his drawings, his future. It's because of Raven he has these dreams, her guidance leading him to connections and schools. I've never seen him so focused.

I swap my sweaty shirt for a gray sweater. It's a little tight in the arms, but it'll do. Sitting on his bed, I pull out my phone to text Raven. I'm practically vibrating to get my hands on my girl. Celebrate this victory. Watching Lily accept Sawyer's proposal stirred my brimming feelings for Raven, and tonight I can finally let them loose. Tonight I'll tell her how much I love her with my hands, my body, and with my words.

Twenty-two

Raven

I've never hated public transportation more than I have tonight. Both buses on my route were late, and I paced restless circles, mumbling curses as I checked my cell a thousand times. The sight of my apartment has me forcing my speed walk into a jog. I bust through my front door, beeline for Rose's room, and I freeze.

The space has been cleaned out. Her clothes are gone, her shoes gone, not a trace of her left in the space. Except for the magazines I bought for her last week. Those are tossed carelessly on the floor, right beside my fractured heart. I scour the rest of the apartment, but her toiletries are history, along with some groceries she bought with my money. She didn't leave a note. I stare down at my phone, willing it to ring.

When it does buzz, I nearly jump out of my skin. Then I slump. *Nico.* Immediately, I chastise myself for my disappointment, almost smacking my head with my hand. Whatever is going on with Rose, at least she texted. This isn't her disappearing again without a word, and this night should be about Nico, not her drama.

Hoping beyond hope his news is good, I click on his message.

The charges against Josh have been dropped.

My heart gives a kick. So happy for you, I reply. And beyond happy for Josh. Now he can go to school, and Nico can breathe easier, and I get more of the man I love.

I need to spend a bit of time with my family, but I want to be with you tonight. Sleepover at my place?

Without more information, there isn't much I can do about Rose, and sleeping with my Sexy Beast is my favorite pastime. National Thoroughly Fucked Day should really be a long weekend. Sounds perfect.

I'll pick you up in half an hour.

I send a demented smiley face—my sticker signature—and sink onto the couch, mind still spinning a mile a minute. Reading Rose's text again, I try to figure out what kind of mess she could be in. Someone from her past screwing with her? The guy she didn't want to talk about? The room may be silent, but my head is full to bursting with noise. My cell rings, adding to my internal chaos. *Please be Rose. Please be Rose.* At the sight of her name, I scramble to hit Talk.

"Where are you?" I wince at the pitch of my voice.

"I'm sorry I left like that, but I needed to get out."

I rub my sweaty palm on the couch. "Why in such a rush? Did something happen?"

Heavy breathing greets me. It goes on so long I almost ask if she butt dialed me while having sex. "An old friend got arrested. I haven't seen the guy in a while, but he's been tossing out names to the cops, hoping to get a slap on the wrist."

"Names? Like your name? What was he arrested for?"

"Dealing drugs. My name and a few others. But I swear I had nothing to do with it. I was in the wrong place a few times over the years, but I haven't hit that scene in ages. Whatever lies he's spinning, I'm just getting caught in the web. I didn't want to involve you, so I split, but…" She trails off.

Nico's warning not to trust Rose crawls up my neck again, leaving a wake of raised hairs in its path. But she didn't have to go. She did that to spare me whatever drama is following her, not to ensnare me. Protect me like she always has. "But…what? What do you need?"

Dead air drops between us, then, "I need an alibi for last night."

I squint at my jean-clad knees and chew my lip. Last night? The night I spent on Nico's couch and in his tub and under his sheets. "Weren't you at work? Can't they vouch for you?"

Rose mumbles something like *back off* from a distance. A few crackles later, she says, "I only had one delivery to make. I didn't feel like hanging at home alone, so I walked around for a while and didn't get back 'til late. All I need is for you to say we spent the night together."

"But I spent the night with Nico." My words are so quiet, she asks me to repeat them. But I don't. She doesn't know what she's asking. Nico isn't some meathead who won't clue in. If I have to make a statement, it will get back to him. Cops talk. I've been to the station a few times to visit him. People know me. If I lie about that night, he has to lie, too.

"Raven, I wouldn't ask if it wasn't important. They're saying I was selling crack on Hastings. If I had someone else to go to, I would. But I don't. It's just you and me. Always has been." Another pause. "*Please.* I could go to jail."

The word *jail* doubles my anxiety, but that's not the part that has the room spinning. *It's just you and me. Always has been.* She doesn't need to remind me she took the beating of a lifetime to keep me safe. It's in every syllable she speaks. She's cashing in my debt.

Last week we shared a blanket, lying on either end of the couch eating Fruit Loops. She even braided my hair like when we were kids. If she were dealing drugs, I would have seen a sign. If she were smoking or getting high, I would have noticed. Her eyes have been clear, her spirits relatively high, and creeps from the street always cast nets when drowning.

Not only do I have a debt to repay, but she deserves this second chance. "If I do this, you have to promise you're clean. That you're not involved in any way."

This time there's no hesitation. "I swear on your stuffed giraffe. I wasn't anywhere near Hastings last night."

I smile at the sentiment, even though there's nothing amusing about this situation. This is do or die. If I don't trust her now, whatever relationship we've forged will be lost, like my stuffed giraffe, Bongo, whose head I ripped off the week after Rose left. I took my fury out on the innocent pile of fluff until the remnants were unsalvageable. Then I held a funeral in our yard. For him. For Rose. I'm either here for her now, or I bury her in my past, too.

I lose my Unconditional Someone.

I can't. Not when I've just found her. Not when everything in my life is falling into place. She wouldn't ask me if she were guilty, wouldn't put me in that kind of position. She's my sister, my blood. She'd do the same for me. She's *done* way more for me.

"Fine." I blink hard. "I'll do it. Tell the cops you were with me."

But my pulse pounds louder than my Reagan Youth album.

"Thanks, Raven. For everything. I'll be in touch."

She hangs up before I can ask if her move out is permanent or how serious the charges are or what being in the wrong place really means. There's still so much about her present life I don't know. Aside from a glimpse of a man at my apartment, the only friend of hers I've met slammed a door in my face. Based on that fact and her current situation, I'd say my sister needs to rethink her priorities. I gulp, remembering her ex, Russ, saying something similar when I spoke with him. But she came to me for help. She would only do that if she truly wants this fresh start. Now I have to deal with Nico. The man who nearly broke down because he *considered* lying for Josh.

But that was a bigger deal with other cops involved and forced confessions. This is a small lie for my sister's safety. A white lie. A lie so insignificant it's a whisper in the wind. He doesn't even have to say a thing. Just needs to let me make this choice like he made his. Support me like I would have supported him, no matter what path he chose to follow.

If he loves me, he'll want to help.

Pacing, I wring my hands and watch the clock, spinning my thoughts, convincing myself he'll do this thing. The seconds drag. A knock sounds, and my attention snaps to the door.

Please, let him love me.

When I open it, I tilt my head back to see Nico's eyes. Azure waves of beauty. His gaze is bright, happy, his cut cheekbones rounded with a grin. He slips an arm around my waist and leans down but looks over my shoulder. "Rose home?"

Stressed and flustered, I shake my head.

He kisses me as though he's starving, deep and thorough, leaving my head in the stars. He tastes like cotton candy and apple juice and giddiness. "Were you at a Princess Party?"

He chuckles against my lips. "Excuse me?"

"Lily had a Princess Party once. Her parents served juice and cupcakes and heaps of candy. We weren't friends then, but I was a pity invite because I was in her class."

He kisses me. Once. Twice. "All Mom had to celebrate with was apple juice and these awful Jolly Ranchers. Should I brush my teeth?"

"No. I like you sweet." I taste him once more and then lead him inside, each step weighting my spirit until it's dragging along the carpet. A beige mess of nerves. "How is Josh?" I ask. *Delay. Delay.*

"High as a kite, in a good way. Talked nonstop about that creature school. Colin and Jack kept begging him to make them creepy masks, and Mom was a puddle of tears. Wouldn't stop hugging him. Nikki, too. Never thought I'd see this day."

Suppressing my anxiety, I reflect his solace back at him. "Josh deserves this. Your family deserves this. I can't wait to hug him in person."

I try to maintain my smile, but my turmoil wins. I look at my feet, at the scuffed toes of my boots that need polishing. He takes my hands, but I don't glance up. Instead I dig my nails into his palms and bite my lip. If this goes wrong, if he gets angry and turns me down, I could lose Rose.

"You okay?" he asks.

That's a hard no. This will be the biggest test of our relationship. Not Aspen. Not letting him back into my life. This. Here. Right now. An X-ray of his heart. Does he love me enough to bend his rules for my family?

Wishing on a wishing star, I say, "I need your help."

He eases a hand out of my grasp and palms my cheek, lifting my gaze. "Babe, anything. You know I'd do anything." When I nearly sever my lip, he frowns. "Now you're worrying me. What's wrong?"

I swallow what little saliva I have. "Rose is in trouble."

His eyes dart to her room, then settle on me. "Trouble how?"

"I don't know exactly. Some guy was arrested, and he's implicated her and some others to catch a break. But she didn't do what he claims and she freaked and moved out because she didn't want to drag me into it, but she's in a real jam and asked for my help, and she's my sister and I couldn't say no, so I told her I'd"—I suck in a breath, my ramble not helping my cause—"I told her I'd be her alibi."

He works his jaw, shadows casting below his cheekbones from the tension. He drops my hand. "Telling her you'd do it implies it's a lie."

"It isn't the truth." My voice squeaks.

"So it's a lie." His voice hardens with each word.

"But she's innocent."

"How do you know?"

"Because she promised. He's just a crackhead, tossing out random names to save his neck."

An eerie quiet expands between us. "What do you mean crackhead? What has Rose done?"

Shit. Drugs. *Shitshitshit.* So worried about Rose and the alibi, I didn't connect the dots. Didn't stop to think about how this would look to Nico. It's the exact thing he worried about after reading my record. And I promised him all that drama was in my past. I open my mouth and close it. Nothing comes out.

"What is she charged with?" he asks again, accusation edging his tone.

There's no easing this blow. "Selling crack."

Nico's face purples, the veins along his neck pulling tight. He turns away from me and grips the kitchen counter. "*Fuck.*" His ragged breaths sound animal, like a caged bull waiting to buck its rider. He doesn't even look at me. "Nikki and Colin were here. *In this apartment.* They met Rose. *In this apartment.* Do you know how dangerous that is for my sister? How reckless of you?"

Oh God. If Rose is lying, he's right. It would mean I'd broken Nico's trust in the most hurtful way. Put Nikki at risk. But she can't be lying. She just can't. Lying means I am nothing to my sister. "Whatever Rose did in her past, it's just that—the past. She swore she's not involved."

He slams his fist on the counter, then flips around. "Jesus, Raven. She's feeding you crap. I told you not to trust her. Not to let her into your life. I knew she'd pull something on you."

He's made his feelings clear about Rose, but he doesn't know her like I do, and his tone sets my hackles up. "She's my sister. I would know if she were lying. I *owe* her."

"No. You believe her lies *because* she's your sister. You're blind where she's concerned. She's not the same person she was. She's playing you. Using your guilt."

"What about Josh? He could've played you, too. But he deserves his second chance. They're not so different."

He steps so close and speaks so low, it's almost intimidating.

"Don't ever compare Rose to Josh. I raised my brother. I know him. And if you think he could pull one over on me, you don't know me as well as I thought you did."

My blood simmers at his insinuation that Rose is beneath Josh, that her transgressions are somehow worse. But yelling at him won't get the answer I need. I school my face and try again. "I told Rose I'd vouch for her, that I'd tell the cops we were together last night. I just need you to let it slide. Not say anything."

I hold my breath as he squints then frowns and shakes his head. When what I'm asking sinks in, his eyes storm. "Last night?"

I nod and reach a hand toward him. "Please," I whisper. "If I don't do this, I lose her. It's just a statement. No big deal."

He curls his lip at my outstretched hand. "Lying to the cops is no big deal?" When I stay silent, he starts wearing a path on the carpet. "This is my job, Raven. This is what I do. Saying yes to her is as good as spitting in my face."

"It's not like that."

He stops and jabs a finger toward me. "It's exactly like that. And you think I'll go along with it? That I'll turn a blind eye?" His face contorts, disappointment shaping his rage. "I've never been as open with a woman as I have been with you. You've seen me with Tim. With my family. I've told you about my father and how hard I've worked to be a better man, and fuck—I even told you I nearly lied for Josh, how disgusted I've been with myself. You should *know* me, Raven. How could you think I'd say yes?"

"I don't have a choice."

"You always have a choice."

Our voices have dropped, anger bleeding into resignation. There's finality to his tone that saps my energy. *I love you*, I want to say. *Us against the world.* I cross the widening rift and place my hand over his heart. "I know how important justice and integrity are to you, but this is about family. Saving mine is more important to me than telling the truth. If you'd chosen to break the law for Josh, I would have stood by you. Why can't you stand by me?"

He winces, like I've slapped him. His heart thuds harder, so strong and fast I could almost touch it. "Because you're right. This is about family. I don't trust yours. Not by a mile. You put Nikki in jeopardy, and you don't even care."

I want nothing but to taste his candy lips again, but he's blinking like he doesn't recognize me. And God, I'm so tired of his righteousness. Of him being so hard-nosed about everything. "I *do* care about Nikki, but Rose promised she's not involved. You're freaking out over nothing."

He steps back, out of reach, and my arm falls to my side. Gone is his anger, all emotion wiped clean. His focused stare is unnerving. "If I were you, I'd keep the hell away from Rose. The only person she's looking out for is herself. And us"—he motions from my chest to his—"I need some space. A break. The fact that Nikki was here, near Rose, isn't okay. You may believe your sister, but I don't. And asking me to lie for you, even by omission, cuts. Deep. I don't know you as well as I thought, and you definitely don't know me."

Bile rises up my throat. No. Fuck, no. *No, no, no.* That's not how things were supposed to go. I expected him to push back, give me hell. Not walk away because he *needs a break.* We've shared so much—at the motel, last night, and every day in between. He asked for more, and I gave him everything.

He strides toward the door before I find my voice. "You can't leave," I croak. "You promised you wouldn't hurt me again."

I'm grasping at straws, trying to figure out how things spiraled so wrong so fast. Maybe he doesn't love me after all, doesn't feel as strongly as I do. He never did say the words.

He spins and pins me with his gaze. "I'm not the one who did the hurting this time."

Then he leaves.

Gone.

Shock and loss and incredulity consume me. My beige walls have never looked so stark, the tiny room massive with him gone. My hands shake. My breath trembles. Nico's sternness just now was the same as it was with Tim, telling the kid if he blew his shot, he wouldn't be welcome at the rec center. This wasn't him needing a break. This was him ending things.

I walk into my room, put on the loudest, angriest music I have, and let it blare, hoping a neighbor complains. *Send the cops*, I think. *Send back* my *sexy cop*. But his words and tone and posture were unmistakable. He's not returning.

Finally, the tears come.

Twenty-three

Raven

Ignorance is bliss. At least that's how my life was *before*. Aspen was my emotional ground zero. The start of my downfall. The straw that broke this camel's back. I don't even understand that saying. Like how much straw, exactly, can a camel carry? And why straw? Why not something useful like apples or goats or bags of rice? But nope. I'm buried under cereal crops, chaffed and flattened and dried out. *Goddamn Nico.*

The past four weeks my hurt has morphed into anger, the emotion thick enough to chew. This is why I never offered up my heart, why I kept men at a distance. The hollow left in Nico's wake is as deep as the chasm Rose chiseled. She's in jail, refusing to speak with me, and Nico, the man who'd promised he'd be my rock, has shut me out.

As a teacher, I gave my classes the same art history assignment each year: Choose a famous work of art—painting, sculpture, or building—and describe how it's a reflection of you. It was an exercise in expression, pushing the kids to look deeper, see art as more than lines and shades. For the most part, it worked. The only kid who thumbed the experience was Eric Trembley. His memorable one line: Michelangelo's David wishes his package was as big as mine. He did *not* get an A.

If I had to write my five hundred words today, I'd ace the project. I'd be the Leaning Tower of Pisa: crooked, birthed with inadequate foundation, one earthquake from crumbling.

Somehow I've held my ground.

I sift through my closet, looking for my Nikon SLR camera. The thing's a dinosaur, but there's something about working with film that's exciting. Sasha and I have been discussing my portfolio, and if I round out the images with hopeful shots of life after living on the street, she thinks she can get me a show. My photos in a real, live gallery.

Yesterday I returned to the slums I visited with Nico. I shouldn't have gone by myself, but it was my personal fuck you to him. Childish and dangerous, but empowering. I brought blankets and nonperishable food and snapped a pile of photos. I didn't see Joe or his nutsack, but there was a couple huddled together, kissing like they were by a fire at the Ritz, not in a rat-infested slum. Their love cracked my thin veneer, and I choked on a sob. Still, the hours I've poured into photography have been my salvation.

Unable to find my camera, I study my room—for the third time—as though I can conjure it. Then I remember the boxes in the hall closet. My phone buzzes on the way, Shay sending me a text: If we have Sawyer kidnapped by pirates until the wedding, do you think Lily will mind?

As annoying as he's been, he and this wedding are the only

other things keeping me sane, but they don't keep me busy at night. That's when the anger I direct at Nico slips. He hasn't messaged me, and I haven't messaged him. Stubbornness seems to be our motto. Instead I listen to music. I watch TV. But the second I close my eyes, I see him, crave him. If I open my eyes, I picture Rose behind bars. Loneliness is my constant companion.

Sawyer's overinvolvement in the wedding is the perfect distraction.

I reply: If we tell him the secret to magic is found at the North Pole, he'll probably go.

Shay: He's driving me crazy. Now he wants to drop from the ceiling and do the vows suspended. The man will ruin our business.

Not on my watch. The first Sawyer hurdle was when he suggested getting married on those water hovercrafts. Then he wanted to have the wedding two weeks after Lily put on the ring, refusing all rehearsals, claiming it ruins the beauty of the moment. We settled on two months. The nuptials are four weeks away, the December date fast approaching, and he keeps throwing us curve balls.

Say yes to everything and then do the opposite. I grin at my reply.

Genius, Shay writes. Come shopping with me. Lily's organizing flowers, and I told her I'd take care of the centerpieces. We can talk bachelorette party.

My Saturday afternoon plan consists of snapping enough photos to neutralize the images of Nico crowding my brain. Time with Shay might prove more successful, and I can still bring my camera.

We decide where to meet, then I pull out the boxes from my closet—two left from my move. I drag them by the couch and sit on the floor. I leaf through the items: a cubist sculpture I made in high school, my first sketchbook, and the squished fishing hat Shay gave me that reads *Bite Me*. Underneath the memorabilia is my coveted camera and a few rolls of film. I rescue them and frown at a white box below. An unfamiliar white box.

I'm about to pull it out when thumping comes from my front door.

Hope floods me at the sound, irrational in its force. Maybe Nico has changed his mind. Maybe he's stopped being such a pig-headed man and has decided helping me isn't a big deal. That leaving me was the worst decision he's ever made. *Maybe, maybe, maybe.* Scrambling to my feet, I reach the door in six long strides. When I swing it open, my hope sinks like a rock.

The man who was at my apartment a while back is shifting from foot to foot. The one Rose wouldn't talk about. He scratches his neck and sniffles up a storm as his gaze darts over my shoulder. The November air is cool and damp, but a sheen of sweat beads on his upper lip. His bloodshot eyes are visible this time, as is the pallor of his gray skin. Again, his familiarity itches at me. Again, I come up short. But the unease I felt the day I saw him here returns. Tenfold.

"Rose around?" he asks.

The second he opens his mouth, it clicks. No, not clicks. The gravity of awareness crushes me with dread. His gapped teeth poke out, teeth I remember seeing outside the shelter the day I found Rose. The creep with the shaggy hair and hard eyes. Rose was awkward and distant that day, until this man appeared with his wife beater and gapped teeth, and she hugged me, facing him. She sang a different tune after that, a tune that included claiming she didn't know the man.

I shift back and close the door an inch, enough to slam it shut if need be. "Rose isn't here. She doesn't live here anymore."

He winces as if I've slapped him, then he mumbles to himself and pulls his hair so hard I'm surprised he doesn't yank out a chunk. "Maybe she's got some stuff still here, left behind? I don't need much. Just enough to get by tonight." He sinks his hand into the pocket of his hoodie and emerges with a handful of crumpled bills. "Just enough for the night. Just to get by," he repeats.

No. No. *Oh God, no.* Bile collects in my throat, and I almost heave. He's looking for a score. At my apartment. The apartment he visited recently and left clutching a white box like the one I just found. Holy fucking shit. "There's nothing here," I shout and slam the door.

I double lock it and press my forehead to the cold wood as the implication sinks in. Rose took my charity and thanked me and told me how *happy* she was, then she used my place to sell drugs. Am I that naive? Was it all an act? I've met with her lawyer, tried umpteen times to set up meetings to see her, but she's frozen me out. With each rejection, I cursed Nico. If he had only said yes, if he trusted me and believed in my sister, she wouldn't be in jail.

Failing her has saturated me with misplaced guilt.

My shock hardens into red-hot anger, my pulse raging as I stomp over to my living room. I yank out the white box and kick the rest away, then I fall onto the couch and drop the offending package on the coffee table. I fold my arms and stare at it. The thing taunts me like a time bomb, *tick tick ticking* toward a truth

I loathe to face. Praying this isn't what I think it is, but knowing better, I pick it up and slice my black thumbnail under the taped edges. I lift the top.

And whimper. It's a wretched sound, weak and shaky.

Tiny crystals are tucked inside, a neat Ziploc full of treachery. It screams sucker, chump, and a thousand insults I deserve. *Stupid. Stupid. Stupid.* I can't piece through her lies, can't even decipher what was real and what wasn't. She used me. My home. My love. My need to have her in my life. My guilt over the dragonfly brooch.

And I let her.

If I'd remembered why that guy was familiar, I wouldn't be here now. If I'd listened to Nico, I could burrow into his arms instead of wishing I could sever mine. I drop the bag and jump to my feet, practically hyperventilating. God, I wish I could scream at her and tell her this is worse than anything our parents ever did. Worse than the neglect. Worse than the sting of my father's backhand across my cheek. This is betrayal of the soul.

Since I can't scream at her, I simply scream. Once. Loudly. So forceful my throat burns. The aftermath is cathartic. Briefly. Until I remember Nico and everything I messed up. I lost him in defense of a liar. He was right to look at me with disdain. I opened my door to Nikki. Let her into my apartment. That creep could have returned that day. The sight of him could have dragged her back to a time she struggles to forget. Rose could have sensed Nikki's history, read into the dark circles always cradling her eyes. Seen her as an easy mark.

Every concern Nico had about me could have come to life.

I pace a hypnotic rhythm, fisting my hands and flexing my joints. There has to be a way to make this right. Apologize to him, admit I was wrong—oh, so wrong—and get these drugs and any memory of my sister out of this house. Shaking out my hands, I take a deep breath, then a few more.

Panic won't help me. I need a plan.

If Nico's not working today, he'll be at the rec center; Saturday afternoons are always busy there. But I have a key to his apartment. He gave it to me when Rose moved in. An escape, he'd said. *If only I'd listened.* He hasn't asked for it back, and I haven't offered. Hope, maybe? Neither of us ready for this to be the end?

I practically dive into the kitchen and wrench a notepad from the drawer. Taking my time, I write him a letter, each word thick with remorse: what Rose did, my fear of losing the only family I had, how blind I was. How sorry I am. The last part blurs with moisture from my tears. What if he says no? I fold the paper, stuffing my hope and heart in an envelope, then I tape it to the offending box. Instead of canceling on Shay, I text that I'll be late. There's no way I'll survive alone this afternoon.

* * *

The second Shay sees me, her already large eyes pop wide. "Are you okay?"

I must look as horrible as I feel. "Nope. Not okay."

We're in Chinatown, pedestrians brushing against us as they hurry by. The day is as gray as my mood, the stores packed with spices and piled vegetables, exhaust billowing from the traffic. Shay grabs my wrist and drags me into the nearest restaurant, a small place with barbecued ducks hanging by their feet, their reddish-orange skin glistening in the window. We sit at a small table against the wall.

"Is it Rose or Nico?" she asks.

I cradle my purse on my lap, needing something to grip. "Both."

"Tell me everything."

My words tumble out, my fury over Rose and a repeat of what I wrote Nico. Shay and Lily know about our argument and how he left, but I haven't bored them with the details of my wretchedness since. Like after Aspen, it was easier to avoid the subject than dwell. But I'm tired of dealing with things on my own. Shay listens as I unload, wincing as I tell her about the box. How I left it in the middle of Nico's floor with the note, asked him to deal with it. Wrote that I'll testify against my sister. Whatever it takes. I couldn't stomach going to the station myself, instead leaning on him. I had no right, but I panicked.

My last line begged him to give us another chance.

"Wow." Shay's monosyllable sums it up. "I wish I had some words of wisdom about Rose, but I'm so angry with her, I'd like to karate chop her in the neck."

"That makes two of us."

"Your life's like a John Grisham novel."

"I could live without the plot twist, and the predictably evil sister."

And the clueless heroine.

Thoughts of Rose have me wanting to light things on fire, but confusion lingers, too. The past six months, so much of my life has revolved around her. She's part of the reason I moved to Vancouver. I fussed over her in my house, tried to keep her happy, thought she was the source of my newfound peace. Believed I needed her forgiveness.

Truth is, I only needed mine. Needed to accept we were both victims. What she did for me back then will always mean something, even in the face of her duplicity, but in the aftermath of her betrayal, Nico's absence is the greater loss. I was so caught up in being angry I didn't realize losing him was a thousand times worse than losing Rose. And Nico didn't falter. He sensed Rose would hurt me, but he knew I needed to figure it out on my own. He gave me his heart and cared for mine, and I threw it all in his face.

Now, maybe, there's a sliver of hope I can get him back. I hang my purse on my chair and remove my jacket, unburdening my body and mind. I rest my elbows on the table. Shay mirrors my pose—her in a bright blue blouse, me in a black, skull-printed top—nothing but old men slurping noodles around us.

"What do you think Nico will do?" I ask.

She rips her wooden chopsticks apart and rolls them over each other. "I think Nico is in love with you, but he's a man of principle. Asking him to lie for Rose, especially when he sensed she was trouble, will be a tough hurdle for him to jump. But he knows why you did it, and I'd like to think he can move past it."

"It's a lot for him to swallow."

"He's a lot for you to swallow." She winks.

I snort, her dirty humor a needed reprieve. My levity doesn't last long. "He never told me he loved me, and I know how freely he's used those words in the past. Maybe he didn't feel that way."

"But you love him?"

My throat burns. "Yes." Denial will get me nowhere.

"I saw how he looked at you, Rave. It's how Sawyer looks at Lily, how Kolton looks at me. That man is head over heels in love with you."

"I don't know," I say, desperate to believe her.

"I do."

If only she were right. But talking about it and admitting my feelings warm me as much as the green tea our waitress pours. A month ago, I was excited to share my love life with Rose, thinking I needed a sister to confide in. It's silly, really, yearning for something so imagined. I was too young when she left, and I built our relationship up in my mind, never stopping to think about what I had. What I *still* have—Lily and Shay. Our friendships are thicker than blood. They won't always fill the void I feel on holidays and birthdays, but I'm luckier than most.

"What if he can't forgive me?" I ask.

She sips her tea. "He'd be a fool. You put it all on the line for him. Give him time. He'll come around."

But nausea clenches my stomach. I'm sick about the evidence I left at Nico's and the statement I'll no doubt have to give. Time for a topic change. "Let's talk wedding. Did you organize the ceiling lights?"

Her green eyes spark. "Taken care of. Sawyer might not be getting his superhero extravaganza"—she gives me jazz hands—"but we're turning that space into a galaxy. It'll be breathtaking."

"You sure you don't need my help?"

"As long as you have the photos covered the night of, we're good. It's best we stick to our strengths. I don't ever want work messing with our friendship."

"Amen to that."

We'd made a pact that Over the Top Events gets burned to the ground before it affects our bond. I was straight with the girls, telling them I was mainly interested in the photography side of the business. I helped with the initial setup, and we brainstorm ideas together, but I don't plan to give up my apprenticeship, and my street project means the world to me. Not like the girls need my help. Lily works part-time for Sawyer and Kolton, using her free hours to shop for flowers and listen to bands. We've chosen the boys' office as the venue, the massive loft with its tall ceilings and industrial vibe the perfect blank canvas for Shay. Her design skills will turn it into the moon and stars and sun.

We order pho and a side of spring rolls, then I pull out my phone. Nico won't be home yet, but rational doesn't define my present state of being. *He will call. He will call.* He has to call. Unless he freaks that I dropped that bomb on him and bolted, because I was scared to deal with him in person. Like an idiot. The more I think about it, the more insane it seems.

As I place my phone on the table—face up *just in case*—Shay says, "Let's talk bachelorette party. It's in two weeks, and we haven't chosen a bar."

But my mind is on that box on Nico's floor. "I can't believe I left drugs in Nico's apartment. What the fuck was I thinking?"

She plays with her chopsticks instead of answering right away. Then, "I'm not sure what I would've done. Maybe gone to the station instead of his place? But it was a pretty big shock, and it's not like the guy hasn't dealt with drugs. I'm sure he'll understand."

Or he'll have me arrested. "Should I text him? I should text him. What if he brings Nikki over or his nephew and the kid grabs the box and opens it and…oh, God."

Moron must run in my family. I grab my phone and pull up his name, hesitating a beat. But I have to tell him what I've done. I made a bad decision. Several. I'm sorry for what I asked of you. For not listening to you. Rose lied. I found drugs in my apartment and kind of freaked and left them in yours with a note. Not sure why. I'm sorry.

I hit Send, but as soon as I do, a million other things I should have written run through my mind. I write them anyway—a barrage of texts, one after another. Our waitress brings us our food, but I don't look up.

I've missed you so much.

I should never have asked you to lie.

I'm sick that Nikki was in my place.

It turns out I don't need Rose. I just need you.

I can't believe I left drugs in your apartment.

The last one sums up my stupidity.

Shay's halfway through her soup, but I can't touch mine. "He's going to hate me."

She puts down her spoon, swirls a spring roll in plum sauce, and bites off the end. Once she swallows, she says, "Have you told him the truth?"

I play with the noodles in my bowl. "Yeah."

"Then he can't hate you. Like I said, give him time."

My phone buzzes then, startling us both. We eye the thing like it's a transformer about to attack. She kicks my foot. "Check it."

Sucking in a large breath, I tap my phone.

I'm taking the box to the station. Detective Crenshaw will meet you there. You'll have to make a statement.

My heart fizzles faster than our neighbor's sizzling beef. He didn't mention the note or my texts. No acknowledgment of my apology or the "break" we're on. With the high bar he's set for those in his life, I shouldn't be surprised.

"Bad news?" Shay's brows are creased, her wild hair framing her concern.

"I have to make a statement, but it doesn't sound like he'll be there. It doesn't sound like he'll forgive me."

She reaches over and grasps my hand. "I'm sorry, but I don't believe this is the end." When I don't answer, she says, "We should get the check. I'll come with."

I mumble thanks as I fish for my wallet, my choices and mistakes so clear they're startling. Nico is everything I want. It took an asshole of a sister and a pile of drugs to figure it out, but I'm ready to put him first. He's a proud man. A man of principle, like Shay said. My request hurt him. Putting Nikki near a bad scene scared him. The fact that I shunned his advice about Rose pushed him away. But he kept the note I wrote in Aspen, rereading it for months afterward. Surely he'll do the same now. He'll reread my letter, and in a day or two or three, he'll call me. He'll accept my apology.

But he doesn't.

Twenty-four

Nico

I don't mind hitting clubs. The dance tunes can be fun, the flirty crowd energetic, but the last thing I feel like doing tonight—or have felt like doing any night the past six weeks—is socializing. Unfortunately, Sawyer's bachelor party isn't something I can miss.

We're in an area at the side, lounging on a group of couches. Everything in this place is white. White walls and furniture, white floor, waitstaff all dressed in white. The second I walked in, I imagined Raven in here, her black ink and clothes and hair shocking against the neutral backdrop. I blinked the image away and ordered a beer.

Some of Sawyer's employees are here, a handful of friends, all of them several drinks in. Laughs and taunts are tossed as Sawyer soaks up the attention. All I can manage is to hang on the periphery and try to look happy.

I should be happy.

My family has never been so solid. Josh has a job, earning money to help pay for school. He should hear any day about his application, but I have no doubt he'll get in. Nikki is sleeping better, Colin even smiling when I walk in the door. Mom buzzes around the place, doting on everyone. I'm the only downer of the group. They shoot me sidelong glances, never prying. Except Josh. The one time he asked about Raven, I snapped so fast, he held up his hands saying, "Sorry, man. I'm here when you're ready to talk."

I'm nothing but a moody troll.

"If you nurse that beer any longer, I'll attach a nipple to the top." Sawyer grins down at me, Kolton behind him. They kick a guy off the couch kitty-corner to mine and take a seat.

Here it comes.

Kolton swirls his bourbon. "We've let you wallow long enough. It's time you tell us what happened."

"And if I don't want to talk about it?"

Sawyer shrugs. "We call Alessi and stick you in an interview room and force you to watch thirty-six hours of *Dora the Explorer*."

I rub my eyes. "You spend too much time with your nieces." But I once threatened Sawyer with something similar. When he screwed things up with Lily, he dropped down a rabbit hole and pushed us away. It took a night out at a club like this to set him straight, along with a threat to book him at the station. The difference between us is he had to find a way to apologize and make up for the shitty things he'd done. Raven's apologized plenty, but I haven't been able to get my head straight.

The boys sip their drinks. They wait me out. The bass pounds in my chest, chasing my angst. Tired of pretending I'm okay, I finish the last of my beer and set it on the white coffee table. "Aside from the fact that I'd warned Raven about her sister, she invited

Nikki over to her place. An apartment with drugs and a drug dealer. And when Raven's sister got arrested, Raven planned to be her false alibi and asked me to go along with it."

Kolton raises his voice over the music. "Sorry, man. That's heavy."

I barely glance at him. "So maybe you guys can lay the fuck off."

He raises a hand in surrender. "Mind my hair when you go for the jugular."

Neck tense, I sigh at my tone. Hostility seems to be all I can manage these days. I count to five before I go on. "Whatever I thought we had went out the window that day. I can't plan a future with someone who thinks that little of me. Who would put my family at risk."

Sawyer leans his elbows on his knees. "Did she know her sister was dealing?"

"No."

"Did she apologize?"

"Yes."

"Then how can you blame her for looking out for *her* family? I bet you would've offered Josh an alibi if things had been that simple."

A fresh wave of anger has me seeing red. "You want to finish your drink before or after I break your face?"

"Dude…I'm getting married in two weeks. Don't even joke about the face." He runs a hand through his hair, all smiles, but I hiss out a breath, unsure why I'm shaking.

I've burned over my argument with Raven a thousand times. Tried to figure out why my rage has felt so wild. Uncontained. I'm furious her bad judgment had Nikki somewhere she could buy drugs. Pissed Raven thought I'd support her lie. I keep spinning back to her record as a teen, wondering if she'll always choose to shirk the law. But this, right now, is something different. This fury is aimed at my own scowling face. Because Sawyer is right: I would have crossed that line for Josh. If it had been a simpler lie, I would have done it. Knew it that night with Raven. Hated myself for it. Didn't want to admit it.

Could my inability to contact her the past month be that base? That childish?

I replay the argument in my mind, the moment she told me if the situation was reversed she would have supported me. That's when I felt sick. Outrage at myself had flared. Embarrassment rose. I realized I would have broken the law for my brother and she was there, an easy target. I unleashed my guilt on her. What kind of man does that make me?

Kolton leans back and crunches on an ice cube. "I hate to say this, but I agree with Captain Immature. I know what toeing the line means to you, how hard you've worked at the rec center and your job and with your family. It doesn't mean you're infallible. And you certainly won't meet a woman who is. When the dust settled, you should've talked it out with her. Tried to understand what drove her actions."

Except I'm an asshole with an attitude. "If I'd opened my mouth, told her how pissed I was, I would've said mean shit that can't be taken back. It was better to say nothing."

Every time I've thought about calling Raven, my temper has flared. Like it did the day I laced into Josh for stealing from our mother. I still haven't forgiven myself for the nasty things I said to him, insults that sent him running to the streets. As mad as I've been, I'd never forgive myself if I hurt Raven that way. I still could have dealt with things better.

"The girls are at a bar across the street," Kolton says. "Why not start over tonight?"

My eyes flit to the entrance, as though I can see Raven through the walls. She could be there, laughing and flirting with some guy. The possibility guts me. I may have been confused and angry lately, but I've thought about her every morning and every night and endless hours in between. I've read her note a thousand times, scrolled through every one of her texts. I've stroked myself to thoughts of her, fast and rough, and it levels me each time. I can't get over her, but facing her, forgiving her, means forgiving myself. I'm more fucked up than Josh ever was.

Instead of answering Kolton, I offer to get the next round.

I suck back my whiskey and order another. Then another. Kolton side-eyes me but doesn't comment. The buzz hits fast. That's what you get when you rarely drink the hard stuff. The music and banter and people blur, my smile no longer forced. At some point, Sawyer gestures to me. "A hundred bucks says King Kong drives his first porcelain bus."

I'm not sure who replies, but I sway on my feet, happy to feel light. My heart has been so saturated, so soaked with barbed thoughts that I've coasted through the days, no idea how to wring it out without getting snagged. My workouts and runs have done nothing to ease my turmoil, but maybe there's something to this alcohol thing.

An hour later, or possibly two, we're on the street, the cold air like a shot of adrenaline. Sawyer grabs my shoulders—to steady himself, or maybe me. He blinks, his pupils blowing wide and shrinking as he focuses. "You're an idiot."

I laugh. After drink two, everything he's said has been hilarious.

"No." He shakes his head, a few too many times to be normal. "Like a real idiot. When I hurt Lily, I did it because I didn't know who I was. I was worried I'd turn out like my family and fuck her over, but you"—he slaps a hand on my cheek—"you're the opposite. You know exactly who you are, but you expect too much of others. Raven loves you, bro. She's been a mess. At least as messy as she gets. Don't lose her because she hurt your pride or whatever. If you expect everyone to be perfect, you'll have one hell of a lonely life." He squishes my face and pats my cheek then stumbles past me.

My boots mold to the cement. It could be the alcohol or wishing Raven would walk out the door across the street, but Sawyer makes more sense than usual. It brings Raven's words after Tim and the Legion rushing back. She said something like that. Scoffed at the hard line I'd taken with the kid. Told me I was setting myself up for a life of disappointment. It's exactly what I've done. Not forgiving Raven her mistakes isn't choosing right over wrong. It's cowardice. Expecting perfection from myself has left me unable to cope with the choices I almost made to free Josh, and I didn't even fucking make them.

I've set myself up for failure.

I really am an idiot. Or drunk. Or both. Trying to rationalize why I've acted as I have is like searching murky waters. The boys shout beside me, hollering some nonsense. I look up, and my knees nearly give out. The girls are dancing across the street, Raven in a sandwich between Lily and Shay. I haven't seen her in six weeks, and I lilt forward, her beauty magnetic. Or the whiskey is unsteady in my veins.

She's in a mini skirt and high boots, a short leather jacket brushing her hips. Fuck, do I want to go over there and hoist her legs around my waist and kiss a thousand apologies into her mouth, but I can't get my feet to move or my thoughts to work or my equilibrium to balance. Something changes, and she squeezes out from her girl sandwich as she pulls her phone from her pocket. Her face falls at whatever she reads, then she looks up.

At me.

I'm sorry, I want to holler. So damn sorry and confused and mad at her and myself, wishing I'd talked this out with her instead of shutting down, like I do. Always festering. Wish I'd found a way to curb my frustration and used the right, *calm* words to explain how her actions messed me up. Instead I sent her to the station alone to deal with Rose. She made a statement and closed the door on her sister's case and their relationship without me by her side. I should have been there for her. Forgiven her. But I couldn't see past my bruised ego and stringent ways.

Such an idiot.

I hold her black gaze as long as I can, but staying on this side of the street is an exercise in determination, and I can't face her like this, sloppy drunk and filled with shame. I drop my head and find a cab. Tomorrow, in the light of day, my mind clearer, I'll make sense of the decisions I've made. I'll pull my head out of my ass and find a way to make things right.

Twenty-five

Raven

Nico can't even look at me. Our gazes collide for a minute, my spirit soars, and then he takes off and slides into a cab. I don't know what's worse, the dejection on his face or the text I just got. Swallowing, I reread Josh's words:

I know something happened with you and Nico. He won't talk to me about it, but I've never seen him so rough. Not sure you want to hear from me, but I got into the film school for their makeup program. Found out today. So, thank you. Wish I could say it in person.

I wish I could congratulate him. The laughter from our bachelorette party fades, any remaining joy seeping out of me like tar. Cold air slaps my face. My bare thighs tremble. Sawyer and Kolton cross the street and hug warmth into their girls, but I can't even muster a hello.

As hard as my initial fight with Nico was, I've fallen into a pit of despair since I dropped that box in his apartment. Not because I signed a statement, sentencing my sister. Not because of her betrayal or the loss of her in my life. I finally understand how much I love the man I hurt, and as painful as this time has been, I want him back.

Lily was worried I'd revert to my old patterns, sleeping with men in a string of meaningless flings. But I'm done pretending. I want someone in my life. I miss trading stupid questions and talking photography and lounging on the couch. I miss sleeping in Nico's big, sturdy arms. I'm ready for something real. If I can't have that with him, I'll find it with someone else. Unfortunately finding a man as good and sweet as my Sexy Beast will be as easy as turning water into wine.

I stare at my phone, oblivious to the Saturday night partiers walking the street. Pride at Josh's accomplishment has me itching to type a reply, but what do I say? Congratulations, and yeah, I fucked up so badly your brother can't even look at me.

"Penny for your thoughts." Kolton nudges my elbow, his brown eyes soft with compassion.

"Seems cheap, and we don't have pennies anymore." My heavy thoughts weigh more than the crown jewels.

The glow from a streetlight cuts across his handsome face. His hair is loose to his shoulders, his cheeks red from the cold. He tucks his hands in his front pockets. "Shouldn't you be celebrating?"

We glance at Sawyer, Lily, and Shay as they break into a drunken version of "Like a Virgin," impromptu busking that has passersby snickering. I'd drop money in a hat if they'd shut up. "My Madonna is rusty. I'm more of a Death Metal girl." He doesn't smile. He waits out my sarcasm as I run my thumb over my phone. Each swipe weakens my defenses. "Josh sent me a message. He got into the creature design program I told him about."

"Isn't that a good thing?"

"Yeah. Awesome. But he also mentioned Nico's been rough, and the way Nico looked at me just now…it's like he can't stand the sight of me." When all I want to do is look and look and *look*.

Kolton glances across the street, as though Nico's hulking shadow still lingers. "It's not my place to say anything, but…"

His pause drags so long I almost wave a hand in front of his face, until I realize the secret he's about to spill. Nico probably fled because he couldn't face me, couldn't tell me he's moved on. That he's dating. The two cosmopolitans I drank churn, and I wrap my arms over my stomach. Gastrointestinal Karma. I should run, spin around, and escape down the street, not let him drop the bomb.

Instead I ask, "Is he seeing someone?"

What if he's seeing someone?

Two girls dart off the sidewalk, and a driver leans on his horn. When Kolton finally says, "No," I nearly crumble to the ground. I am such a mess over this man.

"Then what?" I wish I didn't sound so desperate.

"He's not moving on, Raven. He's just stuck. Since Josh's arrest, Nico's had tunnel vision. He holds people, including himself, to impossible standards." He sighs. "All I know is you guys don't stand a chance if you don't talk, and he's a stubborn mule. I think you should make the move. Force him to hash things out. He misses you."

Hearing he hasn't gotten over me but is too hurt to call has the cracks in my heart widening. Nico is a giant of a man, his size made up of decency and virtue and *righteousness*.

And I asked him to lie for a drug dealer.

I can't decide if I want to throw up the drinks I had or go back in and order more. "I don't know how to make this right." The cold air snaps against my cheeks, and I wish it were colder. Freezing. A bout of frostbite might deaden this deep ache.

Shay weaves our way and loops her arm around Kolton's waist. "This is the best night ever. Isn't this just the best, *best* night ever?"

She's adorable when she drinks, but that's not the word I'd choose. *Wretched* sounds more accurate. Or just plain sucky. Sawyer and Lily holler at us as they fall into a cab, as happy as I've ever seen them. And as wasted. Shay's forehead slumps into Kolton's chest, and he kisses the top of her hair. Envy stings me. I had that in my life, too, and I let it go.

Kolton hugs her tighter. "I should get you home." Then to me, "Fight for him."

I nod, sobering up by the second. "I'm a regular Rocky Balboa."

He winks at me. "You wanna share a cab?"

I shake my head, needing time on my own. As I head for the bus, he calls, "Fight for him!" again.

Unable to turn, I raise a hand in salute, but I'm in quicksand, stuck and sinking. It's kind of hard to show the man I love that I believe in him and understand what makes him tick when I've proven the opposite. That's like claiming I love the color pink.

Buses run less frequently at night, especially this late. Loitering feels cathartic, though. I walk circles around the bus shelter, scuffing my boots along the pavement, wishing I had my iPod to drown my thoughts. My misery. A man and his dog are a block away, huddled against a wall. I walk over, drawn by the image. The man's hair is thick and matted, his beard in need of a trim. Under all that grime and sorrow, I bet he's not much older than me.

I gesture to his dog. "Can I pet her?"

He startles, as though he hasn't heard a voice in ages. His smile reveals straight, white teeth. "Sure. Her name is Spirit."

Of course it is—the name Nico used at Neverland Farms. The pup grins up at me, her black-and-tan fur soft, maybe a cross between a shepherd and a collie. "She's sweet. How old?"

He rubs his nose against hers, both equally fond of each other. "Not sure. I found her roaming the beach and tried to find her owner, but none of the shelters or vets knew anything. I've had her for six months."

He doesn't have a home, but he's given her one. "She seems to like you."

"Man's best friend," he confirms, but the sorrow in his voice pains me.

Many vagrants reek of booze a mile away, but not this guy. This man with the clean teeth. I want to ask him a million questions, find out how he ended up here, what went wrong in his life, but it's not my place to pry. Josh lived like this once, too, calling the street home, no roof over his head. Nico looked haunted when he told me about it, sharing the darkest sides of himself. Now Josh is going to college.

Needing to do something, anything, I clear my throat. "Can I buy you guys a meal?"

Moisture glazes his eyes. "That would be nice."

As I sink my hand into Spirit's fur again, an idea sparks. Crazy, maybe…but maybe not. Josh could be the key to my photographic essay on street life. Sasha said if I pull it together with hope, she thinks she can get me a show. Josh's journey screams *hope*. He's turned his life around, banished the boy he was. If he agrees, I could shoot him at his future school and *show* what he's made of himself. I could show Nico I see his family clearly. That they have thrived because of him. That I want to support their growth and would never jeopardize their progress intentionally. Fight for the man I love.

It's either that or reunite our Painted Hearts band and write a string of power ballads.

Pumped, I hurry into a nearby diner and buy several burgers for the man and his dog to share. Then I hunker down at the bus shelter to blast out a couple of e-mails. To Sasha. To Josh. He replies instantly, thrilled to help me out. We make a plan to meet, and I ask him to keep quiet.

Translation: *Don't tell the big guy I'm fighting for him.*

Poker players don't lead with their hands open. They bluff once or twice, ensuring unpredictability, then they attack. This is my chance to go all in, all chips on the table, win big or fold. For Nico, I'll risk everything.

But he doesn't behave as expected.

The next morning I wake to two messages. Sasha's reply is more than I could have hoped for. She contacted a friend, whose artist pulled out of a show, and he needs a replacement. In two weeks. The night of the wedding. I choke on my toast, unsure fourteen days is long enough to pull this together, but I'll take what I can get. It's a small gallery in the Gaslight District, and the show will only run for a few weeks, but it will be my work and my story and, hopefully, my chance to prove my love to Nico.

The second message is from him. I haven't seen his name light up my phone in six weeks. My belly dips. It plummets. Instead of reading what he wrote, I pace. My plan is too perfect for him to shut me down now. To realize how wrong I was and not have a chance to make things up to him would be the worst kind of evil. The devil's sense of humor.

I drink a cup of coffee and debate another, but nothing will change whatever he sent. A deep breath later, I pull up his message.

Can we get together to talk?

Yes.

Yes.

Yes, yes, yes.

I erase the words I write, my fingers working faster than my head. We can't talk yet. Not like this. Not until I've mounted my show and offered him my best apology. His message might be nothing. It might be him needing closure, not him opening a door. Still, I have to try.

I'm busy with work and the wedding. Can it wait until after? I reread my words and add, But I'd really like to talk. Then I hit Send.

I chew my nail until he responds.

Sure.

His curt reply is hard to swallow, but I try not to focus on the one, lonely, joy-sucking syllable. The big guy messaged me. That has to mean something. Either way I have two weeks to take Josh's photos and print my film and frame my shots. Not to mention making sure everything is organized for Lily's big night. But I can do this. Putting on this show could have the power to make a difference. People who see it might stop and acknowledge the people they pass on the street, even buy them a warm meal or drop off a blanket. Offer them some humanity. If I can get a few school groups through, it could be more effective; often it's kids who teach their parents how to see.

Whatever happens with Nico, I'll still have this, and I'll have Shay and Lily. But pretending I'm not hanging a whole lot of hope on that man is foolishness. This is me, laying my heart on a silver platter, his to accept or toss.

Twenty-six

Nico

I've never been so nervous for a wedding, and it's not even mine. My runs and workouts have done nothing to settle the tension in my bones, and I can't sit still. It's too early to head to the ceremony, but I'd rather drive around in my truck than look at the couch I took Raven on or the tub she slipped into or the sheets we slid against. This is how it's been since the bachelor party. Two weeks of seeing her presence everywhere.

Waking up the next morning taught me two things. Drinking that much whiskey is worse than downing lighter fluid. I didn't puke, but my room spun and my gut ached and I passed out cold. The other lesson, the harder one, is that my revelation about Raven was spot on: I pushed her away because my high standards were the only thing keeping me afloat while my family nearly drowned. Fear is what it was. Pure and simple. Raven was wrong to ask me to lie, but I was wrong to believe one false step had meant she'd failed, or one *more* would mean Josh had failed. Nikki had failed. Tim had failed. *I* had failed.

I'm finally ready to talk it out with her, no longer worried my temper will flare. Only problem is, she won't see me.

Too busy with work and the wedding, she put me off the past two weeks. An excuse? A way to create distance? She might have texted that she wanted to talk, but that could have been to seek closure, move on. Put an end to whatever is still between us. And maybe this is the end. Maybe too much has happened. But if we don't hash things out, we'll never know.

I tuck my handkerchief into my suit pocket, knowing it matches Raven's dress—midnight blue, according to Lily. Lily dropped the handkerchief off and told me I'd be walking Raven down the aisle, both of us standing up for our friends as they say their vows. The news sent my heart slamming into my ribs, where it's been lodged ever since. To see her and touch her and walk next to her might be more than I can take.

Blowing out a breath, I check the mirror one last time. My palms are sweaty, my tux stifling. My shoes feel too tight. I grab my keys and head for the door, and my phone buzzes. My phone displaying Raven's name. When I remember how to inhale, I open her message:

I need a favor. I left my purse at a gallery. I'm with the girls and didn't know who else to call. Can you get it for me on your way?

I deflate at her businesslike tone. She doesn't mention the talk we're supposed to have, or the fact that we've had no contact in two months and we'll be walking down the aisle together. No inkling she's as torn up over this as I am. Sawyer said she's been struggling, but he was wasted and I was three sheets to the wind, and the flatness in her text proves otherwise.

Sure, I type. One word. My standard reply. Not much else to say these days.

She sends me the address and a simple Thanks.

I roll down the window as I drive, the December air like a cold beer on a hot day. I drink it in. Christmas is ten days away, and Raven's present is still burning a hole in my dresser. Knowing how she'd love to skydive, I bought her a pass and haven't been able to ask for a refund. Like I couldn't ask her to return my apartment key. As though, somehow, even before I cleared the mess crowding my head, I knew I didn't want our relationship to end.

It takes a few passes before I find a parking spot a couple blocks away from the gallery. Walking in the Gaslight District in a tux isn't my idea of fun; I'm more conspicuous than in my uniform blues. People stare, two women taking an eyeful. I'd smile back if I had the energy. The gallery is small, the sign outside written in old school lettering. I duck inside, nod to a man at a back desk, and walk toward him with blinders on, barely noting the dark lighting or what's on the walls. Not caring much.

Get her purse. Get to the party. Force Raven to talk things out.

The man at the desk stands as I approach. He has a hipster vibe with his tight pants and checkered shirt, his red hair parted to the side. His eyes—bluer than mine—dance over my suit. "*You* must be Nico."

I nod. "Raven said she left her purse."

He grins, like he knows something I don't. "I see why she's gone to so much trouble." Gaze on my crotch, he licks his lips.

His blatant perusal would be amusing, but I can't focus on anything except his words. "What do you mean trouble?"

Instead of answering me, he pulls an envelope from his desk drawer and holds it out. "You'll see."

If my tux felt stifling before, it's downright suffocating now. It's not Raven's style to be so cryptic. Cagey, yes. Sarcastic, fuck yeah. But not mysterious. Studying the envelope, I rub the back of my neck, my movements jerky.

When I don't grab his offering, he says, "She's put a lot of work into this, and she's a tad intimidating. If nothing else, take it for me. I don't want her chewing me out."

With a tight smile, I grab the envelope and pull out a folded piece of paper. Two words are written on it:

I'm sorry.

She's said them a number of times since I walked out her door, but they steamroll me tonight, flatten my chest. *I'm so fucking sorry, too.* But why isn't she here to say her apology? To listen to mine. To finally get it all out in the open. I look up at the gallery owner, and he lays his hand over his heart. "She said you were a sensitive one."

I don't know how my face looks. I only know how I feel: desperate, dazed, lovesick.

He gestures to the room. "This is her show. She wanted you to see it."

My attention snaps to the walls. They come to life, the space transforming as I take it in. Enlarged photographs hang on the exposed brick, the light dimmer than I'd expect for a gallery. The way a spotlight hits each piece, I can tell it's on purpose, turning me into a voyeur, like the images captured are private.

I return to the entrance and start at the beginning. The first few are familiar. Too familiar. Betty Leroux is in one. It was the day we were at the slums, and she was ranting about her blanket. Her hands are tossed in the air, indignation on her lined face. The next one thickens my throat. Two sets of feet face each other, my boots and Betty's ripped sneakers. The contrast is moving, the lighting making it more powerful. They aren't framed, the images pressed between glass, and after a couple more, I realize small sections have been painted. It wasn't noticeable at first, but as I return to the start, I see Raven's hand in the work. The gray blends with the black-and-white tones, but more blues tint the sections as the images progress.

A little girl's sock. The pillow under a vagrant's head. The flames in a fire.

Still early for tonight's wedding, I take my time. I try to see the photos through Raven's eyes. Although a few scenes are familiar, most aren't. She's been busy, snapping frames when not at work. As I study them, a man and a woman walk in and whisper to each other, taking in her show. The words *strong* and *dynamic* and *talented* drift toward me. Pride fills me like helium.

Halfway through, the air hisses out.

The next image doesn't look like Raven's. The lines aren't as sharp, the photo grainy, like the focus is off, but I'd recognize the face staring at me anywhere. *Josh.* He's on a ratty mattress, crumbling concrete at his back, bottles and garbage littered around his feet. The can of beans in his hand is painted gray-blue, but it's his eyes that hit me: Flat. Dead. No laughter or light. Even knowing how solid he is now, it flays me. Scratches at memories I'd rather let lie. The card at the side of the photograph credits Jericho for taking the picture.

For ruining my brother's life, it should say.

My pulse thunders. Why would she put this here? Why show the world just how far my brother fell? And somehow she's been in contact with Josh.

Shaken, I move through the space. The other couple is long gone, a group of three arriving. Raven's small painted areas get brighter as I near the end, and so do the photos. Hope brightens a child's face as she accepts a gift, the shelter she's living in blurred but noticeable. The blue parcel in her hand pops against the gray tones. In the next, a First Nations man scrubs graffiti from a wall, his few teeth visible in his beaming smile. The word *fallen*, scrawled in blue, is about to be scoured away.

The last one winds me. Knocks the air clean out of my chest. I stand for a good five minutes and stare. This is Raven's apology, the words I never let her say in person.

A portrait of Josh beams at me, his blue eyes—my eyes—painted with so much detail they glow. He's crowded by masks and creature designs, his college acceptance held in his hand. This is why she needed the other photo: To show someone rise, you have to show them fall. Some of my anger the past months stemmed from the fact that I didn't think she understood me. But this photo is everything. It's the work I put into Josh. It's my drive to be better. It's my family and me seen through her eyes. It's beautiful.

A man steps beside me and studies the piece. "They're raw, but really give you a sense of the city. Makes me want to visit a shelter."

Makes me want to tear across town and whisk Raven away to a deserted island. "She's talented," I say. And too far away from me. This isn't her needing distance and closure. This is her hooking my heart and reeling me in.

"Did she do good?" the hipster guy calls as I stride for the door. I pause and turn. "Knocked me straight."

"*That*, sweetheart, is a shame." He blows me a kiss.

Chuckling, I hurry to my car. Hank Williams croons from the stereo, singing about being young and foolish and losing his woman's trust. Hank sure knew how to write. By the time I get to the Moondog office, I'm buzzing. I ride the elevator to the top, the walls barely containing me and the ten thousand things I need to say to Raven. The light flicks from number to number as I climb, my restless energy rising with it. We still need to talk things out, but us not ending up together is no longer an option. That woman is mine.

When the doors slide open, I step off, expecting the usual loft space I visit. Normally it's sparse, half the high-ceilinged room filled with sample ski clothing and jackets, the other taken up with desks.

But this isn't an office; it's a galaxy.

Panels line the walls, floor to ceiling, painted like the night sky. Or maybe wallpapered. The purples, blues, and blacks flow onto the tables, the ceiling covered in something similar. Moving lights dot the ceiling with stars, more candles than I've ever seen filling the space, some as tall as a man, all encased in glass. The flowers are wilder than the ones inked on Raven's chest. It's sexy and otherworldly, and I wish she were on my arm to enjoy it.

I scan the room, ready to bulldoze the place until I find her, but Sawyer's mother blocks my way. "Thank God you're here."

Evelyn West is in a black, sparkly dress, her dark hair pinned on her head. She's all class, as usual. "Did you think I'd bail?"

"Don't be silly. But Sawyer needs your help."

"Has he forgotten how to tie his tie?" My gaze slips past her, scanning, searching. What sounds like a harp plays from somewhere, each strum flowing over the guests. None of them Raven.

She fusses with the handkerchief in my pocket. "If I know my boy, his nerves are getting the best of him. The men's area is sectioned off with the kitchen, and I've been banned. Would you mind checking on him?"

I mind not searching for Raven, but I can't say no to the woman who'd let us boys tear up her lawn with our football games and raid her always-stocked fridge. "Sure. And trust me, nothing will stop him from marrying Lily." Except I've seen Sawyer at his lowest. There's a good chance he's freaking out.

She pats my arm as I push through the crowd to find the groom. I find Kolton and his son instead. "Hey, little man."

Jackson's eyes light up, and he tries to tackle me. At eight years old, four-foot-nothing, and thin as a reed, he doesn't make a dent, but I stumble back. "When did you get so strong?"

"I went to karate with Daddy this week and learned how to stand and do a snap kick and block a punch, and I think my muscles got really big." He steps back, pushes his glasses up his nose, and shows me his kick.

This damn kid. Moving in with him and Kolton was one of the hardest and best experiences of my life. Losing his wife shook Kolton so thoroughly I'd be the one to wake up and feed Jackson, and I'd fall asleep with him on my chest. He peed on me. His diapers were a horror show. But when those brown eyes locked on mine, I was a goner.

I ruffle his hair. "I wouldn't mess with you."

Kolton fixes the little man's suit jacket and squats in front of him. "Can you run this over to Shay?" He holds out a note.

Nodding, Jackson grabs the paper and jogs out.

"You passing notes to your girlfriend?" I ask.

Kolton straightens, a smirk in place. "I write her notes all the time."

"You sure you want your kid accidentally reading it?"

"I kept this one PG and left out the dick pic."

Such a comedian. "Probably for the best. Don't want her thinking you're romantic."

"Too late for that." He punches my shoulder. "Your sappiness rubbed off on me."

Early on, with Raven, the comment would have worried me. I would have wondered if my feelings for her would fade like always, my sentimental side a constant joke with the guys. But everything with her is different. I want her more, think about her more. I wake up wishing she were beside me. I run with my weight vest on, the fire in my lungs no match for the dull ache behind my ribs. An ache that's intensified since seeing her exhibit.

"Pretty sure that's all Shay," I say. "Should I be expecting another wedding soon?"

His blissed-out eyes are answer enough. "Hopefully. I'm trying to figure out the best way to ask. I was thinking of taking her back to Aspen."

"Back to where it all began?"

"Yeah. I just don't want it to be cheesy. And we fought a lot there. Might not be the best place." He looks out over the city, the lights bright against the night sky. More voices drift from the main room. "It feels weird to want to marry someone else."

He doesn't mention Marina's name, but he doesn't have to. He lost so much the day he lost her, but he gained Jackson. "She would have loved Shay. Loved that she doesn't take your shit."

He laughs at that. "She would have."

A makeshift kitchen is set up at the far end of our narrow space, cooks milling about as things sizzle and pop. We watch them fuss over hors d'oeuvres, the bites so small I'd need fifty to stave my hunger.

Kolton turns back to the window. "I'll probably end up rolling over in bed one morning and asking. Not sure how much longer I can wait."

If Raven and I can bridge the distance between us, I don't imagine I'd be much farther behind. But tonight isn't about Kolton or me. We're here for Sawyer and Lily, and as his mother suspected, Sawyer's nowhere to be seen. "Has the groom bailed?"

He frowns. "Took off to the bathroom and never came back. Probably snuck in to see Lily."

Or maybe not. Sawyer's family could be solely responsible for Vancouver's rising divorce rate. Their inability to commit and the fallout have chased him since he was a kid. He's as devoted to Lily as Kolton is to Shay, but chances are his feet are on the ice-block side of cold. I nod to Kolton and slip out to find Sawyer, scanning the room as I go. Still no Raven. But flashes by the bar hint at a camera. As much as I want to see her, I need to make sure Sawyer isn't face-first in a toilet.

He isn't, but it's just as bad.

The few stalls are empty, and he's gripping the sink, staring at his reflection in the mirror, his skin as pale as I've ever seen it. The man looks about to puke. "Should I bring the garbage closer?"

His shaky laugh doesn't inspire confidence. Neither does his suit. I didn't know they made tuxes in dark purple, but I'm not sure they should. Leaning down, he turns the tap on and splashes his face with water. "Is the building spinning? Because it feels like my legs might buckle."

I lean into the wall. "Last I checked, we were stationary."

He blots his face with a paper towel and tosses it in the trash. "What the fuck is wrong with me? I've wanted this for months. I should be ecstatic."

"You're human, and your parents did a number on you growing up. Plus, your extended family is highly dysfunctional. I'd say what you're feeling is pretty normal."

"Thanks for the shrink session, Dr. Downer." He tugs at his tie.

"Getting married is a big deal. If you were your usual obnoxious self, I'd be worried."

Sighing, he rubs his eyes. "I better not hurt her."

"You're damn right, you better not." Just like I better not push Raven away again. If I lose her, I'll likely claim Sawyer's spot, green and noxious and gripping the sink.

"If I hurt her," he says, "I give you permission to paintball me in the nuts."

"I might do that anyway, but glad to see you're taking your commitment seriously. Do I need to stage an intervention, or are you good?"

He shakes out his body, drags his hands through his hair, then smiles at his reflection. "Fuck it. I got this. For the next sixty years, I will devote my life to making sure Lily knows how much I love her." Face pinched, he turns my way. "I think your sappiness rubbed off on me."

These assholes and their jokes. "Get your ugly mug outside before they send in a search party."

Speaking of search parties, it's about time I find a certain dark-haired beauty who's inked herself on my soul. A woman who's only had a taste of my romantic side. The guys can bust my balls all they want, but I'm more than ready to confess my feelings to Raven, tell her I've loved her since Aspen. If our talk goes as well as I hope, she'll witness me in all my sappy glory.

The harpist is still strumming, the room now twice as full as it was. Mrs. West catches my eye, and I give her a thumbs-up. Waitstaff pass champagne as people enter. No, not waitstaff. *Creatures.* Dressed in slim black suits with slicked hair, the men and women carrying trays look like something out of *Star Trek.* Their cheekbones are raised, their colorful brows enhanced. It's the type of makeup Josh will learn. Pride swells at the thought.

Then I see *her.*

The deep blue of Raven's dress matches my handkerchief. Her strapless top hugs her curves, her long skirt flows to the floor, and something on it catches the flickering light. Every time she moves, it shimmers. And my throat burns.

If there's an exotic creature in this room, it's Raven.

A fresh bout of nerves keeps me rooted. She's cagey at the best of times. Too worried her heart will get trampled, she keeps it under lock and key. She let me in twice, neither time ending well. My fault. Her fault. If we end up arguing, she might decide we're not worth the drama.

Her camera is at her face, the flash strobing over the crowd. She floats around, capturing candid moments, even sitting on the floor to change her angle. I've never seen her so happy. Or so stunning. I itch to drag the zipper down the back of her dress and watch all that fabric pool at her feet. I want to kiss every inch of ink on her skin and fill in the gaps with my teeth, branding her. I miss having her at my family dinners and fighting over music.

Love this intense isn't something you toss away at the first sign of trouble. Or the second. You argue, you make up, then you come back together, *stronger*. If Raven pushes me away, I'll only fight harder. I stand by the side wall and watch her through the mingling guests.

Black hair. Sharp bangs. Full lips. Sultry movements.

Then her lens swings toward me, and her body jerks. She freezes, camera in place, and I stand taller. *You're mine*, I want to say. Instead I release a shuddering breath.

She approaches slowly, never lowering her camera. She's taken photos of me before, usually when I'm not looking, but we never got around to those naked pictures she'd talked about. I imagine this is how posing for them would feel: Sexy. Intimate. She works the lens and presses her finger until she's a foot in front of me. There's glitter or something on her chest and arms, making her skin glow. My skin feels too tight, hers looks too delicious.

I press two fingers on top of the lens and lower her camera. "You're beautiful." There's glitter on her face, too, and colored makeup around her dark eyes. There's probably a fancier way to tell her how gorgeous she is, but I'm at a loss.

She smiles at the handkerchief in my pocket. "You don't look half bad yourself."

"As good as I did in that Hawaiian shirt?"

"Do you have to be a virgin to live on the Virgin Islands?"

She's back on those stupid questions. Our questions. Our game. The familiarity has me moving a step closer, but I don't feel much like playing. "If you want to ask me a stupid question, ask me if I've missed you."

The sparkles on her chest glint with each quickened breath. "Have you missed me?"

I lean down and whisper, "Painfully."

Instead of replying, she glances over her shoulder. This is her night. Her gig. And I'm interfering. I scrub my head, the short stubble scratching my palm. "Your photographs were amazing."

Her attention swings back to me, and she grazes her teeth over her bottom lip. "Yeah?"

"Yeah. We really need to talk." So I can tell her I love her. Even now, not saying it is like being gagged, the air in my lungs clawing to get out.

"Or not talk…" There's rasp to her voice, a seductive edge. It's how she sounds when I make love to her slow and deep.

"That, too," I agree.

She looks down, at my thick fingers brushing her thigh. "Unfortunately, both will have to wait." She taps her camera. "I have a job to do. Save a dance for me, though."

"Of course."

Our eyes collide another moment, then she turns, her dress glinting with the sway of her hips.

This better be the fastest ceremony in the history of the world, because we do have to talk. And *not* talk. There are things that need saying, by both of us. Apologies given and received. And I have to tell her how impressed I am with her exhibition and how that photo of Josh lit up the room. And my heart. But having her this close—those lips, that body, and that inked skin within reach—stirs my blood. My hunger for her is a tangible thing. Thickness fists my throat. Tonight, if all goes according to plan, the springs in my bed will be put to the test.

Twenty-seven

Raven

There's nothing subtle in the way Nico's eyes crash over me. This is the look he gets when we have sex, like he can't get close enough or kiss me hard enough or roll his hips deep enough. And I forgot how handsome he is. Even in his penguin suit. All that brawn fills out his jacket and slacks, his tie crooked, the shadows below his cheekbones flickering in the light. I might have to pull a fire alarm and douse myself with water. But this is Lily's night, and I'm on the clock.

Releasing his hand is agonizing, walking away excruciating, but his liquid gaze follows, cascading down my back, lapping at my feet. I don't have to turn around to know he's watching me. And that he wants to fuck me.

What I don't know is if he *loves* me.

Every other woman he's dated has heard those words drop from his lips. Not me. Never me. Still, he seems ready to talk—my exhibit having the desired effect—and I'm ready to listen. I'm ready to drop to my knees and beg forgiveness, especially if I get to look up at his massive cock and climb the ridges of his abs. (With my teeth.) Nico may be as moral as they come, but his body is built for sin.

A deep breath later, my camera is at my eye. The guests mingle in my viewfinder, and I force Nico to the back of my mind.

Click. Lily's father with stars in his eyes.

Click. Moonlight casting over Sawyer's nieces.

Click. Jackson trying to catch a planet.

Sawyer may not have gotten his superhero wedding with spandex costumes and capes, but the girls gave him a galaxy. The room is dark and alluring, a solar system slipping across the ceiling. The harpsichord heightens the mood, the waitstaff taking the theme that much further.

Capturing memories has never been so easy.

A short while later, Sasha taps me on the shoulder. "The ceremony is about to start. I'll take it from here."

"I'll find you after." I hand her my camera.

As much as I'd like to shoot the nuptials, Lily threatened to remove me from speed dial if I didn't stand up for her vows. An impressive threat, from her. Not that she had to worry. Since everything with Rose, I've realized how important my girls are. My sisters, blood or not. They don't judge my taste in music or my ink, they tolerate my snarly moods and sarcasm, and they don't ask me to deal drugs. Since Nico left, they've eaten ice cream with me and offered to egg his house. If he'd deserved it, I would have let them. But I'm largely to blame. The girls were honest about that, too. *Tough love*, they said.

Real love, I thought.

Chairs are put in place for those who need to sit, the rest of the guests ushered toward a small platform and canopy draped in tiny star-shaped lights. I hurry to the back, my velvet skirt trailing behind me, but someone grabs my shoulders and spins me around.

"We might have a client." Shay is always stunning, but with her hair piled on her head and her skin glittered like mine, she's cover-model gorgeous.

"If I dug girls, I'd totally kiss you," I say.

"If I dug girls, I'd press my face into your boobs."

We grin at each other, then I prompt her. "What's this about a client?"

She cranes her neck, searching the crowd, then she points to a ten-million-year-old lady. "That woman wants to throw a baby shower."

That woman's face is about to slide to the floor. "If it's for herself, I'll need a lobotomy to erase the visual."

"Hilarious, but no. You know Kolton's assistant, Stella?"

Of course I know Stella. She's the only woman in this room with as much ink as me. Where my work is black and gray, hers is a swirl of bold colors and fun designs. Her fuchsia hair is hard to miss, too. "Not only do I know Stella, but I'm a member of her fan club. Nico and I were at the office once and walked in as she told Sawyer to stop whining or she'd wax his ass."

Shay cackles. "She keeps Kolton in line, too, and"—she does an imaginary drum roll—"she's having a baby."

"No way."

"Way."

"I thought she was single."

"She is."

"Scandalous."

"Not exactly," Shay says. "She went to the spank bank."

"Shut up."

"Swear to God. She's always wanted kids and got tired of dating Mr. Wrong, so she took matters into her own hands. Her grandmother wants to throw her a shower. Since Stella is into all things ink and sexy, they've asked for a burlesque theme."

Forget member, I'm now her fan club president. "I need to retract my earlier statement. If I dug girls, I'd sex her up."

"Right? And this means we might actually get paid to do this." She gestures around the room.

Another piece of my life falling into place, another milestone reached. It doesn't ease the discomfort lingering from the letter I got this week—Rose's first communication since everything went down. I've reread the single page, trying to assess the sincerity of her apology. It's unclear if she's reaching out because she has no one left, or if she truly realizes how badly she's messed up her life. I doubt I'll ever trust her again, but I'm not sure I can cut her off, either.

I'll write her back, once I get my head around what I want to say. However that plays out, my relationship with Nico is hopefully on the mend, I have an exhibit up in a gallery, and our event business has broken ground. This move to Vancouver was the best decision I ever made.

"Does Lily know?" I ask.

She shakes her head. "I'll tell her after the ceremony."

Speaking of which, the lights illuminating the exterior panels dim, and the galaxy shining on the ceiling casts more magic. A violin joins the harp, and we're ushered toward the back. Kolton and Nico are on the far side of the room, the boys whispering and looking our way.

We're not much better. Shay's in front of me, facing them, and she leans back. "I might ask Kolton to marry me."

Just when this night couldn't get any better. "Seriously?"

"He's taking too long."

This from the girl who stuck with her ex well past their expiration date, waiting on a ring that never came. "Bold move."

"Yeah. It's just, with Jackson and everything, I want it to be more permanent. I want him to have that security, and Kolton is…"

She trails off, and I rest my chin on her shoulder, wrapping my arms around her waist. Both our dresses are the softest of velvet—mine midnight, hers electric blue—both dotted with crystals through the layered skirt. "Yeah, Kolton *is*."

"So is Nico," she says on a sigh.

The big guy is watching us, his gaze unwavering as Jackson runs into his legs. Nico claps Kolton's mini-me on the back, but his focus stays on me.

"Yeah. Nico is, too," I agree, my tone less dreamy. My exhibit clearly affected him, but we're nowhere near out of the woods.

Shay wraps her arms over mine, squeezing us closer. "You'll figure things out."

The alternative is highly unpleasant, but I don't let my mind go there. This night is too special to ruin with what-ifs.

Sawyer's mother fusses with her granddaughters, organizing the twins in front of Shay. Sawyer's father and brother join him on their side. The rhythm of the violin changes, the crowd hushes, and the twins giggle as they walk down the aisle, baskets in hand. Their white petals flutter on the floor, my heart fluttering with them. Shay and Kolton follow, the couple so freaking in love, you'd think it was their wedding.

I'm next.

Nico and me.

The candlelight is soft. Each flicker licks his dark skin, and when I reach him, he pauses so long, whispers float our way. Then he presses his luscious lips to my jaw. This is our first kiss in two months. Sixty-two days. My lips are nowhere near his, but his touch is like the first snowfall and running through puddles and falling into leaves.

I grip his arm to stay upright.

He guides me forward, our elbows hooked, his hand folded over mine. I've never been so aware of his body—the brush of his thigh, the press of his hip. Thankfully we don't talk. I'm not sure what I'd say. So many words have been hoarded I doubt I'd make much sense. When we reach the canopy, I move to pull away, but he tugs me close, and my heart jostles. His gaze is fierce, like he wants to devour me. Like we're not at our friends' wedding in front of two hundred guests.

His blue eyes are liquid, shining like sun-drenched water. He doesn't ravage me, though. He leans down and whispers, "I'm so far gone in love with you."

I die. Melt. Disappear into a puddle of joy.

Then he lets me go. He walks to his side of the aisle, and I rock on my feet, unsteady. Heat flares up my neck. If I were at home, I'd blare the Clash and rock out like I was fourteen being noticed by my first crush. But I'm not at home. And I'm not fourteen.

Somehow I make it to Shay's side. She digs her fingers into my wrist. "What the hell was that?"

I try to listen to her whisper, but my focus is locked on Nico.

Even from here, I can tell his chest rises as fast as mine. "He loves me," I manage.

She gives a little jump. "You guys are gonna have the hottest babies."

I pinch her arm to shut her up, but now I'm picturing my Sexy Beast, shirtless, our kid—a kid I've never cared to envision—pressed to his chest, and I'm a puddle again.

The music shifts, a sign that Sawyer is making his way down the aisle, his mother on his arm, but Nico hasn't looked away. I can't look away, either. My ribs curl inward, struggling to contain my swelling heart. *I love you*, I mouth. His large hand floats up to cover his breastbone, and he taps his fingers twice. His heartbeat? Mine?

He might as well be tapping my inner thigh.

Flushed and flustered, I tear my gaze away. Sawyer is halfway down the aisle, handsome in his purple tux, the color as wild as we'd let him get. It's fun and sexy and suits the man he is, the husband he will become. At the front, his mother whispers in his ear and his shoulders relax.

Then Lily appears.

Shay clutches my hand, and I squeeze back. Our friend is an earthly angel. Her white-blond hair spills down her back in loose waves, pink and purple flowers woven in the strands. Her dress is strapless like ours, but silk instead of satin, the white top blooming into pink and lilac toward the floor. People murmur, and Sawyer's breath hisses out, his brown eyes ablaze. He shifts on his feet, as though not running to her is killing him. His restraint doesn't last long.

As soon as Lily's father leaves her at the altar, Sawyer hauls her into his arms and dips her back, kissing her with abandon. His mother groans, her face full of mirth, and the guests laugh, everyone enjoying the spontaneous show of affection. I check to make sure Sasha captures it. She, of course, hasn't missed a beat, but my heart has. It trips over itself for Lily and this night and the sting of pleasure lingering from Nico's words. The big guy beams, shaking his head at his friend, his attention sliding back to me. Heat. An inferno of heat. And desire, and that thing I've been terrified to wish for: *love love, so much love.*

The ceremony passes with little incident, vows spoken, rings exchanged. Sawyer only cuts off the priest once to kiss Lily again, and red apples bloom on her cheeks. Once, near the end, she fidgets, her trademark anxiety making an appearance. But Sawyer clasps her hands and stills her fingers with his lips. Again, my heart skips. Things don't finish as planned, though. Sawyer must have gotten to someone who wasn't able to resist his charms. He probably promised them a year of Moondog clothing. Without warning the dim lights go black, flickering candles all that are left.

And Pitbull blares from the speakers.

Horns blast as "I Know You Want Me" bounces off the ceiling, neon lights we never okayed lighting up the space. Sawyer leaves Lily, her mouth open in shock and horror, and he joins his nieces for a dance the twins must have choreographed. I doubt he planned to sway his hips quite like that or shake his shoulders.

"That fucker," Shay growls, her eyes as wide as mine.

I'm mute, his willingness to embarrass himself rendering me speechless. But I laugh. Hard. Along with every person in the room. It starts as a nervous burst of air until my stomach rolls with humor, my abs sore by the time his routine ends. Lily's smile could light the solar system. She runs into his arms and he spins her around, the dance music fading into something soft and lyrical. The type of music Lily loves. They dance or maybe float. I don't recognize the song, but it talks of living off love and feeding off love and breathing and drinking and sinking in love.

"'Beauty' by the Shivers," Shay whispers in my ear, knowing this music isn't my thing. The way she bites her lip and dabs her eyes, I'd say she's forgiven Sawyer for hijacking our event.

Afterward the bar opens and the guests schmooze as Lily and Sawyer escape for some privacy. I wanted to shoot posed photos of them after the ceremony, but Sawyer refused. He asked me to capture them in the moment, enjoying their night. The casual cocktails and passed hors d'oeuvres add to the fun atmosphere, neither of them wanting a sit-down dinner.

The second we break ranks, Nico strides my way, those thick thighs of his propelling him forward. "I can't take my eyes off you."

"Even during that dance number?"

His shoulders shake with laughter. "Okay, maybe I looked away for a bit. But"—he steps so close his chest brushes mine—"I'm feeling pretty desperate for that dance." He flexes his fingers as though he needs to get his hands on me.

That makes two of us. "Agreed, but I'm the hired help."

He grabs my hand and traces slow circles on my palm. "Do your work. Just know I'm thinking about you."

My limbs loosen, all sensation gathering in my belly, and lower. I pull away. Another second and my legs will liquefy.

I feel his attention on me as I go, and the weight of his stare for the next few hours. Every time I glance up, those blue stunners are fastened on me, but I do my work. The *other* thing I love. I snap enough shots to fill a library, ensuring there will be winners in the bunch. When I edit them, I'll get to relive Lily jamming a cupcake in Sawyer's mouth, Jackson climbing on Nico's back, and the contentment on Shay's face as she dances with her man. As things wind down, Sasha offers to finish up so I can deal with the tower of tattooed muscle circling me like I'm his prey.

He's on me the second I pass off my camera, his arm curling around my waist. "The last hour has been excruciating."

The band plays something sweet and slow, our hips finding an easy rhythm. "But we're here now."

"We are."

I sink into his arms, so big and strong and reassuring around my back. "I'm sorry."

The words feel too small. Inadequate. Like a swimmer's first stroke across the Pacific.

He tugs me even closer. "So am I. I should have talked out what I was feeling instead of closing down. Cutting you off was like losing a limb."

"I should have listened to you about Rose. Trusted your instincts."

We move and talk—words timed to music, confessions binding us. He runs his nose through my hair. "You were right, warning me not to be so rigid, not to judge every action so severely. It just felt like the only way to keep treading water. I've let you down."

"You haven't. You're the best man I know."

He sighs, soft breath brushing my ear. "But I should never have shut you out. I still hadn't really dealt with my guilt over that stuff with Alessi. Almost breaking the law. What you asked brought it all back, and I was too tough on myself. Too tough on you. And there's so much I want."

"Like what?" All I want is to listen to him, let his deep voice flow through me.

"Everything. I want to wake up with you every day. I want to cook you dinner. I want to picnic with you at the beach and dance like this under the stars and watch you get your next tattoo and have you design mine." Hips swaying, hearts pounding. "I want it all."

And all and all and all. "Your friends were right," I whisper. "You're all marshmallow."

He doesn't laugh. "Makes me easy to burn."

I flinch as if his words do singe. The pain I caused him sank deep, cutting through his muscle and tough exterior. My big, sensitive guy. "I should have listened to you about Rose. I just…I thought she was my one chance at family. But I had it all along. Lily and Shay are my support. Even if I mess up, they're here for me. And you"—I release one hand to rest my palm on his cheek—"you're all I need. *More* than I need. But I'm greedy and want all of you."

Gruff, he says, "I'm yours. And we can't ever fight like this again. Sure, we'll disagree and things will happen, but we can't split up. It's too hard." He kisses my hand and gathers me tight.

Even though I'm tucked into his chest, I feel exposed. As though my heart is made of tracing paper, and he sees into my soul. He's right. We can't do this again, and I want us to be together. But I've also learned a lot about myself these past weeks. "I agree, but…"

His feet pause. He pulls back to study me. "That doesn't sound good."

God, that look of fear in his eyes. "I would do it again."

"Do what?"

"I may have misplaced my trust in Rose, but if Shay or Lily were in trouble and I thought I could do something to help them, even if it meant bending the law, I'd try. I'd ask you to help me." The thing that's rung true since this disaster started is that I'll always fight for those I love. Right or wrong, I'll move heaven and earth to see them well.

Nico sways again, his steps sure as we dance. "If you ask, I'll probably say no. But I won't get mad. Not if the asking comes from the heart."

"Okay," I say, at peace for the first time since Aspen, nothing but honesty between us. "And you need to learn to give yourself a break. You can't be everything for everyone."

He fans his hand across my back and repeats my "Okay."

The song bleeds into another, Nico's warmth bleeding into my veins. I can't imagine dancing with anyone else. "Can I ask you something?"

"Anything."

"Why did it take you so long to tell me how you feel? I know how the guys joke, how you're usually pretty quick to fall. What was different about us?"

Left. Right. Back. Forth. He leads; I follow. "I wanted to wait until there was less stress in our lives, and in the past the saying was always too easy. It never burned me up. The words never lodged in my throat like they did with you. I wanted us to be different. Special. Waiting meant more."

I slip my hands under the bottom of his jacket, his muscles shifting below my touch. "I love you." It's the first time I've whispered this to anyone, and he's right—the words do burn.

He stops dancing. The music plays, but he holds me still. "I love you, Raven, but saying it isn't enough. I plan to show you how much you mean to me."

I look up at his ocean eyes, no longer worried I'll drown. "If your show-and-tell involves more touching and less clothing in the privacy of your place, count me in."

I drop my hand to the curve of his ass, and a growl rumbles from his chest. The kiss that follows is bigger than the galaxy above us and the words we spoke. It's a promise wrapped in low groans and tangled tongues that shivers across my skin. We're not the same, Nico and me. We won't always agree, and we might test each other's limits, but if he kisses me like this and opens his heart, I'll be his and his and his. And he'll always be mine.

Fifteen Months Later

Raven

I must be swaddled in thick blankets and locked in a sauna. Maybe I've been banished to live on the sun. It's the only explanation for this oppressive heat, and the sweltering weight smothering me. The weight moves, tightening and loosening its hold, and my awareness seeps back. Not a blanket. A body. A *large* body. A kiss lands on my cheek, miles of rippling muscle shifting against me. We could be sleeping in an emperor-size bed, and Nico would still wrap his long limbs around me all night. It's one of my favorite things about him.

That and the heat he's packing between his thighs.

He presses his morning wood into my hip. "Hey."

His voice is all rocks and gravel, his lips and hands everywhere at once, like he's a mutant squid with three mouths and eighty fingers, caressing my breasts, my belly, my thighs. I'm surrounded, and I love it. Totally engulfed by Nico.

I move, restlessly, turning in his arms, and my face meets his wide neck. I bite, then I suck, and a red mark blooms on his dark skin. My mark on my husband. His answering groan lights a path through my veins, and my blood turns to molten lava. It's been over a year since the fight that broke us up, and it's like we're still making up for lost time. Apologizing. Forgiving. Over, *and over*. I'm not sure we'll ever get enough of each other.

His busy hands stroke my back, one thick thigh pushing between my legs, rubbing exactly where I want him. "I'm so wet," I murmur. "And I'm ovulating."

Nico grunts and kneads my ass. We slide and drag against each other, nothing but skin for days. Then he says, "I could live like this. With you. Forever. I don't need anything else." My (sexy) gentle giant isn't always much for words, but he sure knows how to make them count.

He only needs me. I only need him. But we *want* a baby.

I wiggle higher until our mouths are lined up, my hand meandering down the dips and grooves of his chest and abs, along the slide of his hipbone. I kiss him and take his cock in my hand, always amazed at how thick and heavy it is, hot to the touch. Hard for me. Our tongues swirl, once, twice, and his hips glide forward, searching for my rhythm, demanding my attention.

I am rapt.

Still stroking him, I shift my head and look into his eyes. The sky has nothing on his blue gaze. "If we can't, if it's not in the cards for us, would you want to adopt?"

I doubt most people would have this conversation while giving their husband a hand job, but we're not most people. We've been known to fall asleep on our front lawn while counting the stars. We choose to stop and kiss in the rain. We dance on the beach. We got married in private, just the two of us and a waterfall. That didn't stop our friends from throwing us the most outrageous party known to man (punk-meets-country theme; think: hay bales, Mohawks, dueling guitars, and cowboy hats), but Nico and I follow our own rules, even choosing tattoos over wedding bands. Or maybe we follow *his* rules. He is, after all, the mushiest, most romantic man birthed this century.

All two hundred and seventy pounds of him.

He traces my lips with his finger. "I'd love to adopt. We can try naturally as long as you want, but I'd rather not go the whole doctor and appointment route, unless your heart is set on it. If we can have our own baby, I'll be thrilled. If we get to give a kid a chance at a good life, I'll be just as excited. More, maybe." He places a gentle kiss to my temple. "It's only been six months. Whatever will be, will be. As long as we're together."

Again his chosen words flatten me. I run my thumb over the head of his cock, spreading around his pre-come, watching how his eyes flutter closed, how his broad chest rises faster. It sends my heart skating across the moon.

"I love you so much," I say.

"Love you, babe. Forever."

He grabs my hips and lifts me over him, like I'm nothing but a feather, and I straddle his bulk. I rock against his length, not taking him inside me yet, just feeling all that power under me, his hardness rubbing me just right, our breaths guiding us. It reminds me of us dancing on the beach, letting the rush of waves set our rhythm. Faster. Slower. Gentle swaying. Then I lift up, and lower myself down. *God.* It never gets less intense. Never ceases to amaze me how perfectly we fit together. Two halves of a whole. A really pleasurable whole.

That's when someone knocks on our door. "You two spend any longer in there, and we're hitting the slopes without you." Shay is way too dedicated of a skier.

"You can mainline Gatorade to replenish your fluids." Sawyer laughs at his own joke and pounds the door once.

I rock against Nico's hips, the two of us grinning at each other. "Give us a minute," I call.

"A minute?" Nico whispers.

"Be quick."

"Only if we get alone time later. I like this baby-making business."

"I like *you*. Now hurry up and make me come."

I swivel my hips, and he growls.

He flips me over and pins my hands above my head, rolling his hips exactly how I like it—short strokes in and out, then deep and hard. It won't take long. It never does. The trouble is keeping quiet. In our Vancouver house, screaming and shouting my pleasure heightens my release, something we've discovered as of late. In our shared Aspen condo it might be best to keep a lid on the vocal side of our performance. I bite my lip instead.

Nico has other ideas. "Fuck 'em. Let them hear how good I make you feel."

He palms my breast with his free hand, his lips crushing mine in a greedy kiss, wet and punishing as our hips meet. It overloads my senses—his thickness filling me, his breath inflating my lungs. Our talk of babies and all the love my husband has to give is bigger than this room. This vacation. It blocks everything out but us.

I shout, "God yes," as we move against each other. I forget where we are, that I have a huge photography show to pull together and events coming up. That our friends can hear our every word. All I can do is *feel*.

"*Fuck*." I'm so close, each snap of his hips pushing me toward the edge. "Yes. Oh God. *Yes*. Just like that." Then I topple over, a symphony of *yes*es hollered.

Nico's "Fuck, I love you. Oh fuck. *Oh fuck*," is loud enough to wake the dead.

I press my face into his neck and cringe; our friends will never let us live this down. I should care. I really should. But they can suck it.

My abdomen clenches, and Nico shudders. He nips my shoulder. "To be continued. Shower now."

He does caveman well.

Twenty minutes later we stride out, long underwear on, humming to ourselves. We planned this group vacation a while back—our three-year Aspenniversary—as a way to have fun and celebrate how we all met. The chalet we've rented has soaring ceilings, Navajo rugs, and a spectacular view of the mountains. Shay and Kolton are cuddled on one end of the living room couch, his face lowered to Shay's still-flat belly, talking to his unborn kid. Lily and Sawyer are at the dining room table, his mouth wide open as she flicks Lucky Charms at his face. He catches most of them and chews happily.

Thankfully our friends don't say boo. Don't even look our way. Maybe the walls are thicker than I thought. Nico pours us each a coffee while I search out bowls and milk.

"What time do you guys want to head out?" I ask.

"Not sure," Sawyer says. "Maybe nine *oh, oh, oh, oooooh* clock." His high-pitched orgasm impersonation stops me cold.

"Really?" Kolton deepens his baritone. "I just *ohfuck ohfuck* don't know. Might be too soon."

Shay joins in with "Oh, baby. *Yes, yes, yes.* Nine is *ohGodyes* perfect."

They get louder and more dramatic, tossing out random exclamations of rapture. Lily face-plants on the table, laughing hysterically, and I can't even be annoyed. Not with the way she and Shay are cackling while Sawyer and Kolton kiss and fondle the air like pornographic mimes.

Nico's cheekbones glow, matching the color of the hickey on his neck. We trade looks. We shrug. Then we high-five each other.

"Be jealous," is all my man says.

No chance they are. Shay and Kolton got married before us, a stunning affair at Whistler Mountain hosted, of course, by Over the Top Events. My favorite photo is of Kolton spinning Shay, her curly hair flying in reckless circles. In seven months they'll be adding a little boy or girl to their perfect slice of life. Sawyer is as immature as ever, but he and Lily are inseparable, too. They've even started a new line of recycled clothing called Saved.

His homage to her effect on him.

When the catcalling dies down, Nico and I sit at the table to drink our coffee and eat our cereal in comfortable silence. As I shovel a spoonful of Lucky Charms into my mouth, a red bra lands in front of me.

"We're tossing them today." Shay is way too chipper for this hour.

Lily's undergarments aren't strewn over the table, but she's already blushing. "I brought my purple one."

I raise my hand. "Black for me. Can't wait."

Kolton steps behind Shay and wraps his hands around her

belly. He's always been a "hands on" kind of guy, but since announcing her pregnancy, he hovers more, touches more, holding her and getting as close as possible. I often forget he lost his first wife during childbirth. Fear must dampen his joy at times, worry about everything that could go wrong.

Today he seems nothing but adorably thrilled. "What's with the bras?"

I sip my coffee. "We're re-creating the Karma Event."

He squints. "I don't follow."

"The Karma Event," I repeat. When his brows crease deeper, I add, "*The bra toss.* You know, like the day you skied into Shay."

His reply: "She skied into me."

Shay cranes her neck to gawk at him. "You really are delusional."

"Just admit it, already."

"We already agreed it was *your* fault. Just like the fact that *you* broke the dishwasher."

"Didn't happen," he tells her. "But what's this about a bra toss?"

Shay rolls her eyes.

"*The bra toss,*" I say again, slower and louder, like English is his second language.

Kolton frowns. "Still in the dark here."

"Me, too." Sawyer picks up the red bra and holds it over his chest. "Can't wait for the details, though."

"Me three," Nico adds.

Lily stares at Shay, her look of confusion likely matching mine. "You never told Kolton?"

"Nope." Shay tries to snatch her bra from Sawyer, but he fends her off.

"But that's the beginning of it all," Lily persists. "How could he not know?"

Kolton steps back from Shay and crosses his arms. "Now's a good time to fill me in. Especially considering Sawyer is a minute from wearing your bra."

Which is exactly what Sawyer does. He slips his arms through the straps and positions the cups over his long-underwear top.

"You're ridiculous," Lily says, all smiles.

He winks at her. "You love me."

She doesn't contradict him.

Kolton, however, isn't sidetracked. "Let's hear it, Shay. What's with the bra toss?"

She waves a dismissive hand. "It's no big deal. Just, the day *you* skied into *me*, I'd seen the bra tree earlier—the one on the mountain with all the bras and tacky necklaces hanging off it—and decided to take mine off and sling it. Wanted to erase my past and start over."

"Does that mean you skied into my boy braless?" Sawyer asks, still dressed in drag.

It's Shay's turn to wink. "It does."

Nico's large hand grips my thigh. "You planning that, then? On slinging yours and skiing without a bra?" The spark in his gaze is all lust.

"That I am." I cover his hand with mine and squeeze.

We proceed to discuss the logistics of our mission and decide to wear our bras until our last run. We'll slip them off at the lodge, ride one final chair, then let our undergarments fly. Our nod to the Karma Event and the place that brought us all together.

Kolton has been quiet awhile. He drags a hand down his long

hair. "Was the bra you tossed last time black?"

Shay nods. "Yep."

"And it hit the tree? It landed on it?" His intensity sucks the levity from the room. Is he pissed she never told him? Mad he didn't know she skied braless?

Shay shakes her head slowly. "I missed. It landed on some guy's head. Why?"

Kolton's jaw tics. "Unfuckingbelievable."

We all trade looks. I stay mute, unsure where his anger is coming from. Kind of annoyed he's making a thing out of this. It's our vacation, after all. We're supposed to laugh and ski and have fun. (And have ridiculously loud sex.) Nothing about Kolton's pursed lips screams *fun*.

Then he laughs. Maybe *loses his shit* is a better description. The man clutches his stomach and doubles over, heaving as he cackles. Jekyll, meet Hyde. The sound is contagious, though. One by one we titter then chuckle then howl, until we're all smacking our thighs, desperate for breath.

Nico comes up for air first. "Why the hell are we laughing?"

Shay punches Kolton's shoulder. "Seriously. What is up with you?"

He opens his mouth, says, "I was…" then doubles over. Each time he tries to speak, he gets out another word or two, then succumbs again, the thirty-two-year-old reduced to thirteen, tears streaming from his eyes.

"Okay, okay." He sucks in a breath. "I was skiing that day and stopped under the chairlift. Like right by that stupid tree. And"—he locks eyes with Shay and shakes his head, his expression dumbstruck—"a black bra landed on my head."

No fucking way. I think back to that moment in time, the memory sharpening: us on that chairlift, Shay's bra sailing through the air, us cracking up as it landed on some dude's helmet.

Shay smacks him again. "Fuck off."

"Swear to God."

"No. Seriously. *Fuck off.*"

Lily's jaw nearly hits the floor. "Oh my God."

I don't bother replying. I tip into Nico and erupt again, my man laughing, too, his huge frame shaking hard enough to cause an earthquake. Once we've relived the event ten thousand times, telling and retelling it until we're beyond giddy, we hurry to finish getting dressed. Tossing our bras today has taken on a whole new meaning.

Nico stops me in our room. "You think it was fate? The bra and everything that followed?"

If Shay weren't braless and full of adrenaline that day, she might not have skied her mogul run and careened into Kolton. If we took a different route together, and Lily didn't fall on our way down, we wouldn't have met Sawyer and Nico. We probably wouldn't have been brave enough to knock on their condo door if they'd been total strangers. There's a chance I wouldn't have married the beautiful man in front of me. "I'll go with fate," I say.

He smooths my hair behind my ear and smiles. "Fate it is."

Acknowledgments

From the moment I started this series, I was dying to get Raven and Nico on the page. Their chemistry came naturally, their banter was a blast to write, and their troubled pasts stole my heart. Another benefit to writing their story: I did a ride along in a cop car to research Nico's character. I got to wear a bulletproof vest. I got to hang out at the precinct. It was pretty freaking cool. Huge thank you to Kristina Klingbeil for taking me under her wing. Your stories as we drove the streets helped shape Nico.

Stacey Donaghy, I hope I get to publish endless books so I can tell you time and again how special it is to have you in my corner. A girl couldn't ask for better support from her agent. Thanks for being you.

Madeleine Colavita, You always push me to deepen my characters and never let me take the easy way out. Your insight has made me a better writer. The team at Forever Yours, from the cover to editing to promotion, thank you for bringing this book to life.

Kristin B. Wright, Esher Hogan, and Brighton Walsh, you have all helped me fine-tune *Hooked on Trouble* and this entire series. I would be lost without your expertise. Tara Wyatt and Heather Van Fleet, your feedback was spot on, and your encouragement meant the world. J.R. Yates, you swooped in at the last minute and saved me from dissolving into a pint of Mint Chocolate Chip. Mad love.

Dayna Bahar, your lawyerly advice helped me flesh out Josh's character—from the charges against him to the clearing of his name. Thank you for fielding my barrage of questions.

To my husband, you put up with my crazy and pick up my slack when I'm busy writing. Thank you for your patience and support, and for keeping me from floating into the clouds. To my family, I love you always.

Heather Van Fleet, Jamie Howard, and the ladies of the Hookup, chatting with you all is a bright spot in my week. You never cease to crack me up and make me swoon. I can't thank you enough for hanging out with me. I also wouldn't survive without the CD, my fellow romance writers in the Life Raft, and my Pitch Wars family.

One of the most amazing things on this journey is the support I receive from the community. A number of bloggers have gone out of their way to promote me and my writing. There aren't enough words to express my gratitude, so a simple thank-you will have to suffice.

And to my readers, you are the reason I do this. Each time I see a review go up, I squee. Each time I get a message from you, my heart soars. Please post and send more, it truly makes my day. Thank you for spending time with Shay and Kolton, Lily and Sawyer, and now Raven and Nico. I hope you had as much fun reading them as I did writing them.

To keep up to date on all my writerly things, subscribe to my newsletter at: www.kellysiskind.com

About the Author

A small-town girl at heart, **Kelly Siskind** moved from the city to open a cheese shop with her husband in northern Ontario. When she's not neck-deep in cheese or out hiking, you can find her, notepad in hand, scribbling down one of the many plot bunnies bouncing around in her head. She laughs at her own jokes and has been known to eat her feelings—gummy bears heal all. She's also an incurable romantic, devouring romance novels into the wee hours of the morning.

Learn more at:
KellySiskind.com
Twitter @KellySiskind
Facebook.com/AuthorKellySiskind